KATY MUNGER

Other Casey Jones Mysteries by
Katy Munger
from Avon Books

LEGWORK
OUT OF TIME
MONEY TO BURN

BAD TO THE BONE

A CASEY JONES MYSTERY

KATY MUNGER

AVON BOOKS

An Imprint of HarperCollins*Publishers*

This is a work of fiction. Names, characters, places, and incidents are products of the author's imagination or are used fictitiously and are not to be construed as real. Any resemblance to actual events, locales, organizations, or persons, living or dead, is entirely coincidental.

AVON BOOKS
An Imprint of HarperCollins*Publishers*
10 East 53rd Street
New York, New York 10022-5299

Copyright © 2000 by Katy Munger
Inside cover author photo by Courtney-Reid Eaton
ISBN: 0-380-80064-0
www.avonbooks.com

First Avon Books paperback printing: June 2000

Avon Trademark Reg. U.S. Pat. Off. and in Other Countries, Marca Registrada, Hecho en U.S.A.
HarperCollins ® is a trademark of HarperCollins Publishers Inc.

Printed in the U.S.A.

WCD 10 9 8 7 6 5 4 3 2 1

This one's for Miss D, the pride of New Orleans—
a woman of passion, courage and loyalty.
We may not be in France, my dear,
but it sure as hell beats where we came from.

Author's Note

This book is a work of fiction. Any resemblance to persons living or dead is not only unintended but a little scary to contemplate. In particular, there is absolutely no connection between the ex–husband depicted in this book and my own ex, Andy. He was—and still is—a great guy. In addition, any mother-in-law you meet in these pages is completely fictional. I have always been blessed with very kind and loving in-laws (thank you Brenda, Tom, George, Pandy, Bill, and Rachel).

ONE

It was one of those desolate, bone-ringing winter days that sweep through the South a handful of times in a century, freezing street bums to building grates and sending the downtown whores shivering home to their grandmas. Anyone with a lick of sense in Raleigh, North Carolina, was huddled indoors, contemplating the bourbon bottle and praying for sunshine.

My ex-husband never had a lick of sense in his life. Except when he married me, of course.

Bobby D. was the first to spot him. "Look at that moron," he said.

I joined him at the window and we stared out at a tall figure hunched against the icy winds. The man was wearing a fleece-lined denim jacket and a cowboy hat—clearly no match for the cold.

Reality slapped me upside of the head. I knew that hat. I knew that hunch. In fact, I knew that moron. Worse, I had slept with him approximately 2,623 times before I wised up. Not that I was counting or anything.

"I can't believe it," I said. "That's my husband."

"Your husband?" Bobby's mouth dropped open. A half-gnawed french fry toppled out and landed on the toe of my boot.

"My *ex-husband*." How the hell had I made that mistake after so many years?

"It's okay, Casey," Bobby said with annoying sympathy. "The tongue is always the last to know." He spoke with

the authority of a man who has been married so many
times he keeps a separate little black book just for ex-
wives.

We stood, shoulder to shoulder, watching the cocky bastard who had once been mine swagger down the deserted
sidewalk toward our door. I'd know his walk anywhere. It
was the bow-legged cowboy rock of a Florida panhandle
hotshot, a strut that could carry him from a hot bean field
to a dark beer joint to the deck of a forty-foot cabin
cruiser—all on someone else's credit card.

Jeffrey Carmichael Jones. There was a time when he
had been my life. But that was then. And this was now.

"What do you want me to do?" Bobby asked nervously.
Was my beloved 360-pound boss quaking in his faux
leather boots?

"Shoot him dead?" I suggested.

"What?" That stopped him, french fry halfway to his
mouth.

"Just kidding. I'll take care of it. But stay close, in case
I need help kicking his sorry butt back out the door."

"That's what I like about you, Casey," Bobby said.
"You're so sentimental."

The door opened and Jeff walked back into my life. Just
for a millisecond, my heart—which had failed to com-
municate with my brain in the matter—improvised a brief
fandango. Then good sense took over. I wanted to rip his
head off and stuff it up his ass.

"Surprise." Jeff spread his hands wide, as if ending a
vaudeville act.

"Fuck off." I followed this suggestion with a look that
was enough to wither a lot more than his enthusiasm.

"Ah, honey." He sounded hurt as only Jeff could sound
hurt. "You don't mean that. It's *me*. The love of your life."

"The love of my life?" I was astonished. "You're the
human equivalent of herpes. Even when I can't see you, I
know you're there. And every day I live in dread that you
might pop up again."

"Honey Bunny," he protested in a slow-as-sludge Florida drawl. "You can't mean that."

"Don't ever call me that idiotic nickname again," I

warned him. "My name is Casey. Use it. You're lucky I don't make you call me Ms. Jones."

"You kept my name," he pointed out. "That must mean something."

"Yeah. It means I'm ashamed to go back to my own name. Thanks to you."

Wordlessly, Bobby D. headed for the bathroom. He knew what was coming. Bobby is the only person in the state of North Carolina who knows that I have served time, operate with a forged P.I. license and carry a gun that I have no business packing. At least, not legally. All thanks to my ex-husband.

It was not good news that Jeff was here. He had a big mouth.

"What the hell do you want?" I asked him. Believe me, it was a lot more polite than what I really wanted to say.

"What makes you think I want something?" Jeff took off his cowboy hat and twisted it in his hands. But he wasn't cute enough these days to pull off the "aw, shucks" routine. At least, not with me. His hair was starting to gray and he had gained weight. A lot of weight. One more Twinkie and he'd explode into just another beach bum whose bloated belly dangled over his belt, gleaming like blubber under the Florida sun.

A stab of satisfaction warmed my innards—is there anything sweeter in life than an ex-spouse who has aged worse than you?

"What do you want?" I demanded again.

"It's private," he mumbled, looking around the office with the same skeptical look a lot of visitors get. Hey, we're a shoestring operation. We don't go in for curtains. Venetian blinds are good enough for me. So is recycled metal furniture and a token plastic plant. Most clients don't complain.

"Back here," I said grimly. I led him to my office. He looked around it, as if fascinated by the peeling green walls. I didn't say a word. He finally sat in the one chair reserved for clients—an uncomfortable leather contraption fished from a Dumpster behind the Legislative Building. I think it's the electric chair the state threw out when they got religion. Too bad I didn't have it hooked up.

I took my seat across the desk from him and waited.

"You look real good, Casey," he said. "Real good."

"I know," I admitted and waited some more.

Jeff shifted uncomfortably. He was a one-hit wonder. If he couldn't sweet-talk a woman into liking him, he had no idea what to do next.

"Why don't you tell me why you're here?" I suggested, once his feigned fascination with the dead plant on my file cabinet had stretched to embarrassing proportions. "Just spit it out." I propped my boots up on the desk and looked at him.

He stared back, mute.

"What?" I asked.

"You have a french fry on your boot." He pointed to it as proof.

I flicked it off, annoyed at how flustered I felt. I refused to give him the satisfaction of commenting.

He fidgeted some more, twisting that damn cowboy hat like a lime above a glass of tequila. Up close, I could see that he had aged a lot more than the fourteen years since I'd last seen him. I didn't much like the reminder that we were both growing old. His hair still flowed to his shoulders in blond waves, streaked with darker, almost black, strands. But gray had invaded his temples and his chin was sandpapered with a salt-and-pepper shadow.

It shocked me. I never thought he'd get old. I guess I imagined he'd also remain the same golden-haired, reckless devil of my long-gone youth. What had I been thinking? We all got old. If we were lucky. Even Jeffrey "Mad Dog" Jones.

Jeff was a Florida cowboy of the beach-and-boat variety, a man who plied his trade beneath the noonday sun. The damage was starting to show. His broad face melted into deep wrinkles around his mouth, and his skin had a sickly green tint to it, if you looked beneath the surface tan. I suspected his drinking, always heavy, had grown worse in the years since I'd last seen him. And god knows what new pharmaceuticals he'd been popping. His blue eyes had a milky quality to them, as if any spark inside had been extinguished in a sea of chemicals.

"What are you looking at?" he asked defensively.

I was looking at his feet. He was, as always, wearing cowboy boots. They were pale green, lizardskin shitkickers that looked like cloven hooves if you squinted at them. How very appropriate.

"Nothing," I lied. "I was just wondering when you were going to explain why you've popped up after almost fifteen years of conspicuous silence."

"Conspicuous silence? Big words for a little lady."

"My words got bigger in prison. There was nothing to do but read."

An even more awkward silence descended. We both knew why I had spent a year and a half in a Jacksonville prison, and we both knew that Jeff had not bothered to visit me once during that time. Which was why the first thing I did when I got paroled was to visit a Tampa divorce lawyer. And why the first thing I did when parole was over was to leave Jeff far behind.

"You could have visited me," I said.

He wouldn't meet my eyes. "They were watching me. Waiting for me to take that chance. We could both have ended up behind bars. Can't we just let all that go? I'm sure we've both changed a lot since then."

"I know I've changed," I said, thinking of the naive, lovesick sap I'd been. I was smarter, stronger, more cynical—and a hell of a lot happier—without him.

"I've changed, too," he claimed.

"How?" I asked, annoyed that he had strung me along this far.

"Have you ever wanted something *really* badly?" he began.

"Sure. The lead singer for the Goo Goo Dolls. Ask me something hard."

"I'm serious. Like respect from other people?"

"What kind of trouble are you in?" I asked, disgusted that Jeff hadn't changed a bit. He was still hot on the trail of some get-rich-quick scheme. "Don't bullshit me about it." I checked my watch. "You have two minutes."

Panic added years to his already haggard expression. "I had the money," he said. "I was going to give it to them."

"Stop," I warned him. "Start at the beginning. You have ninety seconds left."

His explanation gushed out in a rush of words. "These guys fronted me some blow. I was supposed to pay them in a couple of days, but the girl I was with disappeared with the money and the flake. I got left holding nothing. No money. No bump. They'll kill me if I don't come up with something."

"How much coke?" I asked wearily.

"Three kilos. I was just doing it once to get back on my feet."

I lost it at that improbable announcement. I had heard that phrase from him so many times, so long ago, that it just didn't seem possible I could be sucked back into the vortex of time and spewed out into the same old pool of shit.

"Shut up," I said, rising to my feet. "Get out of my office. I don't want to hear any more. Don't insult my intelligence. You don't get fronted three kilos unless you know the sellers pretty damn well. Which means you've been dealing a hell of a lot more than just that once. I told you eighteen years ago to lay off selling that poison and I have not a shred of doubt that you have ignored that advice every day since." My voice had climbed to a screech. I stopped to regain control.

"I swore to myself that when you lied to me about that car being clean, it was going to be the last time you ever lied to me," I told him. "I paid for that lie with a chunk of my life, while you were on the outside drinking margaritas with teenage honeypots and stuffing coke up your nose and popping more pills than Jacqueline Fucking Susann. So don't barge into my life again after almost fifteen years and insult me with the same old prairie shit. You've gotten yourself into real trouble now, Jeff. That's too bad. I saw it coming a long time ago. But I'm not going to bail you out."

"I can't go to the cops," he pleaded.

"No, you can't," I agreed. "And I guess this is one time

your parents won't be able to bail you out, either."

"But she's *here*," he said, his voice almost triumphant, as if the news would surely make me change my mind. "The girl who took off with my stash is in North Carolina. Someone saw her in Charlotte. Even if she's spent the cash, I could still sell the coke, if she has it. If I can get it back, will you help me unload it? They'll kill me if I don't come up with the money, Casey. They'll kill me."

"I don't care. Get out of my office. I already lost almost two years of my life paying for something that you did and I'm not wasting another second on you."

"Just help me sell some of it when I find her. I don't know anyone here."

"Get out."

He rose to his feet, his face a mixture of bafflement and rejection. I wanted to punch him. I had come so far since those days, I had worked so hard to build a new life for myself. How dare he track me down and try to pull me under again? And how had he even found me?

"How did you know where I was?" I demanded.

His eyes slid away from mine.

"Jeff," I warned him. "Tell me."

"Your grandfather," he said. He had the decency to look embarrassed at dragging the one family member I had left in the world into his mess.

"Bullshit. He doesn't even know where I am."

"Yes he *does*, Casey," Jeff insisted. "He told me where to find you."

I sat down again, abruptly, my legs weak. If my grandfather had known where I was all these years, why hadn't he asked me to visit? I'd spoken to him by phone often since I'd left Florida, and he had never once asked me where I was. He always seemed to believe I was someplace far away. Probably because he wanted to. I was the fallen apple on his family tree, the only person in six generations of hard luck scrabbling to have landed in jail.

"So you'll help me?" Jeff asked eagerly. "For old time's sake?"

"Are you insane?"

The look on my face penetrated his self-absorbed fog.

He fumbled for the doorknob. "Just think about it," he pleaded. "I'll call you tomorrow."

"Get out of my office," I warned him. "Get out of my life."

He backed through the door and collided with Bobby, who never seems to move but always manages to be in the perfect position for eavesdropping.

"What was that about?" Bobby asked as Jeff hurried out of the office.

"You don't want to know," I assured him, then stopped as I caught sight of an oddity on the otherwise empty sidewalk. A woman wrapped in a black fur coat stood outside our front door. Her back was to us and her blond hair shimmered in the winter sunlight. She was smoking, as if waiting for someone. Was it Jeff?

No. He walked past her. But then he turned back, mumbling a few words as he eyed her. I couldn't believe it. What a pig. If Jeff was knocking on heaven's gate, he'd turn back toward hell just to warm his pecker.

I watched the scene unfold. He was *hitting* on her. God, I could not believe it. He was still the same sweet-talking swine.

Too bad for Jeff. The woman rebuffed him with a disinterested wave. He slouched away down the sidewalk, gloveless hands wrapped under his armpits to shield them from the cold. I almost felt sorry for him, sucker that I am. But then I remembered that he was a scumbag and that I wanted him to rot in hell.

The woman also watched him go. As soon as Jeff turned the corner, she threw her cigarette down, turned around and walked through our front door.

"Christ," Bobby groaned as the bell tinkled. He sank into his seat without looking up. "We're busier than Krispy damn Kreme. It's too cold for this shit. I'm ordering me some hot wings from Domino's to warm up."

I didn't answer. I was too busy staring. The woman shocked me as much as Jeff. From behind, she'd looked like a Playboy bunny waiting on the steps of an Aspen ski lodge. From the front, she looked like the lead in a driver's ed film the morning after the prom. Ugly bruises crept over her cheeks, a line of stitches stretched beneath her right eye and a huge scab ran off the end of her chin. Her left arm was in a sling tucked beneath her coat. Metal splints bound two fingers together. I'd have guessed she'd been boxing Mike Tyson, except both of her ears were intact and her honey-streaked hair was tucked behind them to prove it.

"Can I help you?" I asked calmly, though the sight of a battered woman always sent a vague fear skittering through the deeper recesses of my brain.

"Are you Casey Jones?" she asked in a cultivated drawl. An old money try, but not quite there.

"Yes," I admitted. "In the flesh." All 170 pounds of it, at the moment, though I was not about to tell this 105-pound beauty what I weighed.

The mention of flesh caused her to unconsciously caress the bruise on one of her cheeks. "My name is Tawny Bledsoe. My husband did this to me. I want you to find him."

"And do what to him?" I asked, imagining the cornucopia of violence I would visit on a wife-beater if I had the chance.

"Get my child back from him," she said. "He's got my little girl. The courts say she's supposed to be with me."

Bobby D. cleared his throat nervously and pretended to rummage in one of his junk food drawers for a snack. We both hated domestic cases involving children. Parents will do things to each other in front of kids they claim to love that will make your faith in mankind shrivel up and die.

"Your husband beat the shit out of you, kidnapped your kid and you just want me to find him?" I asked, to be sure I understood. "That's all? You don't want me to snatch the kid back or anything?"

"That's right," she said, and her accent made it sound more like "That's rat"—which was probably closer to the truth. "Just find him."

"I assume you're separated?" I asked. "You mentioned the courts?"

She nodded, waiting for my answer. Her left eye twitched. Probably permanent muscle damage.

"Come back to my office and we'll talk about it there,"

I said, aware that Bobby was starting to sweat like a hog roasting over an open fire. Bobby hates crying women, and the fact that this one had yet to turn on the faucets was a minor miracle. Tawny Bledsoe must be one tough cookie, even if she had lost her last bout by a knockout.

She followed me without a word and took a seat in the visitor's chair after lining it with her fur coat. I'm not on a first-name basis with domestic pelts, so I had no idea what kind of critters died to make her fashionable. But I could tell that her coat had wiped out a generation's worth of some poor species. Underneath it, she wore a pink cashmere sweater and black designer jeans. This was no thrift shop junkie sitting before me, the lady invested in her wardrobe big time.

She sat with perfect posture and daintily crossed her legs. It was impossible not to stare. She was built like a five-foot Barbie doll, with perky breasts jutting out above a waistline so narrow I fought the urge to ask her to lift her sweater so I could count her ribs. Surely a few had been sacrificed for size.

"Tell me about yourself," I said.

"What do you want to know?" Her plucked eyebrows arched. It was difficult to tell, given the current state of her face, but I was pretty sure she was a stunner beneath the bruises and makeup. Her facial proportions were perfect and her eyes were almond-shaped pools of pale blue. Some people have all the luck.

Not that she looked too lucky at the moment.

"General stuff, like where you come from. That sort of thing," I explained. "I like to know who I'm representing."

"Oh." She stared at the wall. "I was born in Kannopolis, that's near Charlotte. My daddy worked for Canon Mills. In upper management. I went to UNC-Wilmington for a while, but I dropped out to get married."

I examined her more closely. Minute lines were starting to form around her eyes and mouth. The lady was well over thirty, though she wore it well.

"How long ago was that?" I asked. I was being about as subtle as her perfume, which was starting to make me sneeze.

"A lady never tells her age," she said, holding her chin high. "But that was another husband."

"I see." I was starting to sound like a shrink. "Any kids with the first hubby?"

"No." Her lower lip trembled. "That's one reason my first husband left me. The doctors told me I couldn't have children. My frame was too small. That's why it was such a miracle when I had Tiffany." Her eyes filled with tears. "I don't care what it costs. I fear for Tiffany's life. You must find her for me."

"I'm sorry, but I haven't decided whether or not to take on your case." Especially if she had a daughter named Tiffany. Despite her claims about Daddy being in upper management, I'd already gotten a whiff of white-trash-meets-money from Tawny Bledsoe. The kid's name confirmed it. No one with a lick of class would name her kid Tiffany. Still, that made no real difference to me when it came to whether or not I would help her. Seeing a beaten woman like that evoked every protective instinct I had, regardless of social position. What I was really worried about was the fur coat and expensive clothes. When a lot of money's at stake, the kid is often just a bargaining chip in the battle over the jackpot. I wasn't about to get involved unless I was sure it really was the daughter—and not just a fat support check—that this lady wanted.

"What can I do to convince you to help me?" she asked.

"Start by telling me how you found me."

"A friend in the police department recommended you."

"What kind of a friend?" I was reluctant to get caught between an estranged husband and wife, much less between an estranged husband and wifey's new gun-toting boyfriend.

"Not *that* kind of friend. Just someone who has been very helpful to me in my current predicament."

"Name?" I asked impatiently.

"Bill Butler." Her tone was disinterested, but her eyes narrowed as if she knew about my relationship with Bill and was daring me to turn the job down.

"How is good old Bill?" I asked dryly.

"As tall, dark and handsome as ever."

"Today must be my day for exes," I said out loud.

"Pardon me?" she asked.

"Nothing. Why doesn't Bill help you find your kid?" Last I'd heard, he was working the Bod Squad, helping decoy rapists. A little out of this lady's needed area of expertise, but Bill was not one to turn down a damsel in distress.

She swallowed, wincing as if her throat hurt. "My husband is a very powerful man," she explained. "A lot of people don't want to get involved, including the police. They're saying all the right things, but they're really just blowing me off."

A warning flag hit the field with a clunk. "Who's your husband?" I asked.

"Robert Price," she said. "Maybe you know him? He's a Wake County commissioner."

Yeah, I knew him. He was as tall and handsome as Bill Butler—and a hell of a lot darker. What was he doing with the Nordic Ice Queen for a wife? The African-American community would crucify him.

"You're married to Robert Price?" I asked, aware that I was spending most of my time repeating her statements. Seeing Jeff had blown my brain fuses.

She nodded, clutching her pocketbook to her chest, as if to ward off imaginary blows. "It's the second marriage for each of us," she added, seeing my face. "Maybe you're thinking of his first wife?"

It came to me—I was. Robert Price's first wife had dropped out of sight a while ago, before he'd gotten re-elected, if I remembered correctly. I wondered if it was because of Tawny.

"I didn't realize they had divorced," I said. "What was her name? Livinia?"

She nodded. "They divorced about five years ago."

"How old is your daughter?" I asked casually—though I don't think I fooled either one of us.

"She's almost five." She hesitated. "Robert and I met right after his separation. It was love at first sight. We married as soon as we could."

"You don't believe in wasting any time. Looks to me

like the marriage went down the tubes just as fast."

"I should have researched his character a little bit better," she admitted. "But love is blind, as they say."

Love is blind, all right. Deaf, dumb and blind. And I get paid to pick up the pieces once people's eyes have been opened to the madness.

"Got the court papers?" I asked, grateful that at least it had been kept out of the media. Powerful black man beats the crap out of tiny blond wife and absconds with their kid. If this case turned into a race thing, I was going to run the other way. I'm into helping people, not causes.

Tawny Bledsoe pulled a thick envelope from her pocketbook and handed it to me, along with a neatly typed list of information. "Here are his particulars."

I scanned the list. She was pretty damn particular about his particulars. She had detailed all of his personal data— social security number, date of birth, addresses for the past ten years, credit card account numbers, names of friends, even his favorite restaurants. I now knew more about Robert Price than I knew about myself. The woman was more prepared than a frigging Boy Scout.

I looked up. "Have you done this before?"

She shook her head. "I just tried to anticipate what it was you might need to locate him, and I saw this movie once on Lifetime where the—"

"Gotcha," I said, cutting her off. Watch one week of Lifetime programming for women and you'll walk away with a working knowledge of the law—along with a firm conviction that every woman in America is either being stalked, driven crazy by a cheating husband, screwed in a divorce or trying to convince a daughter that her boyfriend is a psycho. Which may be close to the truth.

"Everything looks okay," I admitted as I examined the court papers stored inside the envelope. I skipped over the part about what jerks they were to each other and reached the section about sole custody being granted to the mother, Tawny Anne Bledsoe of blah, blah, blah. Amazing how legalese can reduce a child's future to a handful of words so dry they may as well be referring to the fate of a poodle in a pet store. I double-checked the last page. The court seal was genuine. Now what would I do?

"Please," she said, sensing my hesitation. She leaned forward and the neckline of her pink sweater gaped open, exposing a pair of perfect apple-shaped breasts squeezed into a push-up bra. Were those things real? She was flashing them around like they were brand-new and store-bought. I'm not Miss Modesty, but even I keep my gozongas under wraps until I know the person I'm flashing a little bit better.

For a second, I thought she might be coming on to me, but I dismissed the thought. I'd probably just been watching too much women's golf lately.

"I love Tiffany more than anything in the world," she was saying. "And I don't want anything from Robert, except my daughter back. He can keep his alimony and child support. I have a job selling commercial real estate. I make a good living. I bought this coat myself."

She thrust a furry arm at me as if she wanted me to touch it. When I simply stared, she let it fall over the arm of the chair and began to cry, her tears tracing rivulets through the heavy makeup that failed to conceal her wounds. "I can't sleep at night. I keep thinking he might turn on her next."

I held out a tissue and she took it with her bandaged left hand, plucking it from my grip with robotlike precision. "I would do it myself, go out there and find her," she sobbed. "But I don't know where to begin. Please, I'm begging you, as one woman to another. Help me out. Find it in your heart to help a stranger. Look what he did to me. Just look at this." She tilted her chin up. The scab trailed all the way down her throat, ending in a small ring of bruises that looked like blurred fingerprints.

I sighed, mentally running down the reasons why I ought to take the case, despite my misgivings. There was nothing else on the horizon to pay my rent next month. It wasn't very sisterly of me to refuse. Maybe the kid really was in danger. And it would give me a good excuse for ignoring my ex-husband.

"Okay, I'll do it," I said reluctantly, not quite sure of

my motives, other than that they were green and involved a lot of zeros.

"God bless you," she cried, her tears forgotten. She leaned across the desk and grabbed my hand, then held it up to her mouth and kissed it.

I reclaimed my hand, taken aback by her excessive gratitude. Desperation is always unattractive, no matter how justified.

"What else do you need to know?" she asked, blue eyes fixed on my face.

"Not much. Let's start with your phone number and address." I wrote it down as she gave me the information. She was living in one of the more expensive subdivisions in North Raleigh. I'd seen the address before: on the list of her husband's former residences.

"You've covered everything else here." I held up the sheet of paper with her husband's life detailed on it. "I take it he's not at home right now?" There was an apartment listed as his current residence.

She shook her head. "I've been calling and stopping by his place this whole week. No one's at home."

"When did he take Tiffany?"

Her eyes dropped. "Last weekend. I let him take her to the movies because he begged me. Just for the matinee, he promised. But he never brought her back."

"Have you checked with the hospitals and police?"

She nodded. "They haven't been in an accident. And he hasn't been into his office. His secretary says he's on vacation. She hates me anyway, she'd never tell me where he was."

What secretary did like the boss's wife? "What exactly did the police say to you when you went to them after your daughter disappeared?" I asked.

"A lot of things, but basically that I should go home and wait it out. They said Robert would be back."

"They're probably right," I agreed. It was rare that a man in power willingly left behind a lifetime's worth of career-climbing. On the other hand, people can get pretty crazy when it comes to their kids.

Besides, I realized, Robert Price's career would pretty

much be over if it ever got out that he was a wife-beater—
which was a likely eventuality come the next election.
Maybe he figured he no longer had anything to lose.

"Who's been assigned to your case?" I asked. "I'll need
to talk to them about what they've done so far."

Her voice grew more desperate. "That's what I've been
trying to tell you. No one's been assigned to the case. The
cops aren't doing anything."

"And they saw you in this condition?"

She touched her face again. "I'm not pressing charges.
That's one of the reasons they won't help me. They don't
think I'm serious."

"Why aren't you pressing assault charges?" I asked reasonably.

"That's my business," she snapped back, an edge to her
voice. Her voice dropped. "Look, I'm afraid, okay? He has
my daughter and I'm not going to provoke him while he
has her."

I sighed. My lack of enthusiasm showed.

"What if the police aren't right?" she asked me. "Have
you thought about that? What if he never comes back? I'll
never see my daughter again."

"Sure you will," I promised. If I was going to take the
case, I may as well give it my all. "I'll find them. Do you
have any recent photographs?"

"I have these," she offered, pulling a stack of snapshots
from her purse and setting them on the edge of my desk.
What the hell else did she have in that pocketbook?
Clowns would start piling out of it next.

I looked through the stack, then selected four to keep.
One was a posed preschool portrait of Tiffany, another
showed the child with her mother. They were wearing
matching outfits, which was nauseating, but then I'm not
into pink frilly shit under any circumstances. Another
photo showed Robert Price at a baseball game, holding a
hot dog and eyeing it with comical relish. He looked like
a pretty nice guy, but I guess all wife-beaters do until they
cock a fist. The last photo showed father and daughter
sitting together at the end of a pier, holding fishing poles.
Tiffany was a beautiful child, with her mother's wide blue

eyes, her dad's proud nose and skin the color of caramel. Her hair bunched in tight brown curls that were streaked with blond, and her smile revealed two rows of perfect baby teeth. Father and daughter looked pretty cozy in that photograph, snuggled against each other for Mom's camera. One big happy family. How times change.

"I'll give the photos back when this is all over," I promised.

"When do you think that will be?"

"It depends. But with all the financial information I have on him, it shouldn't be too long. He has to spend money sometime. Call me in two days. I'll let you know how it's going. I'll need a retainer, of course."

"Of course." She removed a leather-bound checkbook from her bottomless purse, along with a Montblanc fountain pen. "How much?"

"A thousand should cover me for a while. I charge a hundred an hour and expenses against that. I'll let you know if I need more."

She wrote the check out without hesitation. I took it, noticing that the ink in her pen was purple and that her handwriting was flowery and precise.

"I do have one more favor to ask," she said softly, unconsciously rubbing the bruised part of her left cheek. "I just deposited a huge commission check in my bank account, but it's out-of-state and it might take a few days to clear. Can you wait and deposit my check on Thursday? It's only three days. I got wiped out with all my medical bills and all . . ." Her voice trailed off sadly, but her face tightened, as if she was afraid I might back out after all.

What could I do? Strip her of her fur coat as collateral? "Sure," I said. "No problem." It was the first week in January and the rent was paid. I could afford to be generous.

Her face brightened. "Thanks. I hate to ask, but with my injuries I've been out of work and it was longer than usual between commission checks."

"Don't worry about it," I assured her, shaking her good hand. Her fingers were long and very soft. This was not a hand that knew hard work.

"Thank you so very, very much," she said. "Really, I promise you—you won't regret it."

"I'm sure I won't." I decided to show her to the front door before she got the notion to kiss my feet. Bobby was in the outer office. He was munching his way through a bag of boiled peanuts as he watched me usher her to the door. When he saw she was about to leave, he coughed loudly and held up one of his ridiculously expensive spy cameras, staring pointedly at her face.

"Oh, yeah," I said. "Just a minute, Tawny. I think it would be a good idea to take some photos of you."

"Of me?" She sounded vaguely pleased, as if I had just suggested she might make a good spokesperson for a cosmetics company. She pulled her fur coat around her chin and tilted her head up in a parody of Marilyn Monroe.

Bobby rolled his eyes as he handed me the camera. We both knew it takes all kinds.

"I need to record your injuries, not your modeling ability," I explained stiffly. I was not in the mood to play around. Maybe she was more unhinged than I realized. On the other hand, she'd been sane enough to sign a thousand-dollar retainer. Why not give her a chance?

"Should I say cheese?" she asked, posing in the doorway.

"No," I barked back. "For godsakes, don't smile. Look like you're hurt."

Her face changed abruptly. "I *am* hurt," she protested.

"I know. That's the point."

She obeyed by slumping dejectedly and looking monumentally unhappy as I snapped about a dozen photographs of her face and neck from different angles.

"Okay, that's enough," I finally said.

"That bastard," she muttered, almost to herself. "I keep forgetting what he did to me."

"He did a number on you, all right," I agreed.

"Could I take a couple of those?" she asked, reaching for the Polaroids. "My lawyer might need them."

I handed over two of the snapshots, wondering why the hell her lawyer hadn't thought to take photos of his own.

"I hope that guy didn't bother you earlier," I said, thinking of my ex-husband. I opened the door for her and a gust of icy wind blasted me in the face.

"What guy?" She seemed oblivious to the cold.

"The one who stopped to talk to you before you came in here." I scrutinized her face. She seemed genuinely bewildered. I doubted they knew each other.

"Oh, *him*," she finally said. She waved dismissively. "He was just some loser. Can you imagine? Trying to pick me up when I look like this?"

Yeah, I could imagine. And she was right—Jeff was just some loser.

"Thank you again," she said, then pulled her fur collar up and headed out into the wind. The heels of her leather boots drummed a staccato rhythm on the sidewalk as she strode away.

"I don't like her," Bobby D. said gruffly, not fifteen seconds after she left. "Wouldn't touch her with my ten-foot pole."

"What do you mean?" I asked, ignoring his delusions of grandeur.

"She's got a screw loose. Too many blows to the head."

"Bobby, that's not funny."

He looked up, perplexed. "Who's being funny? I mean it. I don't like her."

"Someone has to help her. Let's not get into it, okay?" We fought weekly over which sex in divorce cases most often turned out to be right. It was a perpetual girls versus boys debate that neither one of us could ever hope to win.

"What the hell happened to her anyway?" Bobby asked as Tawny Bledsoe reached the end of our block and turned, disappearing from sight.

"Husband beat her up," I said. "As in Robert Price. The Wake County commissioner."

"No shit?" Bobby was interested now. "I figured it was a domestic thing. Wait'll the papers get wind of it."

"They won't," I promised. "A kid is involved and I want to keep it clean."

"Don't blame you." Bobby grabbed his massive fake fur coat off the back of the closet door and wiggled into it. He buttoned it up carefully, then jammed a fuzzy hat with flaps on it over his head and fastened it beneath his chin. He slipped on heavy black gloves and adjusted the hat so low it nearly obscured his eyes. When he was done, he looked like a Kodiak bear lumbering off in search of a cave to hibernate in.

"Where are you going?" I asked. "It's twenty-seven below out there."

"The Domino's delivery truck won't start," he explained. "I'm walking over there for my hot wings."

"My god," I said. "Such dedication."

"You have your causes. I have mine." He patted his enormous stomach and headed out the door, letting another cold blast of wind into the office.

The mention of food made me hungry. I rummaged through one of his drawers and located an unopened box of Twinkies. I unwrapped a couple and started munching away as I sat at his desk and dialed Bill Butler's number.

"Butler," a brusque voice answered.

"Answering your own phone? What's the matter? You get busted down?"

"Casey," he said, making it a statement. "With a mouthful of Hostess cupcakes, if my detective instincts are right."

"Twinkies," I admitted. "I'm trying to eat a more balanced diet these days, so I'm alternating between Twinkies, Snowballs, cupcakes and fruit pies."

"Nice to know someone else in this town is at work besides me." He sounded tired and grumpy.

"Coverage light?"

"Yup. Pipes are freezing. Engines won't start. Furnaces have gone out. Ice on the road. You name it. I've heard it. The RPD is being manned by a few good men right now. I'm one of them." He sighed.

"You ought to move to the country," I told him. "Then you'd have a good excuse not to come in to work, too."

"I'm a city boy," he said. "Remember? I can't breathe unless there's at least a fifteen percent share of carbon monoxide in the air."

We ran out of banter and an expectant silence filled the line. There was a lot I could have said to him, but didn't.

There was a lot he could have said back, but didn't. One of us would have to budge.

"You know a woman named Tawny Bledsoe?" I finally asked.

There was the briefest of pauses. I wondered again about the exact nature of their relationship. "Yeah, I know her," he said carefully.

"Why do you say it that way?"

"She used to work here," he explained. "She left the department about a year and a half ago."

"Are we talking about the same woman? The Tawny Bledsoe who's married to Robert Price?"

"That's her," Bill confirmed.

"She was a cop?"

"No, she worked in public relations. I think that's how she met her husband."

"No kidding? Well, that may have been a bad career move on her part. She was just in my office, beaten black-and-blue. By her husband."

"I knew they were having trouble," Bill said. "I think they've been having trouble from the start."

"I'd call this trouble with a capital T. Her husband pounded her, then absconded with their kid. She says you gave her my name and number."

There was another brief silence. I didn't like it. There was something going on that I didn't know about.

"I gave her your name and number a while ago," Bill finally said. "When she thought her husband was playing around on her."

"So you don't know anything about the husband taking the kid?"

"No," he said too quickly. "I haven't even seen her in months. I'm back in Robbery now. You know I don't like that domestic shit."

"Who does?" I sighed. "So, is she a nut case or what?"

"She's fine," he said. "What makes you think—"

"Nothing," I admitted. "I'm just checking up."

"She held some executive position in public relations, Casey. She was well respected. I think you're safe." There was a silence. "I don't suppose you're holding her perfect body against her?"

"I don't suppose you're holding her perfect body against you?" I countered.

He laughed. "I wish. Nope. I've been celibate for a long time now."

"Yeah, right. And I don't know the difference between shit and apple butter."

"It's true," he protested. "Ever since I heard you had a boyfriend, my heart has been breaking. What can I say?"

"You are so full of crap," I told him. "No wonder your eyes are brown."

"Could be. But I must say, I was surprised to hear you had settled down. With a gimp, no less. You don't strike me as the one-man-woman type."

"I'm not," I said calmly. "And I never settle, down or otherwise. Burly and I have an arrangement. He does his thing, I do mine. Sometimes we meet in the middle. So to speak."

"Really?" His voice perked up. "In that case, if you ever want to arrange anything, give me a call."

"In your dreams." I hung up on him, annoyed.

Bill Butler had the unique ability to piss me off when he was trying to make me laugh, and to make me laugh when he was trying to piss me off. But at least he'd given me the information I was looking for. It was time to tuck him away in my memory until the next time I needed his help.

This inner pep talk, of course, did me no good. I munched Twinkies and daydreamed about Bill Butler's lean-and-mean cop body until Bobby returned from his trek into the wilds.

"You better have left me some of those Twinkies for dessert," he warned as he trundled across the room with a giant box of chicken wings in his hands.

"Those smell great," I admitted. "Got some for me?"

"Yeah. They give me a volume discount." He plopped the box on his desk and struggled out of his coat. "But you're going to lose your appetite when I tell you what I saw walking over to Domino's."

Something in his tone made my stomach dip. "What?" I asked.

"Your ex-husband bending over your newest client's car engine."

"Shit," I said.

"Exactly."

"Jeff doesn't know diddly about cars," I protested.

"I don't think that was the point."

"That means he was sitting out there waiting the whole time I was with her."

"Yup. But which one of you was he waiting for?" Bobby has a knack for cutting to the heart of the matter.

"Do you think they know each other?" I asked as paranoia poked its head up for a peek at my innermost fears.

"They do now," Bobby answered. "But don't worry. I don't think they knew each other before this. They were talking about frozen fuses and shit. And when I walked back by, the client was gone but your ex-hubby was trying to start his own car. He drives a late-model Mustang, by the way. Bright red."

"He would," I muttered.

"You sure lead an interesting life, babe." Bobby tore into a hot wing with the gusto of a vulture attacking a carcass. "These are good. Try one."

"No thanks," I said, thinking of Jeff interfering with my life. "I just lost my appetite."

TWO

I have a short attention span when it comes to men, which I blame entirely on my ex. The moment someone reminds me of Jeff, I show him the other side of the door. This theory lacks introspection, but it does explain why I suddenly had a powerful need to see Burly that night.

Burly is the opposite of Jeff in many ways, including the most important one: while Jeff is ruled by his pecker—making him the modern-day equivalent of the pea-brained dinosaur—Burly can't even feel his. He is my knight in shining armor, though his armor comes with wheels. He couldn't help me forgive, but he might be able to make me forget.

I drove out to Chatham County in weather so cold that the squirrels slipped from ice-covered tree branches like a cartoon gone mad. In the early twilight, Burly's farm looked like a page from a fairy tale. It was frozen over with a layer of frost, and a peaceful column of smoke spiraled from the chimney.

He was in the kitchen cooking Brunswick stew, a process that required the use of at least six pans. Cooking's a great hobby for a guy in a wheelchair, especially one with a total pig for a girlfriend. Did I mention that I don't do dishes? I try to make up for it by licking my plate clean.

I sat down on Burly's lap, ripped his shirt open and starting licking the hollows of his collarbone. There's really no other way to show his world-class shoulders the proper respect.

"Hey," he protested, "you popped my buttons into the stew."

"This is an emergency," I explained. "I just saw my ex-husband."

"Why didn't you say so in the first place?" he complained, turning the stew to low and rolling us toward the bedroom. "By the time I get done, you won't remember his name."

He was right. In fact, by the time he got done, I couldn't remember my own name. Afterward, I ate half a pot of Brunswick stew to regain my energy. When I was done, I put the mixing bowl on the floor for our inert hound to lick, but the effort of raising his head proved too much for Killer. He simply yawned and went back to sleep.

"Incredible," I called out to Burly. "Not only is he too lazy to get up and piss, he's too lazy to eat."

"That hound will have to get his priorities straight one day," Burly yelled back. His mind was on more important matters. In a show of solidarity with all guys after sex, he was watching sports on television.

I wandered lazily into the living room, hoping to complain about my ex. No such luck. I stopped short, knowing that life had just staged one of its infamous schizo-turns and that, warm house and hot sex aside, I was suddenly looking at trouble. Burly was hunched over, staring at the television, his face and body frozen—the way he gets when he's been reminded of what he had to give up. I knew without even looking at the screen that he was watching basketball.

"Why do you do that to yourself?" I asked as I did a U-turn, needing the comfort of chocolate ice cream for what was sure to follow.

"Because I can't play it anymore, I'm not supposed to even watch it?" he yelled back. My good mood evaporated. His tone told me that the whole time I had been in bed with him, thinking of how we owned our own private space, he had been in bed with me, thinking of the things we could not do together.

"You had physical therapy today, didn't you?" I said.

He ignored me and I knew I was right. Physical therapy

always reminds Burly that he lives in a wheelchair and that all the exercise in the world isn't going to change that.

Killer, sensing his mood, actually hefted his tubular body aloft and waddled over to Burly's feet, where he flopped down and began to snore. Traitorous little cur. He always took Burly's side.

We're each difficult to get along with in our own way, so I told myself it was no big deal. I was lying to myself. It was. He had gotten this way before and it scared me. Sometimes his funk only lasted for a few hours. But once it had lasted two weeks. I never knew what to expect until it was over. The thing was, this was not the right time for it to be happening. I had enough on my plate.

I left Burly watching basketball and went to bed early, feeling sorry for myself, since what was the point of having a boyfriend who looked like your very own Nine Inch Nail (dark hair, even darker eyes, cheekbones to die for) when he periodically acted like you weren't even alive? I really, really hated this part of being in a relationship—the being-so-understanding-and-giving-them-personal-space-so-they-can-sulk part.

The black dog had my boyfriend firmly caught in his jaws, but I was the one who was going to get bit.

I went to bed wishing that songs could come true. You be me for a while, I hummed as I fell asleep, and I'll be you.

The next day proved warmer all around. Burly made me waffles for breakfast, and the drive back to Raleigh was filled with sunshine and the crackle of melting ice. Bobby D. and I fueled up on coffee before we got down to work. I was on a new diet kick and refused to eat Krispy Kremes cold; this policy alone saved me thousands of calories a day.

Once sufficiently buzzed on caffeine, we made a number of phone calls to Robert Price's friends. We took turns pretending to be everyone from a credit card company rep to Price's lawyer. Together, Bobby and I were able to confirm that Price was thought to be on vacation by his colleagues and would be back in a few weeks. The family members we reached were less forthcoming. Either he wasn't staying with family, or he had instructed them not to speak to anyone who called, no matter how much we poured on the charm. I'd have to stake out their houses in person to get anywhere, but I didn't feel it was necessary yet. Like I said, he had to spend his money sometime.

Sure enough, the morning of the third day, my clerk contact in the Durham Police Department—Marcus Dupree—called to let me know that Price had made a large ATM withdrawal the afternoon he disappeared with his daughter. This was followed by another withdrawal a few days later in Rocky Mount. His sister lived in Rocky Mount, I knew, as I had just gotten off the phone with her a few minutes before—after being assured that she hadn't seen her brother in months. I'd have called her a lying bitch, but since I'd posed as Price's neighbor, I had no room to talk.

I went back to my friend Marcus for more help. Marcus is a stubborn man. He refuses to give me direct access to his sources at the major card companies. Either he figures he can squeeze more money out of me if he pulls the strings or, more likely, he suspects I lack discretion. Whatever the reason, until I can find a fourteen-year-old computer whiz to seduce in exchange for a way to hack into credit card systems myself, I have to depend on Marcus for real-time financial tracking information. The good news is that Marcus never lets me down.

He called me back later that same afternoon to say that Price had used his Visa card in Kingston, North Carolina, at a Target store two days ago, and later that same day at a restaurant in New Bern.

He was heading toward the beach, I decided, an odd place to go in January when it was cold enough to freeze your nookies off. Unless, of course, you were looking for somewhere totally deserted, yet not too far from home and family.

"Can you let me know the second he uses his card again?" I asked.

"He'll have to use it during my contact's shift," Marcus

explained. "Otherwise I won't be able to find out until she comes in the next day."

"Please tell me that she works the late shift." I was hoping to get another hit before the day was up.

"Noon to eight. If he charges dinner, you'll know within minutes."

I didn't wait for the call. I booted up my iMac and started a property search in all the coastal counties, looking for the names of anyone on the list of Price's friends and relatives. If that failed, I'd start dialing motels.

I got one hit: a married couple listed by Tawny Bledsoe as being among Price's closest friends owned a beach house on Emerald Isle, a protected strip of land that runs east to southwest just below Atlantic Beach. It's one of the few areas to have escaped heavy development along the Carolina coast. This meant it was private. But it was also home to a handful of year-round residents, so Price would have access to heat, water and groceries if he was holed up there.

I was debating whether to take a chance and drive to Emerald Isle when Tawny Bledsoe called from her car. I could barely hear her. Raleigh skirts the Piedmont foothills and, depending on where you are, your reception can run from crystal clear to unintelligible. God, but I hated car phones with a passion. People who talk and drive simultaneously are four times more likely to get in an accident—unless they're driving in front of me, in which case they are four hundred times more likely to get rammed from behind.

"What did you say?" I shouted into the crackling.

"Did you find her yet?" I think she answered. "Do you know where I can go and get her?"

"Not yet," I yelled back. "But we're making good progress. I think he's headed for the coast."

There was a silence and I thought we'd been disconnected, but her voice returned in mid-sentence: "—makes sense. He has a couple of—" Her words were drowned out by more static. I held the phone out, annoyed.

"Car phone?" Bobby asked sympathetically.

I nodded glumly. The receiver squawked at me and I

took a chance at the meaning of her gibberish. "Sounds good," I shouted. "Call me tomorrow."

I hung up, pissed. "I wanted to ask her about that engine thing with Jeff."

"Forget the ex, Casey," Bobby said. "I have a feel for these things. They don't know each other. What I saw was a man trying to pick up a woman. I guarantee it. You're not jealous, are you?"

"God no. Just paranoid."

"Well, don't sit there and mope," he ordered. "Do something. You're making me nervous. Can't you go home and do whatever it is you do with that hell-on-wheels boyfriend of yours?"

"He's getting ready to throw another pity party," I said glumly. "I think I'll stay away."

"Then go get laid. You're bringing me down." He followed this romantic advice by gobbling the last of three cheeseburgers with a gusto most people reserve for their first meal after being lost in the wilderness for weeks.

"It's all food and sex with you, isn't it?"

"It is with everyone," Bobby pointed out. "I'm just willing to admit it."

I was pondering the possible truth of this pronouncement when my phone rang and Marcus Dupree came to my rescue. "You're a lucky woman, Casey."

"Price used his credit card?"

"He just charged an early dinner at the Sanitary Fish Market in Morehead City. The total was twenty-six dollars and change, in case you were wondering."

"I love you, Marcus," I told him. "If you ever decide to bat for my team, I'll give you a signing bonus that will knock your socks off."

"I am no longer a free agent," he said primly and hung up. Spoilsport.

I checked my road trip knapsack. It held a change of clothes, a toothbrush and a spare makeup kit. I added credit cards, identification, cash—and my beloved .357 Colt Python. I stopped for a moment to admire its barrel: six inches of glistening, hard steel. Could a girl ask for anything more? (Well sure, but she'd be unlikely to get it.)

In the past, I'd had as much bad luck with guns as with
boyfriends. They either weren't big enough, went off in
my hand or had a tendency to backfire. I finally decided
that while reliability in a boyfriend is boring, it's a must
when it comes to your roscoe. So I chose the Colt after
careful consultation with a friendly underground arms
dealer who didn't care about my felony conviction. I told
him I was interested in stopping assailants, not making
hamburger out of them. The .357 fit the bill, and the barrel
tucked nicely into my waistband. It even held a tampon in
a pinch. After giving it a good luck kiss, I slipped it into
my knapsack, then grabbed my down jacket and headed
for the front door.

"Where the hell are you going?" Bobby asked as I
dashed past.

"Road trip. I'm hot on the trail."

"You need to cut back on your coffee," he yelled as the
door slammed shut behind me.

There's nothing like a fast highway to clear the mind of
daily jumble. Especially since my car can take the wear
and tear. After a string of clunkers, I'd discovered a 1963
356-b Porsche and had it restored to its former beauty with
a little financial help from Burly. It was an odd shape,
almost like a bathtub, but it ran great, gripping the curves
like a railroad car rocking around a turn. There are two
stretches along Highway 70 between Raleigh and Morehead City where you can put the pedal to the metal, and I
hit a hundred easily on both. By the time I reached the
coast, thoughts of my ex had receded, replaced by the more
immediate need to close my latest case quickly so I could
get on with my life.

I knew from DMV records that Robert Price drove a
gold 1997 Camry with vanity plates that read TIFFGUY,
obviously in honor of his daughter Tiffany. It was better
than TUFFGUY, I'd decided. My first step would be to find
that car.

Just in case he was staying in Morehead City where he
had eaten dinner, I checked the motels in town first. No
luck. I turned back toward Atlantic Beach. As soon as I

crossed the causeway, I began cruising the parking lots of the few restaurants and motels still open for business. Atlantic Beach is a lonely place in the dead of winter. The unoccupied summer houses sag forlornly, and the neon-colored tourist traps look as washed out as over-the-hill strippers counting on sequins for glamour.

It was late and I was the only car on the road. There are twelve motels total in Atlantic Beach and Emerald Isle, and I quickly checked them all. Robert Price's car was not at any of them. It was time to stop by the house that my computer check had indicated was owned by two of his friends.

The road narrowed as I left the commercial strip. Scrub pines grew by the roadside in thick clumps, their gnarly limbs reaching out like beseeching hands. I slowed to a crawl, searching for the address. People don't usually run off into the void, they run to friends or family. If Robert Price was in this area, he was staying either at his friends' house or at a motel. So far, it hadn't been a motel.

I found the road I was looking for and turned onto a sandy lane that wound back through a forest of windswept shrubs. The air had warmed compared to inland. I rolled down the window, and the rich smell of Bogue Sound flooded the car. It was a biting, fertile odor that made me think of tar-colored mud and invisible life teeming in a soup of decaying organisms. There was a salty undertone to it, a hint of fish and something else: smoke. Someone had built a wood fire.

The lane ended abruptly in twin driveways. I checked the mailboxes and chose the one to the right. Cutting off my engine, I stepped out into the cold and crept down a narrow gravel drive. It wound even farther back into the brush, and the smell of wood smoke grew stronger with each step. I spotted lights through the pines and soon found myself at the edge of a circular front yard. A modern gray-shingled duplex had been built out over the sound on a small strip of land. A downstairs light was on in the right-hand unit, and a dimmer light was barely visible beneath a pulled shade on the second floor. A Camry was parked by the front door. Robert Price's car. Was he there alone with his daughter, or were the owners of the house with them? Neither Bobby nor I had been able to reach the couple by telephone. I'd need to find out before I made a move.

The great thing about sand is that you can march through with a parade of elephants and no one can hear you. Without Bobby D. along, I'm not quite that conspicuous and I easily reached what turned out to be the ground-floor bedroom without being heard. The shades were open and I could see enough in the dim light to know that no one was staying there. The bedspread was stretched smooth and there were no personal possessions in the room at all.

There's not a lot of variety when it comes to duplex layouts. I knew the upstairs held two or three bedrooms plus a bathroom. If Price had company, someone would be staying downstairs in the master bedroom while he slept on the second floor near his daughter. That meant Price was probably alone with Tiffany in the beach house.

I followed the exterior wall past a deserted kitchen, and discovered Price alone in the living room. He'd left the shades up on the sound side, maybe for the view of a brightly lit mainland across the water. He was sitting on a pastel-patterned couch drinking a beer and watching golf reruns on television. Pine logs smoldered in the fireplace.

A pair of raggedy-haired Barbie dolls lay sprawled on the carpet at his feet, and a trail of discarded miniature shoes and disco outfits littered the carpet all the way to the second-floor steps. Like all four-year old girls, Tiffany had been reluctant to go to bed. She'd left her version of a bread crumb trail behind her.

If you didn't know that he had unmercifully beaten his wife, you'd think Price looked pretty harmless. He was tall and stocky, but going soft, like an ex-athlete who has kept up his eating routine while cutting down on his exercise one considerably. He was wearing a rugby shirt tucked into khakis and a pair of topsiders on his feet. His outfit blended in perfectly with the golf crowd on the television screen, but the overall effect was a little white bread— even for my Florida cracker tastes. Hell, I hadn't seen a black preppie since the eighties, when I ventured to Atlanta for a weekend of sin with a renegade banker I met on a plane.

I was willing to bet that Tawny Bledsoe had something to do with the J. Crew image—and that Price would start sporting dashikis to make up for his mistake by the time he got through divorcing her.

After a while, my feet and fingers started to ache from the cold. Plus, Price was getting sleepy and his yawning was contagious. When he switched off the television and headed for the stairs, I decided to call it a night. I'd found Robert Price as requested. He was alone with his daughter. Now I could get a good night's sleep and let my client know my mission was done.

I picked up a six-pack of Bud at the Pirate's Cove Pier before heading for the Atlantic Beach Days Inn, where they were happy to rent me a cheap room with a carpet that felt slightly damp to the touch. I didn't want to think about why.

I sat on the bed, popped open a beer, and called Tawny Bledsoe. She wasn't at home. She wasn't in her car. I finally resorted to her beeper number.

She called me back immediately. "This is Tawny," she said in a voice that made me think she was a couple cans ahead of me in the six-pack department.

"Casey Jones," I told her. "I've found them."

"You're kidding? That's great news. Where are they?"

"Emerald Isle. In a private home."

"Those bastards." Her voice grew hard. "It's Linda and Jim's place, isn't it?"

"Yup," I admitted.

"I should have known they would take his side. And they were always so nice to me to my face. When all the time they knew that—"

"If you don't mind," I cut her off. "I'm too tired to listen to who took sides against what."

She was quiet, then said, "I guess you hear that a lot in your job."

"I do. And it's never fun." Talking about the hateful habits of divorce reminded me. "Let me ask you a ques-

tion, Tawny," I said casually. "That guy you met outside
my office hasn't been bothering you or anything, has he?"

"The loser who tried to pick me up? Never saw him
again. Why?"

"No big deal," I answered, wondering why she had just
lied to me. Obviously she had not connected the furry figure who ambled past them while they were bent over her
car engine with Bobby D. "I had some trouble with him.
I figure you have enough complications as it is, and I
wanted to warn you about him."

"Don't worry," she said. "He isn't my type. No money.
If you can't afford a motel room, you can't afford me."
She laughed. I didn't. It seemed a singularly inappropriate
joke for someone in her predicament to make. On the other
hand, the world is full of women who define their lives by
the men in them—and when they lose one romantic partner, the only thing they ever think about is how to replace
him with another. I had a feeling Tawny Bledsoe fell into
this category. You don't spend that much time on your
face and body unless you're trolling for big game.

I realized that, despite what her husband had done to
her, I really didn't like my client all that much.

"Look," I said. "I did my job. I found your daughter. Is
there anything else you need me to do?"

"No," she said. "I'll be there by morning. I'll take care
of the rest."

"Don't try to do this yourself," I warned her. "You need
to be careful. Look what he did the last—"

"I'm not coming down there alone," she interrupted. "I
have help."

With that, she hung up, leaving me to contemplate the
vagaries of love and marriage in the shabby splendor of
an off-season beach motel room. I had a hollow feeling
behind my heart, like maybe I needed to take a break from
all the divorce work I'd been doing lately. It was starting
to affect my personal life. Maybe Bobby was right. Maybe
I did need to get laid. It had been months since I'd had a
no-holds-barred tumble in the hay. And I hadn't missed it
much. That was the scary part.

Just to prove I wasn't Tawny Bledsoe, or even remotely

like her, I called Burly and was as nice as pie.

"It's me," I said when he answered. "I'm down at Emerald Isle on a case. I should be home tomorrow."

"I figured you were up to something." His voice had that same quality it always has, a sort of knowing inflection, like he could see down into my pelvic region and read my hormones like the I'Ching. Which, quite frankly, he could. When he wasn't feeling sorry for himself.

"Sorry you're feeling low this week," I added. It was about the limit of my sympathetic side, a trait I admit is not very admirable.

"It's okay," he said, a little too cheerfully for my tastes. "I'm going out with Debbie for dinner tomorrow night. She'll cheer me up."

"Great, have a good time. I'll call you later in the week."

I hung up feeling even more blue. Maybe Debbie cheered him up, but she did nothing for me. She was a physical therapist—anyone named Debbie is either a physical, occupational or sex therapist—and she had the hots for Burly big-time. I suspected she was going for two therapeutic relationships out of three. They probably fooled around, but that was none of my business. What annoyed me about Debbie was Burly's belief that she understood his predicament better than I ever could. Excuse me for walking on two legs and not spending my days cheering on the afflicted. I couldn't help who I was.

It took me three more beers, but I finally left my bad mood behind and slept. I woke before dawn and dressed quickly, then walked a couple of blocks to the main beach. A spectacular sunrise was unfolding over the pewter-colored ocean. The sun's deep yellow yolk pulsated in the thin winter air, surrounded by fingers of red-orange fire that reached across the pale January sky. Seagulls wheeled above the water, searching for the silver flash of fish surfacing in the morning sun. I felt better after watching the new day arrive, a little less burdened by the unhappiness around me. But then it seemed a shame to waste such a fine morning on going back to bed. So I decided to keep an eye on Robert Price, just to make sure he didn't decamp for new pastures before Tawny arrived.

This time I parked my car beneath the deck of a deserted house at the corner of the main turn-off. I pulled it all the way forward, well under the deck, where shadows hid its shape. A bathtub Porsche is not what you would call an inconspicuous vehicle. I opened a coffee from McDonald's and slumped down to wait. If Robert Price tried to leave with his daughter, he'd have to come out this way. And if Tawny Bledsoe came after him with a truckload of gun-toting cousins, I'd know that, too.

If you don't count my quick trip behind the dunes to pee, nothing happened until just after ten o'clock, when a red Ford Probe made a right turn onto the sandy lane. There was a beefy man with dark hair at the wheel, and a blond seated in the passenger seat that could have been Tawny. They went by too fast for me to get a good look, but I knew enough to get my ass in gear. I checked my gun and slipped it into the back of my waistband. I jogged down the sandy lane, then cut through the pine woods when I got close to the gray-shingled duplex. Although I couldn't see the house, angry voices marred the morning quiet, inspiring a flock of gulls to chime in with their own indignant cries. Hoo boy. I had a bad feeling about this one.

I like to think that, being female, I have an edge over my male counterparts. I'm a bitch under stress, not a bozo. Instead of rushing in under the influence of adrenaline, I am smart enough to think before I join the fray. I hid behind a narrow toolshed at the edge of the yard where I could wait unseen, just in case the adults worked it out on their own. It wasn't looking good.

Robert Price stood on the front porch of the duplex, dressed in a pair of gym shorts and a sweatshirt. His face was contorted with anger and his hands trembled at his side. Tiffany stood behind him, her little girl arms wrapped around his thighs for comfort as she peered out at the scene before her.

It was some scene to see. Tawny Bledsoe stood with her back to me, screaming at the top of her lungs. Her companion was even bigger than I'd expected, with short dark hair and clothes that proved he had money. He stood beside Tawny in menacing support as she called Robert Price every name in the library—never mind the book—including my personal favorite: "you cowardly, limp-dicked pecker-headed pus face."

I shook my head, disgusted. How two people can go at it like this and still think they're acting in the best interests of their kid is beyond me.

"Let's stop this now, Tawny," Price finally shouted. He had waited until his wife's fury ran out of steam. From long practice, I suspected.

"No," she yelled back. "You stop this. That's my daughter you're hiding. She should be with me."

"She's my daughter, too," Price countered. "And I have every right in the world to spend—"

"Rights! You have no rights!" Tawny took a step forward like she was going to smack him. He flinched, leaning away from her reach. He was probably the cowardly type, I figured. The kind who would never dare hit his wife in front of witnesses. Tawny's companion was keeping him in line just by being there.

Unfortunately, Tawny's companion decided to take a more active role. Without warning, he pulled an ugly-looking handgun from his overcoat pocket and pointed it straight at Price's face with total disregard for the child cowering behind him. What a macho asshole. He would have a Colt .45. Personal experience has taught me that the length of a man's barrel is in inverse proportion to the length of his dick. Tiffany began to cry, her pitiful sobs mingling with the retorts of the seagulls circling above.

I was just about to step from behind the shed and make a bad situation worse when Robert Price gave in. Without ever taking his eyes from the gun, he held his hands up and spoke calmly. "Fine, take Tiffany. Just put that thing away. I don't want her to get hurt."

"He's not going to shoot her, you moron," Tawny screamed. "He's going to shoot you if you give me any more trouble." Her face had healed remarkably since I had last seen her, but her hatred made it ugly in a much different way.

Price remained calm, I had to give him that. "No need

to shoot anyone," he said. "Tiff, get in the car with your mother. Do as she says."

The girl took a few steps, stopped and looked back at her father.

"Get in the car *now,* Tiffany," her mother snapped. "I'll buy you new clothes and new toys when we get home."

The girl still seemed reluctant to leave. I didn't like it. Maybe she knew something I didn't.

"Daddy?" she said, her voice quavering.

"Go with her," Price commanded. "I'll call you tomorrow."

"No, you won't." Tawny's beefy companion spoke up. "You won't be bothering her ever again. At all. Understand?" He walked up to Price, gun still in hand, and crowded him against the closed door of the duplex, thrusting his chest against his opponent like a male gorilla warning off a rival. "Call Tawny's house ever again and I'll kill you," he warned Price, then his voice dropped so low I couldn't hear what he said next. But I was pretty sure he wasn't pleading that they all just get along. Price flinched at the words, but he didn't back down.

"Put the gun away," Price begged. "I don't want my daughter hurt."

"Sure, I'll put it away." Tawny's companion raised the gun and brought it down hard, splitting Price's forehead with an ugly thunk. Price crumpled to the ground and the big guy began kicking him.

"This is for Tawny," he said, landing a blow near Price's kidneys. "And this is for me." He stomped on his legs, then kicked him in the head.

God, but I hated domestic cases. I couldn't stand by and watch this. But I didn't like combining guns and a kid.

Tawny Bledsoe made up my mind for me. "Come on, Boomer," she ordered him. "He's not worth it. We have Tiffany. Let's go."

The little girl was sitting in the backseat of the Probe, sobbing. She didn't even look up as her mother got into the car. Tawny glanced at her daughter, then stared out the window at Price's inert body. The aptly named Boomer was reluctant to leave the scene of his triumph and stood over Price, gazing down as if trying to decide where to kick next.

"Boomer, I said to let it go!" Tawny screamed out the car window. She sounded like the head harridan from hell when she issued her orders, and Boomer finally turned away. He slid into the driver's seat and gunned the engine in victory. I half expected him to hop back out and piss on Price as the final insult, but he leaned over to kiss Tawny instead. The kiss lingered. I could practically hear the saliva being swapped as they sucked on each other's tongues. When he was done marking his territory, Boomer put the car into gear and pulled away so quickly that the rear tires gouged the gravel, hitting the soil layer beneath and sending plumes of sand spraying as they sped away.

I was waiting by the side of the shed when the car passed by. Tawny had her head turned for a final peek at her badly beaten husband. She saw me standing in the bushes and her eyes locked on mine. She held the gaze, then reached up to her mouth and slowly wiped away her lover's kiss. She flung the spit out the window onto the ground at my feet, then smiled, as if to say, "So what? I got what I wanted."

Robert Price lay slumped on the ground, immobile, and I was furious with myself for letting it go that far. He had a steady pulse and didn't seem in immediate danger, but I couldn't bring him back to consciousness. Nor did I particularly want to. What would I say? "Hi, I'm Casey Jones, a private detective who got you into this mess. So sorry. How many bones are broken?"

Instead, I found a phone in the duplex. I dialed the emergency number and anonymously reported an injured man. As soon as I gave the address, I hung up and started running. I reached the safety of my car just as the first police cruisers turned off the main road onto the sandy lane. As soon as the first wave of officials disappeared down the turn-off, I got the hell out of Dodge, observing all speed limits on the way home, but not even stopping for a bathroom break.

By the time I was back home in my Durham apartment,

three and a half hours of blasting music had pretty much
erased the memory of Robert Price being kicked like some
junkyard dog in front of his daughter.

But I didn't think I was going to forget the sight of
Tiffany's crumpled four-year-old face any time soon.

THREE

A few days later, my Monday morning was ruined when Bobby announced with "I told you so" satisfaction that the one-thousand-dollar retainer check from Tawny Bledsoe had bounced higher than a superball.

"Insufficient funds?" I asked, figuring maybe the out-of-state commission check just hadn't cleared yet.

"Account closed. I called my guy at the bank. She closed it a month ago."

"That bitch." She had used and abused me to do her dirty work.

"I told you I had a hinky feeling about her." Bobby's voice made it clear that he was getting more than our lost money's worth of satisfaction from my mistake.

"I'll take care of it." I went to work dialing all of Tawny's phone numbers. No luck at any of them. Well, she'd have to surface sooner or later. I could wait. I couldn't forget, but I could wait.

I did a quick accounting and figured out that we had spent a couple grand of our time tracking down her kid. We'd been burned for more than that before, but I wasn't in the mood to cut the little lady any slack. Not after seeing her cheer her Neanderthal boyfriend on to violence in front of her own daughter.

The rest of the week was a madhouse and Tawny Bledsoe got put on the back burner. I didn't hear from Jeff again and figured he had given up and gone back to Florida for his own funeral. I didn't much care. More important matters replaced him. First, the Garner cops asked me to go undercover for a drug buy and there's nothing I love better than dressing up as a biker slut. Thanks to my spectacular cleavage—which could conceal a video camera, much less a microphone—they were able to bring down a 280-pound drug-dealing speed freak who was cooking batches of highly volatile methamphetamine on his trailer stove with the help of his spaced-out wife and two young children. I think everyone involved felt better after that disaster-in-the-making was diffused.

Next, a prominent local businesswoman asked us to investigate her wealthy fiancé. I did her one better. Not only did we discover that he was in hock up to his toupee, I nailed him as a sleazeball. I tailed him to a topless bar and watched him tip the dancers twenty-dollar bills as payment for lap dances (a euphemism if ever I've heard one). He spent hundreds of dollars of my client's money on static cling while I took photos. Then the dunce tried to pick me up at the bar. I got him on tape insisting he was single, unattached, hot to trot and willing to swing with the best of them. I figured we saved our client a whole lot of money with that extra effort on my part. She agreed and insisted on a bonus, then promised to steer some corporate work our way. Music to Bobby D.'s ears.

This last client was so nice, in fact, that she almost made me forget about Tawny Bledsoe and the dozen useless phone calls I made trying to track her down for payment. But on Saturday morning, something happened to remind me that I had been taken in by a 105-pound blond dressed in pink cashmere.

I was sitting at my desk, savoring the smug feeling of accomplishment that a busy week gives me and wondering if Burly's mood had improved any in the few days since I'd last heard from him. My diet had gone belly-up (and out) and there was a box of warm Krispy Kremes and two double lattes at my elbow. I was reading a tabloid and laughing over a photo of Rod Stewart being tongue-lashed in public by his soon-to-be ex-wife when Bobby came into my office, puffing from the exertion of walking the thirty feet from his car to my desk.

"Touch those doughnuts and you draw back a bloody stump," I warned him.

"Relax. I got my own box on the way in."

More like his own truckload, I suspected. "What brings you in on the weekend?" I asked. "Fanny give you the bum's rush?" Fanny was Bobby's wealthy girlfriend. She spent most of her time in Florida, but had been in town for an extended holiday celebration.

"She's headed back to Lauderdale. I'm joining her next week so we can try that new crab joint everyone's talking about."

Fanny and Bobby were on a personal journey to eat at every restaurant in America, without regard to quality or location. A roach coach in San Diego was every bit as desirable as the *Four Seasons* in New York. Eating was their hobby, eating together was their passion. It was a match made in the kitchens of heaven.

"So, you're in the office because you're bored?" I asked. "Does this mean you're actually going to do some work for a change?"

"No, I'm in the office because of this." He tossed a copy of that morning's *News & Observer* on my desk, narrowly missing my latte-in-progress.

"Watch it," I complained.

"Read it," he ordered. "Front page. Didn't you say that guy who pulled the gun down at the beach was named Boomer or something?"

"Yeah, but I pray it's just a nickname."

"That him?" Bobby placed a pudgy finger on a portrait studio photograph of a respectable-looking local businessman identified by its caption as Bernard "Boomer" Cockshutt, owner of Cockshutt Motors.

"What's he done?" I asked warily.

"He died," Bobby said. "Thursday night. They found him in his car out at Lake Johnston, at the back of the parking lot. He'd been shot through the head."

"Suicide?" I asked hopefully.

"Doubt it. He was in the front seat. The gun was on the floor of the backseat. Wiped clean. No fingerprints."

"Shit," I said. "Was it a Colt .45?"

Bobby nodded. "That's what my source says."

"I think I saw that gun. He was holding it on Robert Price."

"I figured." Bobby pulled up my visitor's chair and did his best to fit inside the allotted space. His thighs popped out from under the arms like loaves of bread bulging from their pans. "You gotta go to the cops, Case."

"If I go to the cops, the first person they're going to suspect is Robert Price."

"They already do suspect him. They're looking for him now."

I groaned. "Please don't tell me I helped get a man killed?"

Bobby shrugged. "You were just doing what you get paid for."

"Or don't get paid for," I reminded him.

Bobby nodded sadly. "We'll never get that dame to settle up now. She'll milk the tabloid shows for every penny she can get. Then she'll split and leave Price to rot in jail."

"Maybe she did it?" I asked hopefully.

Bobby shook his head. "My source says she was attending a church retreat in Winston-Salem at the time. Lots of good folk can attest to it."

"How convenient," I muttered, pulling the paper closer. The article was short. Not much information had been made public by the time the edition went to press. It confirmed that Boomer Cockshutt was dead. It offered the tidbit that he had been an All-American tackle from Wake Forest University in his glory days. That figures. Surely the violence I witnessed at the beach was a steroid-inspired flashback of some sort. The article went on to say that he had been shot once through the head and was killed instantly, that police were following several leads and blah, blah, blah.

The story ended with a few predictable quotes from Lake Johnston neighborhood residents complaining of night traffic at the lake and warning teenagers to stay away. Hey, I thought, that's it: it's that mythical guy with the hook for a hand that offed Boomer. The bloody stump is

probably hanging off the door handle of the car right now.
Forensics must have missed it.

"I don't like this." I shoved the paper into the trash can.
"If I'd had to predict, I would have said that Robert Price
would end up the corpse, not this guy."

"You got the photos?" Bobby asked.

"What photos?"

"The photos of Tawny Bledsoe with the shit beat out of
her."

"Sure. Why?"

"You've got to give them to the cops, babe. They need
to know Robert Price is violent. Plus, you were there at
the beach. You witnessed his motive for killing this guy.
Boomer was keeping Price from seeing his kid."

"Actually, it was more like Boomer was caving Price's
skull in."

"Whatever. You have to go to the cops. I can't afford
for them to find out later that we held anything back. We
need their goodwill and my contact says this murder has
them really pissed off."

"Of course it's pissing them off," I said. "It's not like
two teenage punks shot each other over a bag of dope.
Hell, this guy was a member of the chamber of commerce.
Lower the flags. Bring on the bagpipes. Let's give him a
state funeral, why don't we?"

"What's eating you? Maybe the guy was an asshole, but
he didn't deserve to be shot through the head."

"You know what's eating me? This whole case stunk
from the start. It should have been simple. Instead, it
turned ugly. Now it's getting uglier. And, somehow, we're
in the middle of it."

"You're pissed at the blond," Bobby guessed. "You
never like natural blonds."

"Don't be so sure her collar matches her cuff. Besides,
it's not her hair color, it's *her* I don't like. And I didn't
like her boyfriend much, either. Dead or alive."

"What about Robert Price?" Bobby asked reasonably.
"You like him all of a sudden? Look what he did to his
wife." He paused. "If he was the one who did it."

"I don't like anyone but the kid," I said, chewing on

another Krispy Kreme. "And she'll probably get dragged into this soon enough."

"It can't be easy having dear old Dad arrested for murder," Bobby agreed. "And I think that's what'll happen."

"Who's your source?" I asked.

Bobby adopted his Mona Lisa grin. "Sorry. Her identity is confidential."

"But you call her Deep Throat?" I suggested wryly. "Or wish you could?"

"Go talk to the cops," Bobby reminded me. "Do it before they come to you."

I sighed. He was right. An afternoon at the Raleigh Police Department was not my idea of weekend fun. But it would be worse if I didn't go right away.

They know me pretty well down at the RPD, some of them better than others. I saw a couple of ex-boyfriends on my way upstairs and one guy I'd had my eye on just before I met Burly. I flirted with him for a few minutes because I like to keep my options open, then headed for the interview room where a detective working the Cockshutt murder was waiting to see me.

They'd definitely sent in the B-Team. The infamous Detective Roland Dick was waiting for me. Everyone I know calls him Dick-Dick because, well, because he acts like a dick. He'd become a cop for all the wrong reasons and couldn't be trusted alone with a suspect since he managed to violate an average of one constitutional right per minute. At least three cases had been thrown out of court because of him, and there wasn't a person on the force who even wanted to be seen with Dick-Dick, much less work with him. But he couldn't be fired because he claimed to be one-eighth American Indian and had joined all the minority-officer clubs he could find. Consequently, he was tolerated but frequently assigned to backup tasks, well away from the front line.

The fact that he was sitting across from me stuffing his face with cheese straws and slurping Pepsi was proof that the Cockshutt murder team didn't think I had much to offer them.

"Don't I know you?" Dick-Dick asked in a vaguely snide tone of voice.

"No, you don't," I said flatly, not adding that I fervently hoped to keep it that way. Orange flour from the cheese straws coated his liver lips. His mouth seemed to float in his face like some grotesque species of puff fish. I couldn't take my eyes off those lips. They were as gruesomely fascinating as a traffic accident.

"I don't have all day," he barked, annoyed at my rebuff. "What's so important about the Cockshutt murder that you had to pull me away from my real work?"

I forced a smile on my face, then proceeded to give the fat-ass scumbag a summary of what I had seen at the beach involving Robert Price and Boomer Cockshutt. He perked up when I gave him a couple of the blurrier photos I'd taken of a badly beaten Tawny Bledsoe and provided the lurid details on their purported domestic problems. Unfortunately, this inspired Dick-Dick to take notes at the speed of a drugged snail, forcing me to repeat myself endlessly. He made me miserable for over an hour. When I was done, he didn't even bother to thank me for coming in and I made a vow that this would be the last time I went out of my way to perform my civic duty.

"You can go now," he said, slamming his notebook shut. "We'll be in touch."

In your dreams, I thought as I sulked from the room. I was pissed that I had wasted my time trying to do the right thing.

But, as it turned out, the day was not an entire waste. Guess who I ran into in the lobby? Yup. Good old Bill Butler. My favorite man in blue. Suddenly we were nose-to-nose for the first time in months.

"Well, well," I said. "Look who the cat drug in."

"I work here," he countered. "What's your excuse?"

I started to tell him, then stopped. He knew Tawny Bledsoe after all, and who knew if it was in the biblical sense or worse? "Business," I said. "Minor stuff."

"It's all minor stuff. That's my new motto. I'm trying to be very Zen about the job." Neither one of us really heard a word he said.

Being nose-to-nose finally got to him and he took a step back, letting his gaze drop to my high-top tennis shoes. His eyes worked their way up my black thermal stockings to my open coat and, beneath it, my pale pink mohair miniskirt and matching angora sweater. "Isn't it a little cold for an outfit like that?" he asked, staring at the front of my sweater. Okay, so my personal barometers had popped to attention. It wasn't because of the cold.

"Looks like it's warming up," I said, flashing him my biggest smile. I nodded toward his enthusiastic trousers. "Polyester blends give you away every time."

He actually blushed. "You scare me, Casey," he admitted unexpectedly.

"I'll consider that a compliment."

"You should." We stared at each other for a moment in silence.

"You really do have an arrangement worked out with that boyfriend of yours, don't you?" he finally said.

"I really do." I paused. "But that doesn't mean I'm going to arrange things with you."

"That's cold." He turned away. "And here I was going to tell you how much I liked you back as a blond."

"You only like me being taken already," I called after him. "Which is why, when I stray, it will be with another cat."

He shrugged like he really didn't care and marched away. He sure was cute when he was angry. And those black pants of his were a very nice fit.

There had been a lot of truth in what I said to him. Bill Butler was the kind of guy who liked his women married, involved with someone else or otherwise removed from any possibility of actually becoming entangled with him. I didn't want to give him the satisfaction of cooperating with his misogynistic insecurities—even if I was dying for a shot of hips.

By Monday, the local newspapers had uncovered enough information on the Cockshutt murder to take up most of the front page. The first thing that became apparent was that the RPD had sprung a leak as big as Falls of the

Neuse. There was stuff in the main article that no one had any business knowing. Dick-Dick and his orange liver lips had struck again.

"Are you reading what I'm reading?" I yelled to Bobby. The only sounds I'd heard from the front office since I'd arrived had been the steady munch of ham biscuits being consumed. I was once again trying to stick to black coffee in recognition of the fact that my hormones were steering me toward disrobing in front of a yet-to-be-identified new guy soon and I wanted to be ready.

"Yeah, I'm reading it. Who do you think the faucet is?"

"Roland Dick," I yelled back. "Some female reporter probably stroked his leg and he started spouting off like Moby Dick."

"You mean Moby Dick-Dick," Bobby yelled back, then started to har-har in that bull seal bellow of his. I was pleased at his quasi-literary joke. His idea of a great book is *Debbie Does Dallas Restaurants*. It meant I was rubbing off on him.

The article had enough case details to qualify as discovery for the defense team. Protected or not, Dick-Dick was going to be in hot water once the chief got a gander at all the beans he had spilled.

According to the *N&O*, Boomer Cockshutt was legally drunk when slain and had bragged earlier to a coworker that he was meeting a girlfriend that night. Contents of his stomach showed he had enjoyed dinner less than two hours before his death: steak, salad, french fries and bourbon. A Southern last meal, if ever there was one. The gun he'd been killed with had indeed been wiped clean of prints and dropped into the backseat after the fatal shot. Forensic tests were now being conducted on trace fibers and hairs found in the Probe, with results expected later on in the week. After that, the facts petered out in favor of personal details on Boomer and juicy speculation.

Boomer Cockshutt had a wife and two kids, it seemed, though the family was too distraught to comment. I wondered what the wife was most upset about: losing her husband or being publicly humiliated on the front page of her local paper. According to unnamed sources, the article went on to say, Boomer had been seeing an unnamed married woman secretly for months and had bragged to coworkers that the woman's estranged husband was violent.

"Boomer liked to live on the edge, and he liked the ladies," one employee went on record as saying. "I wouldn't be the least bit surprised to hear that he was shot by an irate husband."

Great. The jury was already in. Robert Price was toast.

The cops thought so, too. The article ended by saying that the married woman had cooperated fully and been cleared of suspicion in Boomer's death. But the police were still trying to get in contact with her estranged husband to verify his whereabouts on the night of the killing.

Which meant that so far they had been unable to locate Robert Price. And now they never would. The article was an invitation to flee.

"What do you say, Bobby?" I called out. "Think he's holed up with his sister in Rocky Mount?"

I heard a weird strangling sound in reply, like Bobby had choked on a ham biscuit. I jumped up, prepared to perform a trampoline-style version of the Heimlich maneuver, and rushed into the outer office. I stopped short in surprise.

Robert Price stood uncertainly in our doorway. He glanced back and forth between the newspaper spread open on Bobby's desk and our stunned faces.

"You have to help me." His deep voice broke as his eyes locked on mine. "I know you were at the beach. You saw what she's like. You're the only one who will believe what I have to say."

"Have a seat," I said calmly, though my insides felt like I'd swallowed a fistful of Mexican jumping beans. I'd given Bobby a signal and had no way of knowing whether he'd interpreted it correctly. "How did you find out about me?"

"When they were talking to my lawyer and trying to get me to cut a deal and come in, one of the detectives claimed that you were willing to testify that I had a motive to kill that Cockshutt guy."

I was going to strangle Dick-Dick when I saw him, but odds were good I'd have to wait in line for the privilege.

I didn't know what to say, so I bought some time by looking Price over. He was grimy and his hair was matted. His polo shirt was stained with sweat, his pants wrinkled, his fingernails dirty. He hadn't slept in a bed the night before.

Price noticed me looking him over and dropped his head in shame, then touched the ragged bandage wound around his head. We both winced.

"The detective claims that you saw that Cockshutt guy hit me at the beach in a dispute over Tiffany," he said.

"I was there," I admitted reluctantly. "It was a pretty ugly scene."

"Then you saw what she was like. You'll help me."

"Saw what who was like?" I asked.

"My wife." He paused. "Tawny. She set me up. I know she did."

"Look, Mr. Price," I said, as sympathetically as I could. He was, after all, a hunted man and the smell of fear was starting to fill my office. His eyes were glazed with a watery film rimmed in yellow, and his breath was shallow. Like I said, desperation makes me nervous. "Your wife came in here badly beaten by you, with a legal court order granting her full custody of her child." I forced myself to remember the damage he had done. "She asked me to find out where you had taken the girl. I found you. She came and got her daughter. End of story."

I took a couple snapshots of Tawny from a drawer and tossed them across the desk. "You started it, so don't blame me."

He hardly looked at the photos. "It's a lie," he said, his voice cracking again.

"What's a lie?" I asked, trying not to stare behind him into the hall. Damn it, Bobby—use your head. I'm trapped in my office with a murderer.

"Everything." He picked up a photo and waved it at me. "I didn't do this to her. I hadn't seen her in months until that day at the beach. And I don't ever want to see her again."

"Oh, yeah? Then how did you manage to get your daughter away from your wife to take her to the beach?"

"Their neighbor brought her to me after Tawny dumped Tiffany on her and disappeared for three days."

"What about the court order?" I asked. "Granting her full custody?"

"No way," he said. Anger flashed in his voice. "I'd never give up custody of my daughter. Whatever she showed you was a lie. It's always a lie with her. You don't know her. We have shared custody. It was my week. I didn't kidnap my daughter. Tawny did when she showed up with that maniac to take her back."

"Okay, Mr. Price," I said soothingly, stalling for time. "Make sure you tell that to your lawyer. I'm sure they'll be able to straighten it out."

"You don't understand," he shouted, jumping to his feet. He towered over me, his six and a half feet of anger and frustration intimidating in the extreme. I inched my hand toward the drawer where I stored my gun. God, but I was sorry I'd ever set eyes on Tawny Bledsoe.

"Let me try to understand," I said calmly. "Please, have a seat. I'll listen."

He remained standing. "My wife is . . ." He groped for words. "My wife is empty inside. She lies and she steals as easily as the rest of us breathe. She doesn't care about anyone but herself. She only pretends to care when she thinks she can get something out of you. She doesn't even care about her daughter."

"Then why would she go through the trouble of hiring me to find Tiffany?" I asked. No sounds yet from the outer office. Come on, Bobby, come on.

"Because she was using you to frame me, to make it look like I had a motive to kill. I dumped her and she'll never forgive me for that. She has to *win* and that means taking me down. Forever." His words were a hiss. "She is empty inside. Empty and evil." He slapped a palm on my desk. The sound echoed like a gunshot. My fingers touched the drawer pull and I rested them there, waiting.

"What the fuck is the matter with you people?" Price yelled when I did not respond. "Why can't any of you believe me? Just because she's small and blond and acts so helpless, why the hell can't anyone see her for what she really is? She's been doing this for years, do you understand? For years. Getting away with hurting people, and taking from people, and lying and stealing, and now she's going to get away with murder." His voice dropped to a whisper, making him sound even crazier. "I've been calling people about her. I've been asking them. You go. You ask them. They'll tell you."

"Ask who?" I said, checking the clock. He'd been in my office for eight minutes and it felt like eight months.

"Ask her ex-husband. Ask her kids. Ask the people she's worked with."

"She doesn't have any kids except for Tiffany," I said, knowing then that he was unstable.

"Yes, she does," he shouted back. "That's what I'm saying. She lies and her lies are getting worse. They don't make sense anymore. They can be found out. And do you know why?" Unwillingly, I looked up. He was frightened yet excited, his pupils dilated, the whites of his eyes frozen wide. "She's slipping," he confided in a hoarse whisper. "She's obsessed with getting older. She's getting these wrinkles, you see, little ones around her eyes and mouth." He clawed at his eyes and leaned even closer to me. "She knows she won't be able to get away with her act much longer. The evil is showing on her face. Men aren't going to fall for it anymore. So she's desperate. And if she's desperate, she's dangerous."

I looked away, embarrassed. I was filled with sadness for the broken man standing before me.

His voice came back full force. "Listen to me, please." He grabbed my arm, forcing me to look at him. "She lied to you, so that she could set me up for murder. No one is going to believe me. Don't you see? I'm the perfect fall guy. I'm a black man and she's what she is. And now she has you to tell the world I had a motive. No one will stand up for me. My own people abandoned me when I married her. I have no one to believe me. Except for you. You have to help me. You have to. I don't have anyone else." His voice broke and he began to sob, his shoulders heaving with every ragged breath. "My daughter can't be left with her. She'll destroy Tiffany. You can't let her do this."

"Mr. Price," I began, but, at long last, without so much as a warning cough, four cops burst into my office. Two of them jumped on Price and knocked him to the ground. He hit his head on the chair on the way down, triggering a fresh flow of blood from his scalp wound. He started to struggle and two more cops piled on him. They grabbed his arms and jerked him upright. They threw him against a wall, kicked his legs apart and cuffed his hands behind his back.

"You're making a mistake," he started to say, but one of the cops kneed him in the soft spot of his left calf and he almost crumpled to the floor.

"That's enough," I said more loudly than I'd intended. The cops stared at me. "You have him. Now get him out of here. He's sick. He needs help."

They took turns dragging him through our outer office. Price dwarfed the officers and their vague fear made the four men even more aggressive. They prodded and jerked him along. Price alternated between trying to struggle and allowing himself to be dragged. It was pitiful and it was pathetic. It left a bad taste in my mouth. It wasn't anything I ever wanted to see again.

"Don't you get it?" Price shouted as the cops threw him out the front door. "It was too easy. The way you found me. She knew where I was. She set you up, too. She's using you. Just check the court papers. You'll see it's a lie." His voice faded as the cops hustled him into a waiting squad car.

"God almighty," Bobby said. "What the hell was he saying to you? I was ten seconds away from busting in with my shotgun when the frigging cops arrived."

"I don't know," I said, my stomach filling with an acrid dread. "But I got a real bad feeling that what he was trying to tell me was the truth."

FOUR

"You can't."

"I can."

"You can't."

"I *can*," I told Bobby. "And I am."

"There's no percentage in it. All you're going to do is lose us more money."

"Bobby," I explained. "This isn't about money. This is about some skinny, chicken-necked little twat thinking she can make a fool out of me by batting her eyelashes. If even a little bit of what Robert Price says is true, than that woman sat there in my chair and dredged up some perverted version of sisterhood to get me to help her send an innocent man to jail. She is going to pay for that. No one takes me for a fool. No one."

"Sheesh," Bobby grumbled. "That's *if* what Price said was true. Remind me to stay on your good side."

"Want to stay on my good side? Help me get to the truth."

"Me? No way." He rummaged around in a shopping bag on the floor and came up with a box of Little Debbie Raisin Cakes, which he placed on his desk as reverently as if it were the golden ark. He selected four of the cakes for a snack. "All that excitement is bad for my heart," he confided.

"I'm gonna be bad for your heart if you don't help me."

"What can I do?" he asked indignantly.

"You can find out who the court reporter was on the

Price versus Bledsoe custody case. I want to talk to them."

"What was wrong with the court papers? You saw them."

"I saw them, but they may be fake. And I'll bet you dollars to doughnuts that the actual court papers are sealed. Otherwise, she'd never risk passing off phony ones as genuine. It would be too easy to check."

"This is why I never had children," Bobby said. "It brings out the worst in people." But he reached for the phone anyway, leaving me to ponder the horrifying thought of little no-necked, roly-poly Bobby D.'s populating the earth.

By the next night, I was sitting in a country diner twelve miles east of Raleigh staring at the scrawniest woman I had ever seen. Her dark hair was wound into a protruding bulb on top of her head and she wore a black dress with white cuffs. I felt like I was having dinner with Olive Oyl. I resisted the urge to eat spinach, and ordered a plate of chicken-and-dumplings instead.

My companion was picking at a salad that looked as if it had been hanging around for a week hoping to be noticed. We discussed Bobby for a few minutes, but when it became apparent that the court reporter didn't know he now had a steady girlfriend, I steered the subject to Price versus Bledsoe.

"It was an awful case," she told me. "Judge Poe even ordered a sealed courtroom. Price's lawyer argued that his client's public position would attract the media, to the detriment of the child. Judge Poe agreed."

"So you could technically get in trouble for talking to me?" I asked.

The woman nodded. "More than technically."

"Then why are you doing it?"

She pushed a mushy tomato around. "You said that this was about Robert Price's arrest for murder? Right?"

"Right."

She looked around to see if anyone could overhear her. "I just don't believe he could do something like that," she whispered. "Even if he was a you-know-what. I mean, he may be colored, but he is well-educated. He sounds just like you and me."

Well, not quite. He had at least four years of higher education on both of us—and it showed. But who was I to quibble?

"To be perfectly honest," the court reporter added, "he is quite a nice-looking man. Considering. I can even see how the wife might have crossed that line, you know?" She raised an eyebrow at me and I nodded. "I mean, marrying someone not of her own color and all."

She looked around the diner again. Matched sets of sturdy country folk sat quietly, downing their quotas of starch and fatty meats. No one wore a white hood over his head, so I guess she felt safe enough to continue.

"My ex-husband would kill me for saying so," she whispered. "But for a colored man, Robert Price was deeply concerned about his daughter. More than the mother, if you ask me."

I could tell she was at war with her own bigotry. She had been raised to distrust and fear anyone different from her, especially black men, but being tall and awkward— not to mention homely—she probably didn't dig petite blonds much either. Especially ones who twitched their butts like lightning bugs in heat.

"What made you feel Price was a good father?" I asked.

"A couple of things," she said. "He agreed to the child support amount immediately, though it was quite high. And when the wife said she wanted alimony as well, so she could stay home and take care of the little girl, the husband agreed to that. But," she paused for dramatic effect, "he wanted it stipulated that she could not engage nonfamily baby-sitters for more than ten hours a week."

"In other words, he didn't trust her to stay home with the kid?"

"He did not."

"It sounds like the mother was going to get full custody."

"She was. At first. But then something happened to change that."

"What?" I asked as I worked on a small mountain of

fried okra. Some people won't touch okra. They claim it's hairy on the outside and slimy on the inside. Naturally, most of these people are men.

The court reporter nibbled on a carrot as she thought about my question. "I guess everything changed when Price's lawyer called a man named Joe Scurlock to the stand. There was a big old bunch of excitement at Miss Bledsoe's table, and then her lawyer jumped up and demanded a sidebar conference. Judge Poe listened for a moment, I couldn't hear a word myself, and then she called a recess and everyone trooped back to her office. Except for me, I'm sorry to say. The whole thing was off the record."

I was disappointed and my face showed it.

"When they came back," she said, anxious to help, "Robert Price's lawyer made a motion to grant his client full custody of the girl—and Miss Bledsoe's lawyer didn't make a peep."

"So the *father* got custody?" I asked, confused.

The court reporter shook her head. "Judge Poe decided to bring in a court-appointed child psychiatrist to interview the little girl. The doctor spent all afternoon with Tiffany. The next morning he testified that it would be detrimental for Tiffany to be deprived of her mother's presence during the next six years."

"What happened then?"

"Robert Price started whispering to his lawyer, and then his lawyer jumped up and asked if he could question the psychiatrist again. But all he asked was one thing: would joint custody provide the little girl with enough contact with her mother? The shrink said yes. And that was when Price's lawyer said they wanted to amend their motion to request joint custody instead of sole custody."

"Robert Price suggested joint custody because the shrink thought it was best for Tiffany?"

She nodded. "That was another reason why I thought he really cared about his daughter. No matter what happened, no matter how much money his wife asked for, no matter how horrible her lawyer acted, Mr. Price never lost his

temper. He just sat there calmly while his lawyer worked
out the arrangements."

"So Price was allowed to see Tiffany after the custody
hearing was over?"

"Oh, sure. He was supposed to see her every other week.
And every other major holiday."

"Poor kid," I murmured. "She must have felt like a Ping-
Pong ball."

"He had stuff on her," my companion whispered suddenly, her thin lips barely moving. "I know he did."

"Robert Price had something on Tawny Bledsoe?"

She nodded emphatically. "Toward the end, whenever
her lawyer would make some outrageous demand, his lawyer would call a sidebar conference, they'd whisper, and
then her lawyer would either drop his motion or soften his
demands. She didn't like it *at all,* let me tell you. She was
used to getting her own way, that woman was. You could
tell just by looking at her."

"Who was in the courtroom?" I asked, wondering why
Price had not made his information public. Who had he
been protecting? "Was Tiffany there?"

"Sometimes," the court reporter said. "Not always. Only
if the judge wanted to question her. But the grandmother
was there both days."

"The grandmother on which side?" I asked.

"I think maybe she was *his* mother. Since she was colored."

And here I was the professional detective.

"Anyone else?" I asked, wondering where Tawny's family had been.

"Mr. Price's sister took the little girl in and out of the
courtroom."

"No one from Tawny's side of the family?"

The woman shifted uncomfortably. "I don't think her
family was very happy she had married him."

In that case, they sure as hell weren't thrilled about it
now.

"So, who is Joe Scurlock?" I asked, remembering the
man who had started to testify, then been stopped by
Tawny's lawyer.

The court reporter shook her head. "I don't know. He never came back into the courtroom."

I changed the subject. "How easy is it to fake a court order?" I was thinking about the fat stack of documents Tawny had given me that first day in my office.

The woman pushed her untouched lettuce to the edges of her plate. "It's real easy these days, what with word processing. Except for the seal. That would be hard to fake without going through a lot of trouble."

"But the seal only appears on the final page?" I asked. She nodded.

"So someone could use the back page from a prior court order and attach it to forged front pages?" I asked.

She looked perplexed. "I guess. But why would anyone do that?"

Oh, to fake out some cracker girl PI who doesn't know her ass from a hole in the ground, I thought. "Just speculating," I said out loud. "How about some dessert? Maybe pie?"

"Oh, no. I'm getting fat," she protested. "My husband left me after I gained too much weight when the kids were born. So I lost forty pounds after the divorce and I want to keep it off. In case I start dating again."

As she stood and reached for her check, I watched her bony body unfold like some sort of gawky paper marionette. Jesus, I thought, what women will do just to have some poor dumb-ass man at their side.

Then I remembered Tawny, and thought of how it was true going the other way, too. Stupidity was an equal opportunity inflicter.

"She lied about the court order," Burly acknowledged. "That doesn't mean she's guilty of murder." We were having drinks at MacLaine's later that same night. The evening had started out well, but quickly deteriorated— mostly because I couldn't think of anything but kicking Tawny Bledsoe's ass.

"If it looks like a duck and walks like a duck," I began, but was interrupted by laughter from a group of well-lubricated men I'd never seen at the bar before. I'd have guessed a salesmen convention, except that they weren't polished in that cheesy way. Almost all of them wore eye-glasses and sported haircuts not popular in ten years.

I sat at the bar beside Burly, watching my bartender friend Jack handle the heavy crowd. It was rarely this busy on a weekday night. I caught Jack's eye and exchanged a smile. Jack was more than a friend to me. He was also my sometimes bed partner, though it wasn't a role that we paraded in front of Burly for obvious reasons. I had hesitated at bringing the two men together at all, but my fantasies proved unfounded. They were so busy male bonding, they never got around to fighting over me. I'd had visions of Jack threatening Burly with a corkscrew and Burly retaliating by running over Jack with his wheelchair, but between all the palm slapping and talk about the Broncos, I may as well have been a stuffed moose head on the wall. Men can be so annoying.

"What is up with these guys?" I yelled across the bar at Jack.

"Pathologists' convention!" a fat man with a red face screamed back at me over the din. "Couldn't you just *die*?!"

He was not more than six inches from my elbow and almost perforated my right eardrum as he laughed hysterically at his joke. He turned back to his friends, bumping my arm and nearly knocking over my glass of Johnnie Walker Black. I exchanged a glance with Burly.

"It was your idea to come here," was all Burly said.

Christ, but he was being uncommunicative. Any hopes I'd had that his latest ebony wave would be a fleeting one had evaporated.

"Be right back," Burly said abruptly as he wheeled toward the cigarette machine. Another bad sign. He knew I hated kissing him when he smoked.

"What's up, Casey?" Jack said sympathetically as he stopped by on his way to the sink. "Your boy slipping into darkness again?"

"Looks that way." I sighed.

"We all have our demons," Jack pointed out as he set

up a row of glasses and poured triple shots of whiskey into each. "What's yours these days?"

I fished out the photographs of Tawny Bledsoe that I had kept and arranged them in a row on the bar. "This is my demon."

Jack peered at the Polaroids and winced. "Ouch. She ran into a big door."

"Yeah, she did." I fingered one of the photos, touching a purple bruise thoughtfully. "She claims her husband did this to her. But he denies it."

"Like he's going to admit it?" Jack said. As he slid the drinks down the bar toward a waiting cluster of revelers, the same fat man with the red face who had bumped my elbow earlier leaned forward and stared at Tawny's photos.

"Not bad," he offered loudly. "Pretty authentic. But that one's obviously fake." He touched a bruise that stretched across the top of Tawny's right cheek.

"Fake?" I asked.

"Sure. You a makeup artist or something?" He peered at me closely and a waft of boozy breath brushed my face. "You gals ought to ask the professionals before you jump in with your brushes. Hey, Oscar!" he screamed, attracting the attention of a thin man with wire-rimmed glasses. "Take a look at these and tell the little lady where she went wrong."

Oscar and a couple of his friends crowded around the photos, liquor glasses in hand. They murmured and argued, swapping opinions until Oscar finally held up a hand for silence. "Okay," he said. "These aren't bad." He nodded toward the photos. "You do this to her?"

"No," I said emphatically. "Though something tells me I'm going to want to."

"Well, this side of the face looks pretty authentic." He placed a finger over Tawny's left eye. "But the other side is phony. You shaded this bruise in with too much purple. It's right over a major bone plate, see? The layer of tissue is exceptionally thin at that point. Not enough blood to have bloomed that deeply or so large. And this bruise would have followed an arc this way." He swept his fingers downward over the Polaroid. "But I got to hand it to you—

the rest of the injuries look absolutely genuine. You in theater or something?"

"Sometimes I act happy," I said, sliding the photos off the bar and tucking them into my jeans. "Hey, Jack—buy these guys a round on me, would you?"

"All right," one of them said, pumping a fist in the air. "Southerners sure are a friendly lot." Hah. Wait until he met the Southern patrolman trolling for drunks outside the bar.

Jack gave me a look that let me know I was bringing coals to Newcastle by buying drinks for the pathologists, but I ignored it and worked on my own whiskey instead, pondering why Tawny Bledsoe had found it necessary to enhance her injuries. And wondering who was responsible for the real bruises. Robert Price? Boomer? Someone else? No way they were self-inflicted.

"Ready to get out of here?" Burly asked when he returned with his smokes. His dark stare met mine, and a stab of bittersweet lust tinged with pain shot through me at the haunted look in his eyes. I never loved Burly so much as when he was slipping away from me.

"Sure," I said. "Let's stay at my apartment. It's closer and I can make you breakfast in the morning."

"I wouldn't be very good company right now," he muttered, sliding his bar change into his pocket and unwrapping the pack of cigarettes. "I think I'll head home alone. I'll call you."

I watched him maneuver out the door of MacLaine's, aware that Jack's sympathetic eyes were watching me.

"It's never easy, Casey," he offered, leaning over the bar. "But when you love someone, what choice do you have but to stand by your man?"

"Oh, yeah?" I said. "Look where it got Tammy Wynette."

By the time I got home, I was more depressed than Burly. The evening news did nothing to lift my spirits. The leadoff story was a breathless announcement that Robert Price had been arrested for the murder of Boomer

Cockshutt and was expected to be charged with capital murder. That meant the death penalty.

It wasn't news to me, of course, but what followed was: a three-minute film clip—eternity on television—that began with a shot of a well-dressed man standing on the steps of the downtown courthouse, staring at a row of microphones. It was cold as hell for an outdoor news conference. What was going on?

I turned up the sound just as a caption flashed on the screen, identifying the man as the lawyer for Tawny Bledsoe, estranged wife of murder suspect Robert Price. The man rattled a piece of paper he was holding in his hands, cleared his throat, and began to read from it in a courtroom-trained voice. "The following is a prepared statement put forth by my client, Mrs. Tawny Ann Bledsoe Price."

" 'Although I know the courts are depending on me as a material witness,' " the lawyer read, " 'I fear for my life and that of my young daughter. Because of this, I have gone into hiding with my child until I can be absolutely sure that justice has been served and that my violent and unpredictable husband has been put behind bars forever. Not even my lawyer knows where I am.' "

Here, the lawyer looked soulfully at the cameras, his expression as sincere as that of a man about to ask for your vote. "It's true," he said. "I do not know where she has gone."

Hah—wait until he tried to cash her retainer check. He'd find her soon enough then.

The lawyer began to read again: " 'I beg the court to consider not only my wounds, but those of women everywhere who have ever been threatened or beaten or who have feared for their lives. Hear our cries. Deny my husband bail. To let him go, even for a few months prior to trial, is to put my life and my daughter's life in jeopardy. Please. Protect us. Do not let Robert Price go free.' "

The lawyer stared at the cameras with a sympathetic expression on his face. "I can testify that my client is in genuine fear of her estranged husband," he added. "And I can only repeat her plea. Do not grant Robert Price bail."

What a load of happy horseshit—no judge would grant Price bail under the circumstances anyway. This was grandstanding at its worst.

"That's two strikes against her," I told Bobby angrily. "She lied about the court order. She lied about her bruises. One more strike and I'm taking her out."

Bobby shrugged philosophically. "What's next?" he asked, cheeks packed with food. "Any chance you can get her to make good on her bad check?"

"First, I'm going to track down some guy named Joe Scurlock and find out what the hell he knows about Tawny that keeps her in line."

Bobby was not interested. He had his mind on other things. "Maybe we could sue her for nonpayment," he suggested.

"Thanks for your concern," I muttered and walked away.

I didn't need his help anyway. Thanks to the miracle of the Internet, within five minutes I had found fourteen Scurlocks listed within a twenty-mile radius of Raleigh. There were no Joes or Josephs, but two had the initial J. When I called the first one, an answering machine picked up and announced that Jane and Shebra were not available at the moment. I hung up and stared at the second listing. The address was in Boylan Heights, less than half a mile from my office. I'd be better off just dropping by—it was harder to hang up on me that way.

J. Scurlock lived in a ramshackle Victorian in the center of a downtown residential area that for years had been a run-down reminder of former turn-of-the-century glory. But in the last two decades, new owners had moved in to restore the neighborhood. Some of the nicest homes in Raleigh now graced the blocks of Boylan Heights. J. Scurlock's house was not one of them.

Its white-painted facade had turned gray, the shutters sagged from the windows and the front porch was badly in need of shoring up. No one had bothered to rake the leaves since autumn, and a bin of recycled jars had tipped over at the curb to spill out into the street. There were no cars parked in the driveway or out front, so I pulled into the parking lot of a church across the street and waited for signs of life to appear.

About half an hour later, a tired-looking woman wrapped in a sweater too thin for the weather pulled up in a battered station wagon and began to unload groceries from the trunk. I waited until she was halfway done, then joined her.

"Let me help," I said, reaching for the bag in her arms.

She gripped her groceries tighter. "Who are you?" she asked sharply.

I explained who I was and that I was looking for Joe Scurlock.

"That's my husband. Why do you want to talk to him?" She had a clipped voice and a suspicious attitude that made me think she'd been raised a lot farther north than the Mason-Dixon line.

"I need to talk to him about Tawny Bledsoe."

She stared at me for a moment, then balanced a grocery bag on one hip and reached for another. "What's she done now?" she muttered.

"Your husband knows her?" I asked eagerly.

"He ought to." She thrust both bags into my arms and reached inside the car for more. "He was married to her at one time."

"Oh shit," I answered, the words coming out before I could stop them.

The woman stared at me over an armload of groceries. "You have no idea," she said.

An hour later, I was sitting at a kitchen table across from Joe Scurlock, cups of coffee between us. He was a shy man of medium build with thinning brown hair and a diffident demeanor. Tawny must have chewed him up and spit him out on a daily basis. He wore a yellow jumpsuit smeared with grease, meaning his job was blue-collar at best. Which explained why Tawny had moved on.

Scurlock had left work early to talk to me, but he was having trouble getting started. The clock on the wall ticked loudly in the silence of the house. His wife had tactfully disappeared.

"So you think she had something to do with that man's murder?" he finally asked, avoiding my eyes. He was uneducated, if you went by his voice, but I had a feeling that Tawny had taught him plenty he never wanted to know.

"I think she might be involved," I said. "Do you think she's capable of it?"

"I think she's capable of anything," he answered.

"Have you seen her lately?"

He shook his head. "I spend most of my time making sure I never see her again. That woman scares me. She ain't right in the head."

"That bad?"

"That bad."

A silence descended between us. I thought about how best to approach the subject, then decided that since he was a plainspoken man, I ought to just come right out and say it. "I heard you showed up at the custody hearing for her daughter Tiffany last year," I said. "On Robert Price's behalf."

He nodded. "He was having trouble convincing the judge of Tawny's real character, I guess you could say. He wanted me to tell the judge what I knew. I wanted to help him. I don't care what color he is. He don't deserve what Tawny can dish out and neither do that little girl. So I was happy to oblige."

"And what did you know?"

He looked up at the clock, as if he were waiting for someone to arrive. "I knew that if Tawny got custody of her daughter, the poor kid wouldn't stand a snowball's chance in hell. That woman don't have a maternal bone in her entire body. If she ever did, she starved it out."

"How could you know what kind of mother she was? Some of the worst people on the planet turn out to be good parents."

"Not Tawny," he said emphatically. He wiped his brow and glanced at the clock again. "She ain't seen her other kids in over six years."

"Other kids?" I asked, suddenly remembering that Robert Price had mentioned other children while in my office. "She doesn't have any."

He looked offended. "The hell she don't. She got two of 'em. A daughter and a son. I ought to know. They live with me."

"You're their father?" I asked, a stupid question if ever there was one.

But he surprised me. "No, I ain't. I'm just the sucker who loves 'em."

I looked confused and he explained. "She was married before she met me, but it didn't last. That husband was smart. He lit out for the hills. Me, I ain't stupid, but it took me a while to see that Tawny just married me to have someone to take care of her and her kids. But I didn't mind at first because they wanted so hard to be good kids. So I was their stepdaddy for maybe two years until our marriage busted up. Since their real father was long gone, Tawny got custody of them after our divorce, her being the natural parent and all. But she kept leaving them with me for longer and longer periods of time. First a weekend. Then a week. Finally, a month. And one day, she just never come back for them at all. Poor little things. So I kept 'em. And no one ever said a word to me about it. I don't know what Tawny told her parents, but we ain't never seen the grandparents neither."

"You mean you and your wife have been raising them as your own?"

"That's right," he said, nodding. "We're gonna file to adopt them legally. That lawyer who helped Robert Price last year is helping us do it. For free. Can you believe that? The lady judge said we would have no problem. She was right nice about it. She said we was good people."

I looked around the shabby kitchen. The linoleum floor was worn with black spots gouged out near the doorways. The appliances were outdated, the cabinets badly needed painting and the plumbing was pre–World War II. But the counters and tablecloth were clean and there was a platter of homemade Rice Krispy treats piled on a plate near the stove. No one had bothered to offer me any and I didn't want to ask. For all I knew, it was their dinner.

"What do you do for a living?"

"I'm a mechanic down at Lee's Auto House," he said.

"I'm lucky to still have my job there, especially after what Tawny done."

"What did Tawny do?" I asked slowly, aware that it was a question I was probably going to repeat over and over in the days ahead.

"She went and had an affair with Lee when we were married," he explained, his voice flat. "Busted up my boss's marriage, made a fool of me, and then dumped us both and run away with some guy who sells advertising space or something like that. Married him, but it didn't even last as long as our marriage."

"Married him, too?" I asked, trying to do the math. "That means she's been married four times."

"At least." He took a sip of his coffee. "That woman would just as soon lie as breathe. I only know about one marriage before me. Could be there were others. And who knows how many since? That woman can reel you down the aisle, then clean you out in a heartbeat. She'd make a hell of a fisherman, let me tell you."

"She sounds like a troubled woman," I said.

"She's not troubled," Scurlock answered quickly, his voice sharp. "She's just plain trouble. It don't bother her to be that way. She don't even know she's that way. She don't care who she hurts, long as she gets what she wants. I'm still paying off the debts she run up when we was married." He ran a finger around his collar and looked at the clock again. "I got taken for a fool, but not as bad as that poor man in jail right now. She really did a number on him."

I was about to ask him more, but the front door slammed. Scurlock waited stiffly as the sounds of footsteps echoed through the house. A pudgy girl around thirteen or fourteen burst into the kitchen and made a beeline for the Rice Krispy treats. She jammed one in her mouth before she even put her books down.

"All right," she mumbled through the goo. "My favorites." She was in the middle of reaching for a second one when she noticed me.

"Who are you?" she asked in a voice that bordered on snotty. She was just being a teenager, but I have to admit

I dislike teenagers even more than I dislike small children. At least rugrats are sometimes cute.

"This here lady came to see me about some work on her car," Scurlock interrupted, his hand brushing mine in warning. "I'm gonna get me some extra money to buy you that ten-speed you want."

The child stared at me belligerently, as if doubting that anyone as hopelessly outmoded as *moi* could possibly be the source of her latest dream coming true.

"I'm Casey," I said brightly. "What's your name?"

"Ashley," she admitted in a sullen voice, crossing her arms and glaring.

I tried hard to like her, but failed. She was pale, and her soft body was squeezed into too-tight blue jeans. Her shirt gaped open at the buttons and her stringy brown hair fell in greasy waves to her shoulders. Her features may have been pretty, but it was hard to tell because of her perpetually sullen expression and acne problems. Tiny red scabs dotted her chin and forehead where she had picked at the sores. She was about the unhappiest-looking kid I had ever seen—and the opposite of her mother in looks. I doubted that was a coincidence.

"Where's Roger?" the girl asked her father in a challenging voice.

"Not home yet," he said. "He's got basketball practice."

The girl rolled her eyes and reached for another treat. "Roger is my perfect brother," she told me in a much-practiced suffering tone of voice. "He's tall and smart and a million girls call here each week for him. Roger was a beautiful baby. Roger walked at nine months. Roger has a penis and I have a—"

"That's enough," Scurlock said calmly. "You have homework to do."

The kid didn't argue. She stacked three more treats in her hand, saw the look her father gave her, put one back, and marched defiantly from the room.

As she walked past me, I saw that a series of parallel slashes had been gouged into the flesh of both arms. The wounds started just below her elbows and curved inward toward her wrists. The scabs were picked clean, leaving matching pink trails. Not a suicide attempt. Ritualistic incisions. The girl was a cutter.

I stared at Joe Scurlock in silence.

"Like I said," he explained softly, once the girl had left the room. "Tawny's done a lot of damage in this world."

FIVE

"She could have gotten her claws in *me*," Bobby D. reflected when I told him about Tawny's marital history. He looked vicariously terrified, like a man who has learned that the hitchhiker he almost stopped for was really a serial killer.

"Can you help me out?" I asked him. "I want to know where Tawny's gone. I haven't found anything to connect her to the murder, but I want to be able to get my hands on her when I do."

"Sure, babe. I'll call the moving companies, rental car joints, airlines, the train station. I'm good at that shit." Translation: "I can do it while sitting on my ass."

"I also need to know her real name."

"What do you mean?" Bobby asked.

"She's been married so many times, who the hell knows what her maiden name is. I want to talk to her family."

"Why?"

"The Bad Seed Theory," I said. "Whenever someone seems normal on the surface, but is evil inside, there's one group of people who know the truth—and that's the family. They watched her ripen. They'll know what she really is."

"Yeah, but will they tell you?" Bobby asked sensibly.

"Someone in that family will. Who do you think she sharpened her claws on? Can you track down her maiden name for me or not?"

"I'll call Rachel over at the *N&O*. They must have done background on her."

"Thanks. I'm going to go see Boomer Cockshutt's widow. I want to ask her some questions."

"The widow? Why the hell would you do that?" Bobby asked.

"If Tawny is involved with Cockshutt's murder, there's one big question that bothers me," I explained. "I don't think she ever does anything unless it benefits her in some way. And I can't figure out what she stood to gain by killing Boomer Cockshutt. Maybe the widow can help."

Boomer Cockshutt had been dead for six days. His funeral was over. The grieving friends had departed. His widow would be left alone with two dozen frozen casseroles, facing lots of empty hours to wonder about what she was going to do with the rest of her life.

On the other hand, maybe not.

The surviving Cockshutts lived in North Raleigh on a piece of wooded land worth at least a half million. An old woman who looked like a giant vulture answered the door of the huge house. She was hunched and dressed in black, with dark eyes set deep into crepey gray skin. Her sharp voice gave the impression she was about to tear out a chunk of my flesh.

"We're not talking to the press," she snapped.

"I'm not the press."

"Go away anyway." She tried to shut the door in my face.

"Excuse me," I said loudly, jamming my foot in the way. A television blared loudly in a back room, the distant electronic voices sounding like a static quarrel.

I peered over the old lady and spotted four adults lounging in various poses around an elegantly furnished sunken living room, highball glasses in hand. How quaint. A cocktail party wake.

"Let me in," I said. "I'm a private investigator and I want to talk to Mrs. Cockshutt." I was hoping my conviction might make up for the fact that I had no right to be there whatsoever.

The keeper of the gate was not impressed. "My daughter needs her privacy. She's in mourning."

Laughter broke out in the living room. "Sounds to me like she's managing okay."

The old lady glared at me sourly.

"Who is it, Momma?" a voice called from the living room.

"No one important, Amanda," the old battleax yelled back. "I'll take care of it. Just some private investigator dressed like a slutty war refugee."

"Slutty? I'm not the one wearing combat boots."

Her eyes moved automatically to her feet just as a slender woman with short brown hair appeared in the hallway behind her. Amanda Cockshutt was tall, with a strong face and wide-set eyes that were an unusual greenish-gray. Her hair had been cut short in a style that emphasized the wide angles of her cheekbones. No black for this widow—she was wearing an expensive silk warm-up suit patterned in pink and purple geometric shapes.

"A private investigator?" she asked. "Whatever for?"

"I'm looking into your husband's death." I handed one of my cards over the head of the glowering old lady. Momma glanced at my hand like she was thinking about biting it. I quickly returned it to my side.

Amanda Cockshutt turned the card over in her hand curiously and stared at the back, as if seeking further explanation there. "Who hired you?"

"I can't tell you," I said. "It's confidential."

"Secrets," the old lady snapped, then actually spit on the front stoop. "More secrets. Tell her to go away."

Amanda Cockshutt ignored her mother and gestured for me to step inside. "Please come in. If it's important for someone to know more about my husband's death, I'm happy to help. Some friends and I were sharing memories of Boomer, but they were just leaving."

Her eavesdropping guests took the hint. They obediently placed their drinks on nearby tables and started mumbling about their coats.

I waited in the hallway as Amanda Cockshutt distributed coats, scarves and gloves. The old lady glowered at each guest as they left, leaving no doubt that she thought they had the family silverware stashed in their pockets.

"Mother, I'd like to talk to Miss Jones alone, if I may," Amanda Cockshutt requested. The shrieks of two small children fighting deep within the house erupted. "Perhaps you could get Tommy and Alyssa to stop fighting for five minutes and give us all a break." There was an edge to her voice.

I stared as the old lady clomped belligerently away.

"Don't pay any attention to her," Boomer's widow said. She put a hand on my shoulder and guided me into the living room. "My mother is old-style Italian from New Jersey. She feels out of step down here. She's been living with us for two years now, and she gets crankier every day. Hates the South. But she's an amazing housekeeper. No one wields a broom like my mother."

"Really?" I asked. "Does she sweep with it or ride it?"

"Now, now, Miss Jones," my hostess chided me calmly as she reached for a bottle of gin. "She's my mother, not yours, so I'm the one who gets to make fun of her." She raised her eyebrows and gave me an unexpectedly raffish grin.

"Point taken," I said.

I turned down an offer for a drink and waited until she had settled herself on the sofa and put her feet on the coffee table. Her legs were long and her feet were tiny. They made my size nines look like clodhoppers.

"Your client is confidential?" she asked over highball glass.

"Yes, I'm sorry."

"The police?" she guessed.

I had to laugh at that one. "No. Not the police."

"Robert Price, then? You're trying to get him off the hook?"

"I really can't say," I said politely.

"My husband's insurance companies? They said there were no problems."

I tried shrugging, but she was not to be stopped.

"I know—some lady friend of Boomer's?" she suggested.

I was unable to resist the opening. "Did he have a lot of those?"

"Oh, yes." Her feet fell from the coffee table with a clunk. She leaned forward, a strange smile on her face. "Boomer had more lady friends than I did. And I'm in the Junior League. Am I surprised he was killed by a jealous husband? No. The only thing that surprises me is that it took so long."

"Why did you put up with it?"

She gestured at the room. "We all have a price. Boomer made a very good living. I enjoy not having to work. What can I say? I've never been all that interested in romance, so I was happy to be left alone. Perhaps I am the cold fish Boomer always said I was." She shrugged. "I never put much stock in that romantic crap anyway. It's all an illusion and illusions don't last long."

"Do you think Robert Price killed your husband?" I asked bluntly.

"Sure, why not? And if not him, some other husband. Boomer didn't care where he dipped it. And he didn't particularly care who knew it."

"Wouldn't it bother you if an innocent man went to jail?"

"I did time with Boomer and I deserved better. Let Robert Price do his."

Talk about frosty. Compared to her, the latest cold snap was nothing.

"Did your husband have a lot of life insurance?" I asked, remembering her earlier guess that I worked for an insurance company.

"Of course. He had coverage up to his eyeballs. So do I. Boomer was a smart man financially, if nothing else. I'm rolling in the bucks. But then, I was rolling in them before. The police have already gone through all this with me. I'm sure they're looking at it as a possible motive. Isn't that the first motive everyone thinks of? Money?" She stared at me, amusement in her eyes.

"Not me. I find that money runs a poor second to sex and love."

She gave a sort of bark that was supposed to pass for a

laugh. "That rules me out. I haven't seen a pecker in so long, I couldn't tell you what one looks like."

"That's okay. I don't need any pointers." I stood to go. There was no point in questioning her further. She didn't know anything. Or care, for that matter.

"What are your plans now?" she asked.

"What do you mean?"

"What are you going to look into next?"

"I'm not sure. His business dealings, maybe." It was as specific as I wanted to get. I like to keep my cards as close to my chest as a 38D bustline will allow.

"Was he active in any businesses outside the car dealership?" I asked as we headed for the door. If Tawny Bledsoe was involved in something financial with Boomer, that might give her a motive for killing him.

Amanda Cockshutt shook her head. "I don't know where he would find the time to have outside business dealings. Between his dealership and all the women he saw, my husband was booked solid. But I suppose it's possible."

"There is one more thing," I said, hoping to get something useful out of the interview, no matter how small. "I don't want to upset you by asking this, but did you know the woman your husband was seeing when he died?"

She shook her head again. "I didn't need to know her. They were all alike. Killer bodies. Empty brains. Willing to settle for a schmuck like Boomer."

"Unlike you," I pointed out unkindly.

"At least I got this out of it." She raised both arms in a sweeping gesture.

I wouldn't have called it a good bargain. A great-looking house is still an empty shell filled with dead objects. It was no substitute for a life.

"Thanks for your time," I told her, suddenly anxious to leave Amanda Cockshutt's cold world behind.

"Sure." She touched her throat with a slender hand. "And tell your client, whoever she is, that Boomer didn't really love her and she needs to move on with her life. He didn't love anyone but himself."

"I don't think it was like that with my client," I said evasively.

"Sure it wasn't." She shut the door in my face.

I returned to my car, wondering what it would be like to spend your nights inches away from the body of the person who betrayed you regularly, to count out your days together locked in mutual hate, each unwilling to be the first to crack and show the weakness of true emotion, each silently daring the other to crumble and reveal they had once cared.

It just didn't seem like a game worth playing to me.

Bobby'd had no luck with his routine inquiries, but he promised to keep trying. So far, Tawny Bledsoe had vanished without leaving a trail. But he had come up with a name and an address for her family. Her maiden name was Worth. Her parents lived near Lizard Lick, about twenty-five miles northeast of Raleigh. It was late afternoon and, if I hurried, I could beat the commuter traffic.

The obvious blue-collar status of Tawny's ex-husband Joe Scurlock had perplexed me when I interviewed him. He hardly seemed to satisfy Tawny's cashmere-and-fur tastes. But one look at the home where Tawny had been raised told me that she had come from far humbler roots than blue collar. At the time she married him, Joe Scurlock had probably been a step up.

The Worth home was a sagging clapboard structure barely set back from the highway. The land was muddy and rutted, the house sinking on its foundation, the exterior badly in need of paint. It was a piece of property good for nothing except hanging on to.

As I picked my way over puddles and patches of gravel, a light went on in an upstairs room. There was a flash of white as someone shoved a curtain aside. I caught a glimpse of a face peering out into the twilight before the curtain was pulled shut again.

I climbed the concrete steps to a rickety front porch and reached my hand through a torn screen door to knock. I knew someone was home, but no one answered. I knocked again, and this time heard odd scrambling noises inside.

There was a small window to the right of the door, so I wiped a patch of the surface clean with a corner of my coat sleeve and peered through the dingy glass.

A shrunken head topped with wisps of gray hair peered back at me, its toothless grin and vacant look terrifying in the deepening twilight.

I almost peed in my pants from the shock. I still hadn't recovered when the door flew open a moment later. A small man well into his seventies and dressed in denim coveralls stood in the doorway. There was no sign of the creature I'd just seen.

"Got no money to buy nothing," he said in a gravelly voice as he started to shut the door on me.

"Wait," I told him. "I'm not selling anything. I'm a private investigator. I want to talk to you for a few moments. You are Mr. Worth, aren't you?"

The old man's face turned fearful. His chin was stubbled with whiskers that made a rasping sound when he drew a weathered hand across them. "What's this all about?"

"It's about your daughter, Tawny," I began.

"Ain't got no daughter named Tawny," the old man informed me. A crash echoed in the house behind him, followed by an eerie howling. "Got to go now." The slam of the door was final.

I turned to go, perplexed. Had Bobby gotten the address wrong? Who the hell was that awful shrunken face in the window?

Darkness had fallen during our brief conversation and there was no porch light to guide me back to my car. I bumped my shin on a discarded refrigerator littering the yard and cursed. As I stopped to rub my leg, I heard the groans of a window being opened after years of disuse.

"Pssssttt," a voice floated across the yard. "Wait. Don't go yet."

I looked up at the second floor. A round face seemed to float in an upper window. "I'm coming down," the voice called out.

Nothing about this house was restful, nothing about it inspired confidence. But there was no way I was going to walk away. My curiosity has gotten me in trouble many a time, but I'd rather be curious than bored.

A minute later, a heavyset woman with brown hair permed into frizzy curls stepped out onto the porch. She was wearing tight purple leggings and a screaming pink sweatshirt decorated with a plastic decal of yawning puppies. Her cheap tennis shoes were neon green. If I had been dead, I would have come back from the grave to keep from being buried in an outfit like that.

"I'm Tawny's sister," she whispered as she walked toward me. Her voice was one of those whiny country drawls that lets the whole world know that you were lucky to have squeaked your way through high school. "I heard what you said to my daddy and I want to talk to you."

"Okay," I said. "I'm listening."

"Can we go somewhere first?" she asked. "Anywhere but here?"

I appreciated her sentiment. "Sure," I agreed. "Let's go get a beer. I'll drive." A battered Dodge Dart was parked in the front yard, but the back bumper was held on by clothes hangers and the rear windows had been replaced with packing tape. I didn't want to risk my life in it.

She refused my offer to wait while she got her coat—god knows what color it would have been—and climbed into my car with surprising grace for someone as big as she was. I got a better look at her under the glow of the interior car lights. Only the slightest resemblance to Tawny Bledsoe's perfect face lingered on the time-ravaged woman sitting beside me. Deep wrinkles ran from her eyes and mouth, the nose had broadened under the extra weight she carried and her mouth was a bloodless thin line. Her cheeks were chapped and her callused hands had red knuckles as scaly as lizardskin. Her broad shoulders told me she did heavy manual labor for a living, probably on her knees scrubbing out other people's toilets. My hatred for Tawny Bledsoe flared.

"We going or not?" she asked, and I pulled out of the depressing front yard.

"Head down there," she said. "There's a nice place where the guards from the prison hang out."

Great. Just the ambiance I was seeking.

During the five-minute drive to the bar, all my companion revealed was that her name was Cathy and that she was Tawny's little sister by three years, an admission that made me wince. She also explained that the shrunken face in the window belonged to her mother.

"She's got that dementia thing," she said. "She roams the house all night, knocking things over, turning on the oven. Me and Dad take turns following her around to make sure she don't burn the place down."

"You're talking about Alzheimer's?"

"That's it," she said. "We tried to find a nursing home, but nobody wants no Medicaid patients, so they tell you it's gonna be a couple years of waiting to get in when they hear you're not private pay."

Jesus, I thought. What a way to live. Where was Tawny Bledsoe to help out?

"Your sister Tawny ever give you a break?" I asked.

Surprisingly, Cathy Worth's laughter was genuine, rather than ironic. "No way. And her name's not Tawny. It's Tammy. She changed it when she was nineteen. But she don't fool us none. My daddy refuses to call her Tawny. He still calls her Tammy. Maybe that's why she don't come home none."

I thought back to the house collapsing under the weight of poverty and sickness. "Maybe," I said.

We pulled into the gravel driveway of a gas station that had been converted into a bar. Shania Twain blared from the bar's jukebox and a handful of beefy men in blue jeans sat at metal tables, staring mindlessly at a televised basketball game. The bartender was a fiftyish woman with a drop-dead figure poured into tight blue jeans and a snug white sweater. Her white hair had been piled on top of her head like a mound of soft vanilla ice cream.

"Hiya, Cathy," she said between cracks of gum. She shot me a quick glance, but made no comment. "How's the family? Your mother doing okay?"

"Okay," Cathy said, accepting the Bud Lite that the bartender dredged up from the cooler. "Her teeth finished falling out and we can't find no dentist to take her on account of she's so much trouble. Good thing she likes to eat grits."

As the two women laughed together, I pointed to Cathy's beer. "I'll have the same," I said, pretty sure I'd get nowhere if I asked for anything else.

We took our beers to a table as far away from the crowd as we could get. As we moved past the other patrons, Cathy exchanged a nod with each one of them. Seeing this, I was hit with a sudden stab of remembering, a keen recognition of what it felt like to come from a world so contained that your days were filled with familiar faces and the reassurance of knowing you would encounter nothing more taxing than the routine—even if the routine was sixteen hours of hard work and a few precious moments of rest.

Cathy sat down with a deep sigh and raised the cold beer to her lips, draining a third of it before she spoke again. She shut her eyes to savor the coolness and, probably, the freedom of being out of that house. When she'd stretched the moment out as far as it could go, her beer bottle hit the table with a clunk. I jumped and almost knocked my own over.

"Sorry," I said. "No offense, but your mother spooked me. I didn't expect to see her at the window like that."

"Mom can do that to you." She laughed again—a booming, generous sound. I couldn't believe she could keep her sense of humor in the face of a life like hers.

But the laughter was only a fleeting break from reality. Her face grew serious as she studied me. I knew she was ready to approach the subject of her sister.

"Tawny don't help out none," she finally said. "Says it hurts her to see my momma that way. It's as good an excuse as any. Makes her sound sensitive, I suppose." She took another sip of beer. "I know I ought to get a life. Even Daddy says I should maybe move to California, try to get me a job there and start over. But I can't just leave my momma like that. She spent her whole life doing without, so I could have. I'm not going to leave her now. Know what I mean? You probably feel the same way about your parents."

She glanced at me and I looked away. I was embarrassed, as always, at having to offer up a personal fact that I knew would elicit pity from others. "My parents are dead," I explained. "They died when I was seven."

"Oh," she said, not asking how—like a lot of other people would have done. "You grew up poor?" she said instead.

"It shows?"

"No. But most people would still be talking about what a hellhole my house is and asking me how I can live in it. You act like you've seen it before."

"Up close and personal," I admitted.

I try not to judge other people, but it's not always possible to convince other people of that fact. Cathy Worth now had proof that I didn't think I was better than her. And that made her ready to talk.

"Why are you asking questions about my sister?" she said. "She had something to do with that man being dead, right? She finally went too far." She took a furtive gulp of her beer and stared down at her chapped hands. She was betraying family and, no matter how well-deserved, that was against the grain of the farm community in which she had grown up.

"What makes you think she's involved?" I asked gently.

Her eyes filled with tears. "Because I know Robert Price would never do a thing like that and I know that my sister could."

"You know Robert Price?" I was surprised. Surely Tawny had not brought him home to that house for dinner?

She nodded, her breath coming more rapidly. "Of all the people Tawny has been with, he's the only one who—" She tried to continue, but had to stop and compose herself first. I waited, sipping my beer, until she was ready to go on. "He's the only one who ever bothered to help us," she finished in a whisper. "Tawny didn't even know about it."

"When was that?"

"About two years ago. Daddy fell and hurt his back. He couldn't look after Momma and I couldn't take off work without losing my job. I have to put in two shifts to pay the bills on account of Dad's too old to work anymore. When he was laid low and stuck in bed, I didn't know what to do. I'd already missed two days when this lady showed up at the front door. She was a nurse's aide. She said someone else was paying the bill. That I should go to work and not worry about things. She came for three whole months until Dad got back on his feet. She fixed up the house. She cooked us meals. She made me lie down and rest when I got home from work. She was a real nice woman. I really miss her." She faltered again and I waited it out.

"How did you know Robert Price was the one who paid the bills?"

"I went to the nursing service. I know one of the ladies there on account of I work at the hospital. In maintenance, you know, cleaning the rooms and stuff." I had been right about her rough skin and broad shoulders. "I didn't think Tawny was paying the bills, that wouldn't have been like her at all, she never spent money on anyone but herself. But she was the only one I could think of who knew we were in trouble."

She looked ashamed for a moment. "I had called her, see? Asked her for help. I swore I wouldn't never do it, because I knew she'd make me feel small about it. But I had to call her that time. And, of course, she said she couldn't help us. Said they was having money troubles and she couldn't leave her job to pitch in herself. But then, three days later, that health aide lady showed up. So I thought, you never know, I'd been praying about it, maybe Tawny had sent her. Maybe God had changed my sister. That was pretty stupid of me. She's not going to change, ever. But I thought maybe she had."

"Who did the nursing service say was paying the bills?"

"The lady told me that a man named Robert Price was and that he'd said it didn't matter how long we needed help, he'd pay for it."

"What did you do then?"

"I went to thank him," she explained. "I put on my blue dress, it's the one I use for church and such, and I went down to his office in Raleigh near the courthouse. He had a secretary and everything."

"Did you know he was African-American?" I was curious to see how this deep country woman had handled that bit of news.

She shook her head. "I don't have time to follow politics," she said, sounding ashamed. "So I was surprised. But it didn't matter to me what color he was, and he didn't seem to care what color I was. Or that I maybe didn't fit into his world so good. He could have been real short with me, you know what I'm saying? Him being a public figure and all, and me being nobody. But he saw me right away. He didn't make me wait. And he even told his secretary to hold his calls. He sat me down in this really nice chair and offered me coffee. He asked if I was taking the day off work and if I was going to lose my pay because of it."

"So you liked him?"

The tears began to roll down her cheeks. She turned her face to the wall, so no one who knew her would see her cry. "I liked him and I felt so sorry for him," she whispered. "Married to my sister like that. I knew Tawny would find a way to hurt him bad when he couldn't give her what she wanted. My sister always wants more than what people can give her and if they give her more, she just wants more. And I could see in his eyes that, even back then, he knew it, too."

Her voice rose. "He showed me pictures of their little girl, Tiffany. She's so beautiful. Like a china doll. I don't know where she got it. Well, listen to me, what am I saying? She got it from Tawny, of course." She touched her own face, as if painfully aware that she had lost out in the great genetic lottery. "I'll never have a child like that." She gave a quick laugh. "Never have one at all, probably. I got to take care of Momma and Daddy."

"Did Robert Price find out about your trouble through Tawny?" I asked.

She nodded. "In a way. He heard her talking on the phone to me and asked about us. I could tell from the way he answered my questions that she told him we were nothing but blood-sucking hillbillies who were always after her money." Her hand gripped the beer bottle so hard, I thought it might break.

"I'd never asked her for money before, ever," she said

in a low voice. "That was the first time. We were desperate and I knew she had gotten married again. She always liked to let me know when she married up for more money. I thought even she might want to help out, since it was Momma and all."

"Did Tawny know that her husband was helping you?"

"No." She shook her head emphatically. "He asked me not to say anything to her. He said she would be angry. That was another reason why I knew he was starting to see her for what she really is."

"And what is she, really?" I asked softly.

The answer was a long time coming.

It took two more beers apiece to hear the entire story about the girl named Tammy Worth who had grown up to be Tawny Bledsoe. There was no one who could have told the story better than the plain sister Tawny had left behind—the one who had watched every move her luckier sister made, watched with a sense of shame so mingled with longing that I'm not even sure Cathy herself knew what she really thought of Tawny's deeds.

Tawny may have been born Tammy, but the name didn't matter. It was the face that defined what her life would become—a perfect, symmetrical, Barbie doll face surrounded by loose blond waves. A face born into a family that didn't quite know what to do with all that beauty. Her parents were so startled by it that they remained in awe, treating Tawny as if she were a visitor and doing their best to shield her from the want that the rest of the family endured.

The lesson was not lost on Tawny. She'd started using that face when she wasn't more than seven or eight, bringing home candy bestowed by store owners and strangers, hoarding the sweets as an antidote to the ugliness around her, forbidding her sister to touch the treasured stash because it belonged to her and her alone. Before long, Tawny was bringing home other presents, first bunches of crushed wildflowers, then cheap jewelry, followed by clothing and, finally, by the time she entered high school, real gold and diamonds—the timeless currency of beauty. The gifts were secret payments, Cathy was sure, from men whose identities were hidden. Tawny never talked about who she was seeing because she understood, even back then, that she was engaged in the commerce of silence and that these secrets were her bargaining chips.

"I was glad she was getting those things," Cathy explained, "because she stopped stealing money from my momma's pocketbook and Momma stopped crying all the time."

The world wasn't much help in reining Tawny in. Life was made easy for the girl with the perfect face and astonishing body. She won every crown, led every parade, sat atop each float that made its way down Main Street. When a new regional high school opened its doors to thousands of students, Tawny was queen of their world. High school boys stood in line to have their hearts broken, their wallets stripped and their dreams ground out underneath her high heels.

Even then, Tawny was after bigger game. When Tawny was no more than sixteen, Cathy and a friend followed her after school one day, pedaling furiously on their bikes to keep pace with the white car that had picked Tawny up a few blocks from the high school. They watched, wide-eyed in their junior high school innocence, as Tawny and an older man parked behind a motel on the outskirts of town—the kind of place that always made their parents avert their eyes when they passed it—then disappeared into a room together. They recognized the man as the father of a girl they knew from Bible school.

The two girls listened in at the door and grew frightened by the sounds they heard, sounds not made by Tawny (who apparently even then was silently efficient in her methods) but sounds made by the older man. He moaned and begged, as if something hurtful was being done to him.

"What power did her older sister have over men?" Cathy had wondered that day, then grown afraid that her sister might use that same magic against her.

Cathy would witness Tawny's hold over the opposite sex again and again in the years to come, but, from her voice in the bar that night, I could tell that she still did not quite understand the depth of Tawny's talent.

Tawny had no such trouble understanding her advantage. Though she was never seen doing homework, she always passed her classes; though she repeatedly flaunted the teachings of their preacher, she was clearly his favorite and was never held up to public shame as others were; and though Tawny never lifted a finger at home to help with the farm or the housework, her parents seemed helpless to do anything about it. She left the house at dawn, returned close to midnight, if at all, and no one dared ask where she went on weekends.

On her seventeenth birthday, Tawny came home from school in a bright blue Mustang. No one ever found out who had purchased it for her. Her father demanded she return it; Tawny laughed in his face.

As she grew older, Tawny's clothes and tastes grew more expensive. She was smart enough to protect her assets. When her blond hair faded during her teen years, no one but Cathy ever knew that her older sister discovered the joys of peroxide early on. She had perfected this trick. The fact that she had almost fooled me—the Queen of Clairol—meant that Tawny Bledsoe was dropping a couple hundred a pop on her visits to the hairdresser these days.

As witness to the different way the world chooses to treat its beautiful and less beautiful inhabitants, Cathy Worth felt something of relief when her sister left home for good the day after high school graduation. Tawny's first husband was a truck driver who took her to Phoenix. She hitchhiked back on her own, married and divorced a Chatham County worm farmer, then moved on to Joe Scurlock. I rounded her marriage total up to five and waited for more.

"The worst thing was the way she always treated us," Cathy told me, staring at her nearly destroyed hands. "When I started high school, I still remember the look on everyone's face when they learned I was Tawny's sister. 'She had a sister?' they would all say, in this tone of voice I hated.

"The guys used to call me Cathy Worthless because I didn't look anything like Tawny. Then, one day, my science teacher made me stay after school. She said I was in real trouble. I waited all day, afraid of what I could have done. I was really scared because I couldn't think of what it might be."

Her voice filled with shame at the memory. "Finally, the bell rang and I went to see her. The teacher held up a test she'd made me take home to be signed. Daddy had been real mad, it wasn't a very good grade, but he had signed it and sent it back with me. The teacher pointed to his signature and accused me of lying. She said she knew my parents were dead and that I lived with an uncle and who was I to try and lie to her like that?" Cathy paused.

"Tawny had told everyone my parents were dead, to explain why they never came to any of the high school events. Only they never came because she never told them. She was ashamed of them. The kids from our area knew the truth, but they were afraid to say anything. I had to bring my father with me to school the next day to convince that science teacher I was telling the truth."

Cathy looked up at me. "I know it don't sound like much, she wasn't breaking any laws, but it's the way she thinks that scares me. And she'll never change. She'll only get worse. You don't know what she's like."

"I do know," I told her. "She's like a shiny red apple with a big worm hole in the middle that no one else can see. She has an empty black spot instead of a soul, and she tries to fill it with jewelry and clothes and other people's sorrow."

Cathy Worth stared at me. "I guess that's about right," she admitted.

I explained to her that I, too, thought Robert Price was innocent and asked if she knew where her sister might have gone.

She shook her head. "No, but I can guarantee you that some man is with her. Tawny can't be alone. Not ever. She needs a . . ." She groped for the right word.

"An audience?" I suggested.

She nodded. "I better go home," she said, suddenly sounding very tired. "Dad needs a break. And I have to get up real early for work."

"No problem. I'm sorry I kept you out so late."

"It don't matter." She shrugged her massive shoulders. "When you're as tired as I am, being more tired don't make much difference."

SIX

As I drove home, the moon burned above me in the thin winter sky as brightly as a spotlight, its light illuminating the deserted highway clear up the next hill, making the yellow center line seem as if it just went on and on to the ends of the earth. For a second, I wanted to keep on driving and never look back. I could put Jeff, Burly, even Tawny, far behind. Start over somewhere else. Be someone new.

Here I was chasing someone, yet I felt instead as if I were running away as fast as my legs could carry me. God, but I hated Tawny for what she had gotten away with in life. If there's one thing that people can't help, it's being born poor. Who was she to turn her back on where she had come from? Who was she to discard the people who loved her like so many pieces of used Kleenex?

It went beyond that, of course. I could not shake the memory of Robert Price being dragged from my office. I could see the fear in his eyes, smell the sweat on his body, hear the panic in his voice—and sense the shame overwhelming him.

She had used me to put an innocent man in jail and the only way I could atone was by helping to set him free. I would not be a party to her selfishness.

When I reached Raleigh, the thirty-mile drive home to Durham loomed in front of me like a cross-country trek. I decided to stop off at the Krispy Kreme on Peace Street for sustenance, unable to resist the cheerful glow of the neon sign that promised "HOT." I needed a break from the emotions churning in my gut, and few things in life are as peaceful as watching Krispy Kreme doughnuts being made. Some nights, there's standing room only as dozens of stoners satisfy their munchies in mesmerized silence, their eyes every bit as glazed as the doughnuts being ingeniously created before them.

I sat at one of the tiny tables nestled along the interior glass wall, thinking over my strategy as I munched doughnuts and watched the emerging puffs of hot dough being showered in a waterfall of molten sugar. If I wanted to catch a sociopathic slut like Tawny Bledsoe, I decided, I'd just have to think like a sociopathic slut. Granted, there are a few people in this world who would consider that not much of a stretch for me, but the truth was that I wanted to catch her precisely to prove that we were different animals entirely.

My hatred kept me awake. When my blood sugar reached the stratosphere, I offered the last of my warm dozen to a bum who was lingering wistfully outside Krispy Kreme's doors. I gave him a buck to buy coffee, then fed my spare change into the pay phone so I could call the office and see if Bobby had any news for me. He was long gone, but had left an update on my answering machine.

First, he informed me that Jeff had called, saying it was urgent, but leaving no return phone number. "The guy sounded hysterical," Bobby said. "He was yelling shit like you were going to ruin his life and he was in trouble because of you." That was my ex in spades. Cool-headed and self-aware. Blaming me for his drug troubles.

Next, Bobby let me know that he had run a credit check on Tawny and discovered that she had bounced more than her share of checks and was no longer welcome at most of the banks in town. She had credit cards, but they were at or close to their limits. Perhaps she had used her own car to leave town, he suggested, with maddening obviousness. Maybe I should check?

He reminded me of her address and, as long as my day had been, I was tempted. Her house was a few miles down Capital Boulevard from Krispy Kreme. And there I was, in the midst of an all-time sugar high, with nothing to do but head home and reflect on my depressed boyfriend or sleazy ex-husband.

Come to think of it, it wasn't a very hard choice. And I'd do more than check for her car once I got there.

Tawny's house was better than I could afford. Probably better than Robert Price could afford, too. The redwood-shingled ranch blended into the trees behind it and thick bushes guarded the yard. A side door led from an attached garage into what looked like the kitchen. I could break and enter in perfect solitude.

I parked my car down the block, behind an elementary school, then retrieved my burglary tools from the trunk. As I crept back to the house on foot, using shrubs for cover, my eye caught the flash of something odd going on inside the darkened interior. A faint light was strobing inside one of the rooms. I crouched behind some bushes, unsure if I was imagining it or not.

I inched closer, peered in the living room window and saw it: a dim crescent of white flickering against the far wall. The reflection from a flashlight. Someone was already inside Tawny's house. Tawny herself—or a cohort?

Some people might have called the cops. Some people might have gotten the hell out of there. I pulled my Python out of my knapsack and tucked it into my waistband. I slipped into the garage and rested to bring my breathing under control. Slipping my knapsack to the floor, I found my shimmy blade and began to gently work at the side door. Within a minute, it slid open with a snicker. People really ought to be more security conscious.

My feet made scuffing whispers on the linoleum floor as I passed through the kitchen, but I soon reached a carpeted hallway that cushioned all sound. I was tiptoeing toward the living room when something furry brushed against a patch of exposed skin between my socks and pants leg. I jumped and spun around, banging my knapsack against a door jamb. The metal tools inside clanked. What happened next unfolded in a blur.

Sounds of cursing came from an interior room, then a body pushed past, shoving me to the floor. I smelled tobacco and stale beer in its wake. As I sat back up, a purring cat rubbed against my legs. I shoved it away and listened hard. The intruder was running out the back door with as much grace as a drunken buffalo. A door slammed shut, footsteps thudded across the backyard, then someone crashed through the bushes and knocked over a trashcan.

Dogs began barking on both sides of the house. I had three minutes tops before all hell broke loose. I had to get the hell out of there.

I crawled into the living room and turned on my penlight. It was immaculate. Whatever the other intruder had been looking for, it wasn't in there.

I moved on to a side room. Here I had more luck. An antique wooden desk stood against a wall, its drawers pulled open. Papers fluttered across the rug. The windows faced a side yard, so I stood up slowly, confident I could not be seen from the street. I almost tripped over a table, moved away, and still bumped into it. What the hell? I studied it in the glow of my penlight. It was one of those lamely disguised home safes, a steel box nestled inside a wooden side table, accessible if you knew to lift up the table top and had a key to unlock the inner compartment. Someone had the key. The safe door was hanging open and it was half full of papers. As I reached inside, I heard a sound that made my heart stop.

Sirens. Several of them. Approaching fast. They sounded as close as Capital Boulevard. Abruptly, the sirens stopped and I started to panic as I realized why—the cops had turned into Tawny's subdivision.

I stuffed the contents of the safe into my knapsack, zipping it up even as my feet headed toward the side door. I hit the garage running, took three big steps, then leaped over a row of bushes like a steeplechase winner heading for the home stretch. As I sprinted for the street—judging it to be the fastest route out—lights began blinking on in neighboring houses. More dogs took up the alarm. It sounded like the hounds of hell were on my heels. I ran faster.

I reached the elementary school just as a pair of headlights turned the corner, followed by two more cars. Sheesh. The cops didn't respond like that to break-ins in my neighborhood. The lead patrol car switched on its floodlights and began sweeping the sides and front lawns of each house it passed. The other cars brought up the rear like a pair of silent sharks riding shotgun.

I waited until the taillights of the last police car disappeared down the street, then dashed to my car and pulled out of the school lot, grateful that my recently tuned engine purred as quietly as the cat that had caused all this trouble. I wanted to get to the crowded anonymity of Capital Boulevard fast. Thank god I was familiar with the subdivision. In the dark, every street looked alike. It would be easy to get lost if you didn't know your way around.

I reached the final intersection before the main road and noticed a pair of headlights to my right, approaching the four-way stop at high speed. I had the right of way, but the bastard heading toward me didn't seem like he was in the mood to grant it. He was going way too fast to stop for any sign.

I accelerated, hoping to clear before I was hit. The other driver finally spotted me and slammed on the brakes, but it was too late. The oncoming car swerved, clipped my rear bumper and began to skid in a sweeping arc before slowing to a stop inches from the mailbox of a corner house.

I braked to a halt and jumped from my car. I wanted to check the damage quickly so I could hightail it out of there before the cops arrived. I ran to the rear of my Porsche, wishing I had the time to give the driver a piece of my mind. The jerk would get a free pass he didn't deserve.

As I stared at my mangled bumper in disgust, something made me look up at the other car: an instinct, a chemical bond, perhaps, or maybe some eternal karmic glue that bound us together forever. A bright red Mustang, front end dented from the collision, blocked the intersection. I walked past the blinding headlights, clearing their glare, and peered through the front windshield.

There sat my ex-husband, crouched down in his seat in a pathetic attempt to hide behind the steering wheel. He was staring at me, his face stiff with shock.

My mouth fell open. I could not move.

Jeff—never taking his eyes from mine—sat up straight,

backed out into the road, turned his head away at last, then burned rubber and was gone.

Ten minutes later, my heart was still pounding when I turned into the parking lot of a convenience store off Highway 70. I had escaped without detection by the cops. But I was confused, pissed and in a near panic. What the hell had Jeff been doing in Tawny's house? Was I being set up again in some way?

I opened my knapsack and pulled out the stacks of papers I had grabbed from the safe. Maybe they could tell me more.

My bounty turned out to be about four inches worth of large manila envelopes interspersed with a stack of eight-by-ten-inch black-and-white photographs. The first set of photos showed a naked man dressed in gray socks and black leather bondage gear. His gut bulged out from between the chains that crisscrossed his chest, making his stomach look like a giant Parkerhouse roll. He wore a gag in his mouth, and his hands and legs were bound. It wasn't my cup of tea, but the man's enthusiasm was apparent.

The back of a woman clad in black leather boots and thong underwear appeared in the left third of the photograph. Half of her body was captured on film and I was willing to bet my entire MAC cosmetics collection that it was Tawny Bledsoe. I've seen a lot of female butts in my time, and the one I was staring at belonged to an older woman obsessed with working out: the combination of muscle and incipient cellulite was unmistakable.

In the second photo, the bound man had turned his head, allowing the camera to capture a perfect shot of his face. He was about fifty-five years old and looked familiar, but when a guy is trussed up like a turkey and wearing an expression like an ecstatic sheep, it's pretty hard to place him in context.

Turned out that the first set of photos was just a start. Tawny had photographed a whole series of people in various stages of sexual arousal. I say "people" because one of her partners was a skinny woman with frizzy red hair and pendulous breasts. Without going into detail, let's just say she was doing all the work while Tawny lounged underneath her, hands outstretched as if she were waiting for her nails to dry—an activity that, Tawny's expression made clear, would have been far more interesting than what was actually going on.

Who or what, I wondered, had taken the photos? I had been unable to search her bedroom, but since the setting never varied and the camera angle was always the same, it was probable that Tawny had set up a camera in her wardrobe or through a peephole in the wall and taken the photographs automatically.

How very enterprising of her. How very in character. And I knew why she was doing it: blackmail. Why else keep a collection like this? It certainly wasn't because the photos aroused her. I've seen inflatable dolls that displayed more emotion during sex than Tawny did.

In the chaos of surprising the other intruder, some of Tawny's cache had been knocked to the floor. The bottom half of the stack was out of order. I was shuffling them back into place, so that all the photographs would be image side up, when I saw the face I had been half-expecting to see all along: Bill Butler, Detective First Class. And first class all the way, I must say, if one looked at the photos closely enough.

When I first saw the image of his face held so close to hers, part of me was disappointed. And part of me, I am ashamed to say, was vaguely thrilled at finally getting a look at what I had been missing all those years—those long hands spread out over a pillow, that lean body and graying hair. Those sexy scars on the right cheek. Of his face. And check out those thighs. I considered having a wallet-size print made of that one.

But what a shame to waste him on a total twat like Tawny. For just a second, I hated her more than ever. For having had him. For having used him. For having cheapened something special I was saving for a rainy day. Was this woman just plain born to be on my bad side—or was she intentionally trying to piss me off?

I stared at the photos some more. Bill had beautiful shoulders. They were muscular and stretched taut with the effort of what he was doing, which, I am happy to report, was pretty damn normal, considering. At least he wasn't wearing black leather and being beaten by a cat-o'-nine tails. Thank god for small favors. Not that his favors looked particularly small, I amended, as I discovered a new shot of him in action. It appeared that I'd been missing a lot more than I thought. A wide-angle lens could have told me more.

But where were the rest of the photos? Why only three shots of Bill, when the other victims each appeared in a half dozen or more? I checked the contents of the envelopes and, as expected, they held glassine-sleeved negatives that corresponded to the photos. Tawny had not bothered to print out all the shots on each roll. A quick count confirmed that she had chosen a greatest hits approach and left unprinted most of the photos in which she appeared prominently.

There were no negatives for Bill Butler. The stack had been split in the middle of his file. My ex-husband had the other half.

Oh, my. When worlds collide.

I pulled out of the parking lot and doubled back toward Blue Ridge Road. It was time for a midnight visit.

"Okay, Okay! I'm coming! Don't knock the door down." Bill opened his front door clad in red silk boxers and a 9mm Glock.

"Whoa," I said. "Please put that away."

He glanced down at his shorts.

"Not that. The gun." I nodded toward it, aware that my hands had automatically shot up in the air when confronted with the sight of the barrel.

"Sorry," he mumbled. "Reflex." He glanced at a clock on the hallway wall. "Christ, Casey—it's almost three o'clock in the morning. What the hell are you doing here? If you're trying to bust up a date of mine, forget it. I'm alone."

"It's good to see you, too." I shouldered him aside and headed for his living room, where I plopped down on the sofa. The place still looked like he rented it by the week.

"Got anything to drink?" I asked. "Better make yourself one, too. You're gonna need it."

"Oh, sure," he said. "Can I peel you a grape while I'm at it?"

But he put his gun on top of the refrigerator, grumpily banged ice cubes into a highball glass, splashed Wild Turkey over it and handed it to me with a curt "This better be good."

I hate bourbon, but I took a sip anyway. It didn't seem like the right time to complain. "It is good. Have a seat." I patted the sofa beside me and smiled.

He glanced down at himself again, like he thought I was getting ready to snatch his family jewels and run. "Let me get a bathrobe first," he mumbled.

"Don't bother," I told him. "The cat's out of the bag. The cat and a lot of other things." I spread out the photographs of him and Tawny on the coffee table. "You lied to me," I accused him.

He examined the photos, then turned without a word and marched back into the kitchen. His portion of Wild Turkey turned out to be a hell of a lot bigger than the one he'd poured for me.

"Where did you get these?" he asked after he rejoined me on the couch.

"I broke into her house."

He stared at me. "I'm a sworn officer of the law. You know better than to tell me things like that."

"I hate to tell you this, Bill, but we're gonna have to cross that thin blue line together. If we want to stop her." I took the rest of the photos out of my knapsack and tossed them on the glass-topped table. "You're not the only one. She's got a half-dozen people in here. And I only got half the pile in her safe."

"There's more?"

"I surprised someone else in the house when I got there. They have the other half of her stash, including your negatives. If you want to get them back, you're gonna have to help me. I'm sorry. I know it sounds like blackmail. But then, everything does at three o'clock in the morning."

Bill took another sip of bourbon and stared at the photos

of him doing the horizontal two-step with Tawny. "I'm a single man in the goddamn United States of America. Having sex is perfectly legal."

"I know. But that's not." I pointed to the bedside table. I'd had to look at the photo three times before I could figure out what it was, but blowing up the image even more would make it obvious: a small mirror had been laid flat on the table and its surface was covered with lines of white powder.

"I have never touched that shit in my life," Bill said quickly, his voice rising. "That was for her. I didn't go near it."

"No, but it looks bad." I paused, shocked at how genuinely upset I felt. Seeing him had triggered a regret I had not expected to feel.

"To tell you the truth," I admitted, "I'm a little surprised at how stupid you were. I didn't figure you for the kind of guy who thought with his pecker."

He leaned back against the couch, eyes closed. "I knew this would come back to bite me in the ass."

I stared at him. "You knew she was involved in blackmail and you didn't tell the investigating detectives?"

He opened his eyes, but avoided mine. "It's not like that, Casey. I don't think she had anything to do with the Cockshutt murder. At least not in the legal sense. Besides, Tawny still has friends in the department. She did work there, you know. And I'm not the only one who fell for her talents."

"No, you're not," I agreed, nudging the photographs. "In fact, it looks to me like you missed out on a lot of her talents."

"Do you really want to know what happened?" he asked in a tone of voice that made me think he was offering me more than an explanation.

"Yes," I said, nodding. "It's important to me. For a lot of reasons."

He put his drink down on the table. "It happened about a year and a half ago," he said. "She'd been married to Price for a couple of years by then and she said they were having trouble. Mostly about money. She was quitting her job at the department and getting into commercial real estate because it paid more. So we went out for a few drinks to celebrate her new job.

"At first, there were eight or nine of us. Then everyone else staggered home and she suggested dinner. I gave her your business card during that dinner, after she confided they would probably divorce. I said you might be able to help her out if it ever came to that. Then she started really coming on to me, and I liked it. I drank too much and I was lonely that night. Sorry I wasn't more original, but going home with her was something to do that was better than going home alone. I'd just heard my ex-wife was getting involved with someone I thought was a friend and I felt like shit. So I made a serious lapse in judgment. Can you understand that?"

"Sure," I said. "I've made a career out of serious lapses in judgment, especially when it comes to romance."

"I didn't know she was taking photos. Obviously, I'd have worn my best suit if I had."

"Looks to me like your birthday suit *is* your best suit."

He laughed and I was encouraged he could joke about it. "When did she approach you with the photos?" I asked.

"About a week after they were taken. She took me to lunch and was real upfront about it. She showed me one of the photos and said she'd go to my wife if I didn't help her out at the department."

"Your wife? What wife?"

"Exactly." He reached for his drink. "She thought I was married. And she was pretty pissed when it turned out I wasn't."

"Why would she think you were married?"

He stared at me. "Think hard, Casey," he said in a slow voice that made me nervous. "Why would anyone get that impression? It wouldn't be your fault, now would it? Think back to the last time you were here at my apartment."

"You're kidding?" I said, not knowing whether to laugh or be dismayed at having inadvertently helped Tawny target him. "You mean that time I . . . ?"

"Yes," he said, glaring. "I mean that time."

I started to laugh. This made him madder.

"It's not funny, Casey. It wasn't funny then, and it isn't funny now."

But it was funny and I laughed even harder. Almost two years ago, I had barged in on a hot date of Bill's, only because it was an emergency, understand, and I badly needed his help. I sent his honey scurrying away by claiming to be his wife. She was a department employee and had apparently spread the news. Right to Tawny Bledsoe's ears.

"Whatever happened to that dog-faced woman anyway?" I asked. "She get transferred into the Canine Unit?"

"You're going to seriously piss me off if you don't stop laughing," Bill warned. His face was approaching the shade of his boxer shorts.

Anger always made Bill look more dangerous and that never failed to turn me on. I glanced down at his stomach where the muscles converged in a straight line that ran down into the top of his shorts. For a moment, my mind wandered to what I had seen in the photographs. Bill caught me wandering.

"I guess there are no secrets between us now," he said grimly, rising to pour himself another drink.

"None. But we're on the same side. You help me and I'll help you."

"As if I had a choice," he mumbled. "But I hope you realize that's exactly what she said to me. What do you want me to do?"

"I want to know where she's gone," I explained. "I want to know what my ex-husband has to do with it." I explained about seeing him earlier that evening. "I need your help finding out what's going on."

He sat back down beside me and our bodies brushed. A spark of electricity danced between us. He ignored it, but I filed it away for future reference.

"Help you how?" he asked glumly.

"I want you to run her phone records and give me copies," I said. "Maybe she called someone to help her set this up. And I want you to run her fingerprints nationally to see if she has a record anywhere. Run my ex-husband's name through the network while you're at it."

Bill glanced at me in sudden interest. "You think he's dirty?"

"I think she has some hold over him. And I want to know what it is." I did not want to share with Bill the fact that my ex was being pursued by drug dealers. Yet. "Then there's one other thing."

"Keep it legal. I do have my standards, you know."

I put my hand on his and he didn't pull it away. "I want her arrested. She paid me for finding her kid with a bad check," I explained. "To the tune of a thousand dollars. On a closed bank account."

"Knowingly?"

I nodded. "She'd closed it a month before."

"Okay." He thought for a moment. "I can make a case based on a worthless check charge and obtaining property under false pretenses."

"Those are only misdemeanors," I protested.

He shrugged. "It's the best I can do."

"I still want to swear out a warrant," I decided. "I want it on record. That bitch is fooling the public into thinking she's as pure as Snow White. I'm going to prove she's more like Sleazy the Dwarf."

"There was never a dwarf named Sleazy," Bill said patiently. "You're thinking of Sneezy."

"That, too."

"You'll have to come down to the station and make a complaint."

"I can't. I have too much other stuff to do. Can't you just wing it? Call Bobby for details. Do it for me, please?"

"Do I have a choice?" He pulled the stack of photos toward him as he sipped his drink. "Who else was as stupid as I was?"

He began to thumb through the stack, then held up the photo of the fat man trussed up in black leather. "This is the chief's right-hand man, you know. He's going to shit when he sees this."

"No, he isn't," I said. "Because we're saving it for when we need it."

"We're going to need this?" he asked, sounding alarmed.

"We're going to need all the help we can get to bring her down," I explained. "And that may include this guy. How did Tawny want you to help her when she first tried to blackmail you?"

"She wanted me to run some people through the computer using my log-on code so no one would know it was her. Sort of like you do." I ignored the implication. "Probably hoping to get something on them. She also wanted me to run some credit reports on a couple of guys."

"You're kidding?" I said, incredulous. "Credit reports?"

"What's the big deal about that?" he asked. "My four-year old nephew could do that using his home computer."

"Don't you see? She was shopping for a new husband. She was done with Robert Price and looking for someone who still had money left to spend on her." I stared at him. "Did she have you run Boomer Cockshutt through?"

He started to pretend he didn't remember, saw the look in my eyes and gave up the ruse. "She wanted me to find out where he kept all his assets, if he had any extra bank accounts, that sort of thing. I explained that I wasn't married and didn't care who saw the photos. I also made it clear that I wasn't interested in having anything more to do with her. She wanted to, you know."

"Wanted to what?"

"Wanted to see me again." He didn't look as if he felt complimented.

"Considering all the people she auditioned, it's pretty impressive that you made the cut."

His brown eyes suddenly looked very tired. "Cut the crap, Casey. I wouldn't touch that bitch again with a ten-foot pole."

"It's not quite that long," I pointed out, using the top photograph as proof.

"I said cut the crap," he warned me again.

"Okay. I'm sorry. I will. But why didn't she try and blackmail you using that fairy dust on the mirror as leverage?"

He shrugged. "I don't think she noticed it, to tell you the truth. I get the feeling that bump is a regular fixture in her bedroom. She's a cokehead, Casey. I've seen a hundred of them in my lifetime. And that woman has a problem with it."

"Really?" That interested me greatly. It was the first weak spot of Tawny's I'd discovered. On the other hand, it did not make me feel any better about the fact that she had her young daughter with her—or that my ex might be part of it.

As if he could read my mind, Bill looked up from the stack of photographs. "What the fuck's your ex-husband doing mixed up with her?"

"I don't know. But I intend to find out. Recognize anyone else?"

He nodded. "A couple of married guys from the department. And I see from the redhead that she bats for both teams. You'd think Tawny could do better than that. That girl's tits look like sweet potatoes."

"That's what I like about you, Bill. Your sensitive side."

He shrugged. "Did you think she was a rug muncher?"

"No. And I still don't. Being a dyke requires actually caring about someone else. Tawny could give a shit about anyone but herself. I haven't seen such a bored-looking lesbian since the last episode of *Ellen*."

Bill wasn't really listening. He was staring at the photo of Tawny stretched out on the bed, playacting for the camera. "Do you really think she had something to do with Cockshutt's death, Casey? This isn't just some catfight between the two of you, is it? A female version of dogs pissing to mark their territory?"

"I think she's guilty, Bill," I said. "And I think Robert Price is innocent."

"But why? There's no evidence she had anything to do with it and the evidence against Price is growing."

"Because of the little things," I explained. "The more I learn about Tawny, the more I come to see how dangerous she is—how selfish, how willing to feed on people who aren't as strong as her, how ruthless she is in getting her own way. And the more I hear about Robert Price, the more I believe he's a good man who made a bad mistake when he got involved with Tawny."

"The little things tell you this?" Bill asked skeptically.

"Yes, they do. It's the little things that prove what kind of person you are. The choices you make every day, when no one else is looking. The choices you think don't really count."

Bill nodded again—as if understanding, but not yet agreeing—then put his drink down on the table. His shoulders slumped. "I'm getting too old for this. I can't do it anymore."

"Looks to me like you can," I said with a nod toward the photographs.

"Not that. I meant too old to stop her. She probably did have something to do with Cockshutt's death. But we're never going to find the evidence to prove it. She'll get away with it. I can smell it. You don't know how many people really do get away with murder. And lots of them are dumber than Tawny Bledsoe."

"Don't say that." I moved closer and put my hands on his shoulders, probing for tense muscles. "You don't have to do it alone. We'll stop her together." I massaged his shoulder blades and he groaned in contentment.

"You can be okay," he admitted. "Sometimes."

"Just don't tell anyone I'm being nice. I have a reputation to protect."

"My lips are sealed," he promised. "Now, could you move a little lower, please?"

SEVEN

I woke up alone in Bill's bed late the next morning. The sun was shining through a pair of sliding glass doors that led to a balcony overlooking the tennis courts. I wandered sleepily to the doors and looked out on a beautiful day. Then I noticed that Bill kept a single folding chair on the balcony—with three different grills arranged around it. I had to laugh. Men and their primordial fascinations. If you light it, they will come.

Though I was alone in the apartment, the smell of brewing coffee lured me into the kitchen. No note. But a clean cup lay waiting by the automatic drip machine. How very Bill Butleresque. Welcome, but not too welcome.

It was almost as typical as him falling asleep on the couch under the spell of my magic fingers last night. I'd covered him with a blanket, poured my remaining bourbon down the sink and helped myself to some Scotch instead. Then I'd borrowed a T-shirt, a pair of boxer shorts and his bed. I fell asleep immediately, impressed that his sheets were actually clean.

My morning got off to a good start when Bill's refrigerator yielded a box of chocolate-covered doughnuts. I ate two of them with my first cup of coffee while I enjoyed the solitude of his bachelor pad. Funny how, after all the years of pushing and pulling back and forth, I now felt downright at home in Bill's apartment. Nothing like mutual hatred to bring two people together.

I called home for my messages and felt guilty when I

found one waiting from Burly. Just my luck. My boyfriend rouses himself from the depths of depression to call me for the first time in days and I'm not even there. The time stamp told me he'd called after midnight. I doubted the nuances of my not being home had escaped him. There was nothing I could do about it now.

But I could do something about Tawny Bledsoe. I borrowed one of Bill's work shirts and some clean socks. My jeans could be recycled for another day. It was almost noon and I wondered what the best step to take against Tawny might be.

I sat on the rug in Bill's bedroom, basking in the sunshine, while I thought it out. If my ex was helping Tawny, either he was involved willingly or he was being duped. Knowing Jeff's hormonally induced stupidity, I was willing to give him the benefit of the doubt: he was an idiot, but not an accomplice to murder.

I knew Tawny didn't want to be found until Price had been deemed guilty, so she'd lay low for as long as she could, using her daughter's safety as an excuse. So why had she sent Jeff to get the photographs in the safe? And what would she do when Jeff told her I had been at her house?

Then it hit me: she needed money. The certainty of my guess came in a flash of recognition, a momentary bitter kinship with her devious mind. She needed cash to support both her habits, the shopping and the snorting. But she knew that I'd tracked down Price at the beach through his credit card use, meaning she probably wouldn't touch her own cards for fear of leaving a trail. They were almost maxed out anyway. Plus, she had no money left in her checking accounts. That meant she had to raise cash, probably by squeezing her blackmail victims for more bucks. Conclusion: someone in that pile of pathetically aroused human beings might know where she was.

I wasn't keen on contacting any of Tawny's male victims. They'd already been burned by one blond. Why should they trust another? I'd go for the redhead instead.

Finding her would not be easy. There were zillions of redheads in the Triangle. It wasn't like I could capitalize on Bill's theory and walk around with sweet potatoes, comparing breasts until I stumbled on the right pair. How was I going to work this one? Another cup of coffee and two more doughnuts later, I had it: I'd hit every gay bar in a thirty-mile radius and see if anyone recognized her.

North Carolina may be in the South, but it's not on the planet Mars. There are plenty of gay bars in the area. In fact, there are at least ten between Raleigh, Durham and Chapel Hill. It's the bright lights, big city pull. Not too many gay people born in the rural South stick around the farm, casting hopeful glances at their neighbors. Most of them head south to Atlanta or north to New York. Those who want to stay closer to home, head for the Research Triangle, a rather appropriate destination for the women, in particular, when you think about it.

So, I had a lot of bars to choose from. Too many, in fact. But a quick call to my friend Marcus Dupree allowed me to strike six of the men-only clubs from the list.

"Don't even bother with the boy bars," he advised me. "There's not a lot of mingling." He suggested I try the two lesbian bars located in Durham first. "I'll bet you dinner at the Magnolia Grill that she hangs out at one of them," he said. "Because, honey, when people in our community talk about the Durham Bulls, they don't mean baseball."

"Gee," I said. "Maybe we should let the chamber of commerce know? They could warn the local banks to stop passing out all those free toasters."

"You laugh," he said, "but where would Durham's championship softball team be without our Sappho sisters?" He hung up before I could think of a retort.

There was no point in hitting the bars until early evening, which gave me a whole afternoon to kill. Bobby had nothing to report, my ex-husband had not called back and there was nothing cooking at the office. I needed a way to improve my spirits. I was considering an afternoon of working out when I saw in the *Spectator's* movie listings that the Colony Theater was showing a Chow Yun-Fat retrospective. I spent a glorious five hours eating popcorn and ogling my idea of the world's most perfect man: Cary Grant in a Bruce Lee package.

Having confirmed my heterosexuality, I headed home,
showered and changed into something black, tight and
dyke. By the time I was done, I looked, well, like my usual
self, to tell you the truth. Good enough to eat.

The first bar was a wash. Everyone there seemed barely
old enough to play with Barbie dolls, much less each other.
Their youth lent them a curious asexuality. I felt like a
desperate old hag caught wearing an outdated prom dress
at a convention of the androgynous. I had a quick drink at
the bar, watched two sorority girls swapping spit in the
corner, then wasted twenty dollars on a bartender who not
only didn't recognize the redhead but pointed out that her
technique wasn't all that great, either. "But who's the
blond?" she wanted to know. I assured her that she didn't,
and left.

My second stop of the evening showed more promise.
Rubyfruit Jungle was a bar for dykes with money. The
decor was heavy on tropical murals, potted plants and red
lacquered ceilings. Music played softly in the background:
Joan Armatrading. It was a clear sign that the joint ap-
pealed to the over-thirty crowd. Low lighting levels
confirmed it.

It was just before eight and the bar was nearly deserted.
I figured that most of the after-work crowd had headed
home while the evening revelers were still ironing their
white shirts and creasing their jeans.

Someone with bucks had set the place up. The bar was
mahogany with brass accents. I sat down on a cushioned
stool and looked around. Two glum-looking women sat at
a table in the corner, beer bottles lined up before them.
Maybe I should ask the bartender to bring them a round
of Midol on me.

A table of five nearby was a lot livelier. They were
passing around photographs and laughing. They only made
the table of two look even grumpier.

The only other person alone in the place was a fiftyish
woman sitting on a stool at the far end of the bar. She was
wearing a black pullover sweater that showed off her slender figure, meaning she was either in good shape or in the
middle stages of alcoholism. Her graying hair feathered

back from a handsome, angular face. Al Pacino's younger sister. A glass of whiskey sat on the bar in front of her. She was smoking a cigarette with a relaxed attitude that told me she felt at home where she was and that, while others might be on the prowl, she was content to get quietly drunk. I envied her peace. She'd found a place where she belonged.

"Can I get you something?" the bartender asked, appearing through a doorway behind the bar.

"Jack Daniels straight," I told her, then pretended, just for a minute, that I was checking her out. Hey—I like to walk in other people's shoes. It makes them easier to understand. Besides, she was, in my personal estimation, cute as hell. Her black hair was cropped just below her ears in a way that framed her boyish face. She had a beatific smile and wide green eyes that reminded me of a cat's, eyes that managed to look me over without actually seeming to. She was wearing tight black jeans and a man's white shirt with the sleeves rolled up. As she filled my glass with an extremely generous shot of Jack, I admired her athletic grace. Ah, to be young and gay.

"Run a tab?" she asked.

I nodded. My kind of joint. I waited it out while the bartender checked on the older woman sitting at the far end of the bar, brought a tray of fresh beers over to the large party, then wiped out a couple of glasses. When she came back to check on me, I told her I wanted to ask her some questions.

"Yeah?" she said, putting a toothpick in her mouth and parking one foot high up on a cooler. "Questions about what?" She leaned forward, stretching her back, showing off how limber she was. The road not taken was looking better and better. It was tempting to ask for directions.

"I'm trying to identify someone. If I show you photos of two women, do you promise not to freak?"

Her eyes grew wide in mock horror. "So long as they're not ironing or doing the dishes, I think I can handle it."

"Actually, they're having sex. Or, at least, one of them is. I'm trying to identify the one who's doing all the work."

A shadow crossed her face. "Why?" she asked, averting

her eyes as I took the photos from my knapsack and laid them face down on the bar. "Why are you looking for this woman?"

There was no point in lying. Most gay women automatically protect other gay women unless there's a damn good reason not to. And this gal wasn't the type who would take a twenty to betray her sisters. I explained who I was, what I was doing and why I thought Tawny Bledsoe had taken the photos.

"So you're trying to stop this woman from blackmailing other people?" she asked, moving the toothpick around as she thought it over. "It's not for a custody case or anything like that?"

"Look," I promised. "I'm telling you the truth. But I can't prove it. You'll have to take my word for it. But once you see how bored the woman I'm trying to stop looks, you'll know I'm telling you the truth."

"Let's see it," she said.

As I turned the photos over, I was conscious that the older woman at the far end of the bar was watching carefully. Her relaxed posture became guarded.

The bartender stared at the series of photos in silence, turning the glossies first one way and then the other.

"Recognize either one of them?" I asked, sipping my drink.

"Maybe." She looked up at me. "Could you excuse me for a moment?" She took the photographs and disappeared into the back room. Less than a minute later, the older woman slid off her stool and quietly left the bar area. I had no doubt that she was taking another route to that back room. A minute later, I heard voices murmuring, but I couldn't make out the words.

Finally, long after my drink was gone, the bartender returned. She put the photos down on the bar in front of me, then reached for the bottle of Jack Daniels. She refilled my glass without asking. "Got identification?"

I pulled my fake PI license and photo ID from my pocket. By the time she had finished examining them, the older woman with gray hair was at my elbow. She exchanged a glance with the bartender, then nodded.

"Let's go into my office and talk," she said in a voice made husky by too many cigarettes smoked late at night in bars.

"You're the owner?" I guessed, slinging my knapsack over my shoulder and following her as she led me down a hallway toward a red door.

She unlocked it and motioned for me to enter. "I'm Roberta," she said, not giving me a last name. "Have a seat. Start from the beginning."

I started over, telling her about Tawny Bledsoe and how she had conned me. When I got to the part about Robert Price being dragged from my office, she winced and lit up a fresh cigarette. Her only comment was to ask to see the other photographs when I told her the part about finding them in Tawny's safe.

Her eyes flickered as she looked them over, then she slid them back across her desk toward me. "Continue," she said calmly and I did.

When I was done, she leaned back in her chair and looked up at the ceiling. She blew a series of smoke rings, sending perfect ovals toward the light fixture. "Let me make a call," she finally said. "Wait at the bar. I'll be out in a minute."

I returned to my Jack Daniels and was rewarded by a smile from the bartender. The smile seemed familiar, until I realized that I was looking at the female version of my friend Jack. Weird. And exciting in an odd way.

I killed a few minutes sipping my drink and watching the two unhappy women sitting on the other side of the dance floor. One was starting to cry and the other looked pissed-off. I guess we all have our romantic problems, no matter whom we choose to romance. When some new customers walked in the door and headed toward the happy table of five, the pissed-off woman followed them with her eyes. Her expression changed from anger to envy. She was ready to get on with a new life, her narrowed eyes told me, and her old girlfriend was just dragging her down. I was sorry I'd been privy to the moment.

By the time the bar's owner, Roberta, returned from

making her phone call, I was at the bottom of my triple shot of Jack and starting to feel a little wop-jawed. The more I drank, the cuter the bartender got—a personal phenomenon of mine apparently not confined to straight bars.

"How long do you have?" Roberta asked me.

"As long as it takes," I said.

"Good. I've made a phone call. There's someone on her way in to see you."

"The redhead?"

"That's right." She slipped onto the stool next to mine and leaned closer. Her voice dropped, and what had been a charmingly husky edge became a warning. "If you do anything to harm her," she told me, "I will personally track you down and see that you are very badly hurt. Understand?"

"Perfectly," I said. "I won't harm her."

"You better not. She's been through enough." Roberta settled back as the bartender returned and poured her a new drink: Scotch straight up, no ice. Before I could stop her, she did the same for me, using the bottle of Jack Daniels. I looked at my glass dubiously and considered whether I was close enough to my apartment to walk home—ignoring the fact that once the issue even became a question, it was a sure sign you ought to stop right then and there.

The bar owner saw me looking at my whiskey and raised her glass in salute. "Cheers," she said. "Real women don't eat ice." She downed her drink in a single long shuddering gulp, waved away the bartender and pulled out a fresh cigarette. "I know the blond," she said flatly.

"She's been in here?"

"Sure. Until I had her thrown out."

"What for?" I was relieved that I had finally met someone else who had glimpsed the real Tawny Bledsoe.

"I told her it was because of fighting," she said. "Which it was. But I knew about the other thing, and that was the real reason." She nodded toward the photos. "You got the negatives with you?"

"That's right."

"Good. I expect you're going to leave them when you go."

I measured her gaze. "Probably."

"That's good to hear. Let me tell you more."

I sat back and listened while she filled me in on Tawny Bledsoe.

"We get all kinds in here," she explained. "I've been here twenty years, and I've seen just about every type of woman you could name coming through the door. I get young girls who just got here for college and can't believe that there's other women like them. They come in, the self-hatred just melts off their shoulders, then they hit the dance floor and go wild with freedom." She paused and blew a smoke ring. "I love to see their faces when that happens. Helps me remember why I opened this bar in the first place."

I was just drunk enough to be in the mood to listen—and to start wondering whether there was an advantage to choosing experience over youth.

"Then I get the older dykes," she said, "the ones who feel comfortable with themselves. They have jobs, they have lovers, they have their problems. But they work them out and they're kind to one another, even if they do talk about every detail of their relationships endlessly, usually within my earshot." She shook her head, exasperated, then motioned for a fresh drink. "I think I'm going to get drunk tonight. Feel free to join me."

"About the blond?" I prompted.

"Right. I'm getting to her. Anyway, then you get your dabblers coming in here. Repressed housewives who wander in on their one night out each month, wanting a place where they can get good and drunk without having some salesman slob drooling on them. They're looking to flirt and feel pretty, maybe dance with their bored housewife friends, then go home and tell people how wild they were." She blew another perfect smoke ring toward the ceiling. "Your blond wasn't one of those, either."

"Then what kind was she?"

"The worst kind. The minute she walked in, I knew she was trouble."

"Why?"

"For starters, she was completely femmed out, from head to toe, but she went right for some of my regulars who are, shall we say, a little on the homely side. Created quite a stir at the bar her first night. It was about a year and a half ago, maybe. Something like that. I made it a point to sit near her when she returned."

"And?"

"And I saw her for what she was. A twist looking for a new twist. An aging blond who had always gotten off on wrapping men around her little finger. Only now she was getting old, the wrinkles were starting to show, her ass was falling, her thighs turning to cottage cheese—and the men weren't lining up at her door anymore. She was slipping and she knew it. Because, face it, there's always another younger, prettier blond nipping at your heels." She stared at me. "It's enough to turn you gay, don't you think?"

I took a healthy gulp of my drink. Best to get tipsy after all.

"She was just here for the power play," the owner explained. "For the thrill of being the belle of the ball again. I took one look at her and I could read her mind. She figured, hey, my stock has gone down with the men, let's give it a whirl with the women. They're probably just a bunch of dumpy old dykes anyway. I can have them eating out of my hand."

"Is that what happened?"

She shrugged. "Not really. Believe it or not, most of my customers prefer their women a little more real, a little more genuine."

"I believe it."

"But enough women bought her drinks and fed her ego to keep her coming back. She started showing up regularly. For a while, at the beginning, I think she even hit it off with one those bored housewife-types who wandered in. A real babe, in fact. Looked a bit like Sigourney Weaver. But the housewife disappeared. Which I could have predicted. She was interested in fantasy, not reality."

"But Tawny kept coming in?" I asked.

"Oh, yeah." She hesitated. "Look, I don't condone drugs

on the premises. I could lose my license. But I'm not naive. If I had to guess, I'd say your blond kept coming back
here for two reasons. First, to mooch as much nose candy
as she could. Then, once she wore out her welcome glom-
ming freebies, to pick up extra change blackmailing my
customers so she could pay for her own."

She nodded toward the photos. "That redhead in the
photos? She's a personal friend of mine, so I already knew
about her troubles with the blond. But you said half the
stack was missing. How many of my other customers are
in the same trap?" She wiped her mouth with the back of
her hand and looked sad. "Someone has to stop her. People
come in here to be themselves and that bitch is using it
against them. A lot of these women can't go to the police
because it will get out that they're gay."

"So what?" I said. "In this day and age, what's the big
deal?"

"I'll let Francine explain the big deal. She tells it better
than me. I've been out so long, I couldn't even tell you
where my closet was."

"The redhead?"

"The redhead. She'll be here in a few minutes."

"Thanks for trusting me," I told her, conscious that the
bartender had inched closer and could hear every word.

"Look," Roberta answered quietly. "I'm helping you out
because something has to give. I want you to stop this
bitch. Please."

"I will." I remembered something she had said earlier.
"You said you threw her out of here for fighting. Was it
with Francine?"

"No, a friend of ours named Patsy was trying to protect
Francine. Patsy is one of my regulars and she hates women
like that blond almost as much as I do."

"Or as I do," I added.

She smiled. "Your blond got the worst of it, too. And
no wonder. Picking at your food might make you a size
four, but it's not going to do shit for you in a fistfight.
Patsy doesn't screw around. She takes kick-boxing lessons.
She did a number on that bitch. I kind of enjoyed it, to
tell you the truth."

She stubbed out her cigarette and smiled at me. "I let it go on for a good five minutes before I broke it up. I figured the blond deserved it on general principle. After she left, I found out what the fight was about and Francine told me about the photographs. It made me wish I'd gotten in a few good licks myself."

"This was about three weeks ago?" I asked and, when the bar owner nodded, I had the answer to at least one of my questions: where Tawny Bledsoe's real bruises had come from.

"There she is." The bar owner slid from her stool and greeted a skinny redhead standing in the doorway. The woman looked apprehensive and uncomfortable. At least I had a way to put her at ease. I had planned to swap the photos for information, but seeing how her face looked, I figured she deserved a break.

"These are for you," I said, when the redhead joined us at the bar. I handed her the photos and envelope. I'd held one photo back, just in case I needed it. I hoped I wouldn't. "The negatives are inside," I added. "Do what you want with them. I don't want them. I'm after the woman who did this to you."

She grabbed at the stack, then looked ashamed at her loss of control. Without going through the photos, she held them in her hands and stared at me, waiting until we were alone.

Roberta retrieved her drink and cigarettes, then returned to her seat at the far end of the bar. The bartender, equally discreet, refilled my glass and placed a beer in front of my companion before retreating to a far corner. I could have sworn she threw me a wink on the way down the bar. God help me, I winked back. Maybe it was only the Jack Daniels, but I was hearing the lure of the siren song and the tune sounded mighty sweet.

"Who else saw the photos?" the redhead asked me in a whisper, bringing me back to reality. I knew her first name was Francine and I didn't ask for a last. She'd given up enough of her privacy.

"Only a couple of people," I promised. I noticed the dark circles under her eyes and tried my best not to stare at her bustline, since then all I would be able to think about were "sweet potatoes." Thank you Bill Butler. And Jack Daniels.

"The bartender here saw them," I explained. "And one at another bar, but she didn't recognize you. And Roberta, of course. I'm sorry I showed them around, but I had to find you. If it makes you feel better, no one would recognize you unless they knew it was you."

"That's the problem." She sat next to me and stared down at the photos. "If someone who knows me sees them, I'll lose my job."

"Can you tell me about it?"

It turned out that Francine was a teacher at a Durham elementary school. And even in these supposedly enlightened days, the good people of North Carolina were not going to stand for the homosexual element acting as role models for their young. Plus, she was from a small farming town and a fundamentally religious family. Which meant that Francine had a lot more to lose than her job if her secret was discovered. Tawny Bledsoe, with the instincts of a shark sniffing out a bloody wound, had gone right for her.

"At first I was flattered," she told me in a voice thick with self-disgust. "I couldn't believe that someone that pretty would pick me."

"How long ago was this?" I asked, dismayed that lack of self-esteem apparently transcended all sexual boundaries.

"Three months ago," she said in a low voice. "I only went home with her that one time. I'd just broken up with a girlfriend after ten years together and when she started coming on to me, I don't know. I thought I had to get back out there sometime, so I had a lot to drink this one night and after we had danced, she asked me if I wanted to go home with her and I did."

"What happened then?"

"It took a long time to get to her house in Raleigh. I was following her in my car and before I even got there, I was sorry I had agreed to do it. I had no business being on the road with all I'd had to drink."

I stared guiltily at my own glass of whiskey while she continued.

"When we got near her house, she stopped her car and told me to wait. She said she didn't want her baby-sitter to see me come in with her." She shrugged. "It didn't really offend me," she said quickly, though her voice sounded as if it had. "You have to be careful. I know that. You never know when people are going to freak out." She missed the irony of this last remark. "After a couple of minutes, she knocked on the car window and said the coast was clear."

She took a gulp of her beer, not wanting to relive the experience. "It was a nice house. I could tell she had a lot of money because it was a big, ranch-type thing." She looked down at the photographs and realized where they'd come from. "I forgot. I guess you've seen the house."

I nodded. "I wasn't exactly invited in."

"Be glad you weren't. When we got to her bedroom, I started to get freaked out. All of a sudden, it hit me—I didn't even know her last name. She'd only told me that her name was Cathy, which I later found out was a lie. And I didn't even know why the hell I was doing what I was doing."

She paused again and flushed. "I was trying to think of a way to leave, without hurting her feelings—can you believe how dumb I was to worry about that? But then she started doing this weird dance. I mean, look at me. Do I look like the type of person who'd enjoy seeing someone strip off their clothes? She put on music and everything. With her kid right there in the other room."

"She's used to seducing men," I explained. "Take it from me, they're much more easily entertained."

"Well, it sort of worked. I mean, we did get going." She hesitated. "How much detail do you need?"

"None," I told her. "I'm more interested in what happened afterward."

She looked relieved. "I could tell during it, you know, that her mind was somewhere else. I couldn't figure out why she'd even bothered to invite me home. I thought maybe she didn't like my body when she saw it or something."

"That woman doesn't like anyone's body but her own," I assured Francine. "There is nothing wrong with yours." At least nothing that a few pecans and miniature marshmallows couldn't improve on, I thought.

"Maybe not," she said. "But I got freaked out because after about fifteen minutes, she started in with telling me to hurry it up: I have to go to work in the morning, the kid might wake up. That kind of thing. That was weird, too. Hurry what up? It wasn't like I was having any fun myself. I was just trying to please her. Then the kid did wake up, and started crying for 'Daddy,' and I really freaked out. But she just ignored the poor thing and let it cry. She put her clothes back on, asked for my phone number and said maybe it was better if I left and she'd call me so we could get together again soon." She paused. "I thought that was weird, since she'd acted so cold the whole time we were in bed. But then I thought, maybe I just wasn't very good at dating. I've never been good at it, I was out of practice and it was my first one-night stand ever. It all felt so phony and hollow."

"No one is good at dating," I told her. "It's a necessary evil. And there's no such thing as a meaningful one-night stand. I think that's the point of them."

She nodded. "That's what I figured. So I started to leave and I could hear her yelling at the kid behind me, and I began to feel really bad about that, and so I decided on the drive home that there's no way I want to see her again." She took a gulp of beer and finished in a rush. "A week later, her first phone call came."

What Tawny Bledsoe wanted, it turned out, was money. And if she didn't get it, she would go to the principal of Francine's school with the photographs.

"She didn't show me the actual photos," Francine explained, "but I could tell she had them. I knew when I heard her voice on the phone that I had made a really bad mistake, even before she told me what she wanted. It was so different from the way she had sounded before. All of a sudden, her voice seemed so cold and so distant and so . . ."

"Businesslike?" I suggested.

"Yes. She didn't care what I said. She didn't care that I had been a teacher for fifteen years or that my parents depended on my salary or that it had taken me that long and more to save what little I had."

"She took it all?"

Francine nodded, unable to speak.

"How much?" I asked softly, putting my hand on hers.

She pulled her hand away. "Almost twenty thousand," she whispered. "I gave her twelve thousand from my savings account and then she wanted more, so I took out a cash advance on my Visa. After that, I didn't have anything more to give her."

"So she left you alone?"

"Until three days ago," Francine said, still in a whisper. "I got another call."

I sat up straight. "She called you three days ago?"

Francine shook her head. "No. A man called. He said he was calling for her."

I thought of Jeff and my stomach lurched. "A man? Did he have a deep Southern accent?"

She nodded. "He sounded like a hick, like he was from somewhere even further south from here. Georgia, maybe."

"Or Florida?" I suggested.

She nodded again, biting her lower lip, trying to keep from crying. "He said he was calling to see if I had the money I owed Tawny. He didn't even bother to call her Cathy, so I knew Tawny was her real name."

Another mistake, I thought. She was getting careless. And that was good.

"I asked him 'what money?' and he said that I owed her fifteen thousand dollars and that it was way past time I paid her back."

"Fifteen thousand?" I took a gulp of Jack Daniels. What was she planning to do? Run away to Mexico?

"I don't have the money," Francine whispered, her hands shaking. "I told the man that. He got mad. He said

I owed it to her and she needed it. He scared me."

"Did he say anything about the photos?" I was still hoping that Jeff didn't really know what was going on.

She shook her head. "No. He just said that I ought to have the decency to pay people the money I owe them. Then he said I had a day to come up with the cash and he'd call back for it. But he never did."

"So he didn't give you an address or anything?"

She shook her head and I hid my disappointment.

"I can try and get an address for you if he calls back," she offered timidly.

"He won't call back. They've moved on to threatening someone else. By now they've figured out that without the photos there's nothing they can do to you. You won't have to pay them a penny more."

"You think?" she asked dully, her eyes on the envelope in her lap. "What if they tell anyway?"

"They won't," I promised. "They've got other problems. And if the man ever does call back, just tell them you've got the photos now. They'll know how you got them, and they'll leave you alone."

She looked dubious—and who could blame her?

"Is there anyone else you can think of who might be able to tell me about this woman?" I asked. "Do you know anyone else she may have done this to?"

She shook her head. "I know she came on to a couple of other people, but I don't think she went home with anyone else. At least, not that I know of."

No. She wouldn't. She had found the perfect victim in Francine.

"But she did come back here to the bar?" I said, remembering the owner's story about throwing Tawny out for fighting.

Francine nodded uncomfortably. "A little less than a month ago, when she asked me to meet her here with the money I borrowed from my Visa account. I gave her all I had, but she wanted to know why I couldn't open up some new credit card accounts. That was when my friend lost her temper. They got into a fight. I guess Roberta told you the rest."

I nodded. "What about the other woman Tawny saw for a little while?" I asked. "The one she met here? Roberta described her as a housewife type. Could Tawny have been blackmailing her as well? Roberta said she disappeared suddenly. It would have been a while ago."

Francine furrowed her brow, trying to remember. "She might have been involved with someone before me. I didn't really notice. If it was when I was still with my girlfriend, I wouldn't have been looking."

"Okay, thanks for your help. And don't worry about Tawny. It's over."

"Good." She stared at her beer. "I can't decide what would be worse—the straight world finding out I was gay and my losing my job, or people finding out how stupid I was to let someone like her back me into a corner like that."

"Don't beat yourself up because she's a scumbag. If you do that, she wins."

Francine seemed to be thinking it over. "You're not gay, are you?" she asked in a faintly hopeful voice.

"Not yet," I admitted, sneaking a peek at the cute bartender before checking out the now-crowded main room. It had filled with women moving to the music. I was willing to bet that there were more rat tails bobbing up and down on that dance floor than you'd find in the entire New York City subway system.

"To tell you the truth, after hearing your story about Tawny," I confessed, "I think I'll stick with men. At least men can be controlled."

She nodded, agreeing. "Take it from me. Women are nothing but trouble."

EIGHT

I woke late the next morning with a pugnacious hangover. Over coffee, I suffered murky flashbacks of a churning dance floor, followed by a ride home from some diesel dyke who could have driven her truck through the gap in her front teeth. I didn't remember any groping or goodnight kisses, thank god, but I'd have given up a lot more than that as thanks to anyone sensible enough to make sure I avoided driving when I was drunker than a Kentucky skunk.

The walk back to my car in the cold morning air did nothing for my disposition. Where the hell had I left it? I finally located the damn thing in a municipal parking lot. Someone had draped multicolored metallic tinsel over its radio antennae and it stuck out from a surrounding sea of sedans, looking like the party guest discovered on the host's sofa the morning after. The bumper was still badly dented from my run-in with Jeff a few nights before. Worse still, I detected a rear-end shimmy on the drive to Raleigh—a memento of the banging my ex-husband gave it. I knew how that car felt.

My hangover was so bad that I barely made it to Raleigh without having to pull over on I-40 and puke my guts out all over the median strip. That would teach me to accept free drinks from some vixen of a bartender without at least arranging for a way to sweat it out when I got home. I was starting to realize that sex has a purpose after all—to sober you up before sleep.

All in all, I arrived at the office spoiling for a fight. Bobby D., as disgustingly cheerful as ever, was busy digesting a shopping bag's worth of breakfast biscuits. He was unsympathetic to my plight.

"I could call Brown-Wynne Funeral Home," he offered. "They got some specialists down there who might be able to make you look human again."

"Fuck off," I mumbled, grabbing one of his biscuits.

His indignant shout followed me back to my office. I pawed through my first-aid drawer, searching for aspirin and a can of warm Coke. This was not a good day to feel like shit. I was planning to visit Robert Price.

A munching sound in my doorway distracted me. Bobby held a sausage biscuit in one hand and a newspaper in the other. "Prepare to be even more pissed off," he advised, handing over the *N&O*. It was folded open to an inside page.

I saw what he meant at once. A follow-up story on the Boomer Cockshutt murder featured a slightly blurry photograph of Tawny Bledsoe—my photograph of Tawny, to be precise, one I'd taken when she'd handed me her bullshit story about being beaten by her hubby. The cuts and bruises reproduced nicely in black and white. She looked like she'd lost a fight with a meat grinder. The caption contained a word-for-word account of the statement she'd had her lawyer read on television two nights ago.

"The *N&O* doesn't actually say Price beat her up," Bobby pointed out. "If that makes you feel any better."

"Like it has to say anything at all," I groused. "This photo is the visual equivalent of asking a man when he stopped beating his wife." I stared at it, hatred welling in me. "How did the *N&O* get this?"

"Got a call in. I can find out for you." His voice was so sympathetic, I looked up at him suspiciously. There had to be a catch.

"What's going on?" I asked. He wanted something. I could smell it.

"Maybe you're working too hard," he suggested. He squeezed into my visitor's chair, sending it one week closer to a new home at the town dump. "Let me be frank. I'm worried about you, babe."

"It's just a hangover. I'll be fine."

"I mean with this case." He drummed his sausagelike fingers on his thighs, avoiding my eyes. "You don't maybe kind of think that perhaps you're letting your personal feelings interfere with your professional judgment on this particular case, do you?"

"No, I don't maybe kind of think that perhaps I'm letting my personal feelings interfere with my professional judgment." I glared at him. "Spit it out."

"Obviously this dame has got her claws into your ex-husband. Maybe it hurts a little to think of him with another woman?"

"Robert Dodd, you listen to me and you listen closely." My tone of voice was deadly. "I don't give a shit about Jeff Jones. He can rot in hell. Or end up on the bottom of the Everglades, courtesy of whatever drug dealers are after his sorry ass. I don't care. But Tawny Bledsoe is another matter."

"What is it with you and this dame?" Bobby grumbled. "So she's popular with guys? If there was a law against having hot pants, you and me would be out of business, babe. What hard evidence do you have that she really had anything at all to do with this guy's murder?"

"I don't need hard evidence right now. I have enough to know she's guiltier than shit. And, for your information, I do have direct evidence that she is a blackmailing piece of scum who preys on the weakest, saddest, most fearful people she can find, including her own daughter. Think of it—a four-year-old kid being jerked around so this lady can garner public sympathy while she avoids the cops. Plus, she used me to put an innocent man in jail and now she's using my ex-husband to do her dirty work. That's like prodding a mentally retarded elephant with a stun gun to get it to march faster."

"Surely he's not all that bad?" Bobby asked faintly.

"Jeff is so easy to manipulate, it's pathetic," I explained. "All you have to do is wave a pair of panties in front of that man's face and he's yours for life. If you want him for life. Which I don't." I said this last sentence very distinctly and Bobby looked away, uneasy.

"Jeff is not the point," I added. "This woman needs to be brought down. For starters, she turned her back on her own parents, two good people whose only crimes are being poor and being sick. How could a person do that? If I still had my parents, I'd get down on my knees and thank god I could take care of them. I wouldn't give a good goddamn if they lived in a shack or a shithole."

Bobby started to say something, saw my face and stopped. I kept going.

"She destroyed the first daughter she had. You should see that poor kid now: fat, unhappy, slash marks on her arms, hates herself and, I guarantee you, drugs and sleeping with drug dealers are next. And god knows what Tawny's done to her son, I wouldn't want to guess. I'm sure he's paying, only in a different way.

"As for men, I'd say she marches through husbands like Sherman marching through Atlanta. The only difference is that she wears a silk teddy while she does her dirty work and Sherman, so far as I know, didn't. She deliberately targets married men, Bobby. She takes photos of them having sex with her and then bleeds them dry for money."

"They're adults," Bobby said. "They take their pants off willingly."

"She's just getting started, Bobby," I predicted. "She's blackmailing school teachers, for godsakes. She's ruined a perfectly nice woman whose only crime is that she's trying, against all odds, to be herself. Who knows who else Tawny is taking advantage of right now or what she'll do next? There is no longer any question in my mind about whether this lady will step over some mythical moral boundary. She's doing the Texas two-step over it, with a big smile on her face." I paused for effect. "And you know why? Because she *likes* it. She gets off on doing things the rest of us would never dare try. That means she's going to get worse. Like some junkie who finds one hit isn't enough, this lady will need more."

"That's just a theory," Bobby protested, sweating, as he always does, in the presence of my anger.

"I'll get the evidence." I shook my head, disgusted. "What everyone keeps forgetting is there's a man sitting in jail whose life has been ruined. His daughter's been taken away from him. He may get the death penalty. Don't count on common sense or lack of evidence to save him. I don't care what anyone says—he's a black man and it is easier for a jury to send a black man to death row. If he were poor to boot, I'd say he was toast."

"You make him sound like Martin Luther King," Bobby grumbled.

"Robert Price is someone who has done the right thing his whole life. He was still trying to do the right thing when he left Tawny and tried to protect his daughter from her. For all we know, this whole thing is about Tawny getting back at him for dumping her and wounding her pride. I wouldn't put it past that bitch to kill Cockshutt just to hurt Price."

"But that's what bothers me," Bobby insisted. "I don't buy her going that far just because of pride. So what's her motive? Why would she kill Cockshutt?"

"I don't know. But I'm going to find out."

"If there is anything to find out," he said, still skeptical.

"What is it with you men?" I asked, exasperated. "Is it so hard to believe that just because someone looks good in a pair of jeans she isn't capable of the foulest, most selfish actions a person can take? Because I am here to tell you that there's not a woman in America who doesn't know that women like Tawny Bledsoe exist. We can tell when one of our kind is bad. And this woman is bad to the bone."

Bobby had listened to enough. "Whatever you say," he said, wiggling out of the chair. "I'm sorry I brought it up. But I think you're too involved, and I think you're making a mistake. Besides, if she really is what you say, then you need help on this one. Help I can't give you. You know I'm not good as backup when the going gets rough. I'm a lover, not a fighter. You better call Butler. You need someone like him on this one."

I couldn't tell Bobby that I'd already involved Bill Butler without revealing his trouble with Tawny. So I just shrugged. "I appreciate your worrying about me," I told him. "But I know what I'm doing."

"I hope so," he said as he left.

I arranged to visit Price later that afternoon, then hung up and was contemplating swallowing another handful of aspirin when my phone rang.

I'd hardly mumbled hello when the caller unleashed a string of profanity that would have turned a sailor's ears purple.

"Why, if it isn't herself," I said. "To what do I owe this pleasure?"

"You bitch," Tawny Bledsoe screamed into the phone. "Stay out of my house or I'll have you arrested for breaking and entering."

"That's a good one. Why don't we march down to the police station right now and talk about it?" There was only one person who could have told her I was there—Jeff. Any doubts I had about his involvement were gone.

"Don't fuck with me." Her voice rose even higher. "You think you're so smart, don't you? Well, you have no idea who you're dealing with, you overweight, low-class piece of trash."

"On the contrary," I assured her. "I think I have a very good idea of who I'm dealing with. You're nothing but a swamp coot of the highest order, a white trash road whore who sells her snatch for a handful of credit cards."

She gasped, but I wasn't through yet.

"And, honey, guess what?" I said. "You're getting old. Ain't nobody gonna be buying what you're selling in a year. Your ride is over. Not even liposuction can help you now. You better look for a job at a nursing home if you want to find a husband that can't get away."

"Don't you talk to me like that," she hissed. "I have more class in my little finger than you have in your entire big old *hulking* body."

I had to laugh. She said "hulking" like it was the worst possible thing that could ever happen to a woman. Guess she'd never heard of Janet Reno.

If she was hot before, my laughter pushed her over the edge.

"Don't you dare laugh at me," she screeched into the phone. "I'll track down your family and shoot them in the head while they sleep."

"Go ahead," I said cheerfully. "But bring a shovel. They're already dead."

"Your ex-husband isn't." Her voice dropped. "I can make him do anything I want. I have him wrapped around my little finger."

"Congratulations. That's quite an achievement. Next thing you know, you'll graduate to training dogs."

"Shut up." Her tone was venomous. "I could make one phone call and have him put behind bars for the rest of his life. I know where he keeps his stuff, and a kilo can put a person away for a long, long time."

In that case, the kilo wouldn't be there long. She was no doubt a human Dust Buster when it came to coke. But her words bothered me anyway. They proved that Jeff had lied to me. Not all of his stash was gone. He had a kilo left. There had been no girl who took off with his stuff. He had simply wanted me to help him unload it. How could he think I'd ever do such a thing?

"This is about Bill Butler, isn't it?" Tawny tried again, reading my silence as disinterest. "That's why you're out to get me."

"I don't know how to break this to you," I told her. "But, unlike you, my life does not revolve around a series of penises. Bill Butler has nothing to do with it."

"I know you have my photos. You took them from my safe."

"Sure," I agreed. "I'm using them as an appetite suppressant so I can drop a few pounds off my 'hulking' body."

"You're just jealous I slept with Bill."

"Honey," I told her, "Bill said that sex with you was like dipping his wick in a bucket of dry ice. Now, is that anything to be jealous about?"

She unleashed another barrage of insults, most of them concerning what she would do to which body part of mine if she ever got the chance. I started laughing again and she hung up in frustration. I dialed *69 in hopes of learning what number she had called from, but no such luck. She was outside the calling area.

I sat back and thought. For someone who was supposed to be cool, calm and collected, Tawny Bledsoe sure was losing her shit. Too much nose candy. I could use that against her. The trick was figuring out how—and how far I could go.

I was mulling over the possibilities when I heard the front door open. A male voice said something and Bobby D. laughed. I tiptoed out to the hallway to eavesdrop.

"Yeah, she's in the back," Bobby was saying. "But I'd take it easy with her. She drank her way through Durham last night, and she's got a real bug up her ass about this Bledsoe dame. She's acting a little nutty about it, you ask me. Maybe you can talk some sense into her."

"Me?" an incredulous voice answered: Bill Butler. "If you think I can tell that woman to do anything, you're out of your mind."

"It's impolite to talk about people behind their backs," I yelled.

"Really?" Bill was in my face before I heard him coming. "How about eavesdropping? How polite is that?"

"You have something for me?" I asked, staring at the packages in his hand.

"Afraid I do." I could tell from his expression that it was not good news.

I led him into my office.

"You look like shit," he said, sitting down across from me.

"You say the sweetest things," I mumbled back, acutely aware that I was wearing a gray sweatsuit. When I'd thrown it on earlier that morning, it seemed appropriate for my planned visit to see Robert Price. When you're tromping through a men's jail, it's best to keep your sex appeal on a par with Mother Teresa's. Not so when it came to Bill Butler.

He tossed a thick envelope across the desk. "Tawny's

phone records. And, by the way, she has no criminal record."

"Lucky her. She's not that smart."

"Well, she'll have one now," Bill promised. He pulled several sheets of paper from another envelope. "Sign this and I can have a warrant issued for her arrest on the misdemeanors. It's going to make you real popular, Casey, dragging a battered wife back to face a bad check rap."

"I bet a hell of a lot more people will be happy to see her behind bars than you think." I signed the complaint without looking at it and slid it back to him.

"So what's the bad news?" I asked. "I can see it on your face."

"Your ex has a record. And he's currently wanted in Florida for felony possession with intent to distribute."

"Cocaine?"

Bill nodded. "His convictions are minor stuff, all drug-related, but the outstanding charge is a serious one. It seemed like a big step up to me, so I called a guy I know in St. Pete and he put me in touch with the investigating detective."

"And?" I prompted.

"And your ex is probably in more trouble right now than Tawny Bledsoe could ever cause him."

"Don't be too sure."

"He's hooked in with some big time dealers, distributing for them, doing a little sideline business on his own."

"So what's the scoop on his arrest?"

"They're really looking to bring him in for questioning," Bill explained. "They're after the big fish, not your husband."

"Ex-husband."

"Ex. First he refused to cooperate and then he disappeared, so they issued the warrant for his arrest on the intent charge, mostly to put pressure on him. They'll be glad to cut a deal if he agrees to cooperate."

"He told me a different story."

"I wasn't aware you had conversed about it," Bill said dryly.

"This was weeks ago. When he first showed up here.

He said a deal had gone bad and that a couple of guys were after him. He claims some girlfriend doublecrossed him and left him short, without the money or the drugs. He says that's why he's on the run."

Bill shrugged. "Both stories could be partially true. He might be running from the cops and the dealers."

I sighed. "That sounds like Jeff, all right. He's cursed. Everything he touches turns to shit. Except for me, of course." I opened the envelope with Tawny's phone records in it and started flipping through the pages, searching for calls she'd made around the time of Cockshutt's death.

"What are you looking for?" Bill asked.

"I don't know," I admitted. "I was hoping I'd find something. Maybe the same long-distance number repeated over and over as evidence of who she was in on the murder with. Or where she might have gone."

"Well," Bill said. "There's more bad news."

I stopped reading and stared at him. "What do you mean?"

"Autopsy results and the early forensics workup on the crime scene are in. Cockshutt was shot from a lower angle. The bullet traveled up into his brain." Bill touched the underside of his chin. "Entry point was here."

"Weird," I said. "Like a suicide?"

"It's the right angle for that, but it would have been a hell of a trick for him to shoot himself, then wipe down the gun."

"So someone was crouching down in the car waiting for him?" I suggested.

Bill shrugged. "That's one possibility. Whoever it was, he only needed that one shot. It was right on the money. Then the gun was tossed into the backseat."

"That's even weirder. Lake Johnston was twenty feet away. Why not just throw it into the lake?"

Bill nodded. "A little strange, I agree."

"Who's the gun registered to?"

"It was Boomer's gun," Bill confirmed. "You were right about that."

"There was no evidence of a struggle? As in someone taking it from him?"

"Nope. No defensive wounds. We know he died about midnight. And that no one heard the shot. But there's more."

I stared at him, waiting.

"They found hair and fibers in the car that match Robert Price."

"Bullshit."

Bill held up both hands. "That's what they found. Threads from a sweater he owns were stuck to the butt of the gun. Maybe from wiping it down. Plus there are microscopic blood splatters on a sweater we took from Price's closet. Results aren't in on that yet. And don't give me any O.J. setup bullshit. No one on the job planted evidence. He wasn't even a suspect at the time it was found."

"I agree that no one on the job planted evidence," I said. "It doesn't mean that someone off the job didn't."

"You're going all the way with this, aren't you?"

"Damn right I am. Doesn't anyone but me find Tawny Bledsoe's public pity party a little hard to swallow, given she was banging anyone she could find—including the murder victim?"

"The people who know her from when she worked at the department aren't happy she's disappeared," Bill acknowledged. "They want to question her, but not badly enough to risk alienating public opinion by dragging her in by her hair. Besides, you and I know she's a slimeball, but she still has friends on the job. Plus her alibi checks out. The night Cockshutt was killed, she was in a motel in Winston-Salem with her daughter and thirty other members of her church."

"Says who?" I asked. "Did they actually see her? Winston-Salem is only an hour-and-a-half drive from here."

"The woman who was staying in the motel room next to hers heard the kid crying sometime after midnight. When the kid wouldn't stop, she called Tawny's room and asked if there was anything she could do. Tawny said the kid was fine, she just had an earache, and that the children's aspirin would probably kick in soon. The woman hung up, noted the time, the kid stopped crying soon after and everyone was happy. Tawny was bright and chipper at breakfast."

"Then she had someone else do her dirty work for her," I insisted stubbornly, while silently putting up a prayer that this someone had not been my ex.

"Or she didn't do it at all. It is possible that Tawny Bledsoe is a slimeball who had nothing to do with this particular crime."

"Okay, fine," I agreed. "Who else could have done it? Where was Cockshutt's wife that night, for example? She's not exactly a grieving widow."

"She was in Asheville, with her mother and the kids. They were staying at some fancy hotel up there."

"In the middle of January?" I asked skeptically.

"Casey." Bill was getting impatient. "Some people like snow, okay? I kind of miss it myself. Besides, with all the money riding on Cockshutt's death, you better believe the insurance companies looked into any hint of involvement on the widow's part. She's clean. They're going to cough up the death benefits."

"I guess I'm just a naturally suspicious woman. Which reminds me, Tawny called me."

"You're kidding. When?"

"Just before you got here. But she's out of the calling area. I checked." I looked up at him and smiled. "She said to tell you hello."

"Me?" He blanched.

"Not really. But she did say that you were the best sex she ever had."

"What?" This time he looked scared, with a pinch of confusion thrown in.

"Just kidding." I smiled at him. He did not smile back. "What I want to know is where she called me from." I started thumbing through the phone numbers again, reached the page just after Boomer Cockshutt was killed, then stopped and stared at several identical lines.

"What is it?" Bill asked.

"I know that number." I pointed to a long-distance charge for a Florida call. "The area code is Tampa/ St. Pete."

"You're right. I used the same area code this morning."

"Why do I know that number?" I reached for the phone.
"What are you doing?"

"Calling it." The phone rang twice before a machine answered. I listened to the recorded female voice on the other end for a moment, then slammed the receiver down. I had hoped never to hear that voice again for the rest of my life.

"Who was it?" Bill asked.

"My former mother-in-law." I massaged my temples. My head had started to throb instantly at the mere thought of Clarissa Jones.

"Who?" Bill asked. "Your ex's mother?"

"Yes. My ex's mother," I said irritated. "My former mother-in-law. The very same face-lifted, cellulite-sucked-out, anorexic bitch who hated me twenty-four hours a day, constantly let me know that I was not good enough for her son and who spends her days and nights shopping because god forbid the neighbors look like they have more money than she does. She dotes on Jeff so much it's a wonder they don't chuck public opinion and start shacking up to-gether. God knows his father's not man enough to stop it."

"Your mother-in-law?" Bill repeated, rather stupidly in my opinion. "Why would Tawny be calling her?"

"Maybe Tawny wasn't," I explained slowly. "Maybe my ex-husband was."

"From Tawny's house?" Bill asked. "Why? Is there a connection to Tawny?"

"I don't know," I said, but it was a lie. I thought I finally knew why Tawny had involved Jeff. And I was going to fly down there and find out if I was right.

I booked a seat on a Tampa-bound plane leaving RDU on Monday afternoon. I would need the weekend to set my plan in motion. The fare cost me most of my savings. But no one ever said revenge was cheap. I could only hope they'd give me two bags of peanuts for my four hundred dollars.

Anger, frustration and fear fueled my energy all the way to the front door of the Wake County jail later that afternoon. I left my hangover behind in the cold, but I still looked crummy. Robert Price looked worse.

Prison had changed him. The uniform—a bright orange jumpsuit—reduced him to nothing more than an all-too-familiar stereotype: another black man in jail. Gone was any dignity. Gone was any sense of who he had once been. He could have been a rapist, a drug dealer, a murderer or a thief. That jumpsuit didn't care and, I suspected, neither did the guards who brought him in to me.

He sat down across the table and didn't bother to say hello. He stared at me so long I began to wonder if he remembered who I was. He seemed like a stranger. Even his face looked different, darker and angrier. His hair was disheveled and bulged out on the right side.

I don't know what it was, maybe the contrast between who he had been and who he was right then, or maybe it was just the unfairness of it all, but I felt as sick to my stomach as I had earlier that day.

"I believe you," was all I could think of to say.

His expression flickered. "That makes two of us." His voice was hoarse from worry. "All my lawyer wants to talk about is cutting a deal."

"I looked into Tawny's background. You're right. She's evil."

"Where's my daughter?" he interrupted. Tears welled up in his eyes and he looked at the floor. "Have you found out where she's taken Tiff?"

"No, but I have a lead. I think they may be in Florida."

He looked at me, frightened. "Why Florida?"

"There's a group of people there who maintain a sort of underground railroad for abused women and their kids. I think they've gone underground."

He didn't like that much. "She's not abused," he said flatly.

"I know. But the people who run this organization don't know that. It's a fundamentalist group. They're violently anti-abortion, and they also protect women and children who claim sexual or physical abuse but aren't believed by the courts. The group takes them in and sends them to stay at homes in Florida, Georgia, Alabama and I'm not sure where else. They also help the women take on new identities."

"How do you know all this?" he asked, looking even more alarmed.

"Tawny met my ex-husband outside my offices one day," I explained. "In the very beginning, before all this happened. When she was still planning it, down to her getaway. I think she worked on my ex as a backup plan, then asked him to help hide her when the frame-up of you began. This morning, I found my former mother-in-law's phone number on Tawny's long-distance bill. I think my mother-in-law hooked Tawny up with the underground. She's been active in it for a long time. Makes her feel morally superior to the rest of us. It's not like she gives a shit about the people she's supposedly protecting."

His eyes grew wide with panic. "I'll never find Tiff now," he said. "Not without your help. I don't care about anything but my daughter. You have to bring Tiff back so she can be raised by decent people if they keep me inside here."

Or if they put him to death. "I'll bring her back," I promised. "I know what I need to do." I was silent for a moment, remembering what it felt like to be inside. "I guess they're giving you a pretty hard time."

"You guessed right." His voice was gruff. "Half the Aryan Nation lives in my cell block and my own people don't want anything to do with me. They think I'm an Oreo. I got a crick in my neck from watching my back."

"Then you ought to be in isolation."

"Tell that to the guards." He glanced at the man standing in the small interview room doorway. The guard looked away, embarrassed.

"I'm going to help you get out of here," I promised. "I'll find Tiffany, too, and bring her home to your family. Who should I call?"

"My sister," he said, not sounding very hopeful. "Bring her to my sister in Rocky Mount."

"I'll bring Tawny down, too," I promised. "I'll prove she did it."

Price stared at his shackled hands. "Nobody can do that. She's too smart."

"No, she's not. She's making mistakes. She's snorting too much coke. It's making her sloppy."

Price looked up, alarmed. "She's doing drugs around my baby?"

I nodded. "I'll find her in time. I promise."

"How can you be sure?"

"Because I know how Tawny thinks," I explained.

"Then I wouldn't want to be inside your head."

"I'm one step ahead of her. I'll find a way to stop her."

Price shook his head. He didn't believe anything anymore. "She'll get away with it. She always does. She did a good job of making me look bad."

"Look," I said more loudly, hoping to convince him that I meant what I said. "I'm going to do more than clear you. I'm going to prove she's guilty. You'll get your daughter back and you'll get out of here. I promise you."

Something in his eyes flickered. Hope, maybe, or just more fear. "All I care about is my daughter," he repeated.

"Then you have to help me nail Tawny. I want a favor from you. Or, rather, your lawyer." I told him what I needed.

He didn't like it one bit. "What if she takes it out on Tiffany?"

"She won't. Right now, public opinion is the only thing keeping her from being questioned by the cops. Tawny won't do anything to jeopardize that."

He didn't look convinced. "You don't know her when she gets angry."

I thought back to my earlier phone call with her. "Yes, I do. And I need her angry. It's the only way she'll make mistakes."

"Okay," he agreed reluctantly. "I'll talk to him and ask him to set it up."

"It will be good for you, too," I promised. "Some people will believe us. You've helped a lot of people so far in your lifetime. They'll stand by you."

His mouth curled. "You got a better view of human

nature than I do. Right now, it feels like everyone is assuming I'm a killer."

"Not everyone," I said. "Look, I also need to ask you some questions. They may be painful. But every little thing you can tell me helps."

He nodded, waiting.

"When was the last time you talked to Tawny? Was it that day at the beach when she took Tiffany from you?"

His mouth tightened at the memory. "No. She stopped by my apartment the afternoon after that guy was killed. I didn't even know about the murder yet. I thought she had Tiffany with her, so I opened the door."

"But she was by herself?" I asked, wondering if anyone else had been taking care of Tiffany at the time, or if Tawny simply left her alone.

He nodded. "It was just her. She had some stuff for me, sweaters, clothes and my old dop kit. Stuff I'd left at our house when we separated, because I didn't get a chance to take much at the time. She said I might want my stuff and she'd trade it for the Barbie dolls and clothes that Tiffany left at the beach house."

Bingo. The bitch wasn't half as smart as she thought. Now I knew how Tawny had planted Price's hair and fibers from his clothing in Boomer Cockshutt's car. She'd worn one of his sweaters when she did the killing—or whoever she'd hired had—and she'd gotten his hair from the toiletry kit she'd refused to let him take when they first separated. Then she'd returned everything to Price, just in time for the police to find them.

I shook my head, half in admiration at her cunning. Simply to offer the items would have been too out of character for Tawny and she knew it, so she'd thought up the Barbie doll trade as a cover story.

"Didn't you think it was a little suspicious that she was suddenly offering you these things back?" I asked.

"I was too angry to think. All I noticed was that she didn't have Tiffany with her. I told her I was going to the police if she didn't bring her back by the end of the weekend. I had my court order and I said I would use it."

"What did she do?"

"She laughed and said that I ought to know by now I'd never get the best of her." His fists clenched so hard that his nails gouged into his palms.

"Did you give her the Barbie stuff?" I asked.

He nodded. "Why should I punish my little girl just because her mother's what she is?" His voice started to crack. "At least I know Tiff has her favorite dolls with her right now. A little bit of home, wherever she is."

"I'm sorry, but I have to ask this," I said. "Why did you marry Tawny in the first place?"

"Isn't it obvious?" he answered bitterly.

"Not to me. You seem smarter than that."

"I married her because she was having my baby. And she was having my baby because I was stupid enough to leave the birth control to her. I wasn't thinking at the time. My wife and I were having trouble. When Tawny came along, I was dumb enough to think I could have a fling to get me over my troubles and then forget about it."

"But Tawny got pregnant?"

He nodded. "And wouldn't have an abortion." His face softened. "I'd never have asked her to get one, if I'd known I was talking about Tiffany. When Tawny insisted on having the baby, I knew my wife, Livvy, would find out. She's too smart not to know when something that big is going on. So I came clean, and told my wife. She threw me out that same day, then filed for divorce the next week. Livvy doesn't screw around. There's right and there's wrong in her book. You do wrong and you're out of her life.

"I didn't have anyplace to go after she threw me out, I didn't know what to do. I'd ruined a fifteen-year marriage by listening to my—" He stopped for a second. "By not listening to my brain. Marrying Tawny seemed like a way to make up for it. To make my stupid mistake seem better than it really was."

"So, why—" I stopped, not quite knowing how to put it.

"So why did Tawny marry me, right?" Price guessed correctly. "I've had a lot of time to think about it in here. And I think I know at least one reason why. Before me,

Tawny had been involved with some rich guy who had a lot of snobby friends who didn't buy Tawny's blond hair and pearls. They thought she was trash and they let her know it." He shook his head. "He wouldn't marry her and she blamed it on his friends. It was all she could talk about for a long time. When she gets mad at someone, she doesn't forget. So maybe she just married me to send them a signal. You know what I'm saying? I was nothing more than a big 'fuck you' to all those people at the country club."

"How nice for you to be used in that way."

He shrugged. "I was using her, too. You don't think that me marrying a blond woman wasn't sending a signal to my first wife?" He looked up, eyes clear. "It's hard to hide in this place. From other people. And it's even harder to hide from yourself. But you wouldn't know that."

"I know more than you think. What made your marriage to Tawny go bad?"

His expression hardened. "We'd been married a couple years when she started in on me to use my position as a county commissioner to rezone parcels of land," he explained. "She was going to quit her job at the police department and make a fortune in commercial real estate. At least that's what she thought. If she could promise her clients that a prime piece of land was going to be rezoned for commercial purposes in the near future, she'd have closed dozens of sales a month. When I wouldn't do that, she went bat shit and never forgave me. And when I told her I wanted a divorce, hoo boy, she went ballistic. It didn't make sense. Clearly she hated me. But she wanted to be the first one to leave. I thought she'd come after me with a kitchen knife that afternoon when I told her."

"Was Tawny having affairs when you were still living together?" I asked.

"You're kidding me, right? What do you think?"

"She was doing everyone from the mailman to the mayor?"

He nodded. "That woman was hardly out of the hospital from having Tiffany before she was catting around. Probably did the doctor who delivered Tiff."

"I gather you were the one who first filed for an official divorce?"

He nodded. "I'm man enough to admit it when I make a mistake. I knew I had to get my daughter away from her before she turned Tiff into what she is."

I thought back to what the court reporter had told me about the custody proceedings. "I hear you brought her ex-husband Joe Scurlock into court," I said. "That he was the reason she agreed to joint custody without a fight."

"That's right."

"How did you know about him?" I asked.

"He called me. He said he'd read about me filing for divorce in the public records section of the *N&O* and that he wanted to warn me that she could get real ugly. When I found out she had a son and a daughter with a fellow that I didn't even know about, I couldn't believe it."

"Was that what Joe Scurlock was going to tell the court?" I asked. "That Tawny had abandoned her first two kids and not seen them in years?"

Price nodded. "My lawyer said it was all the judge would need to hear. That I'd get full custody for sure."

"Yet you agreed to joint custody."

He looked up, angry. "Don't you get it, yet?" he asked. "This is about my daughter and what I have to do to give her a decent start in life. The shrink said she needed to be around her mother, so I agreed to joint custody. And look where that got me." He glanced around the desolate room.

The guard caught his eye and motioned to his watch. "Sorry, buddy. Time's up," he warned Price. "Meal call."

I rose to go. There was nothing more Robert Price could tell me anyway. I was officially on my own. "Thank you for talking to me," I told him.

He stood and nodded, then stuck out his shackled hands. I grasped his arms above the handcuffs and he gripped my forearms back. We stood for a moment, locked in a curious embrace that signified—what? I wasn't sure. Thanks, perhaps, a passing of strength between us, or maybe even a blessing.

Whatever it was, I left the room with a feeling of having been honored in some way.

NINE

I spent the weekend trying to track Jeff down in dive bars, watching Burly slide into a depression and talking strategy with Robert Price's lawyer. By Sunday night, I couldn't decide whether to get drunk, slit my wrists or sue someone.

Price's lawyer, at least, was cooperative. He agreed to my idea after his client endorsed it and even made a few suggestions of his own. Now it was show time.

We held the press conference on Monday morning in time for the local noon broadcasts. If Tawny Bledsoe could manipulate the media to weasel out of trouble, I could manipulate the media to start it. Price's lawyer was the perfect man for the job. He was one of North Carolina's liberal elite, an ex-hippie who naturally lived in Chapel Hill with the rest of the state's NPR-loving heathens. Better still, he oozed sincerity and subdued righteousness in just the right proportions.

He now waited solemnly in front of a dozen cameras. The white granite archway of the Wake County Public Safety Building framed him. The jail loomed in the background, an ugly brick tower with horizontal slits for windows. Faces stared out the slits, gazing down curiously at the crowd beneath them.

I was in the array of hangers-on lined up beneath the archway and I wore a tight red dress that stood out in a sea of dark suits. My face was masked by sunglasses as I did my best to project the attitude of a Nation of Islam bodyguard. I looked like I was starring in a Robert Palmer music video, but the outfit was strategically chosen. I wanted Tawny to notice me, so she'd know I'd had a lot to do with what she was about to hear. At the same time, there were still certain people—say, the entire state of Florida—that I wanted to keep in the dark about my whereabouts. I didn't know how far the broadcasts would reach, so I wore the shades just in case.

Price's lawyer cleared his throat promptly at ten o'clock and held up a hand. Television cameras whirred and news anchors quivered with anticipation as they jostled for a good position.

"As you know," he said gravely, "I represent Robert Price, who has been charged with capital murder in the shooting death of Bernard W. Cockshutt. My client is currently being held without bail in the facility you see behind me."

Cameras panned to the jail walls, then zoomed in on the front door as if the cameramen were expecting Sean Penn and Susan Sarandon to come walking out, hand-in-hand.

"As you are also no doubt aware," the lawyer continued, "my client's estranged wife has left the area and is refusing to cooperate with authorities, despite her status as a material witness. She claims that she fears for the safety of herself and her child."

His face hardened and the reporters leaned forward, microphones outstretched. They knew something big was coming. Price's lawyer gave it to them.

"My client has remained silent on the issue of his estranged wife in deference to the feelings of his daughter, but finds that he can no longer remain mute in light of the recent allegations made by Ms. Bledsoe." He paused a moment, letting the "Ms." sink in, knowing it would cost Tawny conservative support. What a ham bone. The media ate it up.

His nostrils flared in lawyerly indignation as he delivered his outraged rebuttal: "My client categorically denies ever having physically hit, abused or emotionally battered his wife in any way. Acting on my advice, he hired an experienced private investigator who has uncovered evidence that Ms. Bledsoe sustained some of her injuries in a barroom brawl and faked the remainder of them for the purposes of the photograph recently printed in a local newspaper."

The assembled crowd murmured at this news, the *N&O* crew looked embarrassed and I resisted the temptation to flip Tawny the bird via news satellite.

"My client Robert Price also denies having had anything to do with the death of Bernard Cockshutt and extends his sympathies to the victim's family. He asks the public to examine the evidence rather than relying on emotional statements made by individuals who have a vested outcome in tainting a future jury pool."

That was tantamount to saying Tawny had done the deed. I tensed, knowing the kicker was coming. "Look like a bad ass," I reminded myself. "So she knows who arranged this all." I smiled into the cameras. *Take that, you blond bitch,* I was thinking. *Let's see if you're woman enough to come after me for this.*

"Tawny Bledsoe is a dangerous, mentally unstable woman with a history of deceit, financial impropriety, moral unfitness, promiscuity and a propensity to make false statements while under oath," the lawyer said loudly. A couple of the news anchors gaped. This was slander territory.

"I challenge Ms. Bledsoe to return to this state and charge me with slander if she believes I am lying," the lawyer continued. "We would welcome the opportunity to prove our charges in a court of law. Particularly since we have hard evidence that she abandoned two earlier children by a prior marriage and that she is currently wanted by the Raleigh Police Department on charges involving financial crimes." Several print reporters pulled out their cell phones and began dialing. If we had not agreed to keep Tawny's blackmail pursuits private, they'd have been hyperventilating.

"In addition," the lawyer said, "Ms. Bledsoe is under investigation by the North Carolina Department of Social Services for abandoning her four-year-old child repeatedly without supervision. Naturally, it causes my client great distress to know that his daughter is in the custody of such an irresponsible individual." A phone call made over the weekend had set this last charge in motion.

"Anyone who believes Ms. Bledsoe's allegations about Robert Price is a fool," the lawyer stated flatly. "Anyone who harbors her is breaking the law. We challenge her to return to this state for questioning and we urge anyone who knows Ms. Bledsoe's whereabouts to contact the Raleigh Police Department. My client believes that his daughter's life is in danger as long as she remains in the custody of Tawny Bledsoe and I concur with his concerns. Thank you."

As the lawyer finished, he folded the prepared statement and stashed it in an inner coat pocket, ignoring the shouts of the reporters. He turned his back to the crowd, glanced at me with a smile, then stepped into a waiting car.

Unsure of what to do, the television crews panned the supporting players. I waited until I was sure a camera was on me, then slid my sunglasses down my nose, stared straight into the lens and stuck out my tongue at Tawny Bledsoe.

The plane to Tampa took off in late afternoon. As always, flying made me melancholy. There was something about leaving the earth beneath and ascending into the clouds that caused my mind to do an inventory of my life below. What, I wondered, was the source of this vague sense of self-loathing that was nibbling at my self-confidence, leaving me with a feeling of impending doom that bubbled in the pit of my stomach like stew gone bad?

Maybe it was just that I had no idea what I would say or do to get my mother-in-law to help me locate Tawny. I had a copy of the press conference video tucked away in my carry-on bag, but who knew if that would be enough. Plus, Bobby D. had been his usual worrywart on hearing my plans to track Tawny to Florida. He'd insisted on knowing exactly where I was going, then tried again to dissuade me from my task. But I stood firm. She had to be stopped.

But the real problem wasn't my mother-in-law or Bobby, I decided. The real problem was that Burly, my boyfriend, was not there for me. It hurt. So did what he did when he was depressed. I had phoned him Saturday night, badly needing to hear his voice. He was nowhere to be found. I called all his favorite bars without luck then, unable to leave it alone, I checked the entertainment section of the *Independent* and saw that his favorite group— Dave's Little Blues Band—was playing at Fat Daddy's. I decided to go find him in person, hoping to atone for my lack of support when he was feeling blue and, probably, in hopes he would be happy to see me.

Fat Daddy's is an unlikely bikers' paradise that looks like just another prefab restaurant from the outside. That night, Harleys lined the parking lot and clouds of smoke wafted out each time the bouncer opened the door. Burly liked the bar because most of it was on one level and it had a pool room with tables spaced far enough apart for him to maneuver his wheelchair between them.

I stood at the front door, hesitating, knowing what I would find inside: Burly, glass of whiskey in hand, cigarette hanging out of his mouth, biker babe drooling over his aluminum handrails in anticipation of sex that would let her lie back while someone else did the dirty work for a change.

In other words, he would be surrounded by all the accouterments of a life that had ended when he'd crashed his Harley into a tree.

Burly never thought about the old days, it seemed, except when he slid into a funk. That was when he returned to his old stomping grounds hoping, I suppose, that by inhaling enough Wild Turkey and tobacco he could convince himself that he was still the baddest neck-stomping biker ass this side of Oakland.

I didn't much like him when he got that way, and I usually avoided being with him when he was. I wondered if that wasn't a good policy to maintain. Should I go inside or not?

"Casey?" Weasel Walters brushed past the bouncer, trailing a cloud of tobacco smoke in his wake. "You coming in? Burly's here."

Weasel was a friend of Burly's from the old days and

one of the few that I liked. He was a tiny man, with thin-ning hair and a pencil-thin mustache that did nothing for his ferretlike face. But he also had a big heart, was gain-fully employed as a computer technician in the Research Triangle Park and, rare among Burly's pals, was a card-carrying member of AA. He also had terrible luck with women. I had a soft spot for him because of his failures and admired his fortitude. If you're going to be a loser, be a sober one. It's far less pathetic that way.

"Hi, Weasel," I said, slapping his palm. "I figured he'd be here."

"Looks like your boy's having a bad one this time," Weasel told me. "Burly's already drunker than a priest after Palm Sunday."

"I'm not surprised. He's been playing nothing but Van Morrison CDs for the last two weeks. That's always a bad sign."

Weasel nodded in agreement; he'd stood by Burly after the wreck and knew his moods as well as I did.

"Who's the biker babe this time?" I asked, wondering which of the always-younger groupies was most curious about the sexual abilities of a paraplegic.

"You got X-ray eyes or something?" Weasel nervously lit up a cigarette.

"I know Burly when he gets like this."

"Bonnie Calhoun's been sniffing around him all night," Weasel admitted as he inhaled with furtive puffs. "Denny's younger sister. The usual. Tall, blond, wearing these killer black suede boots that go up to her thighs. But I wouldn't worry. She's a head case, especially when she gets a snoot-ful." He looked at his watch. "Burly should be figuring that out right about now."

"I'll pass on going in," I decided. "I just wanted to know he was okay."

"Probably a good idea," Weasel mumbled. "It's mighty buzzed in there tonight. Too many Johnston County boys in one place, I expect. I think you'd be too much woman for them to handle." He gave me a crooked grin.

I managed a smile back. "I've got to go out of town

tomorrow. I don't know how long I'll be gone. Keep an eye on him for me, will you?"

"Sure, Casey. I know how to use his hand controls. I'll drive him home, if that's what's worrying you. I can put my bike in the back of his van."

I breathed a sigh of relief. Burly's other bad habit while in a self-destructive mood was trying to finish the job he had started eight years before. No matter that he'd already ruined one person's life other than his own, he still climbed behind the wheel and drove too fast when he was feeding his blues with booze.

"Thanks," I told Weasel. "You're a good friend." I planted a wet one on him and tasted the lingering tang of Marlboros. For a moment, his sharp face was transformed, a wide smile animating his Ratboy features.

"Sure thing," he called after me. "Thank me again any old time."

It was weird, but Weasel's smile was what stayed with me on the plane that afternoon. There was something so familiar about his face. The pointed chin, the sunken eyes and sharp nose. He was straight from the bottom of the Florida genetic pool, the descendant of dirt-poor Scottish outcasts who had been scrambling since time began to make a decent living. I knew the look well, since it was my own heritage, even if I had escaped with cheek and jawbones intact.

Did I really want to be going home again? I wondered, as the plane broke through a cloud bank. Especially when the mother-in-law from hell awaited me in Tampa? I had put off thinking about her but now the memories were inescapable.

Clarissa Jones had made mincemeat out of a girl from the country like me. She'd honed in on my weak spots and tortured me with them, dragging me to dinners at the country club where my manners and clothes could not even match those of the waitresses. She'd perfected a stare that started at my cheap shoes and ended at my home-bleached hair, never mind that her own shade would have looked phony on a woman two decades younger than herself. Everything that Jeff loved about me, she recast as a fault.

I wasn't free-spirited, I was irresponsible. I wasn't spon-
taneous, I was loud. And instead of being smart, I was
manipulative. But the one thing she couldn't argue with
was that I was a hell of a lot younger than she was. And
maybe that's why she really hated me. Because she had
never stopped tearing me down.

Why in god's name was I winging my way willingly
toward this dragon? Did I really want to nail Tawny Bledsoe that bad?

Yes, I thought as the plane began descending near
Tampa, I suppose I did.

I drove by my in-laws on the way to the motel. It was
every bit as gaudy as I remembered. Jeff was the son of a
self-made millionaire who had traded good sense for big
bucks. Just before we married, Jeff's parents had moved
into a white brick monstrosity that my mother-in-law insisted was called Dutch Renaissance. The house looked
like a cross between Tara and Camelot, meaning it was
mighty damn ugly in a turreted sort of way. It fronted
Tampa Bay and had set them back zillions, but then they
had zillions to waste.

Jeff's father had been the first farmer in his rural county
to sell out to developers—after quietly buying up farmland
for a decade before the boom came. He got rich and got
out, which was just as well since his neighbors stopped
speaking to him after he ruined their towns and took advantage of their friendships. Jeff's mother had assumed the
role of socialite after they moved to Tampa, but she had
never quite been able to conceal the desperation in her
eyes. She tried too hard, and she knew it. This knowledge
made her mean. Specifically, it made her mean toward people like me. I guess I reminded her of where she'd come
from.

The house loomed large and white, like the ghost of a
mountain in the deepening twilight. A party was in full
swing. Porsches, Jaguars and BMWs jammed the circular
driveway. I sat in my rental car staring at the well-lit mansion and wondering how much time Jeff had spent there
since we split. His father didn't like him at the house, I

knew. They'd been fighting about Jeff's long hair for a good twenty-five years by now.

I was just about to leave when I noticed a dark sedan parked down the street, facing the house. It was the only curbside car on the entire block. A tiny red ember moved inside the darkened interior as an unseen person smoked. The cops, maybe, watching to see if Jeff tried to come home to Mom and Dad?

Well, no matter who it was, I couldn't just sit there in front of the house being conspicuous. I pulled out a map and studied it, pretending to be lost. Then I started the car again and slowly cruised past the sedan. Two men sat in the front seat, both of them lean with dark, brushed-back hair. They were as sleek as a pair of otters. The men stared at me with blank expressions as I drove past. I was looking as much like a befuddled tourist as I could, but suspected it wasn't enough. I stopped the car, backed up and rolled down my window.

"I'm lost," I told them. "I'm trying to find the bridge to St. Pete."

"That way," the driver said, his voice tinged with an accent that didn't match his vaguely Hispanic coloring. He sounded like he was from the deep South. He jerked a thumb up and pointed it behind him without bothering to look, then dismissed me by rolling up his window. I waved my thanks and drove on, turning back only to memorize their license plate number.

The two men were not good news. They had eyes like sharks, flat, black and lifeless. I sped away, invisible spiders scuttling across the back of my neck. Not cops, I thought. Not cops at all. At least, not good ones.

"What the hell are you trying to prove?" Bobby's bellow cut through the static of his portable phone. I hadn't heard him that upset since the downtown Hilton announced they would no longer serve their All-You-Can-Eat Sunday Brunch.

"I know what I'm doing," I said, annoyed at his fatherly concern. Since when did Bobby worry about my ability to take care of myself? I was sorry I had told him where I was going.

"Both Channel Five and Channel Eleven ran the press conference in its entirety," Bobby said grimly. "It's being replayed all across the state. CNN is probably next. Plus, Channel Five included that cute little trick of you sticking out your tongue. What the hell was that about?"

"They did?" I asked, amazed my taunt had made the cut. "How did they manage that?"

"They used it as background footage for the announcer's wrap-up voice-over," Bobby explained. "What were you trying to do?"

"Flush her out."

"You're going to get shot," Bobby predicted. "If this dame is what you say she is, why are you going out of your way to piss her off?"

"I have to find out where she is," I said. "I can't do that unless she feels the pressure and starts to screw up."

"Have you forgotten that she has her kid with her?" Bobby asked in a voice that reeked of disappointment. "Remember that when you push her to the wall."

"I know," I admitted, not wanting to think about it. "But she would never harm her own daughter."

"I hope to hell you're right," he said. "How long are you going to try this boneheaded scheme?"

"I'll be here for a couple of days. I'm going to visit my in-laws tomorrow."

Bobby let out a breath. "Seeing as how I can't stop you, any way I can help?"

"Run a license check for me?" I asked.

"Why?"

Bobby is pig-headed, not stupid. There's no sense in trying to put one over on him. I explained about the two men watching the house and he exploded again.

"That's it. You have no idea what you're getting into. Come back immediately. I'll hook you up with someone who can back you up and the two of you can—"

"Bobby," I interrupted. "This is a girl thing. Woman-to-woman. Trust me. I'll call you tomorrow."

I hung up and flipped on CNN. You never know. I might

end up with the most famous tongue in America. After Gene Simmons, of course.

I woke the next morning to Florida sunshine. Over country ham and grits with red-eye gravy, I thought about a strategy to take with my former mother-in-law. I decided on the direct approach. I'd torture her, stick bamboo shoots under her fake nails and poke pencils into her liposuction scars if she gave me any shit.

It was past noon before a woman, instead of a machine, answered the phone at Clarissa's house. She had a soft, accented voice. But, of course—Clarissa had probably gotten a couple of Mexican maids, matching pool boys and a cabana boy as accessories for her evergrowing wealth.

After being informed that Mrs. Jones was having a massage and could not be disturbed, I hung up and headed to the house.

The day was obscenely bright, with sunlight flooding every nook and cranny of the monstrosity they called a mansion. The harsh sunlight illuminated the weather stains seeping through the white-painted bricks, making them look like teeth with creeping cavities. Inner decay heading outward.

A maid answered my knock within half a minute and I was inside the front door a few seconds later.

"You can not come in," she protested. "Mrs. Jones is occupied."

"I'm her daughter-in-law," I announced, heading for a vast pink-carpeted stairway that wound around to the second floor. Clarissa had a bedroom as big as a barn up there—probably with livestock to match—and a pink-marbled bathroom spacious enough to accommodate a good-sized harem.

The maid gave a series of squeaks and scurried after me, protesting in broken English. She was cute and I wondered if Jeff had put the moves on her. Then I remembered that he was a scum-sucking pig—and that it didn't matter to me anymore even if he had.

Though I hadn't intended to make a dramatic entrance, the door to Clarissa's dressing room flew open with a bang when I pushed on it. It took me a moment to understand what I was seeing: the Incredible Hunk bending over my former mother-in-law, his hands firmly gripping her buttocks. He was wearing a silver thong bathing suit and matching muscles. And it looked to me like I'd just caught Clarissa with her hand heading for the cookie jar. Both looked up with frozen, automatically guilty expressions.

I was amazed. Clarissa had not aged a day in the past fifteen years. Her plastic surgeon was a maestro. She still looked like a cross between The Joker and Carol Channing, her tautly stretched face dominated by a broad, rigid smile. No wonder she was so skinny. She probably couldn't put her teeth together enough to chew.

"Who are you?" she demanded in her phony old money accent, then stopped, staring in horror as she recognized me. She gaped like the country bumpkin she was beneath all her facialed skin. "You," she sputtered. "Who the hell do you think you are?" This time the accent was pure Panhandle cracker.

"Me, indeed," I said cheerfully as the masseuse quickly pulled a sheet up over her backside. He pivoted on his heels without a word and seemed to melt out the door. It's tough to look dignified when you're wearing eight inches of silver lamé and sporting a boner, but the guy came pretty damn close.

"Goodness," I said, pulling up a prissy French Provincial chair and plopping down in it. It shook beneath my weight. Clarissa winced. "Does your better half know about Bruno?"

She glared at me. I was threatening about eight thousand dollars worth of antique wood. "His name is not Bruno, and Norman could care less. What are you doing in my life again?" She bit off each word and spit them at me like watermelon seeds.

"Jeff is in trouble," I said. "Big trouble. I'm surprised he hasn't called you to bail him out." I was sure that he had. What surprised me was that Clarissa had not taken care of his drug dealer problems for him. Maybe his true occupation was one little fact that Jeff had to keep from his mother. If so, it was a first.

Clarissa Jones had bailed out Jeff more times than I could count over the past thirty years. None of her rescues had ever done her son the slightest bit of good. She had started out by smoothing over his schoolyard fights, greasing his way into college, bribing his professors to give him good grades, arranging abortions for his girlfriends and throwing money at all the right causes so that he could meet and woo moneyed young ladies of appropriate standing.

Marrying me was the first time Jeff had ever opposed his mother and the price he paid was a big one. We'd been married in front of a justice of the peace with only my grandfather in attendance. We'd also been forbidden to visit their house at all for the first year, and when Clarissa finally relented and realized she had to acknowledge me, she pointedly excluded me from as many invitations as possible—or made sure to humiliate me if my presence could not be avoided. Eventually, Jeff broke down and started believing what she said about me. That was the beginning of the end for us.

But what Clarissa Jones hadn't counted on was the effect that her interventions would have on her son. Jeff had never learned to accept responsibility for his actions, was a master at weaseling out of taking the blame, was incapable of guilt and viewed women with a peculiar mixture of distrust and desperation, all courtesy of his doting momma.

She hated me because I knew what she had done to him. Of course, there was also the small matter of my having a prison record. Clarissa still didn't believe the cocaine had been Jeff's. In her mind, I was the reason he had gone bad.

What I wanted to know now was just how bad Jeff had gone—and how much Clarissa knew about it. Find Jeff. Find Tawny.

"Well?" I said. "Has Jeff phoned you for help?"

"That's none of your business," she snapped. She was trapped facedown on the massage table, forced to choose between literally exposing herself to me or toughing it out. She toughed it out. "Get out of my house," she ordered me. "Or I'll have Anna call the cops. One look is all I need to tell me that you're still nothing but trash. The happiest day of my life was when my son divorced you. I don't have to put up with you anymore and I won't. Get out."

"For starters," I said, marveling at the sudden calm that filled me. "I divorced your son, not the other way around. Secondly, you and I both know that I kept him out of jail. All I had to do was open my mouth and he'd still be behind bars to this day. So you owe me, and I'm calling in the marker. I know what he's been doing. Don't pretend he's gone straight. He told me everything."

"You're lying." She angrily propped herself up on her arms, giving me a peek at her ten-thousand-dollar boob job. She saw me looking and snatched a towel from a nearby chair, jamming it down her cleavage with a snarl.

"He came to see me three weeks ago in a lot of trouble," I explained. "He's wanted by the cops, and by people who are a lot worse than the cops. Now he's gotten mixed up with a murderer and he's gotten you mixed up with one, too."

I could have told her about the guys watching her house, but I was hoping they were IRS agents. I'd pay good money to see her get busted like that.

"I haven't the faintest idea of what you're talking about. Jeff sells cabin cruisers. He's the top salesman at his company."

When I started laughing at that whopper, she sat up, clutched the towels around her, jumped to the floor and marched over to a closet. She ripped a kimono from its hanger and threw it over her body, tightening the sash with angry tugs.

"Jeff is mixed up with a woman who killed a man," I said. "The woman you agreed to hide for him. She's gone underground because the cops are looking for her, not because she's abused. I know what she probably told you, but she's lying. She's using you."

"I have no idea what you're talking about," Clarissa insisted. She picked up a brush and began jamming it through her hair. But she didn't call for the maid and she didn't tell me to get out. She wanted to hear what I had to say.

"Clarissa," I suggested. "Let's just accept that you think I'm a white trash social climber who married your precious son so I could horn in on your position at the country club."

Startled, her eyes darted to mine before she looked away.

"Let's also accept," I said, "that I think *you* are a Class A parking lot lizard who is as phony as her 34B tits."

She dropped the brush and glared. "How dare you?" she spat out, unconsciously wrapping her arms around her breasts.

"How dare I what?" I asked. "Are you telling me those babies are real?" I nodded toward them. They looked like two pink puppies trying to escape her embrace. "Give me a break. You've got more saline in your chest than in the entire Gulf of Mexico."

Okay, so insulting her wasn't the smartest thing to do. I had an uncontrollable urge to let her know I wasn't the scared kid she had terrorized in the past.

"What's your point?" she asked through clenched teeth.

"My point is that hating each other doesn't change the fact that Jeff is facing two ugly choices right now. He could be sent to jail for aiding and abetting a murderer, or he could be shot dead by the drug dealers he's ripped off."

Her body wavered slightly, as if she finally heard what I was saying.

"You did help hide her, didn't you?" I asked. "Jeff fed you some line about her trying to escape from a brutal husband."

"She had nowhere else to go!" Clarissa screamed at top volume, scaring the ever-loving shit out of me. I'd never seen Clarissa lose control before, and the fact that she was losing it now made me more nervous than a cat on a hot griddle.

"Her husband is one of the most powerful men in North Carolina," she said angrily. "He'll come after her if he finds out where she is. He'll take her child from her. He's already taken her family money."

"She's not from money," I said quietly. "And her husband's in jail for something she did. He can't possibly do anything to her. She's running away because she took a life, Clarissa, not because she fears for her life. She's a liar and she knows that Jeff is a fool. Just like you know he's a fool. He'll believe anything a woman tells him. She's using him."

I waited out the subsequent silence, hoping my words would penetrate her self-deluded facade. But she would not look at me. I tried again.

"Clarissa," I pleaded. "I've never given you credit for really believing in anything but your charge cards. I always thought that all that fundamentalist, anti-abortion activism was just to make you feel morally superior and balance out all the selfish things you did in life."

She looked away, but she was listening.

"Maybe I was wrong," I continued. "Maybe you do care about the women and kids you help. Maybe it does mean something to you to help them escape."

And, maybe it did. I'd never seen any bruises on her, and Clarissa sure seemed to rule the roost, but she and Norman went through some hard times before they struck it rich. He liked to talk about it; she didn't. Isn't that always the way? Every once in a while I'd seen her wince when he raised his voice, an automatic reflex from the early years, I figured, when Norman's frustration at being poor had not yet turned to pride—and when his aggression had focused on her, instead of a business competitor. So maybe there really was a human being lurking inside her pampered facade, someone who connected with others.

"If you do care about the people you help," I warned her, "or the people who are part of your network, they need to know that this woman is a killer. She's going to be brought down and she'll bring all of you down with her."

"What does this have to do with you?" She stared out a window at the bay.

"She set up a friend of mine," I said. I didn't want Clarissa Jones knowing that I had a new life as a P.I. "She killed a man and made it look like my friend did it."

"Why did she involve Jeff?"

"Because he was convenient," I explained. "Because he believed her lies about what her husband did to her. Because he probably bragged that he could hide her through you, and she knew she might need your help one day. Or maybe she involved him because she just wanted to stick it to me."

"How do I know you're telling me the truth?"

"You don't. But do you really think I would have come all this way, suffer through seeing you again, if I was lying? What do I have to gain? Listen to me, believe me, and tell me where she is. I'll be out of your life forever."

She thought for a moment, then looked at me. "I don't believe you."

"Then watch this tape," I suggested, pulling the video of the press conference from my knapsack and setting it on the massage table. "See if you really want to become part of a public search for her. Then I suggest you call your friends in the underground who are hiding her and ask them a few questions. Listen carefully to what they say."

"What kind of questions?"

"Ask them if Tawny disappears late at night. That's her real name, by the way. Sort of. Ask them if she pays attention to her daughter or just tolerates the kid, letting other people do the work required to take care of her." I was counting on Tawny's lack of a maternal instinct to show up fast, and hoping that it was as appalling to others as it was to me.

"Ask them if Tawny acts like she's entitled to the world on a silver platter," I continued. "Or if she has an endless repertoire of stories where she's always the victim, so many stories, in fact, that it seems as if the whole world is after her. Have they caught her in lies? Has she tried to borrow money? Is her story changing? Do they sense something remote about her?"

"Why those questions?" Clarissa asked, probably because she'd flunk them if she asked them of herself.

"Because if they're good people, in their hearts they'll

know the answers to them. And they'll realize that Tawny Bledsoe is not what she pretends to be."

"It's not enough," Clarissa said. She walked over to a cabinet and opened the doors on a fully stocked bar. She poured herself a tumbler of red wine and didn't bother to offer me anything.

I'd have to give her some of the photos. "Show them these," I said, pulling the blackmail photographs from my knapsack. I selected three of them, two with men and the one remaining shot of the schoolteacher. I didn't want to do it and hoped no one in Florida would know the subjects. But if the people hiding Tawny were the Christian fundamentalists I suspected they were, the only thing that was going to change their minds about her was visual proof. Maybe a few shots of some gal treating Tawny like a box lunch at the Y would bring them around to my way of thinking. Homosexuality was probably not on their list of acceptable traits for a devoted Christian mother—and I doubted that knowing Tawny was only going through the motions for blackmail would make them more tolerant.

"Here." I placed the photos facedown next to the videotape of the press conference. Clarissa stared but did not move. "Take your time," I offered, knowing she'd fall on them like a hyena tearing at a carcass the second I walked out the door. "I'll call you tomorrow. You tell me what you want to do."

"If I decide to tell you where she is?" she asked, turning her back on me.

"Then that's all you have to do. I take it from there."

"If I don't?"

"Then I'll dog your ass until you do."

For a split second, I thought she might throw the wineglass in my face.

"At least call the people hiding her," I said. "Ask them to talk to me."

"I'm not promising anything." Her voice sounded far away, but that was par for the course. I don't think Clarissa Jones ever really liked being where she was, she always seemed to want to be somewhere else.

"I know you'll do the right thing," I lied. In reality,

Clarissa Jones would do the right thing for herself. It was all I could hope for.

I was almost out the door when I heard her voice behind me.

"Is he okay?" she asked.

"Who?"

"Jeff. Is he safe?"

I shrugged. "I couldn't tell you. I don't know where the hell he is."

And neither, her question told me, did she.

TEN

I've always loved cheap motels. They neither ask for nor offer any promises. Even the furnishings seem temporary, creating a sense of impermanence that's exhilarating. There is a lot to be said for just passing through.

That afternoon, though, the usual magic was gone. My room seemed murky and incomplete. Something about the sunlight that leaked through the curtains made me feel trapped, unhealthy, paranoid. I tried to take a nap, but failed in finding rest. Instead, I dreamed about a mirror with a crack down its middle. When I tried to see my image in it, I failed, as if I were blind. I made myself lean closer and closer—aware I was dreaming, but feeling as if I was awake. Every inch of progress seemed to take hours of effort on my part. Finally, the outline of a woman began to materialize in the mirror. Her back was to me, but she started to rotate slowly, like a marble bust on a stand. The figure turned completely around to face me. I was desperate to see her face, but her features remained invisible, obscured by a gray fog. Then, slowly, like a photograph developing in a chemical bath, her head and shoulders emerged.

Who was she? I cried out in my dream at the sight of her. The woman was completely frosted over with a bluish-silver sheen, trapped in a permanent cry for help. She had huge blank orbs for eyes, and a mouth that gaped open in dismay. She was trying to speak, I knew, but could not, was trying to see, but was blind. The terror of emotional exile radiated from her.

I woke, sweating, frightened by the image, my mind racing with sudden doubts: I was wrong about Tawny. Jeff was involved. The whole thing had been a setup. Robert Price was using me. I was walking into a trap.

I worried over each possibility like a sore tooth, until I could stand it no longer. I sat up and considered the chance that Boomer Cockshutt had known Jeff all along. They could have been involved in moving drugs together. Maybe that was why Jeff had showed up in Raleigh, not because he needed somewhere to hide, but because he had met Tawny while dealing drugs with Boomer—and she had convinced him to kill her lover, so they could take over his business together. Were they both now using me in some way? When Jeff had failed to involve me with his sob story, had Tawny moved in with hers?

I picked up the phone and called Boomer's widow. She could help, willingly or not, by providing information on his personal or business connections.

"Hello?" she asked briskly, in a tone people reserve for telemarketers.

"This is Casey Jones," I explained. "The private investigator looking into your husband's death?"

"Of course," she replied, her voice warming. "Have there been any new developments? I saw you on television at that news conference. Now I know who you're working for. Do you really think that woman might be involved?"

"It's possible," I said. "Would it surprise you if she had been?"

"A bit," she said. "Boomer liked women who would roll over and play dead. Or, at least, roll over. I'd be surprised he was seeing someone with enough backbone to kill. I suppose all my cold speculation makes me sound terrible to you."

"Not at all. You had to put up with a lot when he was alive."

"You have no idea."

I paused. "I'm really calling to see if Boomer ever took

any business trips to Florida? Or, if he mentioned friends or associates there?"

"Florida?" she asked, a catch in her voice. "What's Florida have to do with it?"

When I didn't answer, she filled in the blanks on her own.

"Boomer wasn't doing anything illegal, like selling drugs, was he?" she asked. "Because I need every penny he left me, and if the cops are saying he was—"

"Probably not," I interrupted, though it was interesting that her mind had also leaped to the possibility of Boomer moving drugs. "I'm just covering all the bases." Hell, considering her lack of sentiment about Boomer, why not tell her more?

"Actually," I admitted, "I am following up on the possibility that your husband was involved in drug smuggling. It would have been easy for him to move the stuff. I'm sure he transported cars a lot as a dealer."

"I see." Amanda Cockshutt paused, thinking it over. "He did bring cars up from Florida quite a bit, for the used car portion of his business. He said they stayed in good shape, thanks to the lack of salt on the roads down there. But . . ." her voice trailed off. "I'd really have to think about it. Maybe look over some old phone bills. I'd be glad to check for you, if you like."

"Would you?" I was grateful for her offer, but wondered what had prompted her change of heart. She'd gone from being a cold fish to being human.

She could sense my hesitation. "Look," she said. "I know I came off as uncaring at our first meeting. But you have to understand that Boomer put me through a lot. It was humiliating. And with the news of his affairs plastered all over the newspapers, I didn't know how to react. I've had time to think it over now and there's no point in staying mad at a dead man. I've decided there are big sins in life and then there are little sins. Boomer's affairs were pathetic, a bad habit like biting his fingernails, something his aging male ego needed. They don't seem so important now that he's gone. I've started to remember some of the really great things we shared. Like how good he was with the kids. What it was like in the early days. I'm not a robot. I do want to see his killers caught. I'd like you to keep me informed on your progress, in fact."

"Of course," I promised. "I'll let you know what I find."

"I've got to get back to a card game," she apologized. "I have guests waiting on me. Where can I reach you if I find anything of interest?"

I started to give her my phone number, but paranoia took hold. "I'm out of town right now," I explained. "I'll call you back in a couple of days."

"Sure, I get it. Don't forget your sun block," she warned before she hung up.

I lay back down on the bed. What would it mean if Boomer did have a Florida connection? I didn't really know. There were so many unanswered questions, such little proof. I was operating on my own conviction and self-confidence with very little else to back me up.

My mind wandered to how different I had felt with Jeff's mother earlier in the day, how much stronger and in charge. Soon, I found myself thinking about the rest of my old life in Florida. Especially my grandfather. I had not been this close to him in thirteen years. He lived an hour outside of Tampa, in the middle of Panhandle wasteland, surrounded by stingy soil and relentless sun.

Shame was nibbling at the darker edges of my soul. I could not ignore its message. I hated Tawny Bledsoe for turning her back on her family, yet I had done the very same thing. Maybe I should go see my grandfather while I was here, I thought, put to rest the scandal about me being in prison. After all, I'd been the one to decide he was ashamed of me. I'd never heard it from him.

Thinking of my grandfather triggered a rush of childhood memories, flashes of sticky summer days, the brush of Spanish moss against my face, the fertile smell of swamp mud and rotting vegetation. Before I knew it, I was deep in murky dreams again, dreams of my dead parents, my grandfather, long-forgotten songs, tiny details of a past life: the top of a dresser, a broken ballerina on a music box, even dinners I had once eaten. It was as real as being there.

I woke four hours later to a darkened room. It was after
eight o'clock. I had lost an opportunity to go see my grandfather for that day and I was starving.

I struggled into the shower, groggy from too much
sleep. I stood for a long time beneath the hot water, letting
it ease the stiffness from my shoulders while it washed
away the memories of too many dreams from my overstuffed mind. I had to concentrate on the present, I had to
leave the past behind.

Would Clarissa come through with Tawny's whereabouts
or was she tougher than I thought? What would I do if she
refused?

I was so preoccupied that I paid little attention to traffic
as I drove down the highway, searching for a place to eat.
I couldn't find a decent restaurant. My hotel was on the
outskirts of town where several highways converged, and
the area was a franchise mecca. Unfortunately, my stomach
was not in the mood for gut putty drenched in MSG.

Without thinking much about it, I finally took a left turn
that led me away from the plastic and toward the rural
outskirts of town. The flatness of the landscape reassured
me. I knew a roadside tavern would present itself soon.
I'd feel at home in one of those, sitting against the roughhewn back of a corner booth, chowing down on a steak
with a cold beer at my elbow, while the Allman Brothers
played on the jukebox and some fat guy in denim overalls
gave me the eye from his too-small bar stool. Ah, home.

That was when I realized I was heading toward my
grandfather's house.

I thought about it, and kept going.

Twenty miles out, orange groves began to line the narrow two-lane road, their neat rows interspersed with flat,
furrowed fields awaiting a new planting of soy. The flickering lights of the grove torches—lit against the threat of
the far-reaching cold snap—stretched back into the thick
rows of the orange bushes, looking like miniature runways
beckoning a plane to land.

Ahead of me, a creature darted into the road. I swerved
and avoided the critter by inches. Another Florida opossum
would live to cross the road anew. But the incident made

me glance into the rearview mirror and I realized for the first time that there was a car behind me, approaching at rapid speed. Bad news.

I sped up, but the car continued to close ground. Ahead, I saw a crossroads and took a right. If the other car continued on straight, I'd be able to relax.

No such luck. Not only was the new road little more than a glorified asphalt lane, I was barely a quarter mile down it when the other car careened around the turn, taking the corner too quickly. It fishtailed, slid onto the shoulder, then regained the road and began to come at me fast. Shit. I'd left my gun behind in Raleigh, unwilling to unnecessarily risk my fake permit to the scrutiny of RDU's pit-bull security clerks.

I-slammed the accelerator to the floor. After a few seconds' hesitation, the rental car leaped forward. My lead wouldn't last. I doubted that my pursuers were driving anything as anemic as a Ford Taurus. It would only be a matter of moments before I'd have to stop and fight. I had nothing to defend myself with.

Then I noticed a new pair of headlights bearing down on the car that was following me. They were elliptical and low. It was a car built for speed.

The two sets of headlights bounced in my rearview mirror as both cars sped along the bumpy highway behind me. What the hell was going on? I was trying to keep the Taurus on the road, but the lure of the scene unfolding in the mirror proved impossible to resist. I kept running onto the shoulder or crossing the center line as I tried to follow the action behind me.

The car on my tail had obviously noticed the car behind it; it slowed and began to swerve from side to side. I heard a rapid series of pops, like a car backfiring. Gunshots. The red of brake lights glowed behind my first pursuer, but the second car kept coming up on it fast.

I wanted to get the hell out of there and let the two cars duke it out, but I also wanted to watch what happened next. Then a thought occurred to me: suppose *both* cars were after me?

I negotiated a sharp curve in the two-lane road and, as

I came out of the turn, my headlights illuminated a deserted gas station about a quarter mile ahead. The building was abandoned and sagged beneath a rotting roof. I turned off my headlights, made a sharp turn into its gravel lot, then pulled up between two rusting cars and cut the engine. Hidden, I waited in the darkness and watched as both cars almost slid out of the curve, then regained the highway with a screech of tires. The second car was the first to recover. It accelerated quickly, reaching the first car on the straightaway. It bumped it from behind, and sent it into a slow tailspin. The first car was a sedan and its blocky body recovered slowly. The other car bumped it once more and it swerved off onto the shoulder just a few hundred feet away from where I was hiding. It stopped with its front bumper nosed into a shallow ditch.

The crack of rapid gunfire followed. I couldn't tell who was shooting where, but it was plain that both drivers were armed. It was a good time to get the fuck out of view. I ducked as low as I could, my eyes barely clearing the dashboard. The gunfire stopped and I risked a better look. The second car had passed the disabled sedan. Mission accomplished, it accelerated down the narrow highway. Soon, a white Corvette zoomed by the old gas station without slowing. I let out a deep breath as the taillights pulled away into the darkness. The car rounded a curve and disappeared behind a grove of cypress oaks. I was safe for now, or at least I would be as soon as the first car pulled away.

The night grew still again, my pulse returned to normal, and I became aware of frogs peeping in the drainage ditch. Their high-pitched whines harmonized perfectly with the hum of the sedan's engine as it idled by the side of the road. What the hell had I just witnessed? The sedan struggled to break free of the ditch and finally gained a few feet, stopping with its headlights pointed across a field, the beams illuminating an old shed that had been built in a small stand of pine trees. Just as I was wondering if the occupant was too badly injured to drive, the car backed slowly onto the road, pulled a U-turn and headed toward Tampa. The single red glare of a taillight told me that the car itself had taken at least a couple of bullets, if not the driver.

I decided to wait it out. Five long minutes later, I'd heard and seen nothing more alarming than the rhythmic chunk-chunk of faraway farm machinery pumping water to the fields. But the sedan could easily be waiting for me on the road. I'd have to find another route back. On the other hand, car number two might be waiting for me in the other direction. What's a girl to do?

Car number two decided it for me. I'd no sooner restarted my engine and cut my headlights on, when the white Corvette pulled out from behind the cypress grove. Its headlights dimmed to low, it sped down the highway and slid to a stop just a few yards from my front bumper. The driver's side door opened.

I fumbled around on the front seat floor, frantic for anything I could use as a weapon. All I could find was the free map the rental car attendant had given me, and somehow I didn't think that slapping the driver across the face with it would slow him down for long.

A tall figure dressed in black unfolded itself from the Corvette and headed for me, moving like a dark angel through the night. I turned my headlights to bright, hoping to blind him, and the tall figure put a hand up to shield his eyes.

"Jesus, Casey, you trying to blind me?" a familiar voice complained.

What the hell was *he* doing here? I cut off the lights and waited, refusing to say a word. This ought to be good.

Bill Butler sauntered up to my car, his gait even cockier than usual. He was grinning, no doubt from a gun-induced testosterone rush. "Those guys have been parked outside your motel for at least the past three hours," he said calmly. "You ought to be more careful. Who are they?"

"Hell if I know." I stared at him. "What are you doing here?"

"Saving your ass." He patted his shoulder holster. "That was an unlawful discharge of a firearm, in case you're interested."

"I'm not interested in any of your discharges, thank

you." That wasn't what I meant to say, god knows, but the sight of Bill had scrambled my brains.

Why was Bill Butler, a Raleigh Police Department detective, standing in the middle of a deserted slice of godforsaken no man's land in central Florida?

"Nice night," he said, his smug smile hovering. "It's starting to warm up again." We looked up at the thousands of tiny stars visible in the dark countryside. The man had a point. It was a gorgeous evening, with the kind of pristine night sky that made it seem as if man had never arrived to ruin the Earth.

I refused to be distracted. "I'm out of here if you don't tell me why the hell you're following me," I warned.

"Your boss sent me to baby-sit," he said cheerfully.

His flippant attitude was starting to piss me off. I've fired a gun plenty of times, and I don't go around acting like Wyatt Earp on Viagra afterward. Then he really annoyed me by parking his right leg against the side of my car and leaning in my window. There we were, surrounded by twenty miles of empty earth, and this guy had to crowd my personal space.

"I don't have a boss," I reminded him.

"Okay, that fat slob who works with you sent me," he conceded.

"Watch your mouth. He may be a fat slob, but he's my fat slob."

"I'll say." His teeth glowed in the moonlight as he grinned. "He's mighty protective of you. Called me up yelling about drug dealers and cops and god knows what else. What the hell have you gotten yourself into? Is this about Tawny?"

"Bobby really sent you to baby-sit me?" I asked, annoyed.

Bill nodded. "Afraid so."

"I can take care of myself."

"I wasn't worried about you. I was worried about the drug dealers and cops."

"Why are you really here?" I demanded. "Tell me or I'll ram the side of that Corvette you've rented. You're

probably already going to have to pay through the nose
for bullet holes."

"Nope. I checked. Looks like I was the better shot.
Though that dented bumper's going to cost me." He
crouched down on his haunches so that his face was level
with me. His eyes searched my face as if he was trying to
decide on something, then he looked out into the darkness
behind the abandoned gas station without saying anything.

"I'm waiting," I said.

"You said we might have to cross that thin blue line
together to stop Tawny," he answered. "She needs stopping. I'm here to do my part."

"I want the truth," I warned him, knowing he was holding back. "The whole truth and nothing but the truth."

"The sorry truth is this," he admitted. "My ex is getting
married again tomorrow. To someone I used to know."

"That sucks."

"I didn't think it was any big deal, but when I think
about her up there in some church on Long Island marrying some sell-out in an expensive suit while I sit in my
apartment, drinking beer and watching twenty-year old
blonds that I'll never get near parade around in bikinis on
the boob tube while college guys clap like trained seals . . .
What can I say? With thoughts like that, who needs reality? I needed to get the hell out of Dodge for a couple of
days. Thought a change of scenery might help."

"So you came running to me," I said, pleased. My smile
showed it.

He looked embarrassed. "Don't tell me your ex-husband
doesn't matter to you. Look where we're at right now.
Because of him."

"Oh, he matters. They always matter." I put my hand
on Bill's and he didn't pull it away. "Thanks for saving
my butt back there."

"I have one more day off. I can cover your ass until
then."

I thought about it. The smell of the orange groves, the
midnight blue of the sky, the sharp pinpricks of stars all
made me feel dangerously reckless. A flash of freedom

surged through me. No one knew where I was. I had just escaped danger, if not death. I could do whatever I wanted and no one would ever know.

And there were surely worse things in life than sitting across a dinner table, staring at Bill Butler.

"How close do you plan to cover my ass?" I asked.

"As closely as you'd like."

"Buy me dinner first?"

"Deal." His smile was incredibly effective. My mind jumped straight to dessert and beyond in a flash. Perhaps the waitress would give us a doggie bag of whipped cream and honey?

Still, I hesitated. This moment had been a long time in coming. Some things are worth waiting for, and some things are only worth the wait. I hoped Bill fell into the first category.

"How do we know that guy isn't parked somewhere hoping for a second shot at us?" I asked, nodding toward the deserted road.

"Guys," he said. "There were two of them."

I knew then who they were. I just didn't know what they were.

"Same guys who were watching your ex-husband's house?" Bill suggested.

"Bobby told you that, too?"

He nodded. "Like I said, he thinks you're in over your head."

"Is that why you're here?"

"Maybe." His smile grew wider. "Maybe not. It's mighty damn cold up there in Raleigh."

"And you think it's going to be a lot hotter down here?"

"I'm hoping it will."

"What do you think?" I asked. "Do you think I'm in over my head?"

"Definitely."

He leaned in the door and kissed me, his mouth hard against mine. I've got nothing against those kinds of surprises. I kissed him back. God bless gunfire and its aftermath. Cordite is a true aphrodisiac.

"You want to know what I really think?" he said when

we surfaced for air. "I think we should make the most of being out in the middle of nowhere, alone together. Ex-wives and ex-husbands be damned."

We drove straight to the restaurant next door to his hotel. I'm a girl who likes to plan ahead. Bill followed at a distance in his Corvette and proclaimed that I was tail-free when we arrived at our destination. Whoever the two men were, they had called it a night.

We had a drink in the bar area first, surrounded by the excited hum of businessmen on the prowl and the artificial laughter of young girls on the make. My bar stool had an upholstered back and the drink in front of me was enormous. Life wasn't going to get any better.

I'd ordered a gin-and-tonic, but all I could taste was the gin. It burned a line down my throat and into my gut, releasing a surge of relaxation that invaded my bloodstream in warm, overlapping waves. It promised the kind of liquid abandon that man invented alcohol for.

Bill was drinking bourbon and we were both really into our drinks, in a rare "who gives a shit if the rest of the world attends AA, go ahead and call us slushes, because we are really needing this" sort of way.

In other words, I was getting drunk as a skunk. That would teach me to skip meals. "I'm going to eat half a cow," I decided, raising my drink in salute.

"Save the other half for me." Bill raised his glass in return. "I feel better already, Casey. You're a great tonic, you know that? You're always so full of life. No moping around for you."

"Oh, hell," I admitted. "I mope. I just mope in private. It's so much more satisfyingly pitiful that way."

He laughed, then stared at the bottom of his drink. "It's taken us a long time to get here," he said.

"I know," I agreed. "We sure can be assholes."

"At least we have something in common."

By the time we were done laughing, our table was ready. We talked business as we waited for dinner, true cop foreplay: discuss the case, drop an innuendo and retreat, take a drink and talk more shop. It made me giddy to be wallowing in my favorite passions all at once—sex, alcohol and crime.

"Are you going to tell your friend on the St. Pete force about the guys following me?" I asked. "They could be the dealers they're looking for."

Bill shook his head. "They could be, but then I'd be stuck at the station looking at photos for hours. They'd ask about my encounter with them. Right now those two guys don't know who the hell took potshots at them. I'd like to keep it that way. I've got better things to do."

Our eyes locked and we smiled at each other, alcohol making us brave. The waitress interrupted us right in the middle of our unspoken fantasy. Instead of strangling her on the spot, like I wanted to, I ordered another round.

"You're trying to get me drunk," Bill accused me.

"It's not like we have to drive home. So long as we can stagger next door, we're safe."

"In that case, I *need* to get drunk," he agreed, not missing a beat.

"Jeff is in real trouble," I told him after our fresh drinks arrived. "Those guys are watching his house to see if he shows up. I can feel it. He may be telling the truth when he says some girl burned him for his stash and money. Maybe those guys thought I was her?"

"You think they're hoping you'll lead them to Jeff?"

I nodded. "What a jerk. He must owe them a lot of money." I shook my head. "I don't know why I ever married that guy."

"You see," Bill pointed out as our food arrived, "you're proof of my theory. Love is an impermanent state of mind."

"Meaning what?"

"Meaning we'd all be better off just admitting it was temporary lust and leaving it at that."

"To temporary lust," I said, raising my glass in toast. "May it at least last until morning."

"Oh, it'll last," he promised. "It will last."

"What if those two guys you shot at are cops after all?" I asked over a slab of prime rib that was as big as my Aunt Edna's ass. I was shoveling in red meat like a stevedore. There was no point in pretending to be demure. I hoped to demonstrate the advantages of adequate protein in the hours ahead.

Bill shook his head. "I can check for you, but those guys weren't cops."

I sighed.

"What is it?" he asked.

"Every time I think I've left my old life behind, some part of it sneaks up behind me and bites me in the ass. Do you ever feel that way?"

"All the time. Remind me to show you the bite marks later."

Four drinks and two hours later, we were negotiating the third floor hallway of his hotel, holding each other up like a pair of Irish drunks on St. Patrick's Day. The carpet kept undulating beneath my feet and I was trying to stand upright by grabbing at those convenient knobs that line hotel hallways. Unfortunately, the walls were starting to spin. It was like being trapped in a Sonny and Cher anti-drug movie. Soon psychedelic flowers would sprout from Bill's head, his eyes would turn into spinning stars and my hands would morph into hooves.

"Watch it," Bill said, rescuing me as I grabbed the wrong doorknob and nearly fell into some stranger's room. I flopped backward, knocking us both against the opposite wall. "Emergency measures are in order," he declared.

He hoisted me up over his shoulder in a classic fireman's lift just as an old couple stepped out of the elevator in front of us. They stared as Bill staggered by. Blood rushed to my head and I tried to figure out why a pair of upside-down codgers were levitating in my field of vision.

"Just married," Bill explained as he fumbled with his keys. I started to laugh. The old couple tittered along.

"How sweet," the woman said. "And at your age. Such a blessing."

"*My* age?" I called back indignantly as Bill tried to hustle me inside, but a wiggling 170-pound burden can slow a man down. "Wait until you see who carries who out the door in the morning," I yelled drunkenly. "I'll show you who's old."

Bill plopped me down on the bed, then fell facedown beside me. "I may take you up on that offer," he said, breathing hard. "If I can. I'm not convinced I'm even going to survive this experience."

"You might not," I conceded as I rolled him over and started to unbutton his shirt. "But what a way to go."

I woke the next morning feeling ridiculously satisfied. Either I was still drunk or hormonal overload had washed the liquor from my system. I felt like I could run a marathon. Or climb a mountain. But I couldn't find my clothes, so I opted for Bill instead. He proved to be a hard man to wake up. It took us another hour to even think about breakfast. By then, he was a shadow of his former self and I was ready to take on the world. Ah, the advantages of being a woman.

"What?" I asked indignantly, since Bill was lying with his head buried in his pillow and laughing like a demented man.

"I feel like I've been in a train wreck," he said, his words muffled.

"Of course you do," I told him. "Why do you think they call me Casey Jones?" I pulled on his right arm, trying to drag him out from under the sheets. "Come on, we have miles to go before we sleep."

"Sleep?" he mumbled. "What's sleep?"

"The thing you do after breakfast, lunch and dinner. I'm starving. Let's go. Chop, chop. Put some clothes on, Buckwheat."

"How can you be so disgustingly cheerful?" he asked. "I can hardly move."

"Good," I said. "Remember that the next time you ask some skinny hundred-pound bimbo out on a date instead of a real woman."

"You're cruel, Casey." He hit the floor with a thud. "You're going to have to make good on your promise to carry me across the threshold."

"I'll carry you all the way to Devil's Fork."

"Devil's Fork?" he asked, struggling to a sitting position. "What's that?"

"It's a little crossroads an hour from here. I was on my way there last night until we were interrupted. We're going out there this morning." I climbed into his lap, facing him, then kissed him solidly on the mouth. "I'm going to introduce you to my grandfather. So try not to look so pleased with yourself."

"We're going to do what?" he asked weakly.

"Visit my grandfather. He's always wanted to give me a shotgun wedding."

"You're kidding, right?" he asked.

"Only about the wedding."

We stopped by my motel room so I could change into clean clothes before heading out of Tampa. It had been destroyed. The contents of my suitcase were scattered across the floor. My cosmetics bag had been emptied on the bathroom counter with every jar opened. Drawers hung out of the dresser and all the bed sheets had been ripped from the mattress, then tossed to the floor in a heap. Even the bedside table lay on its side, and the rug had been pried from beneath the baseboard in one spot where it lumped up.

"Jesus, Casey," Bill said. "Who are you staying with? Johnny Depp?"

"Now we know where our friends were last night while we were having dinner." I picked up my cosmetics bag, anger rising in me. "Creeps. I had some brand new MAC stuff. It's hard to find in North Carolina. I hope they rot in hell."

I looked around the room, searching for my clothes. A pile of T-shirts and jeans had been dumped on the closet floor. My underwear was scattered across the rug like a trail of bread crumbs for some pervert. "At least my panties didn't have holes in them," I offered.

"Let's hope they stay that way," Bill said with a worried frown. "Those guys are armed and I don't like leaving you to deal with this alone."

I looked up. "You really have to go?"

"I only have two days off. I'm sorry. My plane leaves tonight. I don't have a good feeling about this. Let me make a few calls while you change."

"Calls to who?"

"Backup." He stopped my protests with a warning look. "Don't argue, Casey. I'll find someone we both can trust."

Okay, fine. I could shake unwanted backup as easily as I could shake a tail. Well, better, hopefully. Let Bill fantasize about coming to my rescue if it made him feel more manly. Once he was gone, he wouldn't be able to keep track of what I did.

I stood in the hot shower, letting the spray of water soothe my pleasantly aching muscles. I entertained myself by devising ways I would torture Jeff when this was all over. It had been almost fifteen years since we were together and here I was, once again caught in the middle of one of his drug fiascos. The only thing I could do was contain the trouble.

Then it hit me—containing the trouble meant that I had to assume, wherever I went, that I was being followed. By the time I dressed, I had reached a decision.

"We're not going," I said, sitting down on the bed and toweling my hair dry.

"Not going where?" Bill asked. He'd just hung up the phone with a guilty look and I wondered who he had called.

"To see my grandfather. I can't take the chance."

He was quiet for a moment. "You're sure?" he asked.

"I'm sure. I can't lead those men to him. I can't take the chance, no matter how small. I'd die if anything happened to him because of me."

Bill opened and closed his mouth a couple of times without making a sound, groping in the way that guys do when they're trying to figure out how to be supportive but haven't a clue what to say. "Well," he finally said carefully. "How do you feel about it?"

I laughed. "Jesus, Bill, you sound like you're in marriage counseling."

"I was, believe me. Not that it did any good." He sat down next to me on the bed. "You're sure?"

"I'm sure." I was disappointed, but it was the decision to see my grandfather that was important. I felt released. I would go see him, and I would do it soon. But not until I knew it was safe.

"What do you say we go roust my ex-mother-in-law instead?" I suggested. "I have no problem with leading those yahoos to her front door."

"I can only think of one other thing I'd rather do more," Bill agreed.

"Really?" My tone was hopeful.

"God, no, woman, I'm kidding." He groaned. "I'm not even sure I can drive."

Clarissa herself opened the door. She was no happier to see me than she had been the afternoon before. She glared, but plastered a phony smile on her face when she spotted Bill. He wasn't wearing a silver thong, but I guess he passed muster anyway.

"Oh, my," she said, ever the horn dog in the middle of disaster. "Who might you be?" She waved us in, her eyes never leaving his, then wouldn't let go of his hand after she shook it. I could almost feel the wind from her batting eyelashes.

"I'm Casey's second husband. Didn't she tell you?" Bill gave her a huge grin.

Clarissa's smile faded and her eyes drifted to mine, a dangerous spark glinting behind her cold stare. I did my best to look blissfully married. I know I had "sexually satisfied" stamped on my forehead, thanks to my party-pink complexion. She recognized the glow and hated me for it.

"I guess she forgot to tell you," Bill said cheerfully into the silence. "She's quite a gal, isn't she? Mind if we come in?"

He walked past her without waiting for an answer and headed for the nearest couch. "Nice digs." He sat down with cop confidence and crossed his legs, the crease of his khakis sharply defined. I'll say one thing for Bill Butler. You'll never find a wrinkle on him. Or, at least, not on his clothes.

"What do you do, Mr. . . . ?" Clarissa said, her voice trailing off faintly.

"Bill Butler. I'm a cop." His words hung in the stillness of the room. Clarissa turned pale. "I'm here in an unofficial capacity," he added. "For now."

Clarissa glanced at me, then sat on one arm of an overstuffed easy chair, her movements as brittle as those of a sandpiper pecking for food along the shoreline.

I plopped down next to Bill, holding his hand for good measure. "Bill's helping me out," I explained. "Did you get in touch with the people hiding Tawny?"

Clarissa stared back and forth between us. "You're a police officer with what . . . organization?" she finally asked Bill in a faint voice.

"I'm a detective in Casey's hometown. I guess you know she prefers to keep the exact location confidential on account of your son's business associates." He took out his wallet and flipped it open, giving her a glimpse of his badge. She looked at it, then glanced nervously away.

I didn't want to be ungrateful, but I'd have given up my favorite pair of black leather flats to have been able to hear Bill say, "I'm with the FBI. Up against the wall and spread 'em," at that moment.

Bill waited her out. The more he smiled, the more Clarissa frowned. Her fingernails dug into the upholstered arm of the chair, turning her knuckles white.

"I investigate major crimes," Bill added after a moment of silence. "Drug smuggling. Kidnapping. Felony theft. Evading prosecution. I mention those particular crimes only off the top of my head, of course."

"I see." Clarissa stood, swaying slightly. "Would you excuse me for a moment, please?" She left the room. I figured she was headed for the bar and a stiff drink. Bill was not exactly being subtle.

"My hero," I whispered goonily, rolling my eyes. "Frisk me, please."

"I hate mothers-in-law," he said grimly. "This is going to be fun."

Clarissa surprised me. She returned a few moments later with a tray filled with glasses of iced tea and chicken salad sandwiches. She set the tray on the coffee table in front of us. "Please help yourself," she said politely, though only to Bill. "They'll be here in a moment."

"Who will?" I mumbled, my mouth already crammed with food. Not bad. Sure as hell Clarissa hadn't made the chicken salad. Her idea of cooking was to glare at the chef.

"The people who were . . ." She hesitated. "The people who were assisting the woman you call Tawny Bledsoe."

"I knew you were helping to hide her," I said in disgust, tossing the rest of my sandwich on the tray. "You idiot."

Bill put a warning hand on my thigh. "You used the past tense, Clarissa," he said. "Why?"

Clarissa stared at the window. "She disappeared yesterday. With her daughter. I'll let my friends explain the situation."

Ah, man. I should have tied Clarissa down on her patio without sunscreen and threatened to fry her liposuctioned ass unless she coughed up the info when I still had time. I'd gotten so close. Someone had warned Tawny. Who?

There was nothing we could do but wait, so wait we did. A clock ticked loudly nearby. Clarissa's shoes drummed nervously on the side of her chair. The high-pitched drone of a weed whacker filtered in through an open window. And a flock of gulls pitched a bitch over some bread a boneheaded tourist was tossing off the bow of a party boat on the bay. Gulls are nothing but rats with wings, I thought with disgust. More scavengers in a garbage-filled world.

Not one of us said a word.

Bill closed his eyes and took a catnap, a faint smile curling the corners of his lips. I knew what he was thinking and nudged him back to wakefulness, but he ignored me and kept on daydreaming. Pig. I'd known that the Australian doubleback flex maneuver would knock his socks off. He was reliving past glory.

Clarissa picked up a magazine and pretended to read it, but it was called *Oil & Gas Weekly* so I knew it belonged to her husband. She was only going through the motions.

I passed the time thinking about who had warned Tawny I was near. Either Clarissa herself, Jeff—or possibly a cop in the department who knew that Bill had headed this way. The most likely candidate was Dick-Dick, the big-mouthed detective. A man that desperate to get laid would be Tawny's pawn, and there he was right in the middle of the investigation knowing every move that anyone made. I also wondered if maybe Bobby D. was doing a little double-dealing, keeping the police department abreast of my movements without telling me. He was adamant on the subject of staying in their good graces, and if he had called around for backup, word had probably gotten out. On the other hand, the department was filled with horny men desperate to get laid. So it could be anyone in cahoots with Tawny, a friend from the good old days when she had worked there. The only one I didn't suspect was Bill. No way it was him. Not given the way he was helping me find her. Besides, I knew him, and knew he was better than that. Sometimes you have to go with your gut.

The doorbell finally rang and Clarissa scurried to answer it.

Bill whispered into my ear, "How badly do you want to scare them?"

"Not much. If Tawny's had her claws in them, they've suffered enough. Let me do the talking. Just sit there and look scary."

He tried an evil grin on for size.

"That's good," I said. "It scares even me. You look demented in a very official sort of way."

We were interrupted by the arrival of two of the most miserable-looking people I have ever seen. They were comical in their discomfort, and more out of place in Clarissa's house than even I was. The man was the color of a catfish's belly, no small feat when you live in central Florida. His checkered shirt was tucked into baggy shorts that drooped to his knobby knees. He had a gap between his front teeth, and his black hair was brushed damply against his scalp like that of a three-year-old boy getting gussied up for church.

His wife had her hair teased into a short brown helmet that set off her plain face like a cheap plastic picture frame. She was wearing a polyester dress that clutched her ample middle at exactly the wrong spot. Both blinked at us like apprehensive owls from behind thick glasses.

I felt sorry for them. They were probably just regular, churchgoing, middle-class stiffs who had tried to do the Christian thing by helping out a poor abused woman. Instead, they'd been fleeced and discarded.

"Where is she?" I asked, skipping the preambles. I knew no one much cared what anyone's name was. On the contrary.

"She's gone," the woman announced, then burst into tears. Her husband gave her shoulders an ineffectual pat and stared miserably at his shoes.

"She stole my wife's car," he mumbled.

"When?" I asked.

"Last night. But we knew we were in trouble before then."

"Start from the beginning," I suggested, knowing they were bursting to spill their moral indignation, not to mention their guts. "Clarissa, go get them something to drink," I said as an afterthought. Oooh, that felt good. I searched for more ways to order her around.

She glared at me, but obeyed. The terrified pair perched on the edge of a wicker love seat and clamped their knees together.

"She seemed like a lovely woman at first," the wife began, sniffling. "Going to church with us, playing with her daughter. And then . . ."

Her husband took up the story from there: "Then she began to take off at night, after the girl was in bed. She said she needed to get away and think about her future. She claimed to love looking out over the water at night. So we lent her our car, but the next night she just took it without even asking. She did it again the next night. And again and again. My wife had to start bathing the child and putting her to bed because the mother was never there. I'd hear this woman coming home at three and four o'clock in the morning, and I'd find beer bottles in my car when I drove to work the next day."

His face grew tighter with each word. He was having trouble comprehending that someone who looked so respectable could be so despicable. His villains had dark faces, or sinned in some heinous way, or came from the wrong side of the tracks. I don't think he was used to someone evil who looked and acted just like his friends on the surface. It scared him.

Clarissa returned with iced tea. The man took a glass and gulped most of it before continuing. "I started keeping track of the mileage," he said. "She was driving fifty, sixty miles a night. One day, I found a dent in the fender. I'm sure it wasn't there the night before. Then late last week, she didn't come home at all. I had to drive my wife's car to work the next morning. And my wife had to babysit the child all day until she turned up late in the afternoon. When, this . . . this woman returned, she gave no explanation for her absence."

His wife flushed and nudged him. "Tell her about the thingie," she said.

He looked embarrassed. "I found a . . . birth control device in the car earlier this week. A used device."

What the hell was he talking about? An IUD looped over the rearview mirror? A diaphragm nestled in the ash tray? "Could you be more specific?" I asked.

"It was a . . ." he said, mumbling the final word. I could guess what it was, but his wimpiness annoyed me.

"A *what*?" I asked.

"A condom!" Clarissa snapped, losing her patience with me. "A rubber. A sheepskin. A rascal wrap. Got it?"

Well, wasn't she the expert on party hats? She saw me biting my lip to keep from laughing and glared. Of course, this only made me want to laugh harder.

"Exactly," the man agreed, gulping for air. "A condom. On the floor of my car, where I put my feet in the morning."

The poor guy was as pink as the prime rib I'd eaten the night before. Tawny had made mincemeat of him and his wife.

"It stuck to the sole of my shoe," he added in a whisper, reliving the horror.

God, that *was* disgusting. And the perfect image for

what I thought about Tawny Bledsoe. I couldn't wait to scrape her off my shoe.

"He followed her the next night," the wife explained, sensing a need to uphold her husband's honor. "Tell them what you saw."

"She was . . . *bar-hopping*," he said in a tone of voice I reserve for describing the activities of necrophiliacs. "Going from one disreputable establishment to another, staggering, clutching on to various . . . escorts. And all this after assuring us she did not touch alcohol at all."

"She said it was against her religion," the wife butted in. "But I kept saying I could smell liquor on her in the morning. *He* would not believe me."

The look she gave her husband told me that Tawny had been up to her old tricks. She had flirted shamelessly with the poor schmuck in front of his wife, using her usual methods to divide and conquer. She was like the Johnny Appleseed of disaster, sowing unhappiness wherever she went.

"Bar-hopping where?" I asked, hoping to pick up her trail.

He named a part of north Tampa notorious for its dive bars, in a neighborhood that catered to the circus roustabout crowd during the off-season. God, but it was low-class, even for a road whore like Tawny. It was the drugs, I suspected, and her need to stay off the beaten track.

"Was there one place where she hung out more than the others?"

He gave my question a lot of thought, anxious to be of help. "There was one place where she stayed a fairly long time, it had a neon animal in its front window. I can't remember what it was. An alligator, maybe. But it was green."

That was better than nothing. "Did she give you any reason to suspect she might be using drugs?" I asked, wondering if I could trace her through the drug world. Thanks to my life with Jeff, I'd probably still know some of the players.

I thought they'd both keel over at the mention of drugs.

"Oh my god," the woman whispered, her hand flying to her mouth.

"Drugs?" the man repeated dumbly.

"Yes," I explained. "Cocaine. Blow. Bump. Whiff. It's a white powder and you sniff it. It makes you jumpy and irritable and you talk too much." Kind of like they were making me act right then.

They exchanged a look.

"What?" I demanded.

"She was very irritable with her daughter most mornings," the woman admitted. "Short-tempered. Nasty. I felt sorry for the poor thing. Her mother picked on her about everything. Her hair wasn't brushed, she had chosen the wrong clothes to wear, she wasn't sitting up straight, she didn't smile enough."

Oh, boy. That was Tawny all right. Screaming at her kid for not smiling. Appearance is all-important, so smile, by god, or I'll beat it out of you.

"There were phone calls, too," the wife offered, having made up her mind that Tawny Bledsoe was the devil her minister had been warning her about all these years. "From men. Late at night. The calls woke me up but *he* slept right through them." She aimed another glare at her sheepish husband. "Of course, she was never there when they called. She was always out . . . gallivanting around."

"Did the men ever give a name or leave a number?" I asked.

She shook her head. "I was afraid her husband had tracked her down, so I refused to talk to them. Although I did ask a man one night how he had gotten the number. All he said was that he was a friend trying to help her, and that Tawny had given him the number herself. I think he called himself Hank."

Hank, my ass. Clarissa looked like she was trying to bore a hole through the picture window with X-ray eyes. It was my ex-husband Jeff who had called her, and Clarissa knew it. Was she in touch with him after all?

I shook my head in disgust. "Tell me about last night, when she disappeared with your car."

"She got a phone call," the man said. "I don't know

who it was. She grabbed it before either one of us could get to it."

"She'd been waiting for it," the wife added. "She was sitting on that phone like she was waiting for it to hatch."

"When she hung up, she was in a good mood," the man said. "She'd had good news from up north. She said that her husband was in jail."

Sounded more like old news to me. What had she really been happy about?

"If it had been me, I would never have talked about my husband like that in front of my child," the wife said. "Saying he was in jail and deserved it. It upset the little girl. I could tell. But she cheered up when her mother offered to take her out for ice cream."

"And they never came back?" I guessed.

From the grim look on the wife's face, I knew there was more.

"Tell her," the woman ordered her husband.

"I got a call from my bank this morning," he said. "Someone cashed a check on my account at a branch across town. When they processed it, security kicked it out because the signature looked funny. They called to verify it."

"She had forged your signature?"

He nodded, miserable. "She took twelve hundred dollars, half of all we had in our account."

"What name did she use for identification purposes?" I asked, knowing Tawny probably had IDs in every one of her zillion married names.

"I don't remember. I think Tawny or Tammy. I was too upset to remember what the woman at the bank said," the man replied. "But I knew it had to be her."

"She'd have taken more if she'd known about it," his wife added. "But I'd forgotten to post my last paycheck in our check register. I know she went through my pocketbook. That's how she got the checks. Looking back, I realize she'd been taking money from me. Five or ten dollars here and there. I thought I was just getting careless. I never thought it might be her."

"No one ever does. But consider yourselves lucky," I told them.

"Lucky?" The man was indignant. "How can you say that?"

"She killed the last guy she fleeced."

After giving me the license plate number of their missing car, the two sad sacks left in an even more miserable state. They couldn't report the car stolen without admitting their involvement in the underground safe house network and so, like a sucker, I'd promised to do what I could to get it back for them. They didn't look too impressed with my offer.

Clarissa tried to hustle us out the door the moment we were alone again. "There. Are you happy?" she snapped at me. "You've gotten what you came for. The woman you're looking for is gone. Now get out of my life."

"Not so fast," Bill said, rising to his full height. Normally, I wouldn't be caught dead having a guy stand up for me, but Clarissa was terrified of Bill being a cop and I was enjoying her discomfort.

"What more could you possibly want?" she asked, her voice faltering.

"I want Jeff's phone number," I said. "I know he's been in touch with you."

She looked away.

"Come off it, Clarissa. Jeff's the one who sent them to you in the first place. He's the one who called her late at night at those poor people's house. And I am absolutely sure that he's the one who warned Tawny that I was closing in on her—after *you* let him know I was in Tampa. So don't play Miss Innocent with me."

"I hadn't talked to him in days," she protested.

I stared at her.

"Not until he called last night," she insisted.

"Your son is aiding and abetting a murderer," Bill said. "And so are you."

It was enough for Clarissa. She'd try to keep Jeff out of jail, but she sure as hell wouldn't go in his place. "Are

you going to arrest him?" she asked, marching to a desk
in one corner of the room.

"If Jeff is hanging out with Tawny Bledsoe," I told her,
"getting arrested is the least of his worries."

She took out a note pad and copied a phone number
scrawled across it. "Did that Bledsoe woman really kill
that man?" she asked, handing me Jeff's number.

"Yes, she did," I told her. "Jeff is in real danger. When
she gets done using him, she'll kill him, too. She doesn't
want any witnesses."

A tremor passed across Clarissa's face. I almost felt
sorry for her. She was the kind of person who had never
let herself love anyone in her life. Then her son had come
along, and she had loved him all the more to make up for
the lack of it until then. But it wasn't the right kind of
love. She loved her son more for herself than for him, and
Jeff had always known it. He had used her in retaliation,
he was still using her, and the cycle would never end in
this lifetime.

"I'm sorry, Clarissa," I said. "For what it's worth."

"Just get out of my life," she repeated wearily. She had
to hate me, I understood that, and I didn't hold it against
her. Because if she didn't hate me, she'd have to hate her
son or, worse, admit that she hated herself.

"The tape and photographs." I held out a hand.

She retrieved them wordlessly from a lower desk drawer
and handed them over. I stuffed them in my knapsack.

"I want you to understand something," Bill said suddenly.

"Yes?" she asked in a voice that had lost all pretense at
poise.

"The only thing standing between your son and a long
prison term is this woman." Bill pointed at me. I smiled
gamely. I suspect the effect was more ghastly than reas-
suring. Clarissa looked away.

"If not for Casey," Bill explained, with total disregard
for such minor details as jurisdiction and proof, "I'd have
your son in custody right now. So if you warn him in any
way that we have his telephone number, I will personally
see that he spends the next decade behind bars and that

you are arrested in full view of your friends at the country club."

Her Florida tan lost its luster. I thought she might bite her lower lip off, so I cut her some slack. "If you keep up your end of the bargain, I promise to do my best to keep Jeff out of this mess," I said. "You have my word."

"Your word?" she repeated tonelessly.

"It kept him out of jail once already," I reminded her. "It's the best I can do."

"All right," she whispered. Her composure cracked and a tear slid down one cheek. I never thought I'd live to see the day when Clarissa Jones broke down and cried. But the taste of victory was more bitter than expected. She was just another one of Tawny's victims.

I exchanged a glance with Bill. He shrugged.

"Your house is being watched," I told her.

She looked up, eyes wide. "What do you mean?"

"Two men have been watching it, at least ever since I've been here in Tampa. I saw them on my first day."

"Two men?" Her voice was faint.

I nodded. "You better let Norman know."

She nodded numbly and moved to the telephone to call her husband. Just another disaster created by their son to report.

We found our own way out.

"What are you going to do now?" Bill asked. We were sitting in my car in front of the airline terminal.

"I'm going to find Jeff. He'll know where Tawny's gone." I patted my pocket, where I'd stored the phone number that Clarissa had given me.

"He may not be at that number anymore," Bill said. "It sounds like he's on his way down the I-95 corridor from Raleigh. He could be headed back to here."

Maybe. Bill had made a phone call and traced Jeff's current telephone number to a motel at South of the Border, a tacky tourist trap that straddled the state line between North and South Carolina. Most people only stayed a few hours. Jeff was staying longer. I knew this because I'd already called the number from Bill's hotel room while he showered. Jeff answered and I hung up after pressing the "9" button long enough to make it sound like a fax gone astray. I saw no reason to burden Bill with the news. He'd only worry more. Or, worse, try to baby-sit me.

"Maybe he's not there anymore," I conceded. "But what else am I going to do?" I thought it over. "Of course, I could check out some of the bars Tawny's been hanging out in down here. I'm not going anywhere else tonight."

The more I thought about it, the more I liked the idea. Someone might know where Tawny was headed. No doubt she'd used and abused some new schmuck for help in getting away.

"I wonder why your ex would stop in South Carolina?" Bill said. "It's only about four hours from Raleigh. That's hardly a day's drive."

"I'll beat it out of him when I see him. Trust me."

He glanced at his watch and his expression grew serious. "Be careful, Casey. I don't like leaving you alone on this one."

"I'll be fine. I'm ready to solo. Your version of backup was great." I smiled at him. "But from here on out, I want to take it alone."

He glanced away and mumbled something about thanking me for taking his mind off his ex-wife. It would be the next morning before I figured out why he'd felt the need to change the subject.

"You're not carrying, are you?" he asked.

I shook my head.

"Then I'm going to leave this with you, just in case." He reached into the back seat for his duffel bag and removed a metal box. "This is very special," he told me. "Take good care of it."

He raised the lid slowly, building suspense, like a guy opening a jewelry box to show his girlfriend an enormous diamond engagement ring inside.

"I am not worthy," I murmured.

"Wait until you see it." He pulled back a black velvet cover.

"Holy shit. What is it?" I stared at the gun nestled in

the box. It looked a lot like a Colt semi, except it had a double-stacked, staggered magazine.

"A custom-built .40-caliber Strayer-Voigt," he said reverently. "I had a guy in Atlanta build it for me. It took forever, but it was worth the wait." He stroked the barrel. "It holds fifteen rounds of ammo."

"Double the shooting satisfaction."

"I just hope you won't need it." He took the Strayer-Voigt from its molded compartment and handed it to me.

"I don't know what to say," I admitted. I hefted it, admiring its balance. It was heavier than I was used to, but I liked the wider grip. I'm the kind of girl who really likes to wrap her hands around something and squeeze.

"You sure you want to give me this?" I asked. "What if I have to use it?"

"I'll deal with it then," he promised. "Just don't stick it in your pants. That's a bad habit you have there, Casey."

"I won't," I lied. No point in rubbing in the fact that, unlike him, I didn't have to worry about shooting my pecker off. Besides, where the hell else was I supposed to carry it? In a purse? No fucking way. I could see it now: "Please excuse me while I open my red plastic purse and extract a gun so I can shoot you."

"Just be careful where you point that thing," Bill warned me.

"Hey, I've been telling you that for two days. But did you listen? No."

He smiled, but it seemed sad around the edges. Tired and sad. "I guess this is it." He glanced at his watch again. "Time to return to our real lives."

"Afraid so." I smiled back. "But it's been great while it lasted." I am truly a perverse individual at heart. I had loved every second with him, but suddenly I wanted him to go. The gun in my hand only made it worse. I had Tawny in my sights and I didn't want to lose her.

"If you ever need another tune-up, give me a call."

"You bet," I promised, knowing from his tone of voice that this was the end of our latest truce, at least for a long time to come.

"Be careful," he whispered just before I put my hands

on the back of his head and drew him to me. I kissed him hard. The kiss lingered. I slipped my tongue in his mouth and flashed back to the night before. So did he, apparently. I started to wonder if that was another Strayer-Voigt in his pocket or if he was just happy to see me.

"Don't worry," he whispered. "My safety's on."

We kissed until we both realized that an old lady with a pink poodle was standing on the sidewalk outside our car, glaring in at us. The dog yapped its disapproval.

"Better go," I said. "While you have the strength."

"I still have enough energy to kick that dog on my way past," he promised.

"Kick the old lady instead."

We started to laugh, and it was enough to carry us through those few awkward seconds that it took for him to hop from the car and grab his duffel bag. I busied myself stashing the gun inside my knapsack.

The door slammed and Bill was gone.

I watched him go with a strange mixture of elation and regret. He'd bailed me out when I needed help, he'd taken my mind off my troubles, and he'd given me the strength to keep going.

But I knew it had been one of those times that you can never get back. They're good exactly because you know they won't last.

ELEVEN

As I pulled away from the airport, I checked to make sure no one was following me, then I headed toward the roustabout hangouts where Tawny had been spotted. The cold front had retreated and the night was warm. I rolled the windows down and cruised until I found a strip of seedy storefronts converted into drinking holes for itinerant workers seeking a few hours of oblivion. Boy, did I know how they felt.

The first four bars I tried were filled with snorting, smelly beasts wearing blue jeans and dingy tank tops. Short of a Merchant Marine hangout I once visited in Norfolk, I can't think of when I've breathed air more filled with the unsavory combination of testosterone and sour beer. The women wiggling through the crowds were clearly working girls going down fast. And often. Not even Tawny in the throes of cocaine-induced confidence would venture into one of those joints. Besides, no one recognized her photo, though few people I asked could even focus their eyes.

The fifth place was called the Green Iguana. It was hobbled together out of brick and recycled oak, and looked like it belonged down the road from a Florida swamp. The crowd was mixed. Men and women sat on fifties-style red leather bar stools, sipping draft beer underneath the leering expressions of mounted white-tailed deer heads. The floor was covered in sawdust, the lighting fluorescent and the jukebox big on Jimmie Rodgers.

More to the point, the women were presentable—but not exactly cover girls. This would be Tawny's tramping ground. She'd stand out like a three-carat diamond in a box of lug nuts. The only thing it lacked was a neon green animal in the window, and that mystery was solved when a drunken woman lurched in the door protesting that someone had forgotten to turn on the iguana.

Within minutes, a neon iguana was blinking in the front window and I was sitting beside the drunken woman at the bar.

Most witnesses are reluctant to talk. The key to securing their help is to ease into the subject. Which is why I slapped the photo showing Tawny and her daughter dressed in matching pink outfits on the bar in front of the woman and announced: "I'll buy your drinks for the rest of the evening, if you tell me where I can find this no-good, back-stabbing, coke-snorting bitch."

She peered woozily at the photo, her puffy eyes narrowing in concentration. "You got that right," she finally slurred as her beer-soaked brain cells slowly connected. Her hand inched across the bar and she pressed a finger down on Tawny's face, as if she were trying to obliterate her from the world. "That whore's been acting like she owns this place for the last week. Ask Freddy where her snooty ass is tonight. She's been polishing his knob for the last couple of days."

She cocked a thumb over her shoulder in the direction of a heavy man wearing overalls and a plaid shirt with cut-off sleeves. He was sitting alone in a booth against one wall. He had a Santa Claus face, complete with bushy white beard, but he didn't look too jolly at the moment. He was staring into his beer as if someone had just pissed in it.

"That's Freddy?" I confirmed, pointing.

"Yup. The one with 'stupid' written on his forehead." She hiccoughed and peered closer at the photo. "I knew this bitch was trouble when she first came in here. I could smell it on her. She's a coke hound, too. Bleeds these boys dry. They're too fucking dumb to see her coming. You the cops?" She looked up at me and leered, then brushed a lock of frizzy red hair out of her eyes.

"I'm better than the cops," I promised, taking a twenty-dollar bill out of my pocket and placing it next to her beer. "I'm that bitch's worst enemy."

"All right," she crowed in four-syllable triumph, then circled a fist in the air as if she were twirling an imaginary lasso. I steadied her before she toppled off her stool, then went to twist Freddy's arm.

Poor guy. He was nursing a broken heart. And a broken wallet, too, no doubt.

"You look like a truck just ran over your pecker," I said, sliding onto the empty bench across the table from him.

He glanced at me. "Go away. I ain't interested in no women."

"What's the matter? Afraid I'll steal your car, borrow your credit cards, pick your wallet and leave you to lick your wounds?"

His eyebrows bounced up like a pair of caterpillars doing the jitterbug. "Who told you what happened?"

"You did. Just now." I paused. "Besides, I know the lady in question."

The poor sap stared morosely into the depths of his beer. He was why country music was invented. "She's gone, ain't she?"

I nodded. "What did she take with her? Besides your heart?" I asked this last question kindly. He looked like he had a big heart to break. He was just a teddy bear of a working man, coming here for a cold brew hot from the fields. He was neither equipped for nor deserving of Tawny Bledsoe. I patted his rough hand. He pulled it away like I had scalded him.

"I knew she was too good to be true," he mumbled. "What the hell did I think she'd see in me?"

"Hey," I told him. "A good man is hard to find, and a good woman is even harder. Don't let scum like her win by letting her get to you. She's not worth it. There's plenty of women who appreciate a hardworking, honest man. Just because she used those good things against you doesn't

mean you won't find someone who treasures them." Like
I said, I should have been a shrink.

His glassy eyes blinked at me. "Who the hell are you?"

When I explained who I was and why I was there, he
pushed back into a corner of the booth like he wanted to
disappear into the woodwork. "You really think she did
those things?" he asked.

"Oh, yeah. I do."

"She didn't get my truck or nothing," he said, gulping
at his beer. "Just some money."

"And what else?" I asked, reading his tone of voice.

His mouth twisted sourly. "My Discover card."

"You gave her a credit card?" I tried to hide my surprise,
but failed. Pussy power indeed. Yoko Ono must have had
Tawny in mind when she wrote her anthem. This guy had
handed a credit card over to someone he barely knew.
Geeze, what did she do with that thing to get away with
so much? I suddenly felt as if I were sitting on top of a
Scud missle, though I have far too many morals to use my
cooter for commerce. It's for recreational purposes only.

Freddy sensed my disbelief and launched into an indignant tale about how Tawny's husband was beating her and
she had to get away and blah, blah, blah. Mercifully, we
were interrupted when a skinny guy with a melon head
and a missing front tooth appeared at our booth. He
slapped the table with his palm and began to hee-hee, like
some obnoxious character in a cartoon. The gap in his teeth
added a particularly annoying whistle to the sound and I
started to wonder what his laugh would be like if I
knocked the other front tooth out for him.

"Where's your girlfriend tonight, Freddy?" he asked in
a raspy drawl. "She done run out on you, right? I told you
she was trouble." He tapped his nose.

I stood up and looked the guy in his beady little eyes.
"Listen, bubba," I said. "The only reason you're not the
one in this pickle is that even a slut like Freddy's paramour
has standards. I dare say you didn't measure up on either
end, so get your scrawny ass away from us or I'll knock
you from this booth all the way to the bay. And don't think
I can't." I flexed my biceps and smiled.

His eyes blinked furiously as his brain scrambled to process the unexpected information. He was supposed to do the dissing—how had his little plan gone so horribly wrong? "What's a paramour?" he finally stammered.

"A paramour is someone who gives you the best sex of your life. And Freddy here has just come off a solid week of hot action you would not believe. Just look at how exhausted the man is."

We both looked at Freddy, who did look tired, though probably not from getting any action. He was too confused to play along with my attempt at salvaging his honor, so I forged on without him.

"When's the last time you had sex, by the way?" I asked Melon Head. "I gather you must be the local Don Juan, what with your in-depth knowledge of the female sex and all."

"Who are you?" the guy asked, his eyes darting back and forth between us. "You Freddy's sister or something?"

"I hope not," I said. "Since Freddy and I go at it like weasels at least twice a week. Of course, that wouldn't make much difference to you and your sister."

"I ain't got no sister," he said, perplexed, then added somewhat cryptically, "But I got me a dog."

"Better go home and feed it. Unless you want your friends to see you get your ass kicked by a girl. Because I am perfectly happy to oblige."

The guy bobbed his head and gulped, then scurried away, leaving the decaying scent of old shrimp in his wake.

I flopped back down in the booth and held my head. "I am amazed at how much misery a single person can cause in this world. That woman's disrespect for other people is contagious. I'll never be able to stop her poison from spreading, even if I do stop her."

Freddy was studying me. "Thanks for getting rid of that moron. Dew don't got the sense God gave a possum. But what's in it for you?"

"Stopping her." I looked up. I didn't have time to mope. "What's your credit limit?"

"Eight hundred dollars." He looked ashamed.

"Well, count on that being what she takes you for. Come on, let's go."

He looked alarmed. "Go where?"

"To my motel room. We're going to call your credit card company. I want to know where she's been using your card."

"I can't do that," he protested.

"Sure you can." I grabbed his elbow and hoisted him up. "You're a good man and you need to do the right thing. The right thing is to stop her from doing this to anyone else."

I could have threatened him. I could have raised the possibility of the cops. I could have used my womanly wiles. But, like Tawny Bledsoe, I'd figured out that Freddy was human putty. If I kept on the pressure, he'd bend.

Forty-five minutes later, we were sitting on opposite sides of my motel bed. We'd taken Freddy's pickup truck, since I did not trust him to follow me alone. I was glad for the decision. A dark sedan was parked at an odd angle in a lot across the highway, in a perfect position to allow anyone inside to watch my room. I made Freddy park his truck at the far end of the motel wing, where it would block the sedan's view of my front door, then we scurried inside together. I wasn't worried they'd spot me. They wouldn't be looking for a pickup truck. But I kept the lights off, just in case.

The darkness made Freddy nervous. We sat on either side of the bed, staring at the telephone between us. He was getting cold feet.

"Go on," I urged him. "Just say what I told you."

When he didn't move, I held the phone up to the glow leaking in under the closed bathroom door and dialed the 800 number I'd gotten from information, then handed him the receiver. It took a couple of minutes for him to get through to an actual human being and verify that he was, indeed, the cardholder on the account. I was amused to find out his mother's maiden name had been Ratt, which she had traded up for Fink. It's a good thing hyphenated last names weren't in vogue when Freddy was born.

They were getting down to brass tacks and Freddy was

doing a decent job of lying his ass off. "See," he explained, "I gave my teenage daughter permission to use the card, but I told her don't you go charging no more than a hundred dollars." His furry eyebrows met in the middle as he scrunched his face in concentration. "How much?" he shouted, his eyes wide with panic. He was silent. "Well, I never . . ." He began to chew his lip and I gestured furiously.

"Can you tell me where she's been charging?" he asked. He repeated the answer in a stunned voice. "Jacksonville. Savannah. Where? What the hell is she doing in South Carolina?" He paused again. "No, she did have my permission. It's okay, but . . ." He took a deep breath. "Maybe you better cut her off at your end. Can you do that?"

A moment later, he hung up, his shoulders slumped in defeat. "She done charged six hundred dollars in forty-eight hours. How can a person do that? Most I ever charged in a weekend was sixty."

"Maybe her coke dealer takes credit cards?" I studied the towns on my list. "She's going up the Eastern Seaboard. The I-95 corridor." Same as my ex, I thought. She was meeting Jeff in the middle.

"Why would she head back to where she was in so much trouble?" Freddy asked, his head held between two big paws.

"That's what I want to know."

My determination to immediately track Tawny cooled once I'd retrieved my car from the Green Iguana and driven all the way back to my motel. I had not slept in days, it seemed, though I'd spent plenty of time in bed. There was no way I could go any further without a break. At least the dark sedan was gone. Just to be safe, I parked my rental car in back of the motel, then returned to my room to sleep. I'd head for I-95 in the morning.

That night, I dreamed of Bill Butler, and the images lasted until morning. It was a bonus rerun of torrid sex with no strings attached. Unfortunately, we were just about to get down to brass tacks in my last dream of the night when Bill gazed into my eyes and said, "You forgot to

turn on the iguana." I looked over the edge of the bed, and
there was a big lizard staring up at me, flicking its tongue,
wondering when it was going to be his turn.

That was weird enough to wake me up. Especially since
someone was pounding on my door louder than a beginning bass drum player. I scrambled into some clothes,
grabbed Bill's gun, then peeped out through the curtains.

I could not believe what I saw.

Bobby D. stood on my doorstep, holding a box of
Krispy Kreme doughnuts. His girlfriend Fanny waited behind him. Fanny was, quite possibly, the only human being
on the planet who could even be seen when standing behind Bobby D. Her girth was as big as her heart. Together,
the two of them were a pair of very plump sitting ducks
for the men in the dark sedan.

"Get in here," I said, opening the door and dragging
Bobby inside. Fanny followed him happily, waddling in
on her high heels, chirping about how nice it was to see
me again.

God bless Fanny. She was the happiest human I had
ever met. She'd long since decided what she liked in life—
eating and Bobby D., in that order—and had enough
money to ignore what anyone else said or felt about her.

I slammed the door shut and double-locked it. "What in
god's name are you doing here? I thought you guys would
be in a boat off Fort Lauderdale by now."

Bobby sat on the bed. The mattress collapsed and he
slid to the floor. "These cheap motel mattresses," he grumbled.

"I'll sit on the other side," Fanny offered cheerfully.
"That'll balance it out." The two of them sat on the bed,
opened the doughnut box and began to munch.

"What are you doing here?" I demanded again.

Bobby looked up, annoyed I was distracting him. "Well,
Butler couldn't get anyone else to cover for him, so I
thought I was better than nothing. But I didn't want to
leave Fanny behind. This is our week together. So we both
drove up from Lauderdale."

"Bill called you to back me up?" I asked incredulously.

"Not exactly," Bobby explained, his mouth crammed

with a doughnut. "He just said that he had to go back to work and there was no one else to cover you. He was worried. Said the guys following you were still around."

"Yeah," I agreed, staring pointedly at Fanny. "They are still around. And, frankly, I'm surprised you would drag her into this."

"Me?" Fanny asked. "Don't worry about me, dear. I'll enjoy the excitement."

"Bobby." My voice was low.

"Stop worrying," Bobby advised me. "I've been at this game longer than you. I cruised the joint. There's no one watching. I'd never expose Fanny to harm." He patted her pink hand kindly and they beamed at each other. God, someone give me an insulin shot.

"How do you propose to help if we don't expose Fanny to danger?" I asked.

"Bill figures you're heading back to South Carolina next," Bobby said.

"Oh, he does, does he?" I was annoyed. Smug bastard.

"He said if your ex was there, that was where you would head. So we're going to drive you. We can drive you straight through. You'll make up lost time."

I sat down on the chair that the motel had paired with a cheap desk and lay the Strayer-Voigt on the tabletop. Bobby saw the gun and his eyes widened. He reached to touch it and I slapped his hand away.

"Nice piece," he murmured.

I ignored him. "Okay, so maybe it just so happens that I am heading for South Carolina," I said. "Because that's where Tawny's gone." I filled them in on all of her activities since hitting Tampa. "How in the hell could you help me out?"

Bobby dug two globs of sugar from the corners of his mouth and carefully sucked his fingers. "Number one, the kid. Number two, electronics."

"Explain."

"Tawny still has the kid with her, right?" Bobby asked. I nodded.

"Seems to me, our number one priority ought to be getting the kid away from her before she blows a gasket and goes bonzo on us. I figure she's menopausal and when that hormonal shit kicks in, there'll be real trouble."

"Jesus Christ," I said. "Menopausal? Send in a SWAT team. No one is safe."

"You see, dear," Fanny chimed in, ignoring Bobby's Neanderthal theory. "Robert and I have discussed it in length. It's none of my business, of course, but as a mother myself, I do not believe we should take any chances. The first thing any of us should do is to make sure the child is safe."

A silence fell on the room. They were tactful enough to pretend that selecting new doughnuts required all of their attention, but it didn't lessen my shame any. Of course, they were right. What had I been thinking? I had been so focused on bringing Tawny down, I had lost sight of the danger to her daughter. Tawny's behavior was growing more and more unpredictable. I needed to get Tiffany out of there fast. If I hoped to separate the two of them without losing Tawny's trail, I would need help. But could Bobby and Fanny do it?

"What was that part about electronics?" I asked.

"Suppose something happens to you?" Bobby asked. "You're the only one with proof against that dame."

"So?"

"So I have a long-range microphone and recorder with me," Bobby said. "And a cellular phone. I never leave home without them. You never know."

You never know what? When you might be able to eavesdrop on someone getting it on in the boat next to you during an overnight harbor stay? I could think of no other reason why Bobby would need a long-range microphone while cruising on vacation with Fanny. The old perv.

I tuned him out while he extolled the virtues of modern technology. Bobby D. and his gizmos. If they'd invent an electronic butt wiper, he'd be first in line to buy it. I, on the other hand, hate anything with batteries. Well, almost anything. The exceptions are no one's business but my own.

"Okay," I conceded. "It might be wise to record any future encounters I have with Tawny."

"Wise?" Bobby repeated. "It's essential. You got no real evidence on her, babe. You're going to have to push her buttons and make her spill."

"If we can find her," I said glumly.

"We'll find her," Bobby predicted. He looked at his watch. "It's nine o'clock. The morning's half gone. Get your ass in gear. Let's take this show on the road."

None of us really choose our fates—or even get much of a chance to shape it. And so it was that I, tough chick detective, found myself wedged in the backseat of an opalescent pink Cadillac, feeling like a kid who's been dragged kicking and screaming from the front gates of Disney World because the family vacation was over. Mom and Dad, as in Bobby and Fanny, sat in the front seat and spent much of their time discussing when and where we would stop to eat next. I considered kicking my feet against the front seat and asking repeatedly "Are we there yet?" but soon realized the wisdom of using the ten hours of driving time to plan out what to do if and when I came face-to-face with Tawny again.

Traffic was light once we reached Jacksonville and turned north on I-95. We sped up the superhighway on cruise control, and I had to admit that the incredibly conspicuous pink Cadillac nonetheless had a hell of a suspension system. It was like traveling inside a giant womb.

Some people may have grown tired of manning the wheel, but not Bobby D. It was another activity that required little more than sitting on your butt, and so he was happy to man the helm for the long haul. I fell asleep in mid-afternoon, mostly in defense against Bobby D.'s singing along to the radio. He sounded like Burl Ives on acid. I woke up only long enough to eat the corned beef sandwich Fanny offered me somewhere north of Savannah. When I woke again, Fanny was poking a cup of black coffee at me.

"Wake up, dear," she advised. "We're almost there."

I was clear-headed in an instant, a jolt of adrenaline surging through me. Driving long distances always puts me in a near-dream state, but the prospect of meeting

Tawny again swept all cobwebs from my mind. I could tell she was close. I could almost smell her. Her and her four thousand boyfriends.

"You're the boss," Bobby said from the front seat. "What's next? It's five miles to South of the Border."

I checked the clock on the dashboard. It was just after ten o'clock at night. Bobby had really pushed it. I-95 was almost deserted. Only a few pairs of headlights bobbed in the darkness behind us. "We're going to cruise the parking lots once we get there," I decided. "I'm looking for one of two cars." I described the car Tawny had stolen from her Tampa hosts, plus Jeff's red Mustang. "If we see any of them, don't get near. Don't panic. Just pull over to some discreet spot nearby and I'll take it from there."

"You don't even know the name of your ex's motel?" Bobby complained.

"Bill wouldn't tell me," I admitted. "He didn't want me to come here."

Bobby snorted. "Like that really stopped you."

"What about the daughter?" Fanny interjected bravely.

"I'll try to separate them," I said. "If I pull it off, you both have to promise me that you'll take her immediately to her aunt in Rocky Mount." I would keep my promise to Robert Price. The last thing I wanted was for the kid to enter the social services system.

"You want us to leave you here alone?" Bobby asked, locking eyes with me in the rearview mirror. He knew I was trying to get rid of him.

"I won't do it any other way."

He nodded, but he wasn't happy about it. He'd traded the kid's safety for my own, but both of us were willing to make that bargain.

"What will we do if they've already left South of the Border?" Fanny asked.

"We'll check every Waffle House, every fast-food joint, every diner in all four directions. We'll find out which way they went and we'll go after them. I'm not giving up now."

South of the Border is the world's most garish rest stop, a sort of Las Vegas for toddlers located on the North and South Carolina border. It started out twenty-five years ago

as a single souvenir shop with two hundred decidedly po-
litically incorrect billboards marking the way for seventy-
five miles on either side ("Si Signor! Take the Leap! Pedro
Sells His Trinkets Cheep!")

Over the past two decades, it had grown in neon-and-
plastic spurts, and was now a ten-acre multicolored extrav-
aganza of restaurants, motels, mini-casinos, playgrounds,
bars and souvenir stands. Giant plaster statues of gorillas,
flamingos and other ghastly figments of someone's fevered
imagination dotted the complex in haphazard fashion. I was
surprised the Mexican Consulate didn't demand the place
be shut down on general principle. Instead, it was a thriving
monument to tackiness and, of course, a must-stop on the
long trip from North to South. Ironically, you couldn't get
more American than South of the Border.

It was also possibly the only place on the planet where
a bright pink Cadillac would not look out of place. We
cruised the parking lots slowly. I knew at least one of my
quarry had to be here. Jeff had called his mother from a
motel here several days before, and Tawny had headed this
way.

I spotted Jeff's Mustang first. It was parked at the far
end of a long row of cars fronting the Cactus Flower, a
ground-hugging motel that was painted a virulent shade of
green. Bobby slowed down and I crouched in the backseat,
confirming that it was, indeed, Jeff's car.

"Yup," I said. "That's him. The front end is dented
where the bastard ran into my Porsche."

"Isn't that just like an ex-husband?" Fanny chirped. "To
hit and run like that?" She could afford to be chipper about
the topic. Her ex had given her eighty million dollars as a
good-bye present, while mine had given me the clap.

"There are no lights on in his room. He may be with
her," I told them.

"Let's find out," Bobby said. He turned into the next lot
and we passed the parked cars slowly. No signs of Tawny.
It was slow going because I had to check nearly all the
license plates. Naturally, her former hosts had owned a

Saturn and every other car in the lot could have been theirs.

We cruised three more restaurants and two more motels before I spotted it. She was staying at a place along the southernmost edge of the complex.

"Shit!" I stared at the car. I couldn't believe it. We had done it. "That's it. That's her." I gripped the back of the front seat and tried to keep from bouncing up and down. I felt like a dog that has finally cornered the nasty neighborhood cat and discovered it has arthritis. "I wonder why she's not staying with Jeff?"

"Down, girl," Bobby warned me.

I took a deep breath. "You're right. I wonder which room she's in?"

"My money's on one of the first five," Bobby said. "And you're luckier than you deserve to be that every motel in this place is one- or two-story."

"Thank god for cheap land," I muttered. "Pull over behind the motel office."

Bobby parked the Cadillac in a dark spot between two street lights. We were outside a bar and I could hear the dampened roar of laughter inside. Ah, people with no worries on their minds. What was it like to be one of them?

The Cadillac's trunk was crammed full of Fanny's matching tapestry suitcases. She'd packed enough to clothe an entire Weight Watchers' chapter for the next ten years. "I assume your gizmos are in here somewhere?" I asked.

Bobby grunted and dug around, emerging with a Frisbee-shaped black device that had a small antenna, several dials, a plug-in set of headphones and a mini-cassette recorder.

"This is what you want," he said. "Directional microphone is here." He waggled a triangular protrusion of black wire at me. "You should be able to pick up what's going on in all five rooms with little interference, all from the same spot."

"Excellent. G. Gordon Liddy would be proud." I took the device, held it up to my ear and shook it.

"Watch it." Bobby grabbed it away from me. "It's delicate. A little respect for the circuitry would be nice."

"Sorry," I said. "Habit." I considered electronic devices to have a life of their own until proven otherwise.

Bobby explained the controls, checked to make sure a blank tape was in the recording compartment, then promised to keep Fanny well out of the way.

"She's a nice person," I warned him. "I don't want anything to happen to her."

"Agreed. We'll wait for you over there. Behind the main building." He pointed across the road toward a darkened structure. Someone's dream had gone belly up. The front doors and windows were boarded with plywood.

"Don't go in that dame's room alone," Bobby warned me. "If she's there, come back and we'll discuss how to approach her."

"Sure," I lied. "No problem." There was no way I'd be able to surprise her with Bobby and Fanny along.

The owners had trucked in crushed seashells to fill in the vacant lot bordering the rear of the motel. I crunched like a classroom of kids eating cereal as I made my way behind the rooms. I followed a narrow concrete foundation that was crumbling along its edge. Scraggly weeds and bramble bushes had pushed up through the shells and scratched my ankles as I made my way toward a heap of junk piled in the center of the lot. I could hide in the shadows and still have unimpeded access to most of the motel wing.

The back of the concrete block building was pure utilitarian. Rows of bathroom windows and smaller ventilation openings were my only audio access to the rooms. Bobby had promised that his device could penetrate the Pentagon. This would be a good test of its range.

I found a dark spot, thanked the lord the night was cloudy, turned on the device and leaned against a discarded velour lounger while I fiddled with the dials. At first, all I got was static. But, gradually, the sounds of different lives began to filter through the background buzz. It was eerie, like eavesdropping across space: static, hollow voices, echoes and more static. I adjusted the antenna. That was better. I picked up the first room clearly.

Monitoring those motel rooms was a micro-journey

through the human condition. The first room was filled with teeth-rattling snores that nearly drowned out the competing strains of a radio left on for the night. The second room contained a pair of battling honeymooners, no doubt on their way to Florida. They were arguing about which family had disgraced themselves more at the reception. I gave the marriage a year, at most. The third room was temporary home to a sad sack–sounding guy who was whispering into the phone. A few minutes of listening told me that he was racking up a whopper of a bill to a sex line. The girl's name on the other end was Lureena, and the man kept begging her to call him a cockroach and crush him beneath her spike heels. I wondered how much Lureena was making an hour to put up with such a depressing parade of self-hating men, then turned my attention to the next room.

It was silent. No television. No voices. No snoring. Ditto for the fifth room in the wing. Tawny had to be in one of the two, judging from where she had parked her car. There was no place else to go, except for someone else's motel room, I suspected, or one of the local bars. But it was late—after eleven—and she must have been driving for days. She'd be exhausted. And she'd have a cranky four-year-old on her hands. If this was her room, she was there.

I settled back to wait. A long forty-five minutes later, a phone rang in the fourth room. I adjusted the antenna and pressed the recorder. You never knew.

"Hello?" A woman answered quickly, like she'd been waiting for the call. The hair on the back of my neck prickled. It sounded like Tawny.

"This afternoon," she was saying. "I had to stop for the night north of Savannah. The kid is being a real pain in the ass. What about you?"

When she laughed at the answer, I knew it was Tawny. I gritted my teeth in triumph. She was not going to get away from me.

"God, I miss you," she said. I was surprised—she sounded absolutely sincere. How could anyone feel that way about Jeff? He was a human version of the *Titanic* and sinking fast.

"It's all set up," Tawny was promising. There was a silence. "Yeah, I know. But I got out before then. God, she's a bitch, isn't she? She hates my guts. What did I ever do to her? But I'm not worried. She has no idea who she's up against."

Oh, yeah? A hot, red rage rose in my gut. I knew damn well what I was up against. But did she?

"We'll be on our way to L.A. by then. No one will know." She paused. "I want to drop her off with a guy I know who lives in Phoenix. So we can spend some quality time alone together." She giggled, but stopped abruptly as a small voice interrupted, piping up from another room.

"Mommy," the voice wailed. "It's dark in here."

Tawny's voice grew harsh. "Of course it's dark. It's nighttime. Lie down and go back to sleep, or I'll come in and smack you to sleep." People will talk to their kids in ways you would not believe when they think no one else can hear them.

"I'm thirsty," Tiffany insisted, her little girl's voice sounding desperate as she searched for a way to be comforted.

"No. You'll wet the bed. Lie down and go to sleep or you'll be sorry. I mean it." Tawny turned her attention back to the phone. "We might have to rethink part of this," she said. "We could do a lot with the money from the you-know-what." She was silent. "No, more like fifty thousand." She was quiet again. "You could always visit a lot. Your mother won't care."

So Clarissa had entered the picture.

"I don't think it is," Tawny said. Her voice had an edge to it. "I'm tired of listening to her whine. And I'm tired of hearing about her fucking father. He's a loser, he always has been. I've had my share of that shit from her. It's all she talks about. I've done the mother bit. Now it's my turn to cut loose."

Yeah, poor old Tawny. Working her fingers to the bone taking care of her kids. Spreading maternal love throughout the world. I'd seen cowbirds who were better mothers.

"Of course," she said. "That's up to you. I can live with it." She began to murmur into the phone, but a coughing spell from another room interfered with the signal. I could only catch snatches of her words, but I heard enough to know that she was most definitely planning to jump Jeff's bones the second he walked in the motel room.

"No," Tawny suddenly said loudly. I winced as the sound cut through the headphones. "We have to wait until we're absolutely certain everything clears the bank. Besides, I still have to put the backup plan in place." She paused. "One more night will be worth it. It's all worked out now. Just stay where you are. I'll call as soon as it's ready. We'll be together tomorrow. I promise." She was quiet again. "I know. But it will all be over soon."

I was surprised she was being cautious. How very unlike Tawny. Was she afraid of me? Or the cops? I felt a spark of pride. She might slam me, but she feared me. Even just a little.

"Mommy!" Tiffany's wail cut through the motel room like the scream of a banshee. I jumped, turned the volume down and waited.

"What!" Tawny screamed back, the phone forgotten, any pretense at softness gone. "Go back to sleep or I'll beat the shit out of you." She lowered her voice and whispered into the phone. "I'll call you in the morning."

"I want Daddy!" The child began to cry in earnest. "I'm scared."

"Forget your goddamn father," Tawny yelled. It sounded like she wasn't even bothering to get her ass out of bed. Child abuse while lounging. "Your father will be lucky if he ever gets out of jail again. They've thrown away the key. I'm all you've got. So you better get used to it. And you better start liking it."

Tiffany began to sob even louder.

"That's it," Tawny hollered at the top of her lungs, not caring who heard her. Her carelessness, I knew, was probably caused by cocaine and lack of sleep. "I'm sick to death of this shit. I warned you." I could hear the sounds of a chair being knocked over as she leaped from the bed.

I switched off the recorder, checked to make sure the Strayer-Voigt was properly loaded, then rolled the muscles in my shoulders to loosen them up. It was time to go in and get the girl. I had heard enough.

I reached the motel room in less than a minute. Tiffany was crying loudly on the other side of the door. Lights were flickering on in nearby rooms. The newly married couple had ceased their own argument long enough to eavesdrop on the one down the hall. I pounded loudly on Tawny's door. The crying stopped.

"Manager," I called out in a deep voice.

There was silence. I stepped back, away from the front window. When no one answered, I knocked again. There was a scrambling sound on the other side of the door and a light leaked through the gap in the curtains.

"Sorry about the noise," Tawny apologized from behind the door, her voice dripping peaches-and-cream. "My little girl's just having a nightmare. She's gone back to sleep."

But Tiffany was not cooperating in her mother's cover story. She resumed her crying. Loudly.

"Open up, miss," I bellowed, simultaneously knocking to disguise my voice.

"Oh, for godsakes," Tawny complained impatiently. The lock clicked and the door opened slightly. She spoke through a small opening, the deadbolt chain still firmly fastened. "Haven't you ever had kids stay here before?"

I shifted my weight, dipped my left shoulder and bulled my way inside with one hard push. The chain broke easily. Tawny was thrown back into the room. She stumbled over the chair and fell on the bed. I reached behind me, shut the door against prying eyes, and called out to Tiffany. "It's okay, honey. You can come out here. I'm going to take you home to your father."

The crying stopped abruptly.

Tawny lay on the bed, staring at me, her mouth hanging open. Her ivory negligee had less fabric than a handkerchief and she did nothing to cover herself.

"Hello there," I said pleasantly. "Fancy us meeting again like this."

"Fuck you." She kicked out a leg, even though I was at least six feet away. A spoiled brat throwing a hissy fit.

"You don't have anything on me. What the fuck is your problem?"

Her hair was falling out of a loose ponytail piled on top of her head and she hadn't bothered to remove her makeup before going to bed. Mascara leaked in dark rivulets beneath her puffy eyes and her lipstick was smeared. She looked like a skinny version of Bette Davis in *Whatever Happened to Baby Jane?*

"Over here, honey," I said, gesturing for Tiffany to join me. She had appeared in the doorway that linked her room with her mother's. Her face was solemn. "It's okay. I know your father. He's a friend of mine."

"Don't go near her," her mother screeched. "She'll hurt you, Tiff. She hates little girls. She'll shoot you. I know her. She's a bad woman."

The little girl stood in the doorway, frozen. I was struck again by her beauty. She was small for her age, almost ethereal, her face a tiny sculpted doll face, perfect in every way. Her skin was a pale gold that glowed in the dim lamplight. How could such an exquisite child have come from the body of an ungrateful bitch like Tawny Bledsoe?

"Your Mommy is sick," I explained to Tiffany. I kept my voice calm and resisted the temptation to pull my gun. It would only terrify her. "She needs help. If you come with me, I'll make sure some good people take care of your mommy. Your father would want you to come with me."

"Don't move," Tawny ordered when her daughter took a tentative step my way. "She's lying. Look at her. Does she look like a nice lady to you?"

Excuse me? So I wasn't exactly Glinda the Good Witch. Surely my size wasn't all that imposing to a child.

Tiffany took a step back, resuming her place in the doorway.

"It's over, Tawny," I said. "Let the kid go. You're sick. You're way into the coke. Look at you. You look like shit."

"You're one to talk," she snapped back, but her eyes slid to the mirror. She ran the back of her hand under her nose and sniffed, smearing her lipstick further in the process. "Why the fuck won't you leave me alone? What's it to you?"

Oh, just a small matter of using me to put an innocent man on death row, I thought, by taking advantage of my sense of fairness.

"I'm not going to discuss why I'm here in front of your daughter," I said out loud. "Just let me take her." When she didn't respond, I made a fast decision. Tawny was in worse shape than I thought. That meant she wouldn't be hard to find again. "If you let me take the girl, I'll let you go," I offered.

"Oh, yeah, sure," Tawny answered sarcastically. She scuttled back against the bed pillows, stretched out her legs and glared at me.

"It doesn't have to be a big deal," I lied. At that point I would have done anything to get the kid away from the broken human being that lay splayed on the bed, oblivious to all but her own impulses. "We want the same thing."

"Oh, really?" Tawny asked nastily. She hunched over, wrapping her skinny arms around her body. "Somehow I doubt that. You hate my guts. Think I don't know that? You'll never give it up. You're crazy."

I was crazy? Wasn't that the sociopathic slut calling the kettle black? Tiffany was watching with wide eyes. She had started to suck her thumb furiously.

"They say hate is the closest emotion to love," I said, acutely aware I was verbally tapdancing . I was talking too quickly and could only hope that Tawny was far enough gone to miss my nervousness. "Only a heartbeat separates the two emotions." I forced myself to smile. It was a painful process. It felt like my lips were peeling back from my teeth in a slow grimace.

Tawny was too plowed to care. Empty miniature rum bottles were lined up on the bedside table beside a row of crumpled Coke cans. She'd had to drink herself down from her drug high. She leered at me, let the thin strap of her teddy slide down one shoulder, then leaned forward, licking her lips.

"What's that supposed to mean?" she asked. "You're telling me this is all about you and me?"

God almighty, not in a thousand years. If I was going to walk on the wild side, it sure as hell would not be with the people-eating, used condom of a human being sniveling in front of me. But all I had to work with was Tawny's self-obsession, her belief that the whole world wanted to sleep with her—and her assumption that I was a closet dyke. A small mind and a big ego blinds a person. I could use it against her.

"You might say it's between you and me," I said, easing a step toward Tiffany. If I could get close enough, I'd grab her and head for the door.

"I thought I smelled that on you the first time we met." She smiled slyly at me and I resisted the temptation to pistol-whip the smirk off her face. "You were looking at me a little too much, know what I mean? I get that a lot, you know?" Tawny leaned back and opened her legs slightly. It was amazing, in a truly disgusting way. Her own daughter was watching and she was going to play the sex kitten. "You're not exactly my type, though," she added coyly.

Why not? I wondered to myself. Is it because I have an aversion to diseased swamp coots? So far, everything short of the family dog had been her type.

"What is your type?" I asked her, forcing myself to smile back. I had once given Bobby D. mouth-to-mouth resuscitation, I reminded myself, which meant I could do anything—including flirt with someone who made my skin crawl.

"Let's just say you're a little too macho for my tastes." Her giggle was ghastly, a parody of Scarlett O'Hara at the barbecue.

"Really?" I asked, inching toward Tiffany. "I thought you went in for macho. Haven't you been married four times? Or is it five?" When her face clouded over, I added quickly: "Maybe it's time you tried something different?"

"Like you?" she asked, running a hand through her hair, unconsciously rearranging it for me. Her tongue darted out to wet her lips.

"Maybe." I nodded toward Tiffany. The child was standing silently, perplexed, staring between me and her mother.

"It's not something I think we should go into detail about. Maybe after the kid is gone?" I tried out my cover story. "Come on. Let me take her. Her father's family is giving me a lot of money to find her and bring her back. I'll split it with you, if you let her go."

"How much?" Tawny asked, her eyes darting back and forth between me and Tiffany. She'd definitely been doing coke earlier in the evening, that much was evident in her jerky movements and frequent sniffles.

"Fifty thousand dollars," I said. "You can have half."

She thought it over. "That's if I sleep with you, right?"

The very thought made me want to reach for the penicillin, but I had to play the part. I shrugged. "It would certainly make me more inclined to view your case favorably."

She laughed. "You sound like a lawyer. Hey, remember that time you were hiding in the bushes at the beach, watching that loser Boomer beat up my ex?" Her face flushed, the memory exciting to her. "I passed by you in the car. Just inches away. Remember?"

"I remember."

"I could tell you wanted me then. I saw it in your eyes. You wanted to be the one kissing me, not Boomer. That's what this is all about."

I was almost close enough to grab the child. "If you want something, you have to go for it," I said. "Life's too short to pretend."

"Exactly." She leaned forward earnestly, then gestured to her daughter. "Come here, honey. Let me kiss you good-bye. This nice lady is going to take you home to your father."

"No," I shouted as the child darted toward Tawny.

I was too late. Tawny grabbed her daughter and pulled her onto the bed, then reached beneath a pillow and took out a cheap handgun. It was a Raven, probably bought off some lowlife in one of the Tampa dive bars.

"How stupid do you think I am?" she asked, her forearm locked against Tiffany's throat. The girl had gone mute with terror. "You'd fuck me and turn me in. You'd keep the money. You're no different than anyone else."

"Put the gun down," I said. "You win. I'll let you walk out of here right now."

"You're goddamn right you will."

Then she held the gun to her own daughter's head.

Panic clutched at my guts and I felt dizzy with over-whelming guilt. This was all my fault. I had misjudged Tawny's hatred and underestimated how much her addiction had poisoned her mind. And all of these mistakes had led us to this moment, face-to-face with this horror.

Please god, I prayed silently, don't let this little girl's death be on me.

It isn't often that I pray, god knows. But in that instant, the memories of a childhood spent on my knees in a coun-try church emerged to rescue me from my panic. The room seemed to grow still. Time stopped. Tawny and Tiffany froze in a silent tableau. I could feel my mother's touch on my shoulders, steadying me as I knelt on a roughhewn pew, reminding me to pay attention to the preacher man. And, feeling my mother's touch across the years since, I prayed like I had never prayed before. A calm rose in me, a cooling balm. I closed my eyes, welcoming the strength, and when I opened them again, I knew what to say.

"All I want is the girl," I told Tawny. My voice was low and soothing. "I'm going to sit down on that chair over there while you pack. Take everything you need. Clothes. Money. Car keys. Take my keys, too. So I can't follow you."

I had them on me, where were they? My jeans pocket. That was it. It held the keys to my apartment and my Porsche. She wouldn't know my car was two hundred miles away. "I'm going to reach into my back pocket," I explained. "And give you my car keys. That means I can't follow you. You'll be free. I'll have no way of knowing which way you went. Just leave the girl with me."

"She's my daughter," Tawny said angrily, the gun hov-ering inches from Tiffany's head. "I'll take her with me if I want to."

"Think of what you're saying. If you take her, you'll never be able to disappear. She's a beautiful child. Half black. Half white. She'll stand out anywhere. She'll make it easy for people to find you. The cops, the FBI, whoever. You'll never get far with her. But leave her with me and you get a free walk."

"A free walk?" Tawny repeated, hesitating. "You mean it? You'll sit there and let me pack and just drive away? You won't tell anyone where we met?"

"Yes," I promised. "All I want is the girl."

She pushed Tiffany facedown on the bed and my heart stopped. "Don't look up," she told her daughter. "Don't move until I've left the room."

Oh, god. I'd thought she was getting ready to shoot her. I took a slow breath and spoke again. My knees were wobbly. "Can I sit down in that chair?" I asked.

"Wait until I get closer," Tawny ordered, determined to show she was back in control. She crab-walked off the bed. "Sit down," she ordered, waving her gun.

I sat obediently. Bill's gun was tucked into the back of my jeans. If she looked away for long enough, I could grab it.

"Don't move," she warned. I froze.

Tawny pulled her suitcase from the closet with one hand, keeping the gun trained on me the entire time. No, I couldn't go for my gun. I couldn't risk gunfire in such a small room, not with Tiffany lying on the bed.

"It's too bad," Tawny said. She pulled a button-down shirt from the suitcase and slipped it over her teddy, one arm at a time. Her eyes never left me and the gun held steady. Coke jitters or not, she was determined to get away.

"What's too bad?" I knew that the only thing keeping her calm was her belief that she was in control.

"It's too bad we have to be enemies like this." She unconsciously ran her pointed tongue over her lips, wetting her contrived smile until it glistened. It reminded me of a snake flicking its tongue in warning. "We could have had some fun." She paused. "Even if only for a few hours."

Yeah, right. Until the hidden camera ran out of film. I didn't know what to say so I kept silent as she pulled on jeans and slipped her feet into a pair of flats.

Tiffany was still lying facedown on the bed. She was

too scared to cry. But a stain spread across the sheets beneath her. The poor kid had wet the bed.

"Give me your keys," Tawny ordered. She stuck the gun in my face. "Don't try anything funny."

Yeah, yeah, yeah. I'd seen that late-night movie, too. I reached into my back pocket with one hand and gave them to her without comment.

"Remember," Tawny said, slipping the keys into her pocketbook, "you owe me half of what you're getting for Tiffany. I intend to collect it one day. I know where you live. Cheat me and my friends will come after you."

What a load of grandiose coke-fueled bullshit. But I only nodded, her obedient servant. Just get her out of there so the kid would be all right.

"Count to one hundred," she ordered. She grabbed her suitcase with one hand, then held the gun high in the air and leaned in toward me. I flinched.

She kissed me full on the mouth and held it, the pressure hard though her lips were unexpectedly soft. I kept my mouth clamped shut, unwilling to let that darting tongue inside me.

She pulled away and laughed. "Just so you know what you're missing."

She was still laughing as she walked out the door.

I spit the taste of her onto the rug. I didn't want her poison inside me.

"Is she gone?" Tiffany asked, her voice a whisper.

"Yes." I picked the child up off the bed. She was so light it felt as if she might float away. I sat down and placed her in my lap, cuddling her, hoping to let her know that she was safe. She was wet and trembling, still too frightened to cry.

"Will she stay gone?" the child asked in a barely audible voice.

"Yes," I said. "And you'll never have to see her again if you don't want to."

TWELVE

"You did what?" Bobby was furious. "I told you not to go in alone."

"Keep it down, will you?" Fanny was in the backseat fussing over Tiffany. I'd had to fetch her from the car to change the girl's clothes. When the person I'm dealing with is under four feet tall, I'm in over my head and I know it.

Fanny had arrived in a burst of lilac-scented cooing, an experienced grandmother in full battle cry. Tiffany was washed and changed in a flurry of soft sounds while Bobby and I waited glumly. I'd had to change clothes myself, into a pair of none-too-clean pants. Despite that, I still smelled faintly like a wet diaper.

"Look," I pleaded in response to Bobby's angry silence. "Just take the girl to her aunt and tell her what happened, so she can get the kid professional help if needed. Leave me the recording equipment and the cell phone. I'll do the rest."

"Bad idea."

"She held a gun to her own daughter's head," I said. "What does that tell you about her? She'll do anything now to get her way. How many more people need to be hurt before someone puts her out of commission?"

"You won't even have a car if I leave," Bobby pointed out sensibly.

"I'll take Jeff's."

"What's he going to say about that?"

"Nothing. He won't get the chance. Now go, please. Get

the kid out of here. She's been through enough. Fanny will know what to do."

I glanced at the backseat, where Tiffany was nestled against Fanny's huge bosom, listening to some incredibly insipid story about a teeny-weeny mouse and a teeny-weeny paintbrush. It was making me just a teeny-weeny bit nauseous.

Had I ever been a kid? It sure didn't feel like it at that moment.

"I don't like your plan," Bobby said. "It stinks."

"For godsakes, Robert," Fanny interrupted. "Just get us out of here."

A command from his beloved was all it took. Bobby started the car. "Where to?" he grumbled.

"Drop me off at a corner near Jeff's motel."

"It's your funeral," he said grimly.

A few minutes later, I was standing near the entrance to South of the Border, knapsack nestled on my back and the Strayer-Voigt tucked into my waistband. There are certain advantages to tight pants. The Mexican carry is one of them.

I waved good-bye as the Cadillac turned onto the I-95 ramp. I knew no one was looking back at me, but I felt unexpectedly abandoned to see them go. Now I was really on my own. But the thought of dealing with Jeff calmed me. If I couldn't take on that no-good piss weasel man-to-man, then I had no business being in the business.

I was hiking past an all-night coffee shop when I saw them: the two men from the dark sedan, the ones who had been following me in Tampa. They were seated in a front window booth. There was no way I could mistake them. I'd been nose-to-nose with them the first time I'd seen them and had stopped to ask for bogus directions.

They had followed us all the way from Florida. What a joke that must have been. A giant pink Cadillac poking along an empty highway, stopping frequently for food and fuel. They could have done it blindfolded. Why hadn't I spotted them before we left the motel?

I had led them straight to Jeff.

But no, they must not know where he was, or they'd

have confronted him by now. And we had cruised all the motel parking lots, not just his, so maybe he was still safe. Had they seen me go into Tawny's room and assumed it was Jeff's? From where the two men sat, they could spot any car leaving the complex, heading north or south. And they had watched the pink Cadillac drive by without following. Which meant they either knew I wasn't inside—or didn't care.

I sat on a curb and thought it over. I had to revise my original plan. As much as I loathed my ex-husband, I pitied him more. I didn't want Jeff to be killed over something as stupid as drugs. I wanted him to live to be a wrinkled old man who can't get it up, one who gets rejected by the very girls he used to torture me with.

There was only one thing I could do. I stood up and walked straight toward the diner. They wouldn't kill me in front of a dozen witnesses.

Or would they? The one facing the door spotted me when I was halfway up the entrance stairs. He stopped chewing in mid-bite. He was the one I'd spoken to through the car window my first day in Tampa.

I was sitting beside him before he could swallow. "How are the burgers?" I asked, helping myself to a french fry. My heart pounded in my ears like a hurricane surf. I forced myself to smile anyway, swallowing my fear along with a tasteless french fry.

"They're okay," the second guy stammered, his eyes sliding to his companion.

"Shut up, Denny," the first man said. He turned to me and grinned in a parody of sincerity. "Your parents get on the road okay?"

"I don't know those people. I just hitched a ride north with them," I lied. "I didn't have enough money to keep my rental car, so they made the offer. If I helped drive, I could have a ride. They were picking up their granddaughter here and just trying to do me a favor."

"That's good," the first man said in a flat voice. "You could use some favors right now. You and that boyfriend of yours are in a lot of trouble."

So Jeff had told them the same lame story he'd foisted

on me, the one about a girlfriend taking off with his drugs. And they thought I was the girlfriend. I helped myself to another fry. "I guess you think I'm meeting Jeff here to give him back the stuff?"

The man named Denny looked around nervously at the mention of drugs. I felt a swish against my leg as his friend kicked him under the table. Nothing like having the respect of your colleagues.

"I guess we wouldn't have bothered to follow you for twelve goddamn hours if we'd had a joy ride in mind," the first man said. "I don't know what you two have been trying to pull, but the game is over. We know where Jones is staying, thanks to you, and as soon as we get done eating, we're going to have a little talk with him."

Maybe I could reason with them. "Let's speak hypothetically," I said. "You do know what that means?"

"Let's not be patronizing," Number One whispered back. "Or I'll blow your head off for dessert. You do know what that means?"

"No need to get violent. It was just a figure of speech." So much for reasoning.

"Well, figure this," Number One said. He nodded toward his companion and Denny pulled his sports coat to one side, revealing the butt of a gun tucked into his waistband.

I pretended to be scared. It wasn't hard. "You won't need that," I promised. "You want your drugs back, right?"

"That would be a good start," the first man said. "Money is always good, too."

"If I get you the drugs, will you leave Jeff alone?"

The two men exchanged glances. Both smiled at nothing.

"Sure." Denny's smile widened. "He'll be as safe as a babe in arms."

"What do you know about babes in arms?" Number One asked. He stuck a toothpick in his mouth and stared at the ceiling fan. "Return what belongs to us and then we'll talk."

"He's switched rooms," I said. "It's complicated. Give

me an hour and I'll bring the stuff back to you. Where can
we meet?"

Denny laughed. It was an ugly sound that made the
waitress glance at us, then quickly look away. "Aren't you
the woman in charge? What are you doing with a loser
like Jones?"

I'd asked myself the same question many a time, but I
didn't share my thoughts with him. "Wait here," I said.
"I'll be back in two hours."

"No." The first man took the toothpick from his mouth
and stabbed a french fry with it. "We'll meet you outside
the Red Burro. At half past one."

"That doesn't give me much time," I protested.

"Just do it."

I nodded and got the hell out of there.

I was afraid Tawny might have gone straight to Jeff's
room, but he was alone, sitting on the edge of the bed,
watching television. I could see him through a slit in the
curtains. His gut spilled over the waistband of his boxer
shorts. He had a Budweiser in one hand and was scratching
his crotch with the other. He belched and the low rumble
rose above the canned laughter of some mindless sitcom.
Heavens, how had I ever given up such a gem for the
single life?

I knocked on the door softly. "It's me," I whispered.
"Open up, sugar pie."

That man was dumber than a crab on a stick. He unlocked the door, chain and all. I was inside his room before
he knew it.

"You moron," I said.

He dropped his beer. It splattered across the carpet.

"Sit down and shut up," I told him. "And don't give me
any crap. I'm not in the mood."

He didn't move.

"You were expecting someone else?" I asked. "Someone
like Tawny Bledsoe?"

He stared at me and I could tell he was on something.
Downers, judging from the glazed look in his eyes, and
the inability of his brain to react.

"You're in over your head, Jeff. Way over your head.
You're being set up. You're going to get killed. The two
men who sold you the coke are here. About half a mile
away at a diner."

That penetrated his pharmacological fog. He sat back
down on the edge of the bed and began to moan. I pulled
a chair up so I was knee-to-knee with him. God, but he
looked awful. His skin was the color of uncooked dough
and mottled with red pinpricks from some sort of rash. He
hadn't shaved in a couple of days and his eyes were
rimmed in pink. His hair stuck out in clumps and he
smelled like a combination of sweat, tobacco and stale
beer. Mostly sweat.

"What the fuck is going on?" I asked. "This is your last
chance to tell me the truth. I'll try to save your ass, but
only if you tell me exactly what's going on."

Jeff isn't the kind of guy who can tell the truth easily.
But the mention of the two men in the diner had scared
him.

"How did they find me?" he asked.

I shrugged. I was admitting nothing. "Who knows?
Maybe Tawny told them."

He looked up. "No way. She doesn't even know them."

"Talk," I ordered him.

"I'm only trying to help Tawny out," he said miserably.
"If we can unload the bump, she'll have some money to
start over with. So will I. Her husband beats her, her kid
is terrified of him. The courts won't help. She's a really
nice person, you know. She let me stay at her apartment
in Raleigh."

"You mean her house."

"No, her apartment. Her husband got the house."

Okay, so now I knew how Tawny had gotten him to
break into her house: by lying, of course. And I also now
knew she had a love nest. I didn't know why.

"Keep talking," I told him.

"Can I have a beer?" His eyes focused on a cooler by
the television set. He quivered all over as he eyed it, like
a hound dog who's spotted roast beef.

"Allow me." I dredged a cold one up from the freezing

sludge in the bottom of the cooler and popped it open for him, then held it out of his reach. "What does Tawny have to do with the blow and those two dealers? Why is she here?"

He shook his head. "You've got it wrong. She has nothing to do with those guys. I didn't even know her at the time I ripped them off."

"What time?" I handed him the beer.

He gulped it gratefully. "When I fucked up and took the whiff."

"Tell me quick." I checked my watch. "I have exactly forty-two minutes left to save your ass."

"I meant to sell the stuff, I really did. I had a good record with them. Then I found out the cops were on to them. I was sure they'd get busted, and I'd be home free, with three kilos to sell just for myself."

"Whose 'them'?"

"Those guys." He evaded my eyes. He knew how disgusted I was that he had graduated into being a full-blown dealer. "And I did unload almost a third of it."

That would be nearly a kilo's worth, I thought. He probably did have enough friends left to sell that much coke, if you can call drug buddies "friends." I'd rather have lunched with Jeffrey Dahmer than hung out with stone-cold junkies.

"What about the rest of it?" I asked. "What the hell happened?"

"Well, there was this ball game . . ." he began.

"Oh, god, Jeff." I was disgusted. "You bet it all on a basketball game?"

He was indignant. "The Jazz are really good this year. It was a lock. There was no way they were going to—"

"Stop." I held up a hand. "How much did you lose?"

"Twenty-five thousand dollars," he whispered.

"Jesus, Jeff." I let out a long breath. That was more than enough to kill someone over. "So you traded the second kilo to your bookie to cover the debt?"

He nodded miserably.

"Why did you come to Raleigh to see me?"

"I knew I was in big trouble. I spent the money from

the first kilo, I don't really know where it went. Then I traded away the second. All I had left was one kilo, and I owed those guys sixty-six thousand dollars. I didn't know what else to do. I thought you might be able to think of something." He looked up, his old tricks rising to the surface. "You were always smarter than me, Casey. And I figured I could stay with you until I got on my feet and then maybe we could—"

"You thought the person that spent a year and a half in prison because of you would welcome you with open arms?" I asked. "And help sell your drugs?"

"Ah, Honey Bunny, you know you're an old softie."

"Jeff," I said earnestly, putting my hand on his knee. "If you call me Honey Bunny one more time, I'm going to plug you myself."

He turned white at the joke. "They want to kill me, right?"

"Yes. Slowly and with much pain. Now, how did you meet Tawny and what does she have to do with the drugs?"

"I met her outside your office that day. Her car wouldn't start."

Yeah, right. She'd looked him over during his pathetic pick-up attempt, known he was an easy mark and pounced on him when he proved dumb enough to have hung around for her to leave my office.

"What did you say to her when you first met her at my front door? Think hard. It's very important."

He shrugged. "I asked her what the other guy looked like. Remember, she was all beat up? And then she said I didn't look so hot myself."

"And you said?"

"I said my ex-wife had just given me the deep freeze, so I probably felt worse than she did."

So Tawny had known from the start that Jeff was my ex-husband. It had been personal all along.

"What else?" I demanded.

"I told her I needed a place to stay, and said that maybe we could help each other out. I offered to watch her back, you know, keep the guy who had beat her up away from her, in exchange for her giving me a place to stay. But she turned me down. She said she could take of herself."

That was the understatement of the century.

"What did you talk about when you were fixing her car?"

"I told her again that I needed a place to stay, and asked if she wouldn't think about changing her mind. I didn't tell her why I needed a place, but I was low on cash and afraid to stay at a motel and use a credit card. I knew those guys were going to come after me. I didn't want to leave a trail."

"How clever. They parked themselves outside your mother's house instead."

He looked down at the floor.

"That's right," I said, unwilling to let him off the hook. "You pulled your own mother into your scummy drug activity."

He didn't say anything.

"When did you tell Tawny about the drugs?"

"After I'd been at her place for a couple of days. She wasn't even staying there. Just stopping by. Sometimes she'd ask me to leave for a couple of hours and I'd go shoot pool or something. Once I got back to the apartment and she was still there, in a really good mood. I could tell she'd been partying."

Oh, yeah? I wondered to myself. Where the hell was her kid while she was lounging around her love pad?

"And so you pulled out your remaining kilo and generously offered her more?" I knew Jeff would never be able to resist a chance to play the big man.

He nodded miserably. "I didn't show her how much I really had, but she must have found out."

"Like she didn't go through everything you owned the minute you weren't around? You bonehead."

He stared at his feet. "She told me she knew some people who could unload the bump for me. I said I'd give her part of the profit if she'd help me sell it. I can't do it on my own. I can't go back to Florida, and I don't know anyone in North Carolina. I couldn't take the chance of selling to strangers." He looked at me accusingly. "You wouldn't help me. What was I supposed to do?"

"That's right," I agreed. "It's all my fault."

He missed my sarcasm. "She seemed to know what she was talking about," he said. "I thought she could help me sell it."

"Believe me, she does know what she's talking about. She's on a first-name basis with every scumbag within the state lines. Is that why you're here? To sell the stuff?"

He nodded and gulped from his beer. "I'm supposed to meet her here and then we're going to take the last kilo and unload it in Lumberton. We'll split the difference. Then she goes her way and I go mine."

"Don't insult my intelligence, Jeff," I said patiently. "You think you're going to ride off with her into the sunset, don't you? Come on. Give it up. She's the queen of blow jobs. Think I don't know that? But what you don't know is that it's all part of setting you up. She killed that man in Raleigh, and she is going to blame it on you if it doesn't work to blame it on her husband. Can't you see what she's really like? How did she explain those blackmail photos to you? The ones you stole from her safe?"

He got angry. "Her husband was having her followed by some sleazy detective and I was just stealing the photos back for her."

"Take it from this sleazy detective, it's not often I get an assignment where the cheating spouse is screwing two dozen different people. Didn't that seem a bit odd to you?"

"What's wrong with being open about your sexuality?" He sounded prim, like some phony radio shrink.

"Tawny isn't just open about her sexuality, she never closes. She's the Circle K of sex." I sighed. "Were you the one who called a woman named Francine and demanded more blackmail money?"

"That wasn't blackmail," he protested angrily. "She owed Tawny a commission on some property. It was money rightfully earned."

"Oh, Jeff." I shook my head again, amazed at his gullibility. "When are you supposed to see her next?"

"We're meeting tomorrow. Here."

"What's going down at the bank?"

He stared at me blankly.

"She talked about letting something clear at the bank. Are you stealing checks with her? Has she gotten you involved in that?"

"I don't know what you're talking about," he said sullenly. He drained the rest of his beer and crumpled the can, then tossed it toward the trash. He missed. It hit the TV stand with a clank and rolled across the carpet.

I let my last question go. I'd find out soon enough. "Are you the one who told her I was in Tampa?"

He stared at his bare feet. They were filthy and callused. "I didn't even know you were there, until I called home a couple days ago. You scared the shit out of my mom. Thanks a lot."

"Good. She needs scaring." I scrutinized his face, trying to decide if he was telling the truth or lying to me. "So you never called Tawny when she was staying underground?"

"I didn't say that," he admitted. "She called me and gave me her number. I tried to call back a couple of times, you know, to make sure she was okay. But she was never there."

"You never talked to her once while she was in hiding?"

"Only the one time she called me and gave me her number."

"When's the last time you talked to her at all?" I asked.

He looked uncomfortable. "She called Mom yesterday and asked how to get in touch with me. Mom gave her my number here at the motel. Then Tawny called me and told me to wait here for her."

I wondered if that had been before or after we left Clarissa's house. I also wondered why Jeff would not admit he'd talked to Tawny just a couple of hours ago. But I didn't have enough time to beat the truth out of him. It would have to wait. "Where are the drugs?" I asked.

"Why?" He started to get up, changed his mind, and sat back down.

"Jeff," I explained. "Listen to me very closely. You may think this woman is your friend. You may think you're going to sell your coke and ride off with her, or her on you, or whatever, for a happy life in California. But you are being set up, my friend. She's using you to take the fall in case the cops nab her."

"What are you talking about? It's not her fault her husband blew her boyfriend away."

I shook my head. "Your brain cells are blown. Think about it. How many hints did she drop to you about her boyfriend? Come on, tell me the truth. She probably said Boomer Cockshutt abused her, threatened her, was harming her kid. Just like her husband did. Didn't she?"

Jeff looked away. "People get stuck in patterns," he mumbled.

"Jeff, she was trying to get *you* to kill Cockshutt," I explained. "And when you didn't take the bait, she went to Plan B and killed him herself." I paused. "At least I hope she did. Please tell me you didn't kill him, Jeff."

"No way!" He shot up from the bed and began to pace the room. "I'm scared of guns, Casey. You know that."

What I knew was that he didn't have the balls to kill anyone. He was either too doped up—or too lazy—to hold a grudge.

"Sit down," I said.

He sat. "Why would she want to kill her boyfriend, anyway?" he asked. "All she had to do was walk away from him."

That was a good question. I didn't have an answer for it. I wondered if I ever would.

"Just give me the coke," I said patiently. "Or I'll tear this place apart looking for it."

"Why should I give you anything?"

"Because if you don't, those two junior goombahs sitting half a mile away will come over here and get what's left for themselves. They aren't going to be happy you gambled away or spent the rest of their product and they'll probably blow your brains out. What little you have. That's why."

"They don't know where I am."

"Guess again. Give me the coke. Now. And then I'm going to drop you off on I-95. You can hitchhike back to Raleigh. Meet me in my office in a couple of days. I'll help you get away and start over someplace else."

"They'll find me," he said. "There's no place I can go."

"They won't find you," I promised. "Leave it to me."

"What do you mean, you'll drop me off on I-95?"

"I'm taking your car. Now get dressed and let's go."

In the end, he dragged a sorry-looking brick of coke out from beneath the bed, stuffed it in a plastic bag and handed it to me. While he dressed, I wiped all fingerprints from the thick film wrapped around the kilo and dropped it back into the plastic bag. God, how I hated that shit. How many people's lives would be ruined by it? I wasn't talking about the junkies, either, I'd long since ceased to care about their sorry asses. I was talking about their parents, children, lovers, sisters, brothers. Everyone paid the price but the loser who was stuffing it up his or her nose. Well, this was one kilo going nowhere but straight to the evidence locker. Not if I could help it.

Jeff came out of the bathroom, shaved, dressed and looking enough like a human to give him a chance of hitching a ride along I-95.

He didn't say a word the entire time it took for me to drive him to the entrance ramp. The two men were gone from the diner. I made Jeff crouch in the backseat anyway.

"She was going to set you up," I said again as he got out of the car.

He slammed the door in reply.

When I got back to his motel room, I sat for a few moments, trying to think of a way to make what I was about to try less dangerous. The best I could do was let someone else know where I was—in case it all went bad. I didn't want to leave a trail on Jeff's motel phone, so I pulled out the cellular and called Bill's apartment. His answering machine picked up. I hung up, pressed the redial button, and tried again. Still the machine. I redialed one more time without success, and finally gave up. If he hadn't stumbled from bed yet, the guy was either busy or deep in dreamland. My money was on dreamland. I'd done enough damage to keep him celibate for the next three years.

There was no point in calling Burly. He was my boy-friend, not a police officer. All he'd be able to do was worry. I needed someone who could act.

The thing was, I was a little low on friends in the department. That's the trouble with a love-'em-and-leave-'em policy—it makes it tough to find a partner when the time comes to dance. My one other sure contact was on a leave of absence, and she wouldn't be back for months. In the end, I called Bill again and left a garbled message about what I was about to do.

I thought about not going through with my plan, but thinking about holding back is as far as I ever go when it comes to holding back. Besides, I had to bring the cops into this, not for the dealers but for Tawny. It was the only way to make sure she was kept in custody while I tracked down evidence that she killed Cockshutt. I knew the cops would never arrest her on an out-of-state misdemeanor warrant. But they would if they found her sitting around a motel room with a bunch of big-time drug dealers—and a kilo of cocaine on the premises. All I had to do was get Tawny and the dealers together, then make a call.

The dangerous part was getting away after getting them together.

I hid Jeff's car behind the abandoned building I'd seen earlier and hiked to our meeting place.

Both men were sitting with their backs to the front door of the Red Burro bar, seemingly unconcerned about any-thing but the highballs in front of them.

"Right on time," Number One said. "Like a good little girl."

"I'm in trouble." I leaned in close, brushing his elbow. "Jeff double-crossed me. He was planning to dump me all along. He just used me to hold the stuff for a while. He took off with some other woman a few minutes ago."

The first man picked up his drink and took a sip. "That's a pretty lousy cover story," he said.

"It's not a cover story." I sat next to him and looked scared. We were the only people in the Red Burro except for a hefty woman who was wiping down the far end of the counter, and a group of bored men watching late night television from a table. Probably golfers headed for Myrtle Beach.

"I thought you were smarter than that," Number One said. "Try again."

"It's the truth!" I did my best to sound close to tears. "She's crazy. I know her from Tampa. She chased me down a few nights ago in a white Corvette. She was firing a gun out the window like a maniac. Blew some bystander off the road."

"Hey," the second guy said, excited. "She's telling the truth. We ought to—"

"Shut up, Denny," Number One ordered.

I flung the plastic bag that held the kilo onto the bar. It hit the surface with a clunk. "I grabbed this from them and ran."

"Jesus Christ." Number One swiveled his body away from the package like it was a bomb.

"I was able to get part of it out of his duffel bag while he was in the bathroom. He'll kill me when he finds out," I whispered. "And she'll help."

"Get that fucking thing off the bar," Number One said.

I stashed it back in my knapsack and acted eager to help. "Look, I know what car she's driving now," I offered. "I saw her in it a few minutes ago, driving by. It's a Saturn and I got the license plate number. I bet she stole it for him. He called her when he thought I was in the bathroom. They're meeting tonight. He said he could be at her room in twenty minutes so she must be staying nearby."

I knew Tawny had to be staying close enough to meet Jeff in the morning, but I didn't know where. I had to get these guys to help me find her.

"Be where in twenty minutes?" Number One sounded monumentally bored. But his eyes slid to the knapsack at my feet and I knew I had him.

"I don't know. We can find out by cruising around. You have to help me. When Jeff finds out I took some of his stash, he's going to kill me."

Denny snorted, like the idea of Jeff Jones killing anyone was absurd.

"It's not funny," I protested. "I brought part of what he stole back to you, in good faith. You owe me the chance to prove it wasn't my idea to rip you off."

"We don't have to do anything so far as you're concerned," Number One said. He stood up. "Let's go."

I'd hope to trail them out the door so I could orchestrate a fade after giving them Tawny's license plate number, but it was no go. Denny hopped off his stool and sandwiched me in. I had no choice but to follow the leader out.

Number One opened the backseat of the sedan. "Get in."

"What do you need me for? I'll give you the license plate number. You can take it from there."

"Get in," he repeated, and though his inflection barely changed, the command made my throat go dry. The guy wasn't scary because he sounded angry or pissed, he was scary because he sounded like he didn't care at all.

I slid into the car. It smelled like leather. New seats. Luxury interior. It wasn't the same car Bill Butler had drilled with bullets. But it probably held the same guns they returned fire with, I thought nervously.

Neither man considered me a threat. They let me keep my knapsack and didn't bother to search me. They just climbed in the front, acting bored.

"Let's see it again," Number One said.

I pulled the plastic bag from my knapsack and slid the kilo out onto the front seat between them.

"For fuck's sake," Denny complained, taking off his coat and throwing it over the kilo. "How conspicuous can you get?"

He mispronounced "conspicuous," but somehow I didn't think it was the right time for a vocabulary lesson.

Number One was silent, thinking. He stared at me in the rearview mirror. I forced myself not to look back. I didn't know what he was thinking, but just the fact that he was thinking made me sweat.

"What makes you think he took off with some other bitch?" Number One finally asked. Well, he's half-right, I thought philosophically.

"I told you, he was talking to her on the phone. I was in the bathroom, washing my face. After he hit me." I sniffled for effect. "The water was running. He thought I couldn't hear him. But I was listening at the door."

"You were listening at the door?" Denny asked skeptically.

"Damn right I was." I tried to sound indignant. "I knew something was up. Jeff acted all funny when I got back to the room. I told him you had promised to let us off the hook if we returned everything, but he just looked at me like I was too stupid to bother with."

"Makes sense," Denny offered. "The jerk still doesn't want to give it up. I'm tired of tracking his ass. Let's go in and take care of it."

"Shut up, Denny." The first guy was silent for a minute. "Give me the license plate number."

I reached into my pocket and pulled out the scrap of paper with the license plate number of the car Tawny had "borrowed" on it.

"Florida plates," Denny said. "He had another bitch stored down there. She probably waltzed right past us."

The first man had started to tap the steering wheel with one of his cuff links. The sound was driving me nuts.

"This is the deal," he said, twisting the ignition key. The sudden sound of the engine startled me. "We'll go looking for Jones and this new bimbo he's with. We'll give you half an hour, maybe a little more. But only because you brought us this present." He tapped the kilo. "Denny, get this out of the front seat."

"Put it in the trunk?" Denny asked.

Number One stared at him. "No, Denny. Shove it up your ass." Denny stared at him seriously, as if calculating circumference, enthusiasm and length. "Yes, put it in the trunk," Number One finally said.

Denny scrambled from the car and Number One pounded his head gently against the steering wheel.

"Good help is hard to find," I said. I was just trying to establish rapport.

He turned around and glared at me. "You better not be lying to us, lady."

"Why would I bother to bring you a kilo of coke if I was lying? I could have taken off with it. I came to you, remember?"

He didn't say anything, so I launched into an in-character lament. "Hey," I said angrily. "I'm the victim here. I thought Jeff loved me. He told me just to hold the stuff for him for a few weeks until we could split it. He didn't tell me he'd stolen it from you guys. He was using me. I hate him as much as you do."

"Oh, yeah?" Number One asked dryly. "Funny. He told us you had stolen the stuff and that's why he was in a bind."

"Well, he would say that, wouldn't he? The lying, cheating, no-good, dirty scumbag of a—" I launched into a word-for-word repeat of one of Tawny's more colorful character descriptions. Number One listened in impassive silence until Denny rejoined us in the car.

"What's the matter?" Number One asked his partner. "Get your dick caught in the trunk?"

"Good thing it's not a compact," I chimed in.

Denny began to laugh. "Hey, get it? Compact? It wouldn't be *big* enough." One thing about guys, they'll always laugh at a joke that depicts them as larger than life.

"Shut up, Denny," Number One said as he pulled out from the parking lot. "One idiot to a car is more than enough."

"Hey, where are we going?" I asked. "Let me out. I did my duty."

"You gotta be kidding," Number One said.

"No, I'm not kidding." And I wasn't. This wasn't part of the deal. They didn't need me. They had Tawny's license plate number and a description of her car. And I needed out of their car, so I could sic the cops on all three of them.

There was no response from the front seat.

"Let me out or I'll jump," I threatened.

"Go ahead." Number One accelerated. The car sped up to fifty miles an hour.

"That's smart. Get stopped by the cops with a kilo in your trunk."

Number One slammed on the brakes and the car screeched to a halt. He sat for a moment, hands locked on the steering wheel. I didn't like the silence.

"Listen to me, you dumb bitch," he said quietly. "You're

not getting out of this car. And if we can't find your boyfriend, we'll settle for sending him a message through
you."

"He doesn't care about me. Killing me won't make him
feel bad."

"No, but it will make me feel better." Number One
pulled away again while Denny laughed dutifully at his
joke.

I began to wonder how the hell I would ever get out of
this one. Ten minutes later, I was still wondering.

"Okay," Number One said sourly. "That's every motel
in this entire shithole. No car matching this supposed car.
How does that make me feel?"

"Thorough?" I suggested. No one laughed. "She
wouldn't be stupid enough to stay right next door. She's
probably staying somewhere nearby." God, how I hoped
that I was right.

So did Number One. He looked at his watch. "Let's
hope you're right."

Denny pulled a cellular phone from his pocket and
started to dial.

"What are you doing?" Number One asked, irritated.

"I've got a lot riding on the Lakers game. I'm just calling in to check—"

"Hang up the phone," Number One ordered.

Denny quickly folded it up and stowed it away—but it
gave me an idea.

I waited a moment until Number One's attention was
back on the highway. Then I slipped the cellular phone
out of my knapsack. I didn't want to pull out the gun. Not
when it was two against one. And not when my only op-
tion was to blow one of their heads off, then duck and
pray. When it comes to wholesale carnage, I'll pass every
time.

I held the phone upside down, close to my leg, so the
glow of the LED would not give it away. I'd read a newspaper article a couple of months ago about a woman and
her baby who'd been kidnapped when some yo-yo stole
their car. She'd called the cops on her cellular phone and
kept an open line long enough to signal her whereabouts.

If it had worked for her, it might work for me. But calling 911 cold was useless. They'd have no clue as to what was going on.

Only Bill would know what to do. What the hell was his number?

The redial button. Bill was the last number on it. Shit, which one was it? I closed my eyes and mentally relived those moments in the hotel room. Think, I ordered myself. You were sitting in a chair, you reached for the phone, you dialed, you hung up, you tried again. Your finger is reaching for the—

First button on the left. Top of the row. That had to be it.

I faked a cough and pressed the button. The LED flickered slightly. I held it lower. Please god, don't let them hear Bill's voice on the other end.

"Where are we going?" I asked loudly, after letting enough time pass for Bill's answering machine to pick up and start recording. Both men jumped when I spoke. "Sorry, didn't mean to scare you. I just wondered why we were heading west. I mean, there's not much west of South of the Border. Get it? Get the joke?"

I was prattling, trying to let Bill know where I was and that I needed help.

They ignored me. "Look, I've been along Route 9 a zillion times," I said. "There's hardly any motels on it."

"What are you?" Denny asked. "An expert on motels?" He leered at me. "I bet you are intimately familiar with mattresses from here to Maine."

"Excuse me," I said. "South of the Border is about as racy as I get." I saw a town sign ahead. "What the hell are we doing in Petrie? There's nothing here but a bunch of old farmers."

"Shut up," Number One said. "Or I'll have Denny pistol whip you."

Denny looked alarmed at the suggestion.

"You wouldn't really pistol whip me, would you?" I asked. Hear that, Bill? We're talking pistol whipping. And that's just for starters.

"No," Number One admitted. "I wouldn't risk cracking

my gun on that rock hard head of yours. Just shut up and sit back."

"I can't shut up," I explained in a pleading voice. "It's my worst habit. Jeff says I talk too much. The bastard. He was always telling me what was wrong with me. I want you to find him and kill him. You don't know what he's done to me. He promised me we'd get married and now he's run off with some bitch named Tawny. Who has a name like that anyway? Tawny. What a joke." I raised my voice on her name. If Bill Butler was listening and didn't grasp the implications of that one, he was too dumb to help me.

"If we find him, will you cut me some slack?" I asked. "Give me some credit for returning that kilo and helping you find him and his new girlfriend? We could call it even. Just let me walk away." I was too near hysteria for them to pay much attention to what I said. They'd tuned me out.

"There's nothing here," Denny said. "Maybe we ought to try the eastern road."

"Yeah," I agreed eagerly. "Let's look on Route 9 over toward Dillon. I think there's some cheap motels near the . . ." I searched for a plausible story. ". . . the railroad tracks." Hey, when you come from the wrong side of them, they're never far from your mind.

"How do you know?" Denny asked. "You from around here?"

"Shut up with the small talk," Number One ordered. But he pulled a U-turn and headed back the other way.

"U-turns are illegal on Route 9," I said. Get it, Bill. "It's no joke. South Carolina cops are murder. They'll write you a ticket for jaywalking."

Both men ignored me. The car picked up speed. "This Lumina's got pretty good pickup," I said. "What is it, last year's?"

"You a fucking car enthusiast?" Number One asked. "What the hell do you care what my car is?"

"I care about the color," I said. "I'm a girl, remember?"

"Oh yeah?" His voice was sarcastic. "Well, this is charcoal gray, so don't get your panties in a twist."

"I like charcoal gray," I protested. "It's so . . . classic."

Thanks dickhead, for letting Bill know it was a charcoal gray late model Lumina heading east on Route 9 somewhere near South of the Border.

"There's South of the Border again," I said as we sped past the complex. We kept going on the small southeast-to-west highway that traverses I-95.

"I can do without the fucking travelogue," Number One muttered.

I shut up. I could afford to now. The connection was still open. I'd keep it open. It was my only chance.

"Can we turn on the radio until we get there?" I asked. I wanted to mask any sounds from the other end of the line.

"Get where?" Number One asked sourly. "You've got fifteen minutes left."

"They have to be at a motel between here and Dillon. It makes sense. Except for South of the Border, there are no other motels for sixty miles either way you go on I-95. So this new bitch of his must be staying somewhere on Route 9. If she's nearby and she's not in the other direction, then she has to be staying—"

"Shut up," Number One ordered again.

I sat back and waited. Eight very long minutes later, the glow of a small town appeared up ahead.

"Street lights," I announced. "I didn't even know there was a town between South of the Border and Dillon." We passed a small road sign. "Taylorsville," I said. "There's probably three people who live here: Taylor, Taylor and Taylor."

"Denny," Number One said, "if she keeps it up, shoot her."

"In the car?" Denny asked, appalled. "You said we'd take good care of it if I let you—"

"Shut up, Denny," Number One ordered angrily.

"There's a motel!" I shouted, relieved. "See? The Rainbow Lodge. God, what a tacky sign. You'd think they could come up with something besides a leftover sixties rainbow."

"Quit screaming in my fucking ear!" Number One

yelled. "I'm not blind. I see it. You're really starting to
piss me off with your motor mouth."

I didn't care. I was living on hope, getting my energy
from a fantasy unfolding in my head. Bill had to be on the
other end of the line. He had to be.

"Come on," I urged, "let's check the Rainbow Lodge."

"This is a waste of time," Number One muttered. But
he pulled into the gravel parking lot. Three cars were
parked in front of a low, redwood building.

The car on the far end was Tawny's.

"Holy Christ," Denny said, staring at it. "The bitch was
telling the truth."

"It's her car," I said. "I told you. She's inside with Jeff,
right now. I know she is. They have the rest of your
drugs." If I could get them to go inside, I could slip away
and call the cops.

"There is someone inside with her," Denny added.
"Could be Jones."

"There is?" The words were out before I could stop
them. "How can you tell?"

"Look," he said, pointing to the window. "It's better
than a peep show."

Sure enough, a light shining at the back of the motel
room perfectly silhouetted a slender figure bent over someone on the bed, creating a pornographic puppet show
through the curtains.

"Nice body," Denny pointed out. "Let's break in now
while she's naked."

"Shut up, Denny," Number One said automatically. "I
need to think."

I was too upset to argue. Jeff was even stupider than I
thought. He had hitchhiked back the other way. He had
met Tawny after all. How had he gotten through to her?
He must have known where she'd gone when I ran her out
of her own room. I was so stupid. All he'd had to do was
thumb a ride to a phone and call her. And now they were
having some sort of celebratory boink to commemorate
their victory over me. Oh, god. They'd kill Jeff for sure.
Not even the thought that he'd go while doing the one
thing in the world he was half-decent at calmed me. If he

died, it would be my fault. Well, his really, for being so utterly stupid in the first place, but his blood would still be on my hands.

"We're going in," Number One announced. "Together."

"All of us?" Denny asked, his eyes shifting to me.

"Yes, all of us." Number One was annoyed again. "What the fuck were you planning to do with her while we went inside? Leave her in the car to steal the stuff again and cut out on us? Jesus, Denny. You're dumber than dog shit."

Denny was pissed. It was one insult too many. "Look, we're going to have our hands full with the two of them in there. And now I got to keep an eye on her?"

"We'll manage," Number One said dryly. "Come on. Stop yapping. Let's go." He retrieved something from under the seat, slipping it inside his overcoat. I didn't like it, but I had no time to figure out what it was. They were reaching for their car doors. I bent down quickly. I had five seconds at the most.

"Please tell me you're there," I whispered into the cellular phone.

"Casey?" Bill's voice came back, and relief washed through me. It felt like every blood cell in my body stood up simultaneously to sing the Hallelujah Chorus. "I've called the sheriff on my cellular," he said. "I'm going to keep this line open. Stall them if you can. Don't go inside."

"No time," I started to explain, but could say no more. Both men were stepping from the vehicle and closing their doors. I left the connection open, face down on the floor of the backseat beside my knapsack, and climbed out of the car to join my captors.

"How are we going to do this?" I asked. "That door looks solid." Both men automatically checked the door of the room, then stared at me.

"What?" I asked.

"How are we going to do this?" Number One mimicked. "You think this is the fucking A-Team or something?"

"Hey," the second guy said. "That's funny. The Fucking-A Team. Get it?"

"Shut up, Denny."

"I was just trying to be helpful," I said.

"Use her as a battering ram," Number One told Denny.

"Forget it," I said. "I don't want to be that helpful."

They dragged me to the motel door. Heavy breathing and soft moans came from inside the room. Talk about a big surprise. I had a feeling that once we burst in, I was going to witness yet another wet bed that night.

"What do you want me to do? Just shove her through the door?" Denny asked.

"I was kidding, you fucking moron." Number One pushed him out of the way, raised his right leg, gave the door a full body kick, bounced back, crouched low and then threw his entire body against it. The cheap lock broke from the frame and the door opened partway. Only the chain held it closed.

Denny took his cue from his partner and threw himself against the door. He crashed through more easily than he'd expected and his momentum sent him running straight across the room toward a bed pushed up against the far wall. Both figures had disappeared under the sheets by the time we got the door open. They looked like two ghosts popping up in surprise at the sound of the crash.

Number One shoved me inside and threw me against a side wall. I slid to the floor, acutely aware that there was a .40-caliber semi-automatic pointed straight down at my ass with a clearance of maybe one inch. I eased Bill's gun from my waistband and slid it beneath the television cabinet where I could reach it fast, if I needed it.

Denny landed on the bed, pinning the occupants beneath him. A flurry of screams and shouts erupted. Sheets flew about. Bodies wrestled. High-pitched cursing filled the room—Tawny in full battle cry.

Then Number One pulled a TEC-9 out of the inside of his jacket. I almost threw up when I saw it. It held enough rounds to make hamburger of us all. Number One was the real thing after all. "Shut up everyone and get up against the wall," he yelled at the figures under the sheets. "Top of the bed. Now."

I shrank back, trying to disappear into the wallpaper.

Bedclothes shifted, heads appeared and bodies scrambled to take up a position against the head of the bed. Denny extricated himself from the sheets and tumbled to the floor, panting. "Shit," he said, amazed. "There's two of them."

Crouched against the wall, contorted faces lit by the glow of the lights beaming in the open door, cowered Tawny Bledsoe and Amanda Cockshutt, Boomer's not-so-grieving widow.

"That's not Jeff," I offered, pissed at myself for missing it. Amanda Cockshutt caught between the sheets with Tawny Bledsoe? It explained everything: motive, the warning phone calls, insurance money clearing the bank. It had been so obvious, but I had let my fears for Jeff interfere with my thinking. God, I would never stop paying the price for having married him.

"What the fuck are you doing here?" Tawny screeched when she spotted me. "Who the hell are you guys? What's that bitch doing here?"

Number One silenced Tawny by walking forward and sticking the barrel of the TEC-9 into her mouth. Amanda Cockshutt moaned, grabbed the edge of a sheet and pulled it up to her shoulders. Her body trembled and she looked like she was fighting hard not to cry.

"Where's the rest of it?" Number One asked. He raised the gun barrel a couple of inches, tilting Tawny's head upward. "Or did you store it all up your nose?"

It was a professional guess. Tawny looked like she'd been snorting Peruvian speed bumps a dozen at a time: she was pale-faced, runny-nosed and jumpy. Number One recognized a problem user when he saw one. I didn't need to try and bury Tawny, just the way she looked said it all. Poetic justice. Number One was convinced she was in it with Jeff.

"Where's the rest?" he repeated. "Where's Jones?"

"I don't know what the fuck you're talking about," Tawny mumbled. That woman had steel balls. A gun in her mouth and she could still sound scornful.

Where the hell were the cops?

"Tie up the other one," Number One ordered Denny, letting the TEC-9 drop to his side.

Denny grabbed Amanda Cockshutt by the arm and dragged her from the bed. She was too scared to resist. Her naked body hit the carpet with a thud.

"Get up," Denny told her, staring at her breasts.

Amanda looked to me for help.

I shrugged. "You sleep with the devil, you wake up in hell," I reminded her.

"Don't you dare talk to her that way," Tawny hissed at me. "This isn't over yet, you interfering bitch. Just you remember this: *I know where the old man lives.*"

The room became a vacuum, as if all the air had been sucked from it in an instant. A roaring filled my ears. I could feel my heart pounding in my chest.

"What did you say?" I asked, oblivious to anything but her contorted face. Her tongue darted out again, pointed and pink, like some separate animal that lived inside her mouth. She touched its tip to her lips and smirked.

"I said I know where the old man lives," she said softly. "Jeff told me. The last person left in your family. Boo hoo. And I'm going to make you sorry you ever met me."

I lost it. The roaring in my ears gave way to the buzzing of a million bees. A hard heat exploded in my chest. I went for her, hands outstretched. I leaped across the room, shoving Number One to one side, focused only on grabbing her throat and throttling her into silence.

"Hey!" one of the men shouted, but I was beyond stopping. I didn't care if they shot me, I was going to choke the words from her filthy mouth and make her eat them. She dodged and I missed her throat, but I got part of her ponytail and pulled her across the bed toward me. My fist went back and I put all 170 pounds behind it, smashing it into her nose while holding her in place by her hair. I felt the cartilage crunch beneath my knuckles. She screamed, enraged, and came at me, fingernails slashing. I caught her wrist and threw her down on the mattress, then straddled her and started to pummel. Blood was gushing from her nose, running down her chest, staining my jeans. I hit her again, hard, hating that mouth. I had seen her smirking at me one too many times.

"Knock it off," Number One shouted, but it didn't slow

either one of us down. Tawny was wiggling beneath me, hissing and spitting, trying to grab at my hair. I kneed her hard in the groin and she didn't even flinch. Calluses, I expect. I was about to rip her ponytail off her head when Denny grabbed my arm, clamping down with surprising strength. He dragged me away from Tawny.

"Cool down, princess," he ordered me. "Pick on some-one your own size."

"Get her back over there," Number One said, waving the TEC-9 at the wall where I had been sitting. "You're one stupid bitch," he told me. "I came this close to pulling the trigger."

Tawny was rolling around on the bed, holding her nose, wailing and screeching, trying to stop the bleeding. She sounded like a cat caught in a blender.

"You shut up, too," Number One ordered her. "Where the hell is Jones?"

I had gone for Tawny out of real anger, and the cat fight had strengthened my ruse. "They're looking for Jeff," I screamed at Tawny. "They know you're in on it."

"I'm not in on anything," she started to yell, but she gagged on the TEC-9 when Number One shoved it back in her mouth.

"Take this gun out of my mouth and I'll talk," she said with instant calm, as if her pain and the blood trickling down her body were not real. Her sudden and complete self-control was scary, she was like two different people. At least.

Number One pulled back, his expression close to ad-miration. "A sensible woman. I like that."

"What are you looking for?" Tawny asked, her eyes flickering toward me. "That woman is a psychopath. She's out to get me. Don't believe a word she says. I've got nothing to do with her ex or his drugs."

"Then how did you know we were talking about drugs? Or her ex?" Number One grabbed her by the upper arm and jerked her to her feet. She stood naked on top of the bed, dripping blood, swaying unsteadily on the soft mat-tress.

Near the bathroom door, Denny had tied Amanda Cockshutt to a chair using the cord from the draperies. She still hadn't said a word. I don't think she was able to. This was not the cocktail party ending she had planned.

"What else would a pair of goons waving guns want to know about except drugs?" Tawny spit at him.

Number One drew back the TEC-9, then lashed the butt across her face. It lifted her off the bed and she fell to the floor. Ouch. It had to have hurt.

Tawny didn't make a sound. But I could feel the hatred radiating off her like heat. And a whole hell of a lot of it was radiating my way.

Amanda Cockshutt started to cry.

"Gag her," Number One ordered.

Denny jammed a pillowcase in Amanda's mouth. Her eyes turned to me. I shrugged. I was in no mood to help her. Unlike the other people Tawny had scammed, Amanda had known what Tawny was like when she recruited her to kill her husband. She'd made her choices, not me.

"Back on the bed, skin-and-bones," Number One said. He poked at Tawny with the barrel of the TEC-9. She shrugged it off and scrambled back on the bed, almost snarling at him, a feral animal trapped in its lair.

"Well, aren't you a frisky little—" Number One started to say. He never finished the sentence. An avalanche of shouting, armed, uniformed, pumped-up humanity cascaded through the open door. Commands rang out, shots were fired. Bodies tumbled to the ground. Voices filled the room.

"Freeze!" "Gun, Charlie! Gun!" "Drop it! Drop it! Drop it!" "Look out to the right." "Over here! Over here!" "Get down! Get down!"

I scrambled to safety under a desk, covered my head with my arms and cowered. Then I remembered that I had Bill's Strayer-Voigt. Bad news no matter what. No one was watching me and the room was filling with smoke. Someone had thrown in a flare. I eased the gun out from under the television cabinet and wiped it down. Bill would kill me, but I couldn't afford to be held on a weapons charge. God, he'd never forgive me for losing his beloved gun. Holding it with the edge of my shirt, I flung it across the room. It skittered across the carpet and lodged along one edge of the bed. No one noticed in the confusion.

Around me, the chaos grew. Headlights flickered on in the parking lots, sirens approached, the rasping honk of a fire truck screeching toward the motel surely woke up anyone within a three-mile radius. Outside the door, angry shouts from the motel owner competed with the rough commands of officers.

A man was bellowing for order. "Who set off the smoke bomb?" a fat man in khaki demanded. He stood only a few inches from my hiding spot, his upper body swathed in gray smoke. I stared at his shoes. They gleamed in the glare of the headlights beaming through the front door. I had never seen cleaner shoes in my entire life. For some reason, those shoes made me feel safe.

"It was an accident, Charlie," someone muttered.

"Hold your fire. Let's see what we've got."

It took a while for the smoke and human army to clear. A couple of officers took pillowcases and began flapping the smoke toward the door. As the gray fog lifted, the results of the invasion slowly materialized.

Amanda Cockshutt lay on her side on the carpet, still bound to the chair. She was screaming through the gag wound around her mouth. Denny sprawled over her, his body unmoving. Blood seeped from his torso, flooding Amanda's naked skin as it trickled to the rug.

"One down," someone said. "Not one of us."

Tawny Bledsoe was on her knees, clutching the side of the bed, naked as a jaybird, looking almost as if she were praying. "Thank god you're here, officers," she said. "These men just burst into here and started pushing us around. I think my nose is broken."

"Shut up," the fat man in khaki said. I pegged him as the sheriff. "Cuff her." Two uniforms hurried to obey. They yanked Tawny up and pushed her face down on the bed. She screamed from the pain. They ignored it and cuffed her hands behind her.

"Now cover her," the Sheriff ordered.

A female deputy draped a sheet over Tawny.

"What's going on, Charlie?" a deep voice demanded from the doorway.

A state trooper stood outlined in the door frame, smoke and light swirling around his tall figure. His immaculate uniform gleamed with the crispness of starch, his boots were polished to a high sheen. His Smoky the Bear hat was pushed back on his head, framing a square-jawed face and sharp eyes. We were all in trouble now.

"Some sort of drug deal gone bad," the sheriff said, shaking his head. "We got a tip-off from a cop up in Raleigh. There's been some shooting. None of my men seem hurt. We're trying to sort it out—"

"There's the shooter," someone interrupted. The whole room turned to the speaker. A skinny kid in a too-large deputy uniform was pointing behind a pile of suitcases. Two unmoving legs extended into the room, but the rest of the body was obscured by matching black leather. Number One. Down for the count.

"Dead?" the sheriff asked.

"Not yet," a deputy replied after bending over the body for a moment. He whistled. "But here's one for our collection." He held the TEC-9 up, carefully balancing it on the bottom of his palms to avoid disturbing any fingerprints. "Ralph'll get a kick out of this."

"Excuse me," I said loudly from beneath the desk.

I heard the rustles and clicks of at least six officers assuming a shooting stance in my direction.

"I'm not armed," I said, holding my hands up as high as the desk would let me. "Please, I have nothing to do with this."

"Then why are you here, sister?" the sheriff asked sensibly. He nodded toward a deputy. "Cuff her, too."

THIRTEEN

They shoved me into the backseat of a patrol car with a sullen Amanda Cockshutt. Tawny got her own car, courtesy of the full-blown, coke-induced temper tantrum she threw when they tried to dress her. She'd kicked the sheriff, bitten a trooper, spat on the female officer holding her clothes, flung her blood on a handful of HIV-terrified deputies and unleashed a series of her trademark dressing-downs on anyone within earshot. I thought she was lucky they didn't send her straight to the mental ward, though maybe that was what she'd had in mind. It reminded me of how smart she was, as in smart like a fox dozing by a rabbit hole. This was no time for me to quit the fight.

"Can I talk to you for a minute?" I asked the female officer. She was standing by my open window, watching Tawny being dragged into another deputy's car.

"Why should I listen to you?" she answered.

"Maybe because I had my clothes on when you broke into the motel room and you didn't have to put my panties on for me like the rest of the lowlifes?"

"Make it quick."

"Alone?"

The deputy opened the car door and helped me out. She was smart. She knew that keeping her ego in check might bring a break in the case. She was willing to listen. So was Amanda Cockshutt. I moved out of her earshot.

Activity swirled around us in the parking lot: an ambulance pulled in to cart Denny and Number One away,

troopers poured in to act important, and some of the de-
putys' wives arrived with sandwiches and coffee. It had
been an exciting night in Taylorsville. I expected the hot
dog vendor to arrive at any moment.

"What do you want?" the officer demanded. She was a
stocky black woman, with close-cropped hair and a blunt
face. She had not appreciated two naked women being part
of this bust. I got the feeling she endured enough dyke
jokes from her colleagues as it was, never mind the wedding ring on her finger.

"I'm a private investigator from Raleigh," I explained.
"My ID is in my back pocket. This is part of a murder
investigation."

"Better keep it to yourself until your lawyer gets here,"
she advised. "Charlie don't hold much truck with private
investigators."

"Just hear me out," I begged her. "What's your first
name?"

"Wanda. But you can call me Deputy Castleberry."

I gave her a sanitized version of what had gone down,
telling her about my suspicions that Tawny was guilty of
murder and making it clear why it was so important for
the Raleigh Police Department to know that Amanda
Cockshutt had been caught sleeping with the enemy.

"Even if I believe you," she said when I was done. "It's
another story to convince Charlie over there." She nodded
toward the sheriff. He was in earnest conversation with
two state troopers.

"I'll work on him," I said. "But I need you to do something for me right now." It was a little iffy, she'd have to
mildly contaminate a crime scene. But I convinced her to
give it a try by offering to swap some key information in
exchange for her help. "Deal?" I asked.

She thought it over. "Done. So where's this coke?"

"I saw one of the guys loading it into the trunk of that
car over there." I nodded at the gray Lumina. The crime
team had not yet approached it, they were no doubt too
busy confiscating Bill Butler's gun.

"Get back in the car," she ordered me.

I wiggled into the backseat, smiled at Amanda and received a frosty glare for my trouble. Gosh, it seemed she wasn't speaking to me.

Deputy Castleberry ambled over to the Lumina, opened a back door and starting looking around. She bent over the front seat console and the trunk clicked open. When she slid out of the car, she was holding my knapsack and the cellular phone. She spoke into the phone briefly and then, holding my pack casually to one side, she walked over to the sheriff and handed him the phone.

"It's for you," she told him.

"What the hell is this, Castleberry? I'm busy."

"It's that detective from the Raleigh PD who warned us," she explained. "I found the phone in the backseat of the perps' car."

The men all stared at her.

"It was just sitting there, doors unlocked," she explained. "One of the perps indicated it might contain explosives. I had to look. No explosives. But there is at least a kilo of cocaine in the trunk."

There was a minor stampede toward the Lumina as the sheriff took the phone and Deputy Castleberry returned to her car. She slid into the front seat and adjusted the rearview mirror, then pulled back the bulletproof partition separating the driver from the passenger seat.

"You gals ready to roll?" she asked us.

"I want my lawyer," I said loudly, kicking the backseat.

"Didn't believe you, huh?" Amanda said nastily.

I ignored her.

"You girls need to say something, be sure to knock on the partition, you hear now?" Deputy Castleberry said. "It's soundproof, so I don't have to listen to your bull dookey all the way to the jail." Geeze, but she was laying it on thick. I half expected Barney Fife to pop up and add his two cents' worth.

I started in on Amanda Cockshutt the instant we pulled out of the parking lot. At first she wouldn't bite. I tried appealing to her conscience, her love of her children, public shame. None of it got her talking. But then I wounded her pride. And that's what got her talking.

"You know, Boomer may have been a son-of-a-bitch,"

I said. "But he was a damn sight classier than Tawny. What the hell made you get mixed up with a low-class swamp coot like that? If I'd known you were that desperate for a walk on the wild side, I could have introduced you to my dentist. She's single."

She glared at me. Things had gone from bad to worse. She was wearing mismatched clothes and not happy about it. Her dignity was being stripped away.

"What makes you think I didn't know exactly what I was doing?" she retorted in a scathing tone of voice. "I knew Tawny Bledsoe was trash the first time I saw her. That was the point."

"It was?"

"Trash can be disposed of. Do you really think I was going to spend the rest of my life with her?" She spat on the floor of the car. "Talk about used goods. I shower twice every time she touches me."

"Well, don't the two of you make a lovely couple? Sort of a Bonnie and Bonnie without the Clyde." She didn't react.

"Then why did you get involved with her?" I asked.

"Because she killed Boomer for me, you moron." She looked out the window, enjoying how smart she had been to get someone else to do her dirty work. "There is a certain poetic justice in it, don't you think? Boomer being killed by one of his liaisons. You live by the sword, you die by the sword. Didn't you ever hear that saying?" She laughed, savoring the fact that the father of her children had gotten his brains blown out in the middle of getting his pipes cleaned.

I was truly appalled. But not surprised. Amanda's behavior explained Tawny's descent from liar to murderer. The two of them together were like Molotov cocktails colliding in the air. The momentum was bound to cause an explosion.

"Where did you meet her?" I asked. "I'm always interested in twists of fate."

"Some dyke club in Durham."

"Oh yeah," I said, remembering what the owner of Rubyfruit Jungle had told me about a bored housewife who

looked like Sigourney Weaver. I thought she'd been one
of Tawny's victims, not Tawny's partner. "The owner re-
members you."

She looked confident. "It won't do them any good." We
both knew who she meant by "them." "There's no crime
in being seen at a gay bar."

"So you planned it from the start?"

"I planned it?" She laughed. "I don't think so. Credit
Tawny with the actual idea. I picked her up one night just
for kicks and she went off on me like we were in big love
or something. What a joke. Then I realized she might be
useful. I could use her to get close enough to Boomer to
find out where the bastard had stashed all his assets, so I
could divorce his fat ass. But Tawny figured out he'd be
worth a lot more dead to me than alive, and I sure as hell
went along with the idea. And why not? Fifteen years of
his rubbing my face in some young thing, one after the
other, should be worth something."

"You were willing to let an innocent man go to jail," I
said. "Maybe even death row. How could you live with
that?"

"I lived with Boomer, I can live with anything. From
our first year of marriage, he was like some mongrel who
had to hump every dog in heat he could find. I don't care
who has to pay, I'm just glad he's dead. Do you know it
only took Tawny ten minutes to get a date with him?" She
stared out the window. "I told her what to do, and ten
minutes after walking onto his lot and saying she wanted
to look at cars, that piece of shit I married asked her out
to dinner."

"I'd say that was due more to Tawny's talents than
Boomer's morals."

"He deserved what he got. And I deserved what I got
for killing him."

"Which was what? Money?"

"Lots of it." She laughed. "Especially since I get to keep
it all now."

"You're going to prison," I said incredulously. "Where
do you think this nice deputy is taking us?"

"Not me. They can't pin a thing on me. Tawny did the

killing. I had nothing to do with it. She's crazy. I'll say it
was all her idea."

"But you were in Winston-Salem with her kid the night
Boomer was killed, weren't you? It wasn't Tawny at that
church retreat. It was you. That's why the other church
members heard Tiffany crying. She woke up to find a
stranger in her room. Then you answered the phone in her
motel room late that night, pretending to be her. That's
called accessory to murder, you know."

"You can't prove that," she said. "I made sure of it."

Yeah? I thought, wondering why both she and Tawny
seemed so ready to dismiss Tiffany and all that the little
girl had heard and seen these past few months. Thank god
I got the kid out, I realized, before her mother figured out
what a threat she represented.

"Your mother will testify you were lying," I suggested.
"She'll say you weren't with her in Asheville at that
lodge."

"My mother can't testify to a thing. She drinks herself
into a stupor all day and night. She won't remember what
happened or where we were that weekend. And the kids
were already in bed. There's no way to prove it. It was
Tawny that did it, not me. I'm just the grieving widow."

"I guess you think you're smarter than her," I said.

"Her?" Amanda Cockshutt's voice was full of scorn.
"Tawny Bledsoe is nothing but trailer trash with a coke
habit. She wanted to dump her own kid once we got to
California. Tawny's not smart. She's just good at what she
does. Which isn't much. I'd say she has a limited repertoire."

"Looked to me like you were enjoying her repertoire in
that motel room back there."

Her smile was brief. "A certain amount of posturing was
necessary on my part, even with someone as gullible as
that pathetic coke whore."

"Yeah?" I said, my voice challenging. "Maybe she's
smarter than you think."

"What are you talking about?" Amanda's eyes were
trained on the darkness outside. "I can get her to do whatever I want her to do." She smiled to herself. "Even Na-

poleon had his Waterloo. I'm Tawny's. She loves me. That's power."

I laughed.

"What's so funny?"

"You were being set up," I lied. "She and Jeff were going to clean out your bank account and leave you in their dust. He told me everything."

"You're lying." She looked away in disgust.

"Am I? Let me guess—Tawny didn't want to leave the area until all of your insurance checks had cleared the bank, did she?" Eavesdropping has its benefits. It can make lies a lot more believable. "Well?"

"That doesn't mean anything."

"It means you were being used. She just wanted your money. That's all she ever wants. Why else would Jeff have met you here?"

She was scornful. "That's how much you know. I told Tawny at the start that we better have a backup in case someone political started to believe her ex-husband was innocent." She smirked at me. "Your ex just seemed like the perfect patsy, know what I mean? After all, he'd been stupid enough to marry you. He's only here to take the blame."

"Yeah," I agreed. "Keep telling yourself that. But you and I both know that Jeff can get Tawny drugs, and when push comes to shove, she's going to go with someone who can feed that nose of hers. She was getting ready to double-cross you, cupcake. Wake up and smell the coffee."

I quit while I was ahead—and before I got any hungrier from all my talk about food. Amanda was also quiet for the rest of the trip to the Marlboro County Jail. I didn't care.

Neither did Deputy Castleberry. She gave me a thumbs-up as I was led into processing. The black recording device from my knapsack was tucked under one of her arms. What Amanda Cockshutt had just said would be enough to indict her, probably convict her, and it would sure as hell get her talking about a plea bargain. It would stand up in court, too. There is no expectation of privacy in the backseat of a police car and I had agreed to the tape.

I had brought them both down. Women's prison would
never be the same with those two works of art in it.

The cops in that little South Carolina town didn't appreciate my accomplishment. They strip-searched me,
threw me a jumpsuit and fingerprinted me along with the
rest of the dreck being dragged in to keep the peace.

It was the worst thing that had happened to me yet. I'd
told Deputy Castleberry I was a private investigator, and
now they were sure to get a hit on my fingerprints. They'd
find out I had a felony record and know my P.I. license
was a fake. If they cared enough to do it, they could ruin
my life in Raleigh.

It made for a very long night. Getting caught in a lie
always does.

I was put in an eight-by-eight-foot cell. It reminded me
of bad times and I found it hard to breathe. I had scratches
on my face from where Tawny had slashed me and my
cheek was starting to burn like a son-of-a-bitch.

Tawny was brought in an hour after I arrived, huge
strips of white tape over her nose. They put her in a cell
to my left. Amanda Cockshutt was in the one to my right.
I was glad for the bars between us.

Amanda lasted two hours before she broke. She'd been
thinking about my comments in the car, brooding over the
possibility that Tawny had been planning to double-cross
her. That, plus Tawny's constant coke-induced rustling—
her sniffling, her pacing about her cell, the incessant thump
as she threw herself on her mattress again and again—
combined to push Amanda over the edge.

It was just after five o'clock in the morning when she
called across my holding cell to her lover. "I know what
you tried to do to me, you bitch," she whispered to Tawny.
"I'll get you for it."

"What are you talking about?" Tawny was on her feet
in an instant. Her tiny body looked bloated in the oversized
jumpsuit, making her seem like a grotesque orange neon
tick that glowed in the dim night light of the jail.

This was what I had been waiting for: show time.
Tawny was coming down from what might well be a year-

long coke high. Who knew what she'd do or say? And I
had a front-row seat for the fall-out.

"I know you were setting me up," Amanda hissed.
"Don't think you can treat me like everyone else in your
trailer trash life and get away with it. You're not getting
a dime of my money. I'll teach you to try to screw me
over."

Some people might have had the sense to make up with
the person who held her fate in her hands. Not Tawny
Bledsoe. Not when she had just lost everything, been
stripped of her drugs and plopped in a cell next to me, her
hulking blond nemesis, the one with tree trunk legs and
no appreciation for her charms.

At first Tawny said nothing. That worried me. If
Tawny's feelings for Amanda were genuine, they probably
confused her. She needed a nudge.

"Yeah, Tawny," I said casually. "You seem to be losing
your touch. Did you really think Amanda would stand for
treatment like that? Screwing around on her with a guy.
You must think she's stupid. Jeff told me you called
Amanda 'that rich bimbo' the whole time you guys holed
up together in your love nest apartment and stayed up
every night screwing your brains out. But I didn't think
you really believed she was *that* dumb."

Wee doggies. With those words, a cat fight erupted, the
likes of nothing I venture either Carolina has ever seen.
Tawny began screeching and ripping apart her pillow, then
throwing herself against the bars that divided us. She fast-
balled a shoe at me, but let go too early in her wind-up.
It hit the only light bulb in her cell, shattering it. That
would get the guards' attention.

The names she called me after that exceeded any she
had dredged up in the past. It was a veritable volcano of
invective, and somewhere around the middle of it, Amanda
Cockshutt got it into her head that Tawny was talking to
her. She replied with some Northern expressions I'd never
even dreamed of, and while they lacked the colorful ver-
nacular of the South, they were loud enough and foul
enough to bring two officers running.

"You're gonna carve the zee-zee on her *what* with a

knife?" I asked Amanda as the corridor door slammed and
footsteps headed our way. "What's a zee-zee? Some sort
of gypsy curse?"

I never got my answer. Tawny went bat shit when she
saw the guards. She pulled her mattress from the bed, tried
to rip off her clothes, and then transferred her verbal fury
to the officers. They were afraid to go into her cell. When
she got a whiff of their hesitation, she escalated the volume
and stepped up the insults until both guards went running
for help.

"I'll get you," she hissed at me through the bars.

"And my little dog, too?" I suggested.

This unleashed a new episode of fury. It was like watching a human hurricane unfold before my eyes. She was
unstoppable ferocity, pure energy, the essence of destruc-
tion. Forty years of getting her own way had been thwarted
at last. She imploded with frustration. The display was
awesome. It was a temper tantrum of evil proportions.

And not a second of it was lost on Amanda Cockshutt.
She had grown still as she stared in horror at her partner
through the cell bars. She'd finally figured out that she was
in deep trouble, and that Tawny was going to drag her
down even further.

Tawny unleashed another round of curses.

"Does she eat you with that mouth?" I asked Amanda.

She only stared at me in reply.

The guards returned with reinforcements. It took three
men to pin Tawny facedown on the mattress. Two other
men gripped her arms, and still two more held on to her
feet. One of them was a janitor and the other looked like
some poor guy who had dropped by the station to say hello
to his friends. The Marlboro County Jail didn't have
enough manpower to take on Tawny Bledsoe. They were
borrowing bystanders, and still she was bucking and
shrieking like a rodeo bull with a hot coal up its ass.

"Enjoy rehab," I called after her as she was dragged
screaming down the hallway. Even Sheriff Charlie had
heard enough for one night. She was on her way to the
psych ward.

The last I ever saw of Tawny Bledsoe, her mouth was

running a mile a minute as she went through the family tree of her captors, insulting every member she could name. It was a sight to see and hear: Tawny Bledsoe, unplugged.

And I will never forget what Amanda Cockshutt called out as the guards rushed her lover past that night. The words rang in the hallway, reverberating off the high ceilings, burning themselves into my memory. They would become the words that Bobby D. and I always remember Tawny Bledsoe by:

"You blonde bitch," Amanda screamed after her. "You're not even really a blond!"

Dawn was a long time in coming. When it arrived, it brought a rainy winter day with it. It was noon before they came for me: Deputy Castleberry and another man I didn't recognize. She was holding a cup of coffee from McDonald's. I thought that was a good sign. Especially when she smiled at me.

"Okay," Castleberry said. "You're out of here. The cavalry has arrived."

"The cavalry?"

"Well, at least a knight in shining armor." She pointed to the far end of the hallway where Bill Butler stood waiting, out of Amanda Cockshutt's sight.

"Why's *she* getting out of here?" Amanda complained.

"Shut up," the deputy told her.

Amanda shut up.

"You look good in orange," Bill offered when I rewarded him with a kiss.

I made a face. "Seen my clothes?"

"Upstairs." Deputy Castleberry unlocked my handcuffs.

"Thanks for believing me," I told her.

"Thank him." She nodded at Bill. "Someone's going to have a hell of a cellular phone bill." She was discreet enough to leave us alone at the bottom of the steps.

I slapped Bill a high five. "Thanks, Butler," I told him. "I owe you one."

"Actually," he reminded me. "This whole episode makes us even."

"Oh, yeah," I said, remembering the times I had pulled his bacon from the fire and thrown an arrest his way. Those had been other cases but, right then, they seemed like they had happened in another lifetime to some other creature on a different planet in an alternate universe.

I wanted to go home.

"Come on," Bill said, "I've got to get back to work." He gently touched the scratches on my cheek. "She do that to you?"

"Yeah. You don't look too good yourself, you know."

He sighed and ran his hands through his hair. He suddenly looked very old. "When I heard all that gunshot over the phone last night," he said, then stopped and just shook his head. "I didn't know what the hell was going on, but I knew it was bad. It scared me, Casey. It scared me bad."

We looked at each other and a tentative smile took hold between us, one that turned into an outright grin. "I guess I'm invincible," I said.

"I guess so." He looped an arm over my shoulder. "Ready to go home?"

I nodded as we started up the steps. "How'd you do it?" I asked.

"You've got friends in high places," Bill explained. "One in particular."

"Oh, yeah," I remembered. "The tubby guy in the little gray socks with heavy leather accents. And not much else."

"That's right," Bill confirmed. Neither one of us felt it prudent to discuss further why a high-ranking police officer in Raleigh, North Carolina, had taken it upon himself to pull enough strings to spring me from a South Carolina hoosegow. But I made a mental note to return a certain set of black-and-white photographs plus the negatives of them once I got home. Hell, I'd send everyone their photos, and a lot of sleepless nights would be history.

"Did you get the rest of the photos?" I asked Bill. "I think Tawny had them on her."

"Down, girl. They're coming."

"Here you go," Deputy Castleberry said, handing me a neatly folded pile of clothes.

They smelled, but who cared? "You folded them for me," I said. "How nice."

Her smile took effort. She looked tired and her dark face was etched with sleep lines. They'd stuck her with the paperwork. How typical.

"Give me a moment?" she asked me unexpectedly. "With him."

I stared at Bill, then stepped away. "I'll just go change in the bathroom," I offered, anxious to reclaim my right to the use of the public areas. My stomach bubbled with fear. Fingerprints, I thought. Mine. They'd gotten a hit. This was the end of the line. What would I tell Bill?

I put my clothes on with lightning speed, arriving back in the foyer in time to see Deputy Castleberry handing Bill a cardboard box and a piece of green-and-white computer paper.

Oh, shit. She was handing him my NCN printout.

Bill nodded as he took it, checked the contents of the box, seemed satisfied, signed a clipboarded form she held out to him, then grasped her hand firmly in farewell. Well, weren't they just the best of buddies? Officers of the law united against some poor schmuck like me trying to live down her past.

"Let's go, beautiful," Bill said, his hand resting on the small of my back as he guided me down the stone steps of the jail. A light mist was falling and the air was cold. It felt wonderful on my face. I gulped in the fresh oxygen.

"Your chariot awaits." Bill opened the passenger side door of a white sedan.

"That car looks official," I said, more than a little nervously.

"Relax. It's a final favor from our friend, who was anxious to get all evidence back in my capable hands. You don't think I followed the speed limit on the way down, do you?"

His smile made me suspicious. Why was he being so nice?

"Where are we going?" I asked as I slid into the front seat.

"Home," Bill promised. He placed the box on the seat

behind us. "That's where the heart is, right?"

"What's in the box?" I asked casually. Other than my sordid past, of course.

"My gun," he said. "Potential evidence in a murder case, you know. But only until I get it home. You were worried about that, now weren't you?"

Not as worried as about other things, I thought, and waited. "What else?"

"A nice fat stack of photos from Tawny's suitcase."

"The rest of them?"

"You got it. Including two of yours truly. Nobody recognized me. I guess I have a forgettable face."

"More like no one was looking at your face."

"Guess not," he agreed as he started the engine.

"Oh, come on," I said, staring out at the drizzle. It was turning to rain and the cars on the main drag made hissing sounds as they whizzed past. "I saw her handing over the printout."

Bill had started to pull out into traffic, but stopped abruptly. He turned to me with a hard-to-read smile. "I guess you mean your record?" he said.

I nodded miserably.

"Casey, do you really think that after Tawny Bledsoe, I would have gotten involved with someone else unless I had checked her out pretty thoroughly?"

"You knew? You ran my name?" I asked indignantly.

"And prints. You left them all over my apartment that time."

"I can't believe you did that to me." I paused. "You've known all along?"

"Sure," he said, checking the road and pulling out into the northbound lane. "Everybody deserves a second chance. Even middle-aged burnouts like me."

I don't remember much of the ride home to Raleigh. I remember the squeak of the windshield wipers, the splat of rain on the car, the feeling of safety I got from dozing in the front seat while someone I trusted guided me toward home. I remember a lingering feeling of lightness, as if some weight had been lifted from my soul. Tawny? My

secret? Something else I didn't understand? I was just too
tired to figure it out. And too warm to care.

I woke up near Raleigh when Bill gently pulled my hair.
"Where to?" he asked.

"Home," I said automatically.

"Durham?"

I realized I had been dreaming about Chatham County,
about Burly's farm and the white clapboard house and the
cow pond and our quilt-covered bed. "No," I mumbled,
rubbing the sleep from my eyes. I was too tired to avoid
being tactless. "Head to Pittsboro. I'll show you when we
get there."

I leaned against Bill's shoulder as he steered us over the
rain-slicked highway. A sort of madness had passed
through, and the aftermath left me exhausted. For almost
a month, I had thought of nothing but Tawny Bledsoe,
where she was and how to bring her down. What had
caused my obsession? My need to prove I was nothing
like her? The way she treated people and got away with
it? An innocent man paying for a crime he hadn't com-
mitted? Or that Tawny had assumed I was as disposable
as everyone else? Or was I really just running away from
Burly, for fear he'd expect something from me that I
couldn't give?

I wasn't sure what the reasons were, but I was glad it
was over. Now I could get on with my life.

"What's going to happen?" I wondered out loud.

"They'll get them both," Bill predicted. "The wife will
turn state's evidence and do hard time. Bledsoe may get
the big one. Case, you did a great job. No one else could
have done it. You've done a good thing today."

"No, I mean what's going to happen with us?"

"Oh." His shoulder stiffened beneath my head. "Well,
am I or am I not driving you out to your boyfriend's
house?"

"You are," I admitted.

He relaxed again. "So, the two of you are still going
strong?"

"I think so," I said. "If he's back from the dark side."
A stab of longing for Burly hit me. I wanted to be home

with him. I wanted him to be back, to be really back, to
have survived this latest funk of his, so we could both
return to our life together. It felt, somehow, that if we
didn't make that happen, Tawny would have won out after
all.

Bill was nodding. "I can live with that. You and him, I
mean."

"You can?" I was vaguely disappointed that he was taking it so calmly. I've always wanted to have my cake and
eat it, too. Even when I'm full.

"To tell you the truth, Casey," Bill said, "you're one
hell of a woman, but you're exhausting. I'm going to need
at least a three-week vacation before I can muster the energy to even have coffee with you. I'm too old. I can't
keep up." He laughed. "But it sure is nice once in a while."

"Yes," I decided. "It is."

I stared out the window at the foggy skyline of downtown Raleigh and wondered if Jeff had come by my office
yet.

"Can we keep him out of it?" I asked Bill.

"Who? Your ex?"

I nodded.

"So far as I know, he's not involved," Bill said. "Unless
I get evidence from you otherwise, that's the way it stays."

"I guess that's it then," I decided. "One last bail-out, for
old time's sake."

Mist cloaked the farmhouse. The pond was as flat and
gray as gun metal, a nickel nestled among the hills. It was
a dreary day outside, but the lights were on in the kitchen
and smoke billowed from the chimney. That meant Burly
was home and my heart lifted at the thought. I wanted
everything back the way it had been before Tawny Bledsoe
entered my life.

I found Burly in the kitchen, his wheelchair pulled up
close to the stove. He was tasting lamb stew and nodding
his head in satisfaction. It smelled great and I was suddenly
starving.

Killer was asleep on the hearth, snoring in front of the
fire. He smelled me finally—not even lamb stew could

mask my on-the-road-again funk—and he opened one eye. His tail quivered in his version of a wildly enthusiastic greeting.

"Honey, I'm home," I announced, helping myself to Burly's lap. I snuggled against him. "Of course, the drawback is that I stink."

"Mmmm," he said. "No problem. I'm part French, remember?"

"Which part?"

"All the right parts."

We laughed and I inhaled the air around him. I could feel and smell the change in him, there was no stale tobacco odor lingering around him and his body chemicals were different, they were back in balance. His face was relaxed, his hair was washed, he had on clean clothes and had shaved. The black dog had moved on to bite someone else. The man I knew and loved had returned.

I ran my hands over his cheeks. "I'm impressed." I rubbed my face against his, feeling our skin pressed together. "You must be doing better."

"I guess you could say I'm back, too," he admitted.

"It was a bad one, wasn't it?"

He nodded. "But it's over now."

"For a while." The words hung in the air. I hurried to soften them. "I'm sorry I'm so lousy at being there for you. I hate that in myself."

He gripped my arms, his voice strong. "Don't be. This is something I have to go through alone. There's nothing you can do."

"You're just saying that to make me feel better."

"Does it matter why I'm saying it?" he asked. "You did the right thing for you. I don't want you to be any other way. I mean that."

I buried my head back in his shoulder. "Did anyone get killed, arrested or otherwise compromised this time around?"

He ran his hands up and down my waist, moving them up to cup my breasts. "The only damage done was to my liver. And my dignity, if I have any left."

"I'm glad you're back," I whispered, sliding my hands

under his shirt and rubbing them across his chest. He had the smoothest skin I'd ever touched, it was like corn silk beneath my fingers.

"And I'm glad you're back." He paused, noticed my scratches and touched them lightly with a finger. "You had me worried."

"I did it. I found her. I got the proof. She's in custody."

He smiled. "I knew you could do it; I never doubted it for a moment. Without exception, you're the most stubborn woman I ever met."

"Lucky for you," I pointed out.

"Lucky for me."

"Want me to tell you about it?" I offered.

He shifted in his wheelchair. "Oh, yeah, baby. You know I like that Xena Warrior Princess stuff."

"Well," I whispered into his ear. "We had a cat fight. A really knock-down, drag-out one."

"Hair pulling?" he asked hopefully, his hands sliding over my stomach to find the zipper of my jeans.

"Yup. Some bitch-slapping, too."

He started to breathe harder. I licked his ear and whispered into it. "I had to rip her clothes off, but it was worth it. She was begging me for mercy in the end."

His voice was thick as he fumbled with the top button on my jeans. "You kicked her ass?"

"Of course," I said. "And I kicked in a couple of doors, too. There was even gunfire. I had to hit the floor."

That did it for Burly. His hand slid down the front of my pants as he pressed his mouth against mine. When I felt the familiar touch of his lips, a jolt went through me like it did every time our bodies met. Four hundred volts of direct current and then some. It had the power to make me leave everything else far behind. Which was exactly what I needed to do just then.

Four days later, I was sleeping late when I got the call.

"He's here," Bobby D. said. "In the office. And he doesn't look too good."

"Be there soon," I promised, wondering what I would say when I saw him.

Jeff looked even worse than I expected. His skin had a yellowish cast to it, and his eyes drooped at the edges. His hair was dirty and his clothes looked as if he had slept in them for days. There was a sour air around him, like the beer slop that ferments on barroom floors.

"How are you holding up?" I asked. I slid behind my desk, anxious to put room between us.

"Not so good," he admitted, staring down at his grimy fingernails. "I can't sleep. I never know when those guys are going to show up. And I had to leave Tawny's apartment. I heard she got arrested and all."

I was amazed at his paranoid isolation from the real world. Jeff hadn't heard about the drug dealers. One of them, Denny, was dead and Number One was in a Florence hospital, under arrest for narcotics trafficking. He'd be in jail for decades. But such an unremarkable event along the I-95 corridor would never have made the papers up here, not when Tawny Bledsoe and Amanda Cockshutt were being splashed across every inch of available newsprint. All anyone knew was that they had been arrested together, the details were still coming out.

"You're lucky you're not in jail with Tawny," I told him.

"I know. She really had me fooled." He took off his cowboy hat and stared at the tattered rim. "Thanks," he mumbled, like it was a big effort. "It's too bad we had to lose the coke, you know. It would have brought in a lot of money. Given me a stake so I could start over."

When I heard those words, I knew what I had to do. "I didn't have a choice. I had to give it back to them," I said. "But I don't think you'll have to worry about those two guys. At least not for a couple of weeks."

He looked up hopefully. "What do you mean?"

"I sent them to Arizona," I lied. "I said you went to Tucson."

"You did?" He threw back his head, laughing. "You're a piece of work, Casey."

If only he knew.

He paused. "Hey, where's my car? I need my car. I gotta go while the going's good."

"Forget your car, Jeff. They're just waiting for you to go back to it."

"Who?" he asked, alarmed.

I shrugged. "The cops. The SBI. The FBI. Those goombahs. Who knows?" I stared at him, wishing I could somehow get through. There had to be someone deep inside him. I could never have fallen in love with such an empty man. Could I? Where had he gone? What had happened to him? Had I really been so different back then?

All the hatred I felt for my ex-husband was gone, replaced by a sort of sadness for what we had been, what we had lost and who we had left behind. Sometimes not knowing is a good thing. Sometimes not caring is even better.

"You're going to have to do something to turn your life around, Jeff," I told him. Unexpected feelings welled in me. I knew he'd never make it. I knew it was only a matter of time. One day I would open the paper and read about a body found in some canal in Miami, a thousand miles away, and I'd wonder if it was him. And it would be him. Until then, though, I had to try.

"You got pulled into some bad things this time," I said. "Really bad things. A lot of people could have been hurt. An innocent man could have gone to jail for life. A little girl could have lost her father."

"What did happen to the dude?" Jeff asked guiltily. "They let him out?"

"They let him out of jail two days ago. He was happy to be with his daughter again."

I did not tell Jeff that I had been there for the release, that Robert Price had asked for me to be waiting for him on the outside. Nor did I tell him how Robert had locked his eyes on mine when he walked through the front door, a free man again, how he had taken my hand and held it in his, or about the tears he blinked back—and the gratitude on the faces of the friends and family members who had gathered to welcome him back into the world.

"Thank you," he had whispered, unable to say more.

"Hey, man," I said. "No problem. Just doing the right thing."

"Why *did* you do it?" Price's lawyer had asked me a minute later. We were watching a car door open down the block. A young girl dangled her long legs over the sidewalk, gauging the distance, then hopped down and started running toward her father. She called to him as she ran: "Daddy! Daddy! Daddy!"

"That's why I did it," I told him as Tiffany flung herself into her father's arms. Price's sister hurried up the sidewalk after her niece, crying. I got a little teary-eyed myself. "I feel like I'm in a goddamn Hallmark commercial," I muttered.

Price's lawyer patted my shoulder. "Tough chick to the end," he said. "I like that in a private investigator."

"It's only allergies," I lied, then I caught sight of a regal-looking woman standing at the edge of the family crowd. "Holy shit," I said, tears forgotten as I stared at her beaded braids, the colorful strip of cloth binding them on top of her head, and the vibrant colors of the robes she wore.

"What?" Price's lawyer asked. "What is it?"

"Isn't that Robert's first wife?" I asked.

The lawyer nodded. "Sure is. And they say women and elephants never forget."

"We don't forget," I assured him. "It's just that sometimes we manage to forgive."

Jeff had been talking to me, but I was lost in the memory. I hadn't heard a word he said.

"What?" I asked blankly, looking up at him. "What did you say?"

"I said I'm sorry I lied about your grandfather," he mumbled. "I'm sorry I pulled him into this mess."

"So he didn't tell you where I was?" I asked. "He doesn't know?"

Jeff shook his head. "You remember Rocky Road Reed?" he asked.

"Despite years of trying to forget him, yes."

"He saw a photo of you in a Jacksonville paper a while ago. Something about a lady politician."

Oh, yeah. I had tried to stay out of the papers for that one. I thought I had succeeded.

"He remembered that the photo had been taken in Raleigh. You were pretty easy to find once I knew that. You don't exactly blend in with the crowd."

He laughed nervously. I didn't.

"Ah, Honey Bunny, don't be mad," he pleaded.

I think it was the Honey Bunny that did it. Jeff never really heard a single word I said. Like every other junkie on the planet, he was far too busy scheming to ever listen. No amount of caring for him or wishing it otherwise would change that simple fact. Any guilt I felt at what I was about to do vanished.

They say you're not supposed to interfere in other people's lives. But if I had followed that advice, Robert Price would still be in jail and a lot of rotten people would be walking around free.

I stood up. "Good luck, Jeff," I said.

"Where are you going?" he asked, alarmed.

"I'm giving you some privacy, so you can call your mother."

"Why would I want to call her?"

"Jeff," I told him, "one day soon those two men are going to be back for the rest of their drug money. And you better not be around when they get here. They told me they would kill you if it was the last thing they ever did. Ask your mother for the money to go away. She'll give it to you. She always has. Tell her you need it to start over. Somewhere far away where you don't know anyone and where those men will never find you. Go someplace where you have a chance to be someone new."

"Someone new?" he asked. "Why would I want to be someone new?"

"Because your nose is running, your eyes are bleeding, your head is pounding and one day you, my friend, are going to either run out of pills or do something else stupid. And, believe me, next time I will not be there to bail you out."

He stared at me in silence.

"Get out now, Jeff," I warned him. "Stop the world, tell it you want to get off. Go someplace far away. Go to Alaska."

"Alaska? I'm from Florida."

"Bring mittens. Sign up for a work crew and build pipelines. Do some hard labor. Use your body for a change, instead of abusing it. If you stay away long enough, those guys will move on to someone else. It's your only chance. Take it. Just do something different, so you can get on with your life."

"Like you have?" he mumbled resentfully.

"Like I have," I agreed. I walked to my door and took my knapsack off the hook on the back of it.

"Where are you going now?" he asked.

"To the Amtrak station," I explained. "To check out the fares to Florida."

"Florida?" he said. "You hate that place."

"No, I don't. You're what I hated about that place. You and the people we used to know. But I love Florida. It's my home. It's where I come from. It's who I am. And I am not Tawny Bledsoe. Or anything like her. I am not going to turn my back on the people who love me."

"Meaning what?" Jeff asked hopefully. "You'll help me after all?"

He would never change. "This has nothing to do with you," I explained. "Nothing I ever do in my life again will ever have anything to do with you. It means that I am going home to see my grandfather. And I'm going to pray every mile of the way that he forgives me for staying away for so long, all because of something as stupid as pride."

Jeff stared at me, not understanding. "I don't get it," he finally said.

"I didn't think you would. But I learned something important from Tawny Bledsoe and I don't plan to forget it. Maybe you ought to remember it, too."

"Remember what?" he mumbled resentfully.

"You can run from yourself," I told him gently, "but you cannot hide."